BLOO

By

H A Culley

Book three about the Earls of Northumbria

Published by

oHp

Orchard House Publishing

Cover Image: © *Henry Hustava*

First Kindle Edition 2019

Text copyright © 2019 H A Culley

TABLE OF CONTENTS

Author's Note

This book is set in a period when Northumbria encompassed a large part of Northern England. In addition to today's Northumberland, Bernicia covered County Durham, Tyne and Wear and Cleveland in England. Deira, the southern part of Northumbria, corresponded roughly to the three counties that make up modern Yorkshire.

I am indebted to Richard Fletcher for his invaluable book *Bloodfeud – Murder and Revenge in Anglo-Saxon England* which provided much of the background information about the period and, in particular, the blood feud between Uhtred's family and Thurbrand's. I also drew on *Anglo-Saxon England* by Sir Frank Stenton during my research. I do not pretend that this is a factual account of what happened in Northumbria in the early eleventh century but I have tried to weave the story around the most likely series of events as far as possible.

In the last book of the series '*The Kings of Northumbria*' I said in the historical note that Uhtred the Bold died at the Battle of Carham and, indeed, several sources reflect this account of his death. However, further research on my part leads me to believe that Uhtred was killed two years before the battle by Thurbrand the Hold, possibly on the orders of King Cnut (also spelt Canute). As a blood feud evidently followed his murder this makes it the more likely of the two versions of Uhtred's death.

In past books about the Anglo-Saxon period I have used the ancient names for places, where known, to add authenticity to the story. However several reviewers have said that this is confusing, especially when the reader has also had to cope with the unfamiliar names of the characters. I have therefore used the modern names for places with two notable exceptions. I have retained the Anglo-Saxon name for Bamburgh – Bebbanburg - as that will be more familiar to readers who like this period, and I have used the Saxon name for what is now Yorkshire - Deira. As this would have been divided up into a number of administrative shires at this time, to call it Yorkshire would be confusing.

I have also used Aldred instead of Ealdred for Uhtred's eldest son. This is to save confusion when so many characters have names beginning Ea.

I felt it would be wrong to use the word *knight* for Aldred's mounted warriors as it applied to horse warriors on the Continent at this time. I have therefore opted for the word militar (pl. militares) which is a Latin term which preceded knight as the term for a mounter warrior. Another was miles, but this could lead to obvious confusion.

The idea of using heavy cavalry had been introduced into Europe by Charlemagne in the eight century. The French and the Normans developed the concept until these mounted warriors became minor nobility, partially because only the upper class could afford the horses, armour, weapons and servants required to maintain themselves as militares.

Heavy cavalrymen needed attendants and the Franks, later the French and the Normans, employed boys and youths of noble birth in this role. At the same time they learned to become mounted warriors themselves. The Medieval term squire derives from the French word escuier, which derives from the Latin scutifer (shield bearer). An alternative word in Latin was armiger (armour bearer) and this is the term I have opted to use.

The other term I have used which didn't come into usage until later is gambeson – a quilted or padded tunic worn under chainmail, or sometime worn on its own to offer more protection than a plain woollen tunic. Sometime the outer layer was leather but more often it was cotton or linen. Although the word gambeson wasn't the term in use then, even the Romans are thought to have worn this type of garment under their mail.

At the time that this novel begins Northumbria, or what remained of the ancient northern kingdom, was divided into two; Deira in the south centred on York; and Bernicia between the River Tees and the Firth of Forth. Lothian, between the River Tweed and the Firth of Forth, had been absorbed by Bernicia in the seventh century but in 1018 Malcolm, King of Scots, had defeated the Bernician army at Carham and from then on it remained part of Scotland, only Berwick upon Tweed being contested. The town changed hands over a dozen times after Carham but eventually it became part of England.

The inhabitants of Lothian were mainly descended from the Goddodin, a tribe of Britons who had more in common with the Welsh and the people of Strathclyde than they did with their conquerors – the Angles from Bernicia. Over the centuries three peoples – the Picts, the Scots of Dalraida and eventually the Britons of Strathclyde – had united to become the Kingdom of Alba. However, again to save confusion, I have used the modern name of Scotland and the Scots for the inhabitants.

Although the first King of the English, Æthelstan, had subjugated the Danes of Yorvik – the Danish name for York – and brought them under his rule, they had retained their Viking identity and their relationship with a king who lived in Wessex was a fragile one. Since Æthelstan's time the differences between the Danes and the Angles – the occupants of Deira before the time of the Danelaw – had been somewhat eroded by the passing of the years, inter-marriage and conversion to Christianity; nevertheless Deira stood out as a largely Danish ghetto in the midst of an Anglo-Saxon England. Although people of Danish descent lived in other parts of England as well, they were in the minority.

Since the demise of Northumbria as a separate kingdom it had been split in two, the Danes ruling the former Saxon Kingdom of Deira, centred on York, in the south and the hereditary lords of Bebbanburg governing Bernicia in the north.

Æthelred (King of the English from 978 to 1013 and again from 1014 until his death in 1016) had re-united Northumbria under Earl Uhtred the Bold but, shortly after Cnut invaded England, Uhtred was ambushed and killed. Once more Northumbria was split in two. Uhtred was succeeded in Bernicia by his brother Eadwulf Cudel and the Norwegian Erik Håkonsson became Earl of Deira. It isn't clear whether Erik was in fact Earl of Northumbria with Eadwulf as his junior or whether there were two quite separate earldoms.

Siward, who succeeded Erik as earl after his death, married Aldred's half-sister and their son, Waltheof, eventually became Earl of Northumbria, thus continuing Uhtred's line. Unfortunately he was the last Earl of Northumbria, but that's another story.

List of Earls of Northumbria & Bernicia

Northumbria

Uhtred the Bold	1006 - 1016
Erik Håkonsson	1016 – 1023
Siward Bjornsson	1023(?) – 1055
Tostig Godwinson	1055 – 1065
Morcar	1065 – 1066
Copsi	1066
Oswulf	1067
Gospatric	1067 – 1068
Robert de Comines	1068 – 1069 *[Norman]*
Gospatric (restored)	1070 -1072
Waltheof	1072 – 1075 *[last Anglo-Saxon*

earl]

Bernicia

Eadwulf Cudel	1016 – 1020
Aldred	1020 – 1038
Eadulf	1038 – 1041
Under Northumbria	*1041 – 1065*
Oswulf	1065 – 1067
Under Northumbria	*1067 onwards*

NOTE: Names in bold are members of the Bebbanburg dynasty

List of Principal Characters

In alphabetical order, historical characters are shown in bold:

Acca - One of Aldred's armigers

Ælfflæd - Uhtred's posthumous daughter, later wife of Siward

Ælfgifu – Uhtred's third wife. Daughter of King Æthelred and Emma of Normandy

Ælfric Puttoc – Archbishop of York

Æsc – Rowena's brother

Æthelnoth – Archbishop of Canterbury

Aldred – The late Earl Uhtred's eldest son, now Earl of Bernicia

Alwyn – Ealdorman of Alnwick

Beda – Ealdorman of Durham

Beorhtric – Rowena's brother, later head of scouts

Carl – Thurbrand's son and heir to Holderness

Ceatta – Former captain of Aldred's warriors, now serving Aodghan and Sigfrida

Cerdic – Oeric's elder son

Cille – Oeric's daughter

Cnut – King of England, Denmark and Norway

Colby – Another of Aldred's militar; a former scout

Cynric – Armiger to Oeric, Colby, Acca and Osric

Duncan – Malcolm's eldest grandson and his successor on the throne of Scotland

Dunstan – One of Oeric's scouts

Durfel – Aldred's body servant after Uuen

Eadulf – Uhtred's second son

Ealdgyth – Uhtred's elder daughter, later married Maldred

Edith – Aldred's eldest daughter

Edmund – Bishop of Durham

Emma of Normandy – Former wife of King Æthelred of England, now Cnut's queen

Fiske – A Norseman, body servant to Eadulf

Gillecomgan - Máel Coluim's younger brother, who succeeded him as mormaer

Godric – Captain of Aldred's militares

Gospatric – Aldred's nephew, son of Maldred and Eadgyth

Gunwald – Illegitimate son of Cnut; now a militar (knight) in Aldred's warband

Iden – An armiger, enemy of Oeric

Kjetil and Hakon – Captured Norse boys who had become militares in Aldred's warband

Leof – An armiger with Colby's section of militares

Macbeth – A disposed Scottish noble; one of Malcolm's grandsons, later King of Scots

Máel Coluim mac Máel Brigti –Mormaer of Moray

Malcolm - Nicknamed Forranach (the destroyer), King of Scots

Maldred - Brother of Duncan, King of Scots

Mildred – Heiress of Lesbury; Acca's wife

Morcar – Aldred's grandson, son of Edith and Ligulf, Thane of Lumley

Oeric – The narrator. The son of a tenant farmer, now serving Aldred as an armiger

Osbjorn - Aldred's nephew, son of Siward and Ælfflaed

Osric – A former novice at Melrose Monastery; now a militar serving Aldred

Oswin – Oeric's younger son

Regnwald – One of King Cnut's housecarls

Rowena – Daughter of the Reeve of Pirnie, later Oeric's wife

Sigfrida – Aldred's half-sister and Eadwulf's widow, later Eadulf's wife

Sihtric – A thane. Iden's father

Siward Bjornsson – Earl of Northumbria from 1023

Synne – Aldred's wife, a former street urchin in York

Thurbrand the Hold – A wealthy Danish jarl who had conspired with Eadwulf to kill Uhtred, father of Aldred, Eadulf, Ealdgyth and Ælfflæd

Uuen – Body servant to Aldred

Glossary

Organisation of Society

King – the male ruler of an independent country. In Anglo-Saxon England the king was elected by the Witenagemot (Witan for short), the council of nobles and senior churchmen

Queen – the crowned wife of a king. Many early royal wives were merely called lady, not queen. Ælfthryth, wife of King Edgar, was the first to be crowned as Queen of the English in 973 and most consorts after that date were accorded the title queen.

Earl – a member of the nobility. Akin to the Scandinavian *jarl* and meaning chieftain; the ruler of a territory directly under the king

Ealdorman – a senior official appointed by the king, who was responsible for governing his shire in accordance with the law and for leading the shire's fyrd in battle

Thane – a man holding land of a certain size from the king or from a superior in rank

Reeve - an official supervising a landowner's estate or the magistrate of a town or district in Anglo-Saxon England. The latter was sometime called high reeve or shire reeve (later corrupted to sherrif)

Ceorl – a free peasant who formed the basis of society in Anglo-Saxon England, ranking directly below a thane. Often a minor landowner or artisan.

Villein - a feudal tenant subject to a lord to whom he paid dues and services in return for land. Although free, he or she was bound to their lord.

Serf – also termed a slave or a thrall. Held in bondage and forced to obey their master, they were regarded as property and could be bought and sold.

Weapons, Nautical & Military Terms

Armiger – Essentially the same as a squire, which came from the French word escuier, which derives from the Latin scutifer (shield bearer). An alternative word in Latin was armiger (armour bearer) and this is the term used here. They looked after a militar's horses, armour and weapons whilst training to become mounted warriors themselves.

Battleaxe – a large broad-bladed axe used solely as a weapon, often two-handed

Bodkin Arrow Heads – Thin, tapering round or square heads with no barb which were designed to force their way through the links in chainmail.

Birlinn - a clinker-built wooden warship propelled by sail and oar with a single mast and a square sail. Narrower that a Viking longship, they carried a crew of between twelve and forty rowers

Byrnie – A coat of mail, sometimes sleeveless, designed to protect the torso and upper thighs. It was usually worn by those who fought on foot

Dagger – a double edged blade used as a weapon in close combat. It was primarily meant for stabbing or thrusting and was usually less than a foot long

Fyrd – the Anglo-Saxon militia consisting of freemen raised to defend their shire or to join a royal campaign. Each man was expected to provide their own weapons and provisions

Hauberk – a full-length coat of mail coming down to below the knee and split front and back to allow the wearer to ride. Sleeves usually came down to mid-forearm and it was typically worn by knights and other armoured horsemen

Housecarl – a member of the bodyguard of a Danish or English king or noble

Gunwale - the upper edge or planking of the side of a boat or ship

Knarr - a cargo ship whose hull was wider, deeper and shorter than a longship. It could take more cargo and be operated by a small crews, relying on its sail as the main means of propulsion

Militar – a professional warrior trained to fight on horseback as well as on foot. The mounted equivalent to a housecarl. Also termed miles, knecht or knight

Seax – a single edged blade longer than a dagger but shorter than a sword. Used in close combat primarily for slashing

Shell Keep - A stone fortification, often circular, usually built on top of a motte or mound within an outer timber palisade or stone wall.

Shield – an Anglo-Saxon shield was circular, up to three feet (1 m) in diameter and was usually made of lengths of hard wood glued together. Most had a central metal boss and were covered in leather. Many had a metal rim

Sword - a double bladed weapon intended for both slashing and thrusting; usually significantly longer than a seax

Targe – a round shield between 18 in and 21 in (45–55 cm) in diameter made of iron or iron plated wood. Instead of a central boss, some targes had a blade similar to that of a dagger protruding from the centre so that it could also be used as a weapon

Chapter One – The Enemy in the West

1018 - 1022

My name is Oeric. I was born in the spring of 1008 on a small farm in Lothian where I lived with my parents, an elder brother and my two sisters.

Our family were subjects of the King of Scots, just like the warriors who raided our farm, but that made no difference. I was just ten when they killed my father and elder brother, and then raped my mother and both my sisters - even Æffe who was only eight - before putting their bodies inside our hut and setting fire to it.

I watched all of this from the safety of the trees. I wanted to stop them, but what could an unarmed boy do against two dozen grown men armed with swords, spears and axes? But I still felt like a coward for doing nothing, and there are times even now when I feel depressed by my failure to act. I should have died with them.

These Scots had come from north of the Firth of Forth and were intent on stealing our livestock. They were led by King Malcolm who I later learned was hell bent on conquering Berwickshire and Selkirkshire - the remaining part of Lothian which was still part of Bernicia. He had already captured the other part of Lothian – Edinburghshire – some years previously.

Of course, I wasn't aware of who ruled what in those days. My life was filled with work, looking after the animals, planting crops, weeding, watering, and harvesting. I knew nothing of kings, kingdoms and border disputes. My one relaxation was riding. We owned a mare which my father used for pulling our cart full of produce to market and sometimes I was allowed to ride her. My father said I was a natural horseman. The comment was even more unusual as he never praised me. In fact he normally ignored me and at times I felt that he might even hate me. If he did I had no idea why he should do so. What made it even worse was the affection he plainly had for my siblings.

Now he was dead, along with the rest of my family. I didn't know what to do but I was determined to put as much distance between myself and the invaders as I could. That night I tried to steal a horse from a lone man asleep by a small stream, but either I made a noise or he had a sixth sense. He caught me and I fully expected him to kill me. Frankly at that moment death would have been a merciful release, but he didn't. Instead he listened to my tale of woe and took me with him.

We eventually arrived at a vill called Duns in Berwickshire whose thane was called Aldred, the eldest son of the famous Uhtred who had been Earl of Northumbria before he was murdered two years ago. I'd started as a stable boy but Aldred's captain, Ceatta, had noticed what a good rider I was whilst I was exercising one of the horses and he mentioned me to Lord Aldred. He had come to watch me himself and put me through my paces.

I was as nervous as hell and I didn't think I'd done as well as I could have done, so I didn't quite believe what happened next. Aldred made me an armiger – a trainee horse warrior, or militar in Latin - and I joined young nobles like Aldred's brother, Eadulf, and Gunwald, Cnut's bastard son.

It was hard work. There were eight of us to look after the horses, armour and weapons of forty mounted militares. The best way of describing them is as Anglo-Saxon versions of Norman knights. We also had to prepare their food and treat wounds on campaign. I served five militares at first but that was the easy part of my duties. I spent most of my time with my fellow armigers being taught how to fight on both horseback with spear and sword and on foot with everything from a bow to a seax. I had never been so tired - or so happy.

You might have thought that those of our fellow armigers who were nobly-born would have looked down on a peasant like me, especially as I was the youngest by two years, but there was a strong sense of camaraderie that bound us all together. I had become good friends with two other armigers, Colby and Osric, and we helped each other out as a matter of course.

Then came the day that Eadulf, Gunwald, Colby and Osric became militares themselves. By then the ranks of both militares and armigers had grown; there were now fifty two of the former and a dozen armigers. Although still only fourteen, I was one of the most experienced and I was chosen to serve the four new militares.

It could have been difficult as the day before we'd all been equal, but none felt they had to demonstrate their new status by bullying me and I treated them with the respect they deserved.

Soon after I'd joined the service of Lord Aldred King Cnut made him Earl of Bernicia in the place of his uncle, Eadwulf Cudel. I didn't know the details at the time but I gathered that there was a blood feud between Aldred and Eadulf on the one hand and Eadwulf and a man called Thurbrand the Hold on the other. Word had it that Thurbrand and Eadwulf had murdered Uhtred, the father of the two brothers. Whatever the truth of the matter, Eadwulf was killed by Eadulf when the two brothers took the fortress of Bebbanburg on the edge of the North Sea. That then became our home.

We had just settled down as a group when news came that the Britons in Cumbria had invaded Upper Teesdale in the shire of Durham. For some time they had been pushed eastwards by the Norse, who were encroaching further and further inland from their enclave along the Cumbrian coast, and now the Britons had come east in search of new territory.

Durham was part of Bernicia and so Earl Aldred was bound to defend the shire in any case, but he also owned several vills in Lower Teesdale and that added to the urgency of the situation. Unfortunately it was now August; the beginning of harvest time. No doubt the earl would have liked to have called out the fyrd, but every available body would shortly be needed to help in the fields, or else we would go hungry this winter. Instead, he decided to find out how great an invasion he faced. That evening Eadulf told me to get everything ready to leave the next day.

Leaving young boys and the elderly to man the fortress, we rode out of Bebbanburg on a bright sunny morning heading for Hexham, the muster point. Aldred might not have called out the fyrd, but word had gone out for every ealdorman and thane to meet him there with their housecarls. From there Upper Teesdale lay thirty miles to the south.

†††

Fiske, an eighteen year old Norseman who'd been Eadulf's body servant since he was a young boy, wasn't exactly happy that I was looking after his master's horse and war gear, but he accepted it. However, in all other matters such as cooking, washing clothes and putting up the tent he would brook no interference. I know he resented me at first, but I had three other militares to look after and it wasn't long before we learnt to at least tolerate each other.

We stayed that night at Morpeth. Aldred and the militares shared the floor of the thane's hall whilst the rest of us made do with the stables. There wasn't room for our horses, of course, so they were tethered to a line in a nearby pasture. Although this was friendly territory, Godric - the captain who had replaced Ceatta when he had retired - insisted that four of us guarded them at all times. Britons weren't the only ones who might steal a valuable war horse or even a packhorse, given the opportunity.

I shared my watch with Kjetil, Hakon and another armiger called Iden. The two militares had been captured Norse ship's boys who had earned their release and their place as militares through ability. Iden was the son of a wealthy thane who was the same age as me. He had only recently joined the warband and I suspected that he looked down his nose at me because of my humble background. God knows what he made of the two Norsemen.

Iden made a lousy sentry. The trick of guarding the horses successfully was not to be seen. Many was the tale I'd heard of enemy sentries who had been quietly removed by our men. It didn't matter how stealthily you could move if you couldn't find the guards. Kjetil, Hakon and I stood still in positions we could see the horses from. In the dark it is very difficult to see someone who is perfectly stationary, especially if they stand beside a tree trunk. Movement catches the eye but Iden was incapable of standing still. In the end Hakon crept up on him and knocked him out.

When he awoke the next morning complaining bitterly about his sore head, I went over and pressed my dagger against his throat.

'If there had been an enemy out there last night you wouldn't have a headache, your throat would have been cut,' I said softly. 'Unless you can keep still when on guard we would be better off without you.'

I'd hoped that Iden had learnt a lesson but I feared that he was too full of his own self-importance and all I had done was to make an enemy of him. It didn't bother me. The other armigers applauded, which just intensified the boy's resentment.

When we set off after a quick meal of cold pottage left over from the previous evening's meal the sunshine of the previous day had been replaced by dark clouds. I'd heard that Aldred had planned to take the shortest route to Hexham which was across open country heading south-east until we hit the old Roman Wall that ran from the mouth of the River Tyne to the Solway Firth. Once we had crossed it at Chesters Fort Hexham would only be a mere four miles or so due south. It was an easy day's ride if we didn't get lost but, without the sun to help us to determine directions, it was more than possible that we would miss our way.

Therefore Aldred decided against the cross country route and instead we took the safer, but longer, option and headed north-west for a while to hit the Roman road which ran from Berwick to York via Hexham. The Romans had left six centuries before and parts of the road were in better repair than others but, although the distance was greater, we could make much better speed along it. Encouragingly we passed three contingents led by thanes also heading for Hexham. However, apart from the thanes, they were on foot and so they wouldn't arrive until the day after we did.

We stopped briefly three times to rest the horses and fill our water skins. Our midday meal consisted of stale bread, fruit and cheese. At one of these stops Fiske sought me out. He'd brought Uuen, Earl Aldred's body servant, with him.

'We've just overheard Iden boasting that he is going to cut your throat when you are asleep tonight,' Fiske said.

'Do you want me to have a quiet word with Lord Aldred,' Uuen asked.

'Who was he talking to?' I asked out of curiosity. 'I didn't think Iden had many friends.'

'Just a couple of other armigers. I don't think they thought he was serious; just letting off steam. At any rate they made fun of him,' Uuen replied.

'I don't suppose that would have improved his mood,' I said grimly. 'Thank you for your warning; I appreciate it. I'll deal with it so don't bother the earl; not yet at any rate.'

I may have made an enemy of Iden but it seemed that I had a couple of allies in the two servants. They had the ear of their respective masters and that might be helpful to me at some stage in the future. Now, however, I had to think about what to do about Iden.

When we reached Hexham we camped in the ruins of the old monastery which had been destroyed during a Viking raid. There used to be a Bishop of

26

Hexham as well as an abbot, but it was now part of the Diocese of Durham. Leaving Fiske to put up the tent which would house Eadulf and his three companions, I took care of the horses and then took my master's hauberk, helmet and chainmail coif for cleaning.

The militares didn't wear armour on the march in friendly country; it was too heavy and uncomfortable. Instead it resided in leather bags on the packhorses together with the shields and spears. There was hardly a speck of rust on any of it but I put it in a sack of sand and whirled it around so that the grains polished the steel. When I returned the armour in its leather bag to my packhorse I put one item aside to take back with me.

That night I unsheathed my dagger and put it beside me, pulled the hood of my cloak over my head and went to sleep. I woke when I felt a sudden pressure on my throat. I opened my eyes to see the astonished look on Iden's face. He had thrust the point of his dagger into my throat but, instead of piercing my flesh it had struck the chain mail links of Eadulf's coif.

Before I had gone to sleep I had put it on. It covered my head, shoulders and, most importantly, my throat up as far as my chin. I had then carefully arranged my cloak so that it was out of sight. The steel links were sewn onto a padded leather liner so, although I might suffer slight bruising from the blow, no real damage had been done.

I grabbed my own dagger and thrust it into the kneeling boy's thigh. He screamed in agony like a girl and tried to rise, but his leg gave way under him and he fell on his side. The scream had awoken the rest of the camp and the first to reach me was Erian, one of the militares who Iden served.

'What's happened? Stop making that noise, Iden, what's the matter with you?'

'He tried to kill me,' he yelled, pointing a finger at me.

'I think you'll find that it was the other way around. I was merely defending myself,' I replied calmly.

At that moment Aldred arrived with Uuen who was carrying a torch. He pushed his way through the gathering crowd and I took off the coif to examine it under the flickering light of the flame. Where Iden's dagger had struck there was a bright scar on three of the links.

'This is where he thrust his dagger into my neck whilst I was sleeping, lord.'

I handed it to Aldred so that he could see for himself. As he did so I picked up the dagger that Iden had dropped.

'Do you deny that this is yours?' I asked my assailant coldly.

Aldred handed the coif back to me without comment.

'Back to bed all of you. Fiske, pull Oeric's dagger out and deal with the wound. Iden shut up for the love of God. It's only a flesh wound. You will be kept under guard until the morning when I'll find out what exactly happened.'

I waited as Fiske pulled out my dagger and handed it back to me after wiping it clean on Iden's trousers. Presumably he thought a little more gore wouldn't make much difference. Then he ripped them apart so that he could wash and sew up the cut.

I lay down again and tried to sleep but found that I was trembling and the incident kept replaying in my mind. It was the first time someone had tried to kill me and I found the experience unnerving. By the time I eventually dropped off Iden had been carted away to be tied to a nearby post, once the door frame of the monastery church.

✝✝✝

The evidence of Uuen, Fiske and those of my colleagues who Iden had told that he planned to kill me was enough to condemn him without my testimony. What I said under oath was just the nail in the coffin. However I didn't escape without a reprimand. Earl Aldred told me that a punch to the jaw would have been sufficient to defend myself. A stab in the thigh in the dark could have cut the femoral artery and then I would have been accused of causing the boy's death.

Eadulf was also displeased with me for borrowing his coif without permission.

'You should have come to me and complained, Oeric,' he told me.

'Is that what you would have done in the same circumstances, Eadulf? Whined like a baby?'

He was about to rebuke me for insolence when he suddenly grinned.

'No, but I would have probably killed him; but then I have the funds to pay the weregild to his family.'

Weregild was the amount of compensation paid to the victim or, in case of death, to his family, by a person committing an offence. There was a sliding scale according to the status of the victim. As I had no money to pay anyone anything there was an alternative – blood feud. The family would be entitled to kill me without fear of retribution – at least under the law. The problem with blood feud was that things tended to escalate with each side killing more of their enemies each time. However, I had no family so it would end with my death. Thankfully Iden lived and, as he'd been found to be the offender, weregild wasn't applicable.

Aldred decided to send the boy back to his father in disgrace and let him decide how to punish him. I thought that was the end of the matter but, as I was going to find out, Iden was not a person to forgive and forget.

†††

Colby, Osric and I approached the last ridge below which lay Upper Teesdale. We dismounted and, leaving our horses with Eadulf and Gunwald, we slithered on our bellies until we reached the top of a tall cliff. From the base of the rock face the heather stretched away, gently sloping down to the river as it flowed to the east. On the other bank a grassy slope led up a slight incline to a low hill. Beyond that I could see ridge after ridge, growing bigger with distance, until the vista ended in the range of high hills that divided Teesdale from Weardale.

The hot August sun beat down on us and sparkled on the broken waters of the shallow river as it found its way around the mass of boulders and smaller rocks that littered its bed. I was glad that I was only wearing my padded leather gambeson, though that was hot enough to make me swelter. I pitied my companions in their hauberks and coifs.

At first I saw nothing and then I spotted movement some distance to the west. Below us the river followed a winding course for about two miles and then disappeared behind a spur that jutted out into the valley. It reappeared again perhaps four miles away. It was there that I had seen something in motion along the north bank. I looked away and looked again obliquely. I had learned some time ago that you could often detect movement better out of the side of your eye than if you looked directly at it.

And so it proved this time. There was a dark mass against the green of the hills and there was a faint yellow something hovering above it. I looked away and looked back again. The dark blob was in a different position, as was the yellowish cloud. It had to be a large number of people on the move and the yellow haze was undoubtedly the dust cloud kicked up by hundreds, perhaps thousands, of feet.

I touched Colby's shoulder and pointed. He shook his head, indicating that he could see nothing, but then he gripped my shoulder. He studied the distant river bank and then turned his head to the side as I had done.

'You're right,' he whispered. 'It has to be the invading Britons. We need to get closer so we can make an estimate of their numbers.'

The three of us scrambled back down the far side of the ridge and briefed the others on what I'd seen. A few minutes later all five of us were riding at a moderate pace along the south bank of the River Tees. At first the ground was fairly open but as we rode further the trees and shrubs grew ever closer to the river itself. It was the same on the other bank and I knew that any large body of people, no doubt driving livestock to add to their difficulties, would be forced to make a detour away from the river.

Crossing the Tees just west of a series of waterfalls, we headed north to try and intercept what Colby thought was almost certainly the main body of the invading Britons. We heard them before we saw them; not the noises made by an army on the march, but the lowing of cattle, the bleating of sheep and the cries of boys trying to keep them moving in the right direction.

The first of them appeared out of dead ground preceded by a dozen men on hill ponies – presumably their scouts. Then the Britons appeared in family and clan groups driving their livestock before them and accompanied by carts stacked high with crude furniture, provisions and tired children hitching a ride. This wasn't an invading army or even a large scale raid, it was a migration.

We stayed in the shadows of the trees, being eaten alive by midges, whilst we tried to estimate their numbers. Once the passing horde had dwindled to a trickle of those struggling to keep up, Colby asked us how many each of us had counted. There was little difference in our individual estimates: a thousand men and older boys of fighting age and some four thousand old people, women and children.

Then, just as we were about to head back to the river and make our circuitous way back to Aldred's camp, we saw some five hundred more Britons emerge. Only a few wore helmets and even fewer a vest or byrnie of chainmail, but they were relatively well armed. They were led by two dozen men on ponies and three on good quality horses.

Evidently they were the rear guard. As we watched the warriors turned to face back the way they had come to deal with an attack by several hundred Norsemen. Then, when the skirmish was over and the Norse had retreated, they turned around and put as much distance as they could between the two sides before the next assault. I was mystified. Why had the Norsemen broken off their attack? There was no obvious reason to do so as far as I could see. Had they maintained their attack they would have lost men but they would surely have overcome the read guard. It was Eadulf who realised what they were doing.

'They're just harrying them to keep the Britons moving,' he said. 'Obviously the Norse have decided to drive them out of Cumbria completely.'

'They seem to have succeeded,' Gunwald replied, 'so why are they still pursuing them?'

'To make sure they don't try and return to their homes I imagine. They are probably also after the livestock and provisions that the Britons have with them, but they won't want to lose more men than they have to.'

'If we attack these people and drive them back into Cumbria they are just going to be slaughtered by the Norse. What can we do?' Colby asked.

'Thankfully that's not our problem; it's my brother's,' Eadulf said with a wry smile. 'I wouldn't want to be in his shoes. Shouldn't we get back across the river before dark and then return to the main body first thing tomorrow?'

'Just a moment,' Gunwald said before anyone could make a move. 'Earl Aldred will want an assessment of the Norseman's strength.'

Reluctantly the others agreed and we waited until the Last of the Norsemen had passed our position before we made a move. We would be travelling back in the dark for at least part of the way now but it had been worth waiting. We now knew that there were between six and seven hundred Norsemen herding the Britons eastwards.

Chapter Two – The Battle of Cotherstone

August 1022

We found Aldred and his small army camped at Hunderthwaite about ten miles downstream from where we had encountered the Britons and their Norse pursuers. In addition to his fifty militares, Aldred commanded some forty nobles and three hundred and fifty housecarls who had answered the call to arms.

Bernicia was still suffering from the losses inflicted by Malcolm and his Scots at Carham four years before. Some vills had been inherited by thanes who were too young to bear arms and so many housecarls had been killed on that infamous day that it was taking time to replace them.

Being a lowly armiger I didn't attend the earl's war council but Eadulf told me what had been decided. Upper Teesdale was relatively sparsely populated but it was a different story once the Tees reached the vill of Startforth where Teesdale met Deepdale. As you travelled ever eastwards the area got more and more populous. Many of the vills in Lower Teesdale belonged to Aldred, either in his own right, such as Aycliffe, or as Earl of Bernicia. One such vill was Gainford, the centre of a large and prosperous estate. He was determined to halt the Britons before they reached Startforth.

The real problem was the Norsemen. If they could be defeated and sent back to Cumbria with their tails between their legs, the Britons could probably be halted without having to kill too many of them; at least that was the earl's theory. There was much discussion in the camp as how we might effect this. However, when we found out the plan it wasn't what anybody had expected.

Aldred proposed to split his small army in two. The main body would be deployed against the Norsemen whilst a smaller force would confront the Britons and negotiate with them to prevent them advancing further whilst their pursuers were dealt with. No one thought that splitting our force of four hundred was very sensible, but Aldred's reputation as a successful leader was such that practically everyone was willing to give it a try.

The one notable exception was a thane called Sihtric. He spoke vehemently against the plan to anyone who would listen; so much so that he was causing dissention in the army. Then I saw him with Iden and things began to fall into place. I wasn't surprised when I found out that Sihtric was Iden's father. Perhaps the public shaming of his son had turned the father against the earl.

Aldred's solution was to order Sihtric to go home with his son and the housecarls he'd brought with him.

'I'm better off without you if you aren't prepared to be loyal,' he had told Sihtric. 'Instead of the military service due to me, I will levy an additional tax. My steward will be in touch with you in due course.'

I had a nasty feeling that, if I had made a sworn enemy of Iden, the earl had also made one of his father.

Beda, the Ealdorman of Durham, was chosen to lead the party tasked with negotiating with the Britons whilst the rest of us set off to go around them and locate the Norsemen. Aldred left the contingent from the shire of Durham with Beda. That reduced our force to three hundred and twenty men, fifty of whom were the militares. We knew that there were twice as many Norsemen and they had a grudge against Aldred. He was the man responsible for annihilating hundreds of their compatriots four years previously in the run up to the Battle of Carham.

Unlike us, who had to wait until boys grew up and were trained as warriors in order to replenish our numbers, Norsemen were continually arriving from Ireland in the aftermath of their defeat at Clontarf near Dublin in 1014. Although the High King of Ireland, Brian Boru, had been killed in the battle, the Irish had won the day and thereafter the Norse settlers had become subjects of the local Irish kings.

This didn't suit many who left to try their luck elsewhere. Unfortunately for the Britons of Cumbria, and for us, many of them decided to head across the Irish Sea to the Norse settlements on the Isle of Man and, when it got too crowded, across the sea to Cumbria once more.

✝✝✝

The battlefield chosen by Aldred was near the small village of Cotherstone in the Pennine Hills. The Tees was shallow at this point but wide enough to present something of an obstacle to men on foot, especially as the river bed was rock strewn, making crossing slow. The terrain on the south bank sloped gently down to the river and was wooded. Conversely the hills to the north sloped steeply away from the Tees leaving only a narrow path along that bank. In many places no more than ten men could walk abreast. For small stretches it was narrower still.

At the ambush site chosen by Aldred there was a re-entrant that led into the hills that was level for a several hundred yards before the gap in the hills curved to the west and suddenly got steeper. The main advantage for horsemen was that it was free of boulders.

Toland, Ealdorman of Hexham, had been placed in command of the housecarls who were fighting on foot and Iuwine was put in charge of the archers, of whom there were sixty or so. The archers took up their position in the trees on the south bank whilst Toland's men hid high on the hillside near the re-entrant waiting for the last of the Britons to pass below.

38

The militares lay in wait out of sight in the re-entrant under the command of Godric, Aldred's new captain. The militares I served stayed with Aldred as his bodyguard. I had no specific orders so I went with them whilst the rest of the armigers waited with spare spears and horses at the far end of the re-entrant.

Aldred needed to direct operations and so he and Uuen, with a horn and coloured banners, sited themselves on the top of the slope above the re-entrant from where the earl had a good view of the battleground and, more importantly, from where he could be seen by his commanders. He was on foot as were the rest of us. My job was to hold the horses but I took a risk, tying them to a tree and moving a short distance away to where I could see what was happening.

We were ready, now we waited for the first of the Britons to appear.

†††

It seemed ages before the last of the long column of fleeing men, women, children and livestock passed below us. Surprisingly there was a gap after the rear-guard passed below before the Norsemen appeared. It seemed as if they were hanging back, and there didn't appear to be as many of them as there had been when I had last seen them. I thought for a moment that a lot of them had turned back. That was a reasonable assumption as they had clearly driven the Britons out of Cumbria.

It was then that I spotted movement along the tops of the hills opposite me, above the woods where our archers were concealed. Evidently some of the Norsemen, perhaps half, were hurrying to overtake the Britons and presumably they intended to come down further along, re-cross the river, and cut the Britons off. I wondered why they would do that if they just wanted to take the land that the Britons used to own. Then I realised that they were after slaves and the livestock.

Aldred had also seen the Norsemen on the south side of the Tees.

'Oeric, ride and find Toland and then cross over to Iuwine. I want them to engage the Norse this side of the river. I'll collect the militares from the re-entrant, find somewhere safe to cross and try and catch up with the enemy on the ridgeline opposite before they encounter Beda; otherwise they'll slaughter him and his men.'

I nodded and was away on my horse just before Aldred and his bodyguard arrived to mount theirs. Some of the Norsemen on the north bank had heard the shouted exchange and were now looking up at the hills in alarm. The time for secrecy was past and so I yelled at the top of my voice for Ealdorman Toland to attack the enemy on this side of the river and signalled for Iuwine's archers to engage the enemy above them.

The ambush had been sprung too early. The people immediately below Toland were the Britons' rear guard and not Norsemen. However, those of Tolands's men who could speak the Brythonic tongue called out 'friends' and 'we come to your aid' as they made their way down the hillside.

Thankfully whoever was in command of the rear guard gathered what was happening and his men turned and ran at the bewildered Norsemen. That gave Toland's housecarls time to reach the river bank and form up behind them. When the Briton's heroic, but ultimately doomed, charge was beaten off, they fled and Toland yelled for his men to let them through.

The shield wall reformed and the Norsemen found themselves facing a solid block of housecarls stretching from the river to the steep hillside. At the same time our archers sent volley after volley across the river into the rear half of the Norse column.

Even standing ten ranks deep, the shield wall only required a third of our housecarls because of the narrowness of the level ground. The Norsemen stood undecided whilst a few at the rear, infuriated by the archer's bombardment from the other side of the river, started to wade across. They didn't get very far before they decided that had been a bad idea and they retreated leaving a score of men face down in the water.

Toland took advantage of the Norsemen's indecision and charged into their packed ranks. They now found themselves assaulted on two sides – by housecarls in front and by volleys of arrows in the flank.

I didn't think that it would be long before they broke but my role was over. I rode along the river bank until I was well clear of the fighting and then looked for a place to cross. I walked my horse through the water slowly to avoid any risk of a broken leg and, once safely on the south side, I urged the mare up the slope to get above the wood. Once there, I set off after Aldred and his militares.

✝✝✝

From the ridge I could see a fair way along Teesdale below me. I could see the column of migrating Britons, which had come to a halt. At the front, just where the Deepdale Beck joined the Tees, there was a small group of mounted men and, to the east of them, a shield wall of what had to be the Durham housecarls.

The Norsemen further along the ridge realised that Aldred and his militares had nearly caught them up and had turned to face them. There were some three hundred of them and worse, the ground wasn't suited to a massed charge on horseback. Consequently Aldred had halted two hundred yards back from the Norsemen, who had now formed a shield wall. I wondered what on earth the earl could do, apart from ride away. It appeared to be a stalemate as our men couldn't tackle the enemy on foot; they outnumbered the militares by six to one.

Then I had an idea. There was a narrow animal trail leading from the ridge where we were down to the confluence of the Tees and Deepdale Beck.

'I'll fetch help, Lord Aldred,' I called to him and kicked my mare into motion down the steep and narrow trail.

It took me a little while to reach the bottom and then I rode eastwards as fast as I dared over the broken ground towards where Beda was negotiating with the leaders of the Britons. I had come down to river level two hundred yards away from them and was faced by a mass of people and animals between me and Beda.

I yelled for them to get out of my way and rode like a madman into the throng. The men were armed and anyone of them could have either killed my horse or me, but they were bemused and everyone and everything scattered out of my way. It was like the prow of a ship parting the waves.

'Lord Beda, the Norse at the back of this column have been taken care of by our men but Lord Aldred needs your help up there,' I shouted excitedly, pointing back the way I'd come.

The leader of the Britons, an imposing looking man mounted on a tall stallion and dressed in colourful checked trousers, a red wool tunic and a byrnie, looked bemused but another rider beside him hurriedly explained what I had said. Everyone looked up at the ridgeline where Aldred's men were riding carefully through the rock strewn area in front of the Norse shield wall in small groups before casting their spears at them once they got within range. Then they withdrew to collect another spear from the armigers. However, the pack horses the latter were leading didn't have an inexhaustible supply and they would soon run out.

The Norse decided that they had had enough of standing still for target practice and, with a roar of rage, they broke formation and ran at the horsemen. The militares calmly turned and trotted gently away from the Norsemen, who soon tired of running after them.

'Will your warriors help us kill your enemy and ours?' Beda asked the leader of the Britons, who I later learned was the Earl of Cumbria.

Before the translator had finished the earl yelled something and several hundred men left the column armed with a variety of spears, swords and axes. Some had shields of varying types, but not many. He turned his horse and pointed up the hill towards the Norsemen and, with a roar, they followed him up the steep hillside. Beda was tempted to follow him, but there were still a great number of migrants in the valley and, in any case, his housecarls in their heavy byrnies and carrying their yard-wide round shields, would never have arrived in time to make any difference.

Even Aldred and his men played no further part in the battle once the Britons reached the crest. They tore into the Norse, intent on revenge for being driven from their lands. A great number of Britons were killed or wounded but, by the time they had finished, there wasn't a Norseman left alive.

We camped that night a mile to the east of the Britons and Aldred put out pickets in case of a surprise attack. Just before dusk Toland and the rest of the army joined us, marching along the north bank of the Tees and straight through the migrants' camp. Instead of opposing them the Britons had cheered them.

Word soon spread that Toland had inflicted a crushing defeat on the other half of the Norse army, killing well over a hundred of them for the loss of forty on our side. The rest had fled back to the west.

'Get ready to leave at dawn, Oeric,' Eadulf told me later than evening, 'the five of us are to track the Norsemen who were routed and make sure they return to Cumbria.'

It proved to be an uneventful journey. All we found were the wounded who had fallen by the wayside. We stopped to give them a merciful release from pain via a quick slash across their throats and then we pressed on. A few miles after we'd found the last Norse body – a boy of about my age who'd lost half an arm and who had presumably bled to death despite efforts to cauterise the severed stump, we came to a farmstead. The family spoke Norse and told Colby, who spoke some Danish, that their lord was a jarl called Gunnar of Gilderdale.

Gilderdale Forest was several miles over the ill-defined border with Northumbria. The remainder of the invading Norse were now back in Cumbria and had presumably dispersed to their homes. There was nothing more for us to do so Eadulf gave the order to head back home.

✝✝✝

In our absence Aldred had held several meetings with the former Earl of Cumbria. It transpired that he only had some six hundred men of fighting age left, the rest had been killed or had been enslaved by the Norse. There were over eighteen hundred old men, women and young children though. Upper Teesdale was only sparsely populated and Aldred thought that establishing new vills there with palisades and well trained warriors would help defend it against any future incursions from Cumbria.

However, he didn't want the area to become an enclave of Britons and so he rewarded some of his own thanes, their housecarls and his married militares by giving them title to these new vills. The Britons would be freemen, but tenants, not landowners.

That would only absorb a portion of the migrants and so those who didn't want to stay in Teesdale were offered an escort north to the River Tweed. From there they could cross into Scotland where they would become Malcolm's problem, or head west into Strathclyde and hope that their fellow Britons would welcome them.

It was a neat solution which increased the population of Bernicia and gave Aldred another five

hundred members of the fyrd. The only downside
was the loss of six of the militares. However, there
were three armigers who had reached the age of
seventeen and another four who were sixteen.
Although ability and the maturity of the body were
more important than actual age in deciding when an
armiger could be promoted to militar, all seven now
became militares.

The loss of seven armigers left the remaining five
of us to serve fifty two militares. Looking after four
had been bad enough; serving ten or eleven was
never going to work. Aldred solved the problem by
opening up our ranks to any boy over the age of
twelve who was the son of a noble, militar or
housecarl throughout Bernicia. I found myself as the
senior armiger and so I would have the unenviable
task of training the new batch of recruits as and when
they arrived.

When we returned to Bebbanburg we learned that
Sihtric had abandoned the two vills he owned and
had fled with his wife, Iden, his other children and his
housecarls into Deira. My reaction was to think that
we were well rid of them. It was much later that we
heard that he'd sought service with Thurbrand the
Hold, who had given Sihtric one of his vills. That
wouldn't have been so bad, but the vill bordered
Aycliffe to the south.

There was also a letter from King Cnut waiting for
the earl. Now that his illegitimate son was a man, his
father had decided to honour his promise and give
Gunwald lands of his own. The problem was that he

had been given an earldom, not in England, but in Norway.

Gunwald didn't know anything about the land of the Norse but, in view of the fact that we had just been fighting them, the prospect of ruling some of them didn't fill him with joy. It also meant that he would be parted from his friends and that hit him hard, especially Eadulf who he'd been close to since they were young boys.

However, an award of lands from the king was not something that he could turn down. We were in for a further surprise though. Two days later Eadulf asked his brother for permission to go with Gunwald.

Chapter Three – A Changing World

1023

The news that Archbishop Wulfstan had died didn't impinge on my world very much. I knew vaguely that the Bishop of Worcester in Mercia, a man called Ælfric Puttoc, had been chosen to succeed him. What I hadn't realised was that, unlike Wulfstan, he would only hold one diocese and he wouldn't be kept busy as Cnut's chief lawyer in London. This was a man who would devote himself to his new province.

One of the first things he did was resolve the impasse over consecrating a new Bishop of Durham. Prior Edmund had been fulfilling the role for a couple of years but Wulfstan's opposition had prevented him from election to the vacant see. Now the way ahead was clear and Archbishop Ælfric lost no time in enthroning him. Now, at last, Bernicia had a proper bishop again.

The next event was even more earth shattering. Erik Håkonsson had died suddenly. His body servant had gone into his chamber to wake him one morning and found him stiff and cold. He was childless and so Cnut had chosen Bjorn, Ealdorman of Beverley, to succeed him. It wasn't a surprising choice as Bjorn had been one of the king's council for several years as well as foster father to Cnut's illegitimate son, Gunwald, when he was younger. The king knew that he was completely trustworthy.

Unfortunately Bjorn didn't have long to enjoy his new earldom. I heard the tale later from Colby. Three months after he had become earl, Bjorn had gone hunting with several of his ealdormen and a few thanes, one of whom was Sihtric. Bjorn and Sihtric had somehow got separated from the rest of the group and Siward, the earl's fourteen year old son, and several of his companions had gone looking for them.

They found Bjorn in a clearing with a boar spear in his chest. It must have only just happened because Sihtric was still in the clearing. He tried to make a run for it but Siward threw his boar spear at him and it struck Sihtric's horse in the rear quarters. It reared up, depositing its rider on the ground.

Colby wasn't clear about the details but thought that Sihtric must have broken his neck in the fall. He'd heard later that Iden and the rest of Sihtric's family had fled to Scotland.

That left the earldom vacant once more and we had hopes that the king would appoint Aldred, especially as his father had been Earl of Northumbria. However, he didn't and he allowed Siward to succeed his father, despite his youth. However, Cnut did ask Aldred to guide him and, to bind the two families together, he arranged for Siward to be betrothed to Ælfflæd, Earl Aldred's half-sister.

The girl was only seven years old and so, although they would be married later in the year, consummation would have to wait at least another five or six years. What Siward thought about the arrangement no one knew. I didn't imagine that he was very happy about it.

Sihtric was dead and Iden was in Scotland but Thurbrand, the person who had sent Sihtric to kill Bjorn was still at large. I wondered why Thurbrand had arranged for Earl Bjorn's death, but then I learned that Bjorn had killed Thurbrand's son, Edgar, in a fight at sea. Bjorn and Thurbrand were already engaged in a land dispute and the death of the latter's eldest son turned their enmity into a blood feud.

Thurbrand had got his revenge but I was fairly certain that Siward wouldn't let it rest there; nor would Aldred and Eadulf who had sworn to kill him in retaliation for the slaying of Uhtred. It seemed that Thurbrand's days were numbered.

✝✝✝

It was just after my fifteenth birthday, not that I could remember the actual date but I knew it was sometime in May, that Aldred sent for me. I'd been busy assessing the skills of three new armigers with Colby and Kjetil, both of whom helped me to train the armigers as riders. Other militares taught them swordsmanship, fighting on horseback and archery but I was involved in every aspect of their training. As I still looked after Colby and Osric my life was very full, too full I sometimes thought.

'You know that I have been asked by the king to counsel Earl Siward until he is older, Oeric?' Aldred asked me when I entered the hall.

'Yes, lord. It's rumoured that you will be moving to York as a result.'

'The rumour is true,' he said with a wry smile.

Nothing stayed secret for very long in our little community on top of the rock.

'I've done without an armiger up until now as Uuen looks after me and I've not felt the need. However, he is ill with a fever and I'm not sure he'll be able to travel, or indeed if he will survive at all.'

I'd heard that Uuen was ill, of course, but I hadn't appreciated how serious it was.

'Consequently I have been forced to choose a new servant to accompany me. Come forward Durfel.'

A boy about ten or eleven years of age stepped forward into the light afforded by the sun streaming through the hole in the roof that let out smoke from the central hearth. He was dressed in a simple blue wool tunic and brown trousers which were of a quality more appropriate to the son of a freeman than a slave. His face was unusually clean for one too. He had a pleasant face with a mouth that looked as if it was about to break into a smile and a mop of long brown hair, which also looked remarkably clean. The name was British and I guessed that he was one of the migrants who had invaded Upper Teesdale last year.

'Durfel is an orphan and was a present to me from the former Earl of Cumbria when we agreed on the grants of lands in Teesdale. He isn't a slave but a servant none the less. He will replace Uuen as my body servant for now. His English is limited and his Danish almost non-existent. He will need to improve the one and learn the other from you.'

'From me, lord?'

'Yes, I would like you to become my armiger and accompany me to York.'

I was taken aback. This was a great honour but several thoughts occurred to me almost immediately. Who would be in charge of the armigers now? Would any of the militares who now trained them be coming with us as part of his escort? How long did Aldred intend me to remain as his armiger? I was still growing, both in height and in body mass, but I had hopes of being made a militar next year or, at the very latest, the following year. Wouldn't it have made more sense to appoint a younger boy as his armiger and then he could serve Aldred for longer? Would I still be serving Colby, Kjetil, Osric and Hakon as well as Aldred? But I said none of this.

'I would be overjoyed to serve you, lord.'

Perhaps I was being a bit too effusive but what I had said was true. Aldred was my hero and all that I aspired to be in a man and I asked for nothing more than to serve him. However, my other dream was to be one of his militares.

'You will continue to oversee the armigers who will accompany us, of course, but Godric, who will remain here as castellan of Bebbanburg until Eadulf can return and take over, will sort out a replacement for your role here. You will need to discuss that with him as you know them best, and find someone to take over from you as armiger to your present militares. Do you have any questions?'

'Just one, lord. When do we leave?'

✝✝✝

It would be an understatement to say that Siward was less than pleased by the arrival of his mentor. He made it quite plain that he could manage his earldom very well on his own without interference from the man who looked after Bernicia for him. The implication of that statement was quite clear. Siward evidently intended to be seen as lord of the whole of Northumbria and not just Deira, like Earl Erik and his father.

I was there when they first met and admired how Aldred handled the young puppy. He ignored Siward's claim to be overlord of Bernicia and concentrated on the reason he was there.

'Of course, lord,' Aldred replied smoothly and without giving any indication of the anger he must have felt at being treated like a subordinate, and a barely tolerated one at that. 'I am here at the request of the king to give you whatever assistance you require until you officially come of age on your sixteenth birthday. To that end I suggest that I might attend meetings of your council and I will be, of course, available for you to consult privately whenever you think it necessary or helpful.'

Siward gave him a baleful look.

'I already have quite enough advice from the archbishop, thank you. I don't think I need anyone else interfering with my government of Northumbria.'

'I'm sure that Archbishop Ælfric can guide your spiritual welfare but I understand that he is an unworldly man with little experience of life outside the cloister. On the other hand I have some military knowledge and expertise in the management of my own earldom. It is not as simple as you might imagine. You will need to be judge, arbiter in disputes, commander in the field when necessary and a leader that your nobles will willingly follow. You also need to care for the people who call you lord. You may be called earl but it is an empty title until you earn the respect of your nobles.'

I watched Siward carefully during Aldred's little homily and I could see the boy earl getting more annoyed and impatient with every word he uttered.

'I don't need you to teach me how to rule,' he spat. 'My father brought me up to succeed him as Ealdorman of Beverley. I learned all I need to know from him. Now you may return to Bernicia just as soon as you have knelt and given me your oath of allegiance as your superior. One other thing, it is inappropriate for you to call yourself earl. In future you will be called the High Reeve of Bebbanburg and will be my deputy in Bernicia.'

I could hardly believe what I was hearing. This jumped-up child was acting like a tyrant. I looked in alarm at Aldred, knowing that he could lose his temper quite spectacularly if provoked enough.

'The king made me Earl of Bernicia and it is not for you to overturn his decision. He asked me to guide and help you but I fear I shall have to tell him that he has given me an impossible task. You think you know it all, Siward, but let me tell you, you know nothing. Your father once told me that you were a headstrong, opinionated boy who wouldn't be told. I now see how right he was. Well, you have made your bed, now you must lie in it. I hope you never need my help in the future because, after your treatment of me today, it will not be forthcoming.'

Siward was spluttering with rage and almost incoherent; however, he recovered sufficiently to call out to his guards to arrest Aldred. However, as the two in the door moved to intercept Aldred and myself the door opened and Colby and Hakon stepped in, pointing their spears at Siward's two housecarls.

'I wouldn't if I were you,' Hakon said grimly and the two guards dropped their spears.

We walked out of the hall to find our men already mounted and holding our horses ready for us.

'I gather your fears about the meeting were justified, lord, Kjetil said as we mounted.'

'Yes, the king has made a bad error of judgement in appointing him, but I know he won't change his mind. He'd be seen as weak if he did. So I'm afraid that we are lumbered with the little shit.'

Siward came running out of the hall just as we cantered towards the gates that led into the narrow streets of York. He called for the guards on the gates to stop us but there was nothing they could do unless they wanted to be trampled to death. Five minutes later we shook the dust of York from our horses' hooves and headed back north.

✝✝✝

'What does Cnut say?' Synne asked Aldred.

I was sitting in their chamber polishing the earl's helmet and playing with little Edith at the same time. The new baby, also a girl, lay asleep in her cradle being gently rocked by one of Synne's maids whilst Durfel put the earl's freshly washed and dried tunics and trousers away in a coffer. It was a peaceful domestic scene on the surface but the letter from the king, which had just arrived, brought with it tension and angst.

Aldred finished reading it and put it down. The expression on his face was not encouraging.

'He blames me for handling my meeting with Siward badly. It seems that his version of events reached Cnut first. He apparently wrote to complain that I was practically insisting on governing the earldom myself until he became of age. He says that, because of my past service, he doesn't intend to punish me but he has asked Archbishop Ælfric to mediate between us. I am to return to York forthwith.'

'Ælfric will be as much use as a nun in a brothel at making that boy see sense,' Synne said with a snort.

There were times when her childhood as a street urchin in York showed.

'Nevertheless I must obey. However, this time I shall take all my militares and their armigers and we will camp outside the town. I shall insist on meeting somewhere neutral. I wouldn't put it past Siward to arrest me as soon as I entered York.'

'He wouldn't dare!'

'I suspect that Siward is someone who acts first and thinks afterwards. At any rate I'm not about to put it to the test.'

✝✝✝

It seemed that whatever Cnut had written to Siward had chastened him somewhat. We met in a large tent erected between our campsite and the northern gates of York. Negotiations beforehand had arranged the details: the archbishop would chair the meeting and each earl was allowed to bring two advisers and two servants.

Siward was accompanied by two ealdormen: Ansgar of York and Folke of Leeds. Aldred chose Beda of Durham and, to my surprise, Bishop Edmund of Durham. Durfel and I were chosen as the servants on Aldred's side and we were there to dispense ale, mead and food. Of course, it also meant that I was privy to what was discussed so I wasn't upset by being cast in the role of servant.

The archbishop had the reputation of being venerable and wise, but his nickname of Puttoc, which meant buzzard, struck a rather different note. I later formed the opinion that he was self-serving and would always act in his own best interests. His pious demeanour hid an avaricious and ambitious nature.

'My lords, we are here at the request of the king to resolve a misunderstanding which I understand occurred when you, Lord Aldred, came to make obeisance to Earl Siward.'

If Aldred was upset at being addressed as lord, a title even the lowest thane was entitled to, whilst Siward was called earl he hid it well, for now.

'Then you understand incorrectly, archbishop,' Aldred said, interrupting Ælfric's somewhat unctuous opening remarks. 'Cnut send me to York, against my will I might add, to act as mentor to Siward whilst he was still a child.'

Ælfric seemed rather taken aback by Aldred's statement and sat there opening and closing his mouth in a fair imitation of a trout. I saw Siward's grin of triumph out of the corner of my eye. By butting in Aldred had upset the archbishop, which would naturally incline him towards the boy's side.

'I see, well if this is true...'

Poor Ælfric got no further. Aldred handed him the king's original letter asking him to guide and advise Siward. The archbishop read it and pursed his lips.

'Yes, well. This does seem to bear out what you claim, Lord Aldred.'

'Would you care to be a little more specific, archbishop? Does the king's letter ask me to mentor the boy or doesn't it?'

'Yes, it does,' he said, clearly uncomfortable at the turn the proceedings had taken.

'I don't need a mentor,' Siward loudly declared, 'and if I did, Aldred of Bebbanburg would be the last man I'd choose.'

'And you would be the last person I'd want to have to steer along a sensible path,' Aldred shot back. 'Unfortunately, the king has dictated otherwise and we've both got to make the best of it.'

'How can Cnut expect me to listen to a man who is my inferior? He shouldn't be called an earl, he's no more than a glorified ealdorman.'

'I'm afraid that isn't quite the case, Earl Siward,' Ælfric said, looking even more uncomfortable. 'In his letter to Earl Aldred King Cnut makes it quite clear that your earldom covers only Deira, not all of Northumbria. So you are both of equal status.'

His voice tailed off as he quailed before the look of fury on the boy's face.

'Why is it that only you know of this? What hasn't the king written to me? I don't believe you. You're siding with Aldred.'

'I assure you that I'm not lying to you, lord earl,' Ælfric said stiffly.

If Ælfric had started on Siward's side, which was understandable seeing as how he was the boy's senior prelate, that didn't seem to be the case any longer.

Siward didn't respond. He got up, knocking his chair back as he did so, and stormed out of the tent, hastily followed by his bemused ealdormen.

'How can anyone be expected to advise such a spoilt brat?' Aldred asked no one in particular. 'God help Deira with such an earl.'

'I'm sure he will,' Ælfric muttered piously, but he didn't sound as if he believed it.

'I presume that you'll write to the king to advise him of the failure of your attempts to mediate, and making it clear why you failed?'

'I er, um.'

A look of panic crossed Ælfric's face. He wasn't about to admit any such thing to Cnut.

'No, we'll meet here again at the same time tomorrow. In the meantime I'll try and calm Earl Siward down.'

Aldred nodded, reluctantly accepting that Cnut wouldn't understand if he refused a second attempt at mediation.

'I don't envy my poor sister, having to marry that wretch,' Aldred muttered to Beda as they left the tent.

'Hopefully he might have grown up a bit before then,' Beda replied, but without much conviction.

✝✝✝

Siward came into the tent the next morning looking sulky. Nevertheless, he was there and he seemed prepared to listen to what the archbishop had to say.

'It's unfortunate, to say the least, that we got off to such a poor start yesterday,' Ælfric Puttoc said with an ingratiating smile.

'Pardon me for interrupting,' Bishop Edmund said, speaking for the first time, 'but shouldn't we begin our deliberations with a prayer, lord archbishop?'

'What, oh, yes. Of course. How remiss of me; especially as we need God's guidance to avoid any further misunderstandings.'

The archbishop looked disconcerted at being rebuked, if ever so politely, by his junior.

'Perhaps you would be good enough to lead us in prayer, Bishop Edmund?' Ælfric suggested rather peevishly.

'Of course, archbishop. Lord God, we beseech you to guide our thoughts and utterances in the ways of cooperation and friendliness so that the peoples of Bernicia and Deira, and especially those entrusted with their leadership, may live in harmony and affability from now on. In the name of God the Father, God the Son and God the Holy Ghost. Amen.'

It was a pious hope, but also a cleverly worded rebuke to both of the argumentative earls.

Everyone joined in saying *amen* except Siward who continued to look like a boy denied something he'd been promised.

'Well, now that we have clarified the matter of the relationship between the two of you, it seems to me that the one remaining question is providing advice to Earl Siward until he reaches adulthood,' Ælfric said brightly.

He was about to continue when Bishop Edmund spoke again.

'If I may make a suggestion, lord archbishop,' he said tentatively. 'Perhaps the answer might be to form a small council where matter of policy and complex problems could be discussed and resolved.'

'Rather like the king's council, you mean?'

'Precisely.'

'Would that be a sensible arrangement, Earl Siward?' the archbishop asked.

'Provided that man isn't part of it, I suppose so.'

That man was obviously Aldred who nodded his head.

'I have no reason to interest myself in the affairs of Deira,' Aldred said with some relief. 'I am only here because of the king's instructions. If you can get me excused, archbishop, I would be most grateful.'

Much to my surprise Siward greeted these words with a faint smile and was almost affable as we took our leave.

'Well, that ended rather better than I'd expected,' Beda said as we mounted our horses to ride back to our camp.

'Yes, I must say I hadn't anticipated such a volte face after you suggested a council to support him, bishop. I had rather thought that he was determined to rule alone,' Aldred said.

'Oh, I don't think it was taking advice that he objected to,' Edmund replied. 'It was taking advice from you. I rather think it was a simple case of jealousy. He knew of your reputation and feared that you would try and take over the running of Deira, using him as a mere figurehead.'

'That I would become de facto the Earl of Northumbria, you mean?'

'Yes, after all Uhtred was and he probably thinks that you desire what your father had.'

'Well, at least Siward is one less problem to worry about,' Aldred said with finality.

It was a pious hope but Edmund was only partially correct. Siward was jealous, but he was also ambitious and he never gave up his desire to unite Northumbria once more.

Chapter Four – Vengeance at Last

Spring 1024

My back ached and my arms felt as if they were falling off as we rowed out to sea with the wind on our bows. The day was typical for late April: brief interludes of warm sunshine followed by overcast skies and then squally showers before the sun put in another brief appearance. Then we turned to head south with the wind on our beam and the ships boys hauled up the sail. At last we could rest our weary bodies for a spell and I collapsed beside my sea chest, which served as my rowing seat.

We were heading for Holderness and a reckoning with Thurbrand the Hold, the other man responsible for the plot to kill Aldred's father, Uhtred. The mood was one of excited expectancy tinged with a little apprehension as we didn't know any of the details.

One of the youngest armigers, a boy called Acca, handed me a ladle full of water and a lump of bread with a cheeky grin. No doubt he found it amusing to see the earl's armiger exhausted but I summoned up enough energy to sit on my chest and take what he offered before clipping him around the ear for his impudence. His grin broadened and I scowled back at him.

He had only just joined us at the age of thirteen but already I found his irrepressible good humour irritating in the extreme. Whenever he messed up, which he did quite a lot, he would accept his punishment with a cheery smile. It seemed the disapproval of his seniors made little impression on him. What Erian, who had taken over from me as the senior armiger when I went to serve the earl, thought about him I didn't know. I was just grateful he wasn't my responsibility.

Acca moved along to the next rower who, like most of the oarsmen, was one of the militares. Aldred needed a crew of thirty rowers and four ship's boys, together with a helmsman, for each of the two birlinns that he was taking on this raid. Fifty of the rowers were militares so he had made up the numbers with the ten oldest armigers. Some were younger and less muscular than me and I pitied them. If I found it hard I dreaded to think what they felt. I imagine that they thought they had entered Hell. It didn't matter how strong we were, we weren't used to rowing and we were using muscles we didn't know we had.

Acca and the other boys finished giving us refreshments and he was sent up the mast as lookout. Our two birlinns had left Budle Bay, the natural harbour under the looming mass of Bebbanburg, at midday. We had a voyage of a hundred and forty miles ahead of us which would take us a whole day and night to complete, and that was if the wind held.

We gathered that Aldred's plan was to arrive off Spurn Head in the afternoon of the second day. We would then wait over the horizon until dusk. Rowing into the mouth of the Humber in the dark was perilous as there were sand bars and the only illumination, other than the moon if we were lucky, would be from the candlelit huts in the villages along the shore of Holderness and from the port of Grimsby on the Mercian shore of the estuary.

As the afternoon drew to a close the armigers helped the militares don their hauberks, coifs, helmets and then they prepared their weapons. I belted Aldred's sword around his waist but the others left theirs beside their chests; it was too difficult to row wearing them.

The sun sank over the horizon to the west, painting the sky in vivid hues of orange, red and dark purple, which were reflected in dappled patterns on the surface of the water. Not having sailed a great deal, I was mesmerised by the colourful display of a sunset at sea. However, my reverie was rudely interrupted by Aldred's shouted command and we pushed our oars out through the holes in the hull just below the gunwale and started to pull for the coast.

An hour later we rounded Spurn Head under cover of darkness. Sailing at night was always a risky undertaking, but it was the only way that we could get near to Newsham, where Thurband's hall was located, clandestinely.

We passed the dim lights of Grimsby to our left and a stretch of mudflats called Foul Holme Sands now lay to our right all along the north shore. Halfway along there was a narrow inlet that led into the wetlands behind the mud. Thankfully the entrance was marked by poles sunk into the mud or we would never have spotted it. This led to a small basin where Thurbrand moored his knarrs and small longships, called snekkjas. There were huts nearby to store the merchandise he traded in and, so Aldred had been told, another hut to house the housecarls on guard duty to protect the small harbour and its contents. The rest of the crews lived at Newsham with their lord or in one of the nearby fishing villages that dotted the North Sea coast.

The entrance to the harbour was only wide enough for one ship at a time. It seemed obvious to Aldred that there would be a watchtower at the entrance and he had his best archer in the bows ready to put an arrow into the lookout before he could raise the alarm. However, there was nothing and we glided silently up the channel that led to the basin beyond. The only sounds were the gently splashing water at the bows and the hooting of owls in the distance as they hunted small rodents.

As we drew closer we heard the faint sound of singing coming from dead ahead and then several huts silhouetted against the slightly lighter night sky appeared out of the darkness. In one of them a feeble light escaped from the gaps in the poorly made shutters over a window.

We drifted in towards the wooden jetty and bumped alongside a snekkja. Acca leaped aboard it from the bows and someone threw him a rope which he made fast whilst another ship's boy did the same at the stern.

The warriors clambered ashore, trying to keep any noise to a minimum, whilst we armigers stayed behind with the two steersmen to guard our respective ships. Acca came and stood beside me as we watched the dark shapes move stealthily towards the hut with the light. I couldn't believe that Thurbrand's housecarls were so lax; they should have put out at least one sentry. I suppose they felt themselves safe so far inside their lord's territory.

Suddenly light spilled out from the open doorway and we saw half a dozen of our men rush inside. Startled shouts, screams and a brief clash of metal on metal shattered the quiet of the night and then silence returned. I heard later that there were half a dozen men drinking and playing a game of chance inside the hut. Only one had managed to reach his sword before the killing started. They were all dead without so much as a scratch on any of our men.

†††

An hour later the huts and their contents were burning merrily. We had moved the ships out into the middle of the basin, away from the flames, towing Thurbrand's two longships and three knarrs with us. Whilst the militares melted into the darkness away from the flames we boys set about chopping holes in the hulls of the two snekkjas so that they would sink. It seemed a shame not to take them back with us as the spoils of the raid, but we simply didn't have the men to man them, especially as they required a bigger crew than our birlinns did.

The knarrs were a different proposition. They were dependent on wind power for propulsion and only had a few oars for manoeuvring in harbour. Therefore they could make do with a crew of half a dozen each and, although that would leave our two birlinns undermanned, it didn't matter overmuch as we would all have to rely on wind power if we were to escort the knarrs.

I brought my axe down time and time again against the stout oak planks and eventually they began to give way. There was no way my fellow armigers and I could chop through the thick wood; our task was to loosen the bronze nails that held them in place so that water could seep in through the gaps that we'd created. Hopefully we would have plenty of time to regain our own ships before they sank beneath the water. I paused in my labours and wiped the sweat from my brow with my hand. Although it was a chilly evening I was hot and stripped off my padded leather gambeson. Underneath, my thin woollen tunic was drenched.

'Don't be an idiot, Oeric, you'll catch a chill,' Acca scolded me. 'The drying sweat will lower your body temperature quickly in the cool of the evening.'

At first my reaction was the familiar one of irritation with him and I was about to rebuke him for insolence, but the boy's strictures reminded me that I'd heard that he was the son of some thane before the loss of Lothian. After that he'd been sent as a novice to the twin monasteries of Wearmouth and

70

Jarrow. He'd been one of the assistants to the infirmarian and had gained a basic knowledge of the ills of the body. However, he had got up to a lot of mischief and the Abbot complained about him to Aldred during one of his infrequent visits. The earl had interviewed him and thought the boy had promise as a warrior, so he agreed to take him on as an armiger.

I glared at Acca but I doubt if he saw it in the darkness. However, I put my gambeson back on before attacking the planking of the hull with renewed vigour. I knew Acca was right but that made it worse. I was angry with myself for looking an idiot in his eyes. I wouldn't have minded so much if it was anyone else, but he'd succeeded in getting under my skin.

We had just done enough damage for me to feel confident that the snekkja was irreparably damaged when we heard shouts coming from the shore. We scrambled back aboard our birlinn and rowed it slowly away from the sinking ship before dropping the anchor again. Then we rushed to the side nearest the burning huts and tried to make out what was happening.

We could see figures silhouetted against the flames as they rushed to the jetty to fill buckets and then ran back to throw them on the conflagration. It did little good but the fires were dying down now in any case. Then we spotted our own men as they arose from the marshy ground where they'd been hiding and silently killed the men on the periphery of the fire fighters. Perhaps a dozen men had been slain before someone noticed them and a cry of alarm went up.

The militares quickly formed a shield wall whilst their opponents tried to organise themselves. They were unprepared for combat; most hadn't bothered to put on byrnies and helmets in their rush to deal with the fire and few had anything to fight with other than swords and daggers. None had shields.

Three of the enemy were mounted, presumably Thurbrand and two of his sons. I knew that he had three surviving sons. Edgar, the eldest, had been killed by Siward's father, Bjorn, years before. The others were Sumarlithr, Carl and Thurbrand the younger. If my assumption that the horsemen were indeed Thurbrand and two of his sons, it would mean that one had avoided the trap.

Several of the men on foot had fled and Aldred let them go. It was Thurbrand he was after and his militares now concentrated on surrounding the three riders. My focus on what was happening on shore was suddenly interrupted as Acca tugged at my sleeve and pointed at something on the water. The moon had reappeared and the line of silver across the natural harbour was suddenly broken by a dark shape. At first I couldn't make it out, and then I realised that it was a fishing boat that we hadn't spotted when we first landed.

It seemed to be making straight for us and it was full of men. I tried to count them but they moved out of the light on the water and it was difficult to make out men individually. From the size of the craft I estimated that there could be up to ten enemy housecarls aboard her. It was fairly obvious that they were going to board us as we were the nearest of the five ships.

†††

'What do we do, Oeric?' Acca asked and I realised that the four ship's boys and even the steersman were looking to me for leadership.

We had our daggers, of course, but no other weapons of our own. The steersman, an old sailor called Gifre, only had his eating knife. I looked around, trying not to panic, then I remembered that there were three spare shields, several bows and quivers and two spare spears in a bundle at the base of the mast.

'Who can use a bow?' I yelled.

None of the boys answered. It required a certain strength to use a war bow and of those on board only I had the physique required to pull and release properly. The bows that the others used in training were smaller and required far less effort.

'I can, though it's many years since I used one,' Gifre said picking up a bow and two quivers full of arrows.

He rushed to the side of the ship and a few seconds later the first arrow flew towards the oncoming boat. It missed, plunging into the water a foot to one side of the bows. Gifre cursed and sent several more arrows on their way in the next minute or so. At least one hit someone, judging by the cries from the boat.

Meanwhile I'd picked up another bow and quiver and ran to join Gifre.

'Acca, bring me a shield and those spears. The rest of you, grab an oar. Your task is to fend that boat off.'

The fishing boat was much smaller than the birlinn and its gunwale was several feet below ours. The housecarls would have difficulty in climbing aboard and they would probably have to hoist each other up – not an easy task from a relatively unstable small boat. If my companions could fend them off with the oars, then it would be quite impossible for them to get aboard.

I joined Gifre at the rail and managed to send two arrows into the mass of men in the boat. I heard one squeal in pain and felt some satisfaction. However, even those with arrows in their limbs seemed determined to board us and wreak their revenge on us. Acca and the other boys leaned down holding an oar each and pushed the fishing boat away whilst I took careful aim and managed to send an arrow into the chest of the man in the prow. He toppled into the water with a splash, which only served to drive the rest to greater efforts.

I dropped the bow and armed myself with spear and shield. One of the housecarls grabbed one of our oars and tugged. The armiger holding it had to let go or he would have been pulled overboard. A second or two later their boat banged against our hull. The first man was lifted up by his companions in the boat so that he could grasp the gunwale. As soon as he did so

I stabbed down and drove the point of my spear into his neck. He fell down into the boat, knocking another man into the water. It was plain that he couldn't swim because he thrashed around and eventually sank beneath the surface.

I threw my spear at another man and hit him in the stomach, then grabbed the second spear. Two more men were lifted up and I managed to stab one in the shoulder. He fell away but now I realised that the second man had managed to get aboard and had killed poor old Gifre. The moonlight illuminated half the man's face and I was unnerved by it. There was a livid scar running from a milk white eye down his cheek and into his beard. The scar evidently continued to his chin as the line of it under his beard had turned the hair white.

He had drawn his sword and his dagger and now eyed me like a wolf eyes the lamb destined to be its next meal. His face split into a lopsided grin and he hacked at my shield with his sword whilst thrusting his dagger towards my unprotected side. I'd made the mistake of letting him get inside my spear and the damned thing was next to useless. I felt the jar of the sword on my right arm, and even protected by the shield, it went numb for a while.

The dagger cut into my padded leather gambeson and I felt a sudden pain in my side. I knew that he'd drawn blood but I didn't know how serious the wound was. I was dimly aware of a cry of triumph as the armigers managed to push the fishing boat away from the side of our ship, accompanied by a splash as another man fell into the water. I thought fleetingly that there couldn't be many more left now, but that didn't help me.

I had faced many an adversary on the training field but had never fought in anger before. I was now acutely aware that mock combat is very different to the real thing. Scarface moved around to my left and made a feint at my head. I instinctively raised my shield to block it and he dropped to one knee in order to make a sweeping cut at my lower legs.

The counter-move was something that I had practiced many times and, almost without thinking, I jumped in the air as the blade swept underneath me. Scarface was now at a disadvantage. He was kneeling and off balance as his blow hadn't landed. I let go of my spear and, as he tried to rise, I pulled out my dagger and aimed it at the back of his neck. Unfortunately, I hadn't allowed for movement as he tried to regain his feet and the blade plunged into his left shoulder instead.

He gave a roar, whether of pain or fury I wasn't quite sure, and jumped to his feet, my dagger still impaled in his shoulder. Having thrown away my spear and lost my dagger, I only had my shield with which to defend myself. I noticed that he had dropped his own dagger when I'd wounded him and I decided my only chance was to grab it. As he raised his sword and stepped towards me I shoved my shield with all the force I could muster at his face and had the satisfaction of hearing the metal boss crush his nose and break his cheekbone.

He cursed and staggered away from me, blinded by pain, and I bent down to scoop up the dagger.

Unfortunately, he had retained his grip on his sword despite the agony he must have been in and thrust it at me with all his might. So great was the force behind it that the point of the sword went through my shield and cut into my forearm.

I staggered back, letting go of my shield. He saw his opportunity and, with a cry of triumph, he charged at me with his sword drawn back to cut my head from my shoulders. I had never been so scared in my life and, albeit briefly, I shut my eyes and waited for the killing blow. When I opened them again a moment later I could scarce believe my eyes.

Acca had jumped on Scarface's back, wrapped his skinny legs around the man's waist. Holding on grimly whilst the man tried to dislodge him, the boy had calmly plunged his dagger into Scarface's neck. He missed the carotid artery but it gave me the opportunity I needed. I thrust my borrowed dagger into his chest and, more by luck than judgement, found his heart. He collapsed onto the deck with Acca still wrapped about his back.

I went to pull the dead man off my rescuer and to thank him profusely for saving my life, but instead the world went black.

✝✝✝

When I awoke my side hurt like hell and my forearm wasn't much better. Gradually I became aware that the deck under me was moving about quite violently and I realised that, not only were we at sea, but we were being tossed about with the wind howling in the rigging. Salt water cascaded over the side of the ship and splashed my face. I spluttered and spat out a mouthful of brine. I was now fully awake.

'He's back in the land of the living,' I heard Acca call out cheerfully and I looked to my right to find him kneeling by my side.

'We thought we'd lost you. Don't you ever give me a scare like that again,' he said with a broad grin on his face.

'Wha... what happened?' I asked. 'Did the earl kill Thurbrand?'

'No, you did. Earl Aldred wasn't best pleased as he wanted that pleasure for himself.'

'Scarface was Thurbrand the Hold?'

'Apparently so. He and two of his sons got others to take their place on horseback whilst they tried to escape by boat. He obviously thought that taking a birlinn guarded by a few boys would be easy. How wrong he was. They attacked us with eight housecarls but we managed to kill all but two of them. They were captured and turned out to be two of Thurbrand's sons. They confirmed that the man you killed was their father before Earl Aldred hanged them.'

'Ah, so the boy who robbed me of my revenge is back with us, is he?' I looked up to see the earl looking down at me as he struggled to keep his footing on the heaving deck.

I was worried until I saw the smile on his face.

'Well done lad. I need to reward you for your courage when you recover. In the meantime I fear I'll need to replace you as my armiger.'

'I'm sorry lord,'

'What for? It's not many boys your age who can beat an experienced warrior like Thurbrand.'

'I did have a little help, lord. If it wasn't for Acca I'd be dead.'

'So I hear. He has earned my gratitude too.'

Acca brought me some water to sip and covered me with an oiled wool cloak to keep the waves that were still breaking over the ship from soaking me. I thanked him and then drifted back into unconsciousness. I learned later that I had lost a lot of blood and looked like death. Acca had cleaned and sewed up my side whilst Durfel took care of the less serious cut on my forearm. We had other casualties including two dead, but none of the wounded were as severely injured as I was.

As I lay there I re-evaluated my opinion of Acca. I had thought him nothing but a flippant child. Certainly he was annoyingly cheerful all the time and didn't take my rebukes seriously, or at least he appeared not to. But he had saved my life, and that had taken courage and showed a certain strength of character. Furthermore, for some reason he seemed to have attached himself to me. I found that I no longer disliked him quite so much; in fact I came to the conclusion that I quite liked him.

After the storm had passed he brought me more water and some cold meats. There was little enough of the latter on board and I did wonder where he got it from. The thought that he might have stolen it for me was rather touching. For the rest of our slow return voyage we talked whenever he got a spare moment, which wasn't that often. He didn't talk much about himself or his family, but he was full of amusing stories about his time as a novice. By the time that we docked back in Budle Bay he and I had become friends.

The mission had been a great success. Of course, one of Thurband's sons, Carl, had escaped but no one thought much about it at the time. That was a mistake. Carl would prove to be more of a threat to the lords of Bebbanburg than his father ever was.

Chapter Five – The Return of Macbeth

1024/1025

Of course the slaying of Thurbrand and two of his sons became common knowledge very quickly. Most had no doubts as to who was to blame. Thurbrand had been responsible for Uhtred's death and, without the payment of weregild, the pursuit of a blood feud was the inevitable response in our culture. However, one or two thought that Siward might have ordered his death. It was a reasonable assumption in view of the fact that Thurbrand was strongly suspected of being the man behind the murder of Earl Bjorn. King Cnut did nothing, not that we expected him to, and life in Bernicia carried on as before.

It took me a long time to fully recover. After a few weeks my side had healed well enough for me to walk short distances and I was impatient to wield a sword and ride again. However, Acca convinced me that to rush things would be folly. He had three militares of his own to look after but he seemed to think that he also had to be my body servant. To be honest I found that his fussing over me like a mother hen with a chick a little embarrassing, especially when the other armigers teased him about it.

I had expected him to be annoyed by this but he treated their jibes with his normal good humour and they soon stopped. I was something of a hero for having killed Thurbrand and Acca shared in the esteem in which I was held because of the vital part he'd played. Consequently he was respected by his peers, even if they didn't understand his evident devotion to me.

By the time autumn turned into winter and the first snow fell I was able to move normally once more and, despite a bit of stiffness in my side, I began to train with sword and shield again. My muscles had wasted away through lack of use and I was slow and clumsy at first. Acca made an ideal fighting partner initially but I soon began to beat him regularly and Godric pitted me against other armigers who were nearer my age and then, when I could beat them, against Colby and some of the younger militares.

I also began to ride again, usually with the ever faithful Acca as my companion. Two inches of snow lay on the ground when I commenced my combat training on horseback. I found it difficult keeping control of my horse in the slippery conditions whilst using spear, axe and sword against my opponents but gradually I improved.

One day the blizzard conditions kept us all indoors. I was helping Acca to clean his masters' hauberks, as I had not yet been allocated militares of my own to look after when the boy who had replaced me as the earl's armiger came to tell me that Aldred wanted to see me. I assumed that he wanted to tell me it was time that I returned to full duty. However, I was puzzled because that would be left to Godric, or even the current senior armiger.

'Oeric, come and sit down.'

I was startled as few were invited to sit in Aldred's presence, but the smile that Synne bestowed on me was encouraging. Durfel came and gave me a goblet of mead which I took nervously, feeling quite out of my depth. When we had returned from Holderness it was to find that Uuen had died in our absence and Durfel had now been confirmed as the earl's body servant.

Aldred mourned Uuen's passing as they had been together for some time and Uuen had been the last link with his father. He had been Uhtred's body servant before he was Aldred's and he and Wictred, who had been killed at Melrose during the Carham campaign in 1018, had been the only ones to escape the massacre when Uhtred and his warband were slain by Thurbrand and Eadwulf.

'I'm told that you are now fully fit again and have done well against your opponents, not only the older armigers but also some of the militares,' Aldred said, jerking my mind back to the present.

'Thank you, lord. I'm only sorry that it has taken me so long to get fit again.'

'It was only to be expected; after all, we nearly lost you. At the time,' he continued, 'I said that I would reward you for killing Thurbrand. Now that you are completely recovered I've decided to make you one of my militares. I know that you are young for this – you won't be sixteen for a few months yet and normally I wait until armigers are seventeen or eighteen - but I think you have earned it.'

'Lord earl, I don't know what to say. You do me great honour.'

'It's no more than you deserve. One more thing. I've noticed how devoted young Acca is to you. I've therefore asked Godric to allocate him as armiger to you, Colby and Osric. I don't think he was best pleased as it means making several changes to the established sections so don't expect Godric to go easy on you.'

'I wouldn't have it any other way, lord,' I said with a grin.

He half smiled and I rose, handed my still full goblet back to Durfel, bowed to the earl and then his lady, and left his chamber feeling euphoric.

✝✝✝

Colby and Osric seemed pleased to have me as part of their section. We had been good friends when we'd all been armigers and we took up again where that had left off. Needless to say Acca was delighted. Now he could go on looking after me legitimately.

'I can't think why he seems so devoted to me,' I said to the two of them one day.

'Don't you know?' Colby replied. 'He told me that you remind him very much of his elder brother; the one who died at Carham. I gather that they were very close.'

That explained a lot. I didn't think it was only hero-worship for killing Thurbrand. In fact he saved my life, not the other way around. He had tried to befriend me before that and that had made me a little uncomfortable. The senior armiger needed to keep the younger ones at a distance if he was going to impose discipline. Now I knew the probable reason I was somewhat relieved.

We heard sporadically what was happening in the rest of the world. In Scotland Malcolm was still having problems in Galloway and with the Norse of Cumbria, whilst fresh trouble had broken out in the north. Like Findlay before him, Máel Coluim of Moray was too fond of his independence for his king's liking. In particular, he had stopped sending Malcolm the taxes he owed him.

We did speculate what he'd do about Moray but none of us came close to his next move.

'I have a task for you three,' Aldred told us at the beginning of March.

The temperature had risen and the thaw has started, helped along by quite a lot of rain.

'You all remember Macbeth? He arrives at Sunderland by sea in four days' time. I want you to meet his ship and escort him north to the crossing over the Tweed at Norham. He'll be met there by an escort of Earl Hacca's men.'

'Is Cnut turning him over to Malcolm?' Colby asked in alarm. 'The Scots will kill him.'

'No, apparently Malcolm has forgiven him. He has promised him lands near the southern boundary of Moray. Obviously he expects him to harass Máel

Coluim in return, perhaps even kill him. Macbeth must have jumped at the opportunity to get his revenge on his father's killers.'

'I wouldn't have thought he'd find that very easy. He's what now, barely eighteen? And with no power base in Scotland,' I said. 'It seems more likely to me that he's the one likely to end up dead.'

'That's not our concern,' Aldred reminded me. 'Our task is to get him across the Tweed safely.'

It was at least a two day ride to Sunderland and so we set out early the next morning. The journey was uneventful, if uncomfortable thanks to frequent rain showers and a road deep in slush that was rapidly turning into thick mud. We arrived in Sunderland tired, saddle sore and soaked to the skin just as the sun was setting on the second day. Even Acca's sunny disposition had taken a hit. He didn't complain – he never did – but he was very quiet, which wasn't like him at all.

Once we had found a tavern near the jetty his spirits soon picked up. He was everywhere, taking care of our horses in the stables, much to the annoyance of the tavern's ostler and his stable lads; polishing our chain mail and helmets; drying our clothes and making a vain attempt to rid the filthy woollen blanket that covered the one bed in the shared room of bugs and lice. In the end he gave up and we ended up sleeping on the floor wrapped in our cloaks.

Macbeth arrived at noon the next day. He'd changed a great deal since the last time that any of us had seen him. Then he'd been a gangling thirteen year old and now he was a broad-shouldered young man with a bushy red beard that was a few shades darker than his flaming red head of hair.

He greeted us warmly enough and seemed pleased to be re-united with Osric and Colby. He didn't remember me, but there was no reason he should have. He ignored Acca when he was introduced, which annoyed me, but the boy didn't seem bothered.

Macbeth's only companion was a surly Scot who Malcolm had sent to act as his body servant. He was a man in his thirties from Fife called Fibh. I strongly suspected that he'd been sent to spy on Macbeth as well as serve him. In the time that we were together he kept himself apart from us and never spoke to us. He only responded to Macbeth when spoken to.

That first night we camped by a stream. Thankfully the weather had improved and, although the ground was saturated, the rain had stopped and practically all the slush and snow had gone. Macbeth and my fellow militares were busy talking about the time he was rescued from Malcolm's camp at Melrose and I was feeling a bit left out until Acca came and sat beside me, his chores for the evening all done.

'I gather you think I look like your brother,' I said, thinking to find out a bit more about his family.

Immediately his face clouded over and I saw that I'd upset him.

'Yes,' he said quietly, 'but not just similar to him, you could be Horsa's twin.'

'Horsa was your elder brother who was killed at Carham?'

'Yes, along with my father. He was the Thane of Torphichen, which some filthy Scot now owns, he said, giving Fibh a dirty look.

That stunned me; my father's farm had been near Torphichen and had been owned by Acca's father. Most of the Lothian thanes had followed Hacca of Edinburgh and joined Malcolm's army before Carham but a few had refused and had fought for the Bernicians. Evidently Acca's father and brother were amongst the latter.

'My father's farm was near Torphichen,' I said quietly, 'before the Scots burned our home to the ground and killed the rest of my family.'

Acca gave me a startled look.

'What?'

I suddenly had a thought that I found disturbing in the extreme. I got up and muttering something about needing to go for a piss I wandered off along the stream. It was too dark to see much until the moon suddenly appeared. I found myself beside a still pool cut into the bank of the stream. I could only make out my reflection dimly in the silvery light but it was enough for me to be able to study my reflection. It confirmed what I had suspected. I might look the same as Acca's dead brother, but there was also a certain resemblance to him.

I sat down, my mind in a whirl. It couldn't be a coincidence that I looked like both of them. My father had always been cold towards me; unlike the way he treated my siblings. Perhaps he had known what I now strongly suspected. He and my mother were close enough and they had the girls after me, so he didn't hold a grudge against her for straying; just against me. I could only think of one reason for that.

Eventually it began to rain and that drove me back to the campsite. By then I had reached a conclusion which seemed to fit with what I knew. Acca's father had to be my natural father. My mother wouldn't have cuckolded her husband willingly, therefore she must have been raped. I felt sick and when Acca looked at me anxiously from where he was lying near the embers of the fire, I ignored him. I wrapped myself in my cloak and lay down on the opposite side of the fire. I couldn't sleep; I kept turning things over in my mind time and time again. It made no difference. I always came to the same conclusion. I was the product of rape and Acca was my half-brother.

✝✝✝

A priest came out to meet us when we rode into the village of Norham and shortly afterwards a rotund man came waddling up to join him. As we were now near the border the three of us had donned our war gear.

'I'm Father Bealdric and this is Cedric, the reeve. We don't often see the earl's men here as these are the bishop's lands. What are you doing here?' he asked self-importantly.

'We're here to meet Earl Hacca at the ford,' Colby, who was the senior, told him brusquely.

'Oh, you haven't heard?'

'Heard? Heard what?'

'Hacca is dead,' Bealdric said, not without a certain amount of glee.

'Dead? How?' Osric asked.

The priest shrugged.

'His wife woke up beside his corpse one morning, or so we heard.'

'Serve him right for betraying us,' Cedric added.

'Who is Earl of Lothian now then?' I asked.

'Not sure,' Cedric replied. 'We believe that Malcom the Destroyer has moved into the fortress on Edinburgh Rock.'

We thanked them and rode eastwards out of the village to the ford.

'What do we do now?' Colby asked.

'Does it matter if Hacca is dead?' Macbeth asked. 'It's Malcolm who sent for me and, if he's in Edinburgh, surely he'll send an escort to collect me?'

We camped by the ford just outside Norham for three days but the only people who crossed in either direction were farmers with produce to sell and shepherds moving their flocks from one pasture to the next. Borders didn't seem to apply to them.

'Do you think one of us should try and find out what is happening?' Osric asked us that evening. 'We can't sit here for ever; for a start our supplies are nearly exhausted.

'You can always buy more in the village,' Macbeth said, in a tone that implied that Osric was stupid.

'And pay for them how? I'm not spending what little money I have just so we can go on sitting here until Judgement Day.'

Aldred had given us a small purse of silver sceattas but that had been spent on the room at the tavern and provisions that we had already eaten.

'I suggest that you cross the river tomorrow and ride into Berwick. Whoever is now the lord must know what is happening,' Colby suggested. 'Take Acca with you.'

'No, not Acca. I'll go on my own.' I replied.

Acca looked close to tears but I hardened my heart. I just didn't want to be alone with him right now. Colby and Osric both gave me strange looks but said nothing. We had avoided each other up until now but my refusal to take him had made it obvious that there was some sort of rift between us. The silence lengthened until Macbeth broke it.

'I suppose we could always kill a few of those sheep,' he suggested, pointing at the flock on the north bank of the Tweed.

'And break the treaty between Cnut and Malcolm? I don't suppose either of them would thank us for that.'

Osric was exaggerating somewhat. Small raids across the Tweed still occurred and none had threatened the peace between England and Scotland so far. Nevertheless Aldred would not be pleased with us if he found out.

Acca dejectedly saddled my horse the next morning. I nearly said something to him but I still felt sick when I thought about how I'd been conceived and I just couldn't look at him. It wasn't his fault, of course, but I felt so ashamed. He stumbled away and I mounted without his help.

However, before I reached the ford I saw two riders with a packhorse coming towards us from the east. I rode back and dismounted. We armed ourselves ready for trouble but, as they descended the steep path from the bluff overlooking the ford to the campsite, we relaxed.

'It's Wulfgar and an armiger,' Colby said in relief.

Wulfgar had been at Carham and had rescued Iuwine, the former Ealdorman of Berwick, when the fyrd had followed Earl Eadwulf's example and fled. He had been accepted by Aldred as one of the first armigers and had now been a militar for several years.

'I'm glad I've found you,' Wulfgar said as he dismounted. 'Aldred wasn't sure you'd still be here.'

'What's happening? We were on the point of leaving because we're almost out of supplies.'

'You know Hacca is dead, of course, well Malcolm has now appointed Hacca's son, Wigbehrt, to be the new Earl of Lothian.'

'Not Duncan?' Macbeth asked, surprised. 'Wigbehrt can't be more than fourteen or fifteen; I would have thought he wanted someone reliable to defend his southern border.'

'No, Duncan is to be called King of Strathclyde apparently, but it means nothing. It merely signifies that he is Malcolm's chosen heir.'

'What happens to me?' Macbeth asked. 'I didn't trust Hacca overmuch but at least I knew him. I'm not about to entrust my life to a child.'

'No, you are to return with me to Bebbanburg. King Malcolm has sent a ship to take you to Angus.'

Chapter Six – Family Matters

Spring 1025

The journey back to Bebbanburg was uneventful except for an unpleasant conversation I had with Colby.

'What on earth is wrong between you and Acca?' he asked quietly as he rode away from Norham beside me. 'You are both as miserable as sin and you're making Osric and me depressed as well. Why have you fallen out?'

'We haven't' I said curtly. 'I can't explain.'

'Well, you're going to have to. We can't go on like this. We depend on each other in combat and we need to be a team. We used to be a good one; not anymore.'

'You don't need to worry. I'm going to ask Earl Aldred to release me from my oath of allegiance when we reach Bebbanburg.'

'You're what? Why on earth would you do that? Being part of the militares is your life.'

'Yes,' I said sadly, 'but I'm not worthy. I'm unclean and not fit to serve with you.'

It was more than I had intended to say and, of course, Colby wouldn't leave it there. He dropped back and I was conscious that he was having an earnest conversation with Osric.

'What on earth is the matter, Oeric? What's upset you so much that you would leave us? Is it Acca? Has he done something unforgivable?'

'No, not at all. He is innocent of any involvement. It's me. I just can't go on now that I know.....'

I broke off, unwilling to explain.

Both of them tried to get me to say more as we travelled but I refused. I saw Colby ask Acca if he knew what was wrong with me but the boy just shrugged and looked away. I felt even worse, knowing how much he must be hurting inside.

'You asked have a word with me, Oeric,' Aldred said the day after we had arrived back at Bebbanburg. We had just said goodbye to Macbeth and we were riding back from the jetty in Budle Bay to the sea gate. I looked around me and saw Colby and Osric within earshot.

'Yes, please lord, but in private.'

He nodded.

'Come to the hall once you have taken care of your horse.'

When I was shown into his private chamber by Durfel I was dismayed to see Synne was there as well.

'Well, what it is? Is it to do with Acca? The whole garrison seems to be rife with rumours about you two.'

'Is it possible for us to speak alone, lord?' I asked, giving Synne an apologetic look.

'No, it is not. I discuss all my problems with my wife and if she hears what it's about first hand it saves me having to explain later.'

It seems that I would have to speak in front of her or not at all. I debated whether to leave it, but in the end I shrugged and took a deep breath.

'I have learned something recently which means that I am not fit to serve you and I ask you to release me from my vow of service.'

Of course I knew that he wouldn't leave it there and would demand to know more, but I didn't want anyone to know my disgraceful background.

'What is this awful secret that is bothering you so much? You are one of my most promising militares and I cannot believe that you are guilty of acting dishonourably.'

'The dishonour is not my fault but still I must bear it, lord.'

'Stop beating about the bush, Oeric,' Synne suddenly said. 'You know about my childhood, I'm sure, and I cannot believe that whatever is bothering you is worse than what has happened to me in the past.'

That was a very revealing statement. We all knew that the earl's wife had been a street urchin before he rescued her but I hadn't thought about the indignities and awful suffering that she must have been subjected to.

'Very well, lady. I am a bastard and, worse, I was the end result of rape.'

Neither of them said anything for a moment but I saw real compassion in Synne's eyes. I wondered at that moment if the circumstances of her own birth might have been similar to mine. It certainly seemed possible, and for some reason it made me feel better about myself.

'You and Acca both come from Torphichen I think?' Aldred asked quietly.

I knew how intelligent the earl was, of course, and at that moment I realised what a shrewd mind he had as well.

'I had heard that you looked very like Acca's elder brother and my wife had commented to me some time ago that she detected a resemblance between you and Acca, although others don't seem to have noticed. Am I barking up the wrong tree?'

'No, lord. I am almost certain that Acca and I are half-brothers.'

'And you suspect that your mother didn't go willingly to the Thane of Torphichen's bed?' Synne surmised.

'The man I believed to be my father until recently would hardly have welcomed her back and given her two more children if she had been agreeable, lady.'

'And this is the cause of your shame? The reason you want to run away like a coward instead of facing the truth like a man?' Aldred asked.

Of course, I had never thought of it in those terms. I had been staring at the ground; now I looked him in the eye and I saw no condemnation there. I felt that a great weight had been lifted off my shoulders.

'Yes, lord. But you are right. The shame is not mine. It lies squarely at the door of Acca's father, or rather mine, God curse him. You have helped me to see that and I'm grateful.'

'Good,' he said with a smile. 'Be proud of who you are, Oeric. You have every right to be. Now I think you had better go and find Acca and tell him that he has a brother.'

✝✝✝

I found him in the stables morosely grooming my horse.

'Acca, come with me,' I said gently.

He looked at me warily, unsure of my mood. It was the first time I had wanted to talk to him since that fateful night and I didn't blame him for being cautious. He wiped his hands clean on a piece of cloth and followed me up onto the walkway around the palisade where we wouldn't be overheard.

'First of all I owe you an apology; no, more than an apology,' I began. 'I have treated your abominably for something that wasn't your fault – or mine come to that, but I didn't see it at the time.'

'I don't understand what it was that I said that got you so upset, Oeric. I've been over our conversation that night again and again, but I cannot understand what could have caused you to react so cruelly. The only thing I can think of is that it's something to do with the fact that we both come from Torphichen.'

'There is more that connects us than that.'

'What, the fact that you look very like my brother?'

'And you. Lady Synne saw it. There is a family resemblance between us.'

'A family resemblance? You mean we are related?'

'I think so, in fact I am certain of it.'

'Why would you be so ashamed, if that's the case, that you shunned me as if I had the plague?' he said, his voice vibrant with resentment.

'It had nothing to do with you; well, nothing that you were in any way responsible for.'

'Then what?' he asked angrily.

'When I tell you I know that you will hate me.'

'Why would I do that? I admire you and I was never happier than when you allowed me to get close to you. When you spurned me I wanted to die.'

'I know and I can't tell you how much I regret that now. Things changed when I came to the conclusion that we were brothers.'

'Brothers? How can that be? There's no connection between our families as far as I know and, even if there was, we don't have the same parents.'

'We do, that's the problem. We have the same father.'

'But that would mean...' His voice tailed off. 'My father and your mother,' he began. 'Were they lovers?'

'No,' I said bitterly. 'If that was the case my supposed father would have disowned my mother. As it was they were happy together and had two more children after... after I was born. My father barely tolerated me and I always wondered why. Now I know; I was the cuckoo in the nest.'

'But if they weren't lovers, how...?'

'Because I was the product of rape,' I cried out bitterly.

I didn't mean it to come out like that, but the knowledge still gnawed away at my insides.

I saw Acca stiffen and turn away from me.

'Are you sure?' he asked in a small voice.

'How else do you explain the coldness that the person I had thought of as my father always showed to me, yet he showed every sign of affection to my mother and siblings?'

'But you don't know for certain. They may have had an affair and he may have forgiven her.'

'I don't think that's likely,' I said shaking my head; my father wasn't the type of man to forgive such a deliberate betrayal.

'I need some time alone to think,' he said and walked away from me.

We lived in a hard world where every day might be our last. To survive you needed to be confident of your own abilities. Your opponent had to fear you if you were to beat him. That was why my loss of belief in myself could have been fatal. I was beginning to recover from the blow to my self-esteem but I needed Acca's forgiveness, not for my illegitimacy, but for destroying his idealised memory of his, or rather our, father.

✝✝✝

It was late the next day before he sought me out.

'Whatever the truth of what you told me, you are certain that you are my brother?' he asked earnestly.

'I truly believe so.'

He suddenly smiled in the way I remembered.

'Then let's forget the rest of it; it's all in the past. To dwell on it achieves nothing. I am really glad to have a family again,' he said with sincerity. 'But don't imagine that I'm going to respect you just because you're my elder brother,' he added with a cheeky grin.

Chapter Seven – A Plot Foiled

1027

It seemed wrong to me but Cnut had decided that the time had come for Ælfflæd to wed Earl Siward. They had been betrothed for four years but the girl was still only eleven. The king was about to depart on pilgrimage to Rome and no doubt he wanted the most powerful magnate in the north of his kingdom tied more closely to him.

Apparently Earl Aldred felt the same and, as the senior male member of their family, he'd managed to extract a promise from Siward that he wouldn't bed his new wife until she was at least thirteen. Whether he trusted Siward to keep his promise or not I couldn't say. Then I heard that both her mother, Ælgifu, and her elder sister, Eadgyth, would be staying on at York after the wedding to help Ælfflæd to settle in.

I doubt that Siward thought much of this arrangement, and his sour expression on the day of the wedding tended to confirm that he didn't, but as Ælgifu was the queen's daughter he could hardly object.

The king and Queen Emma attended the celebrations and the day went off as well as could be expected, given the torrential rain and the gale force winds that buffeted York all day. Aldred was given a seat on the high table next to the queen with his step-mother, Ælgifu, on his other side. The bride sat between Cnut and Earl Siward and the archbishop, who had officiated, and the bride's sister, the thirteen year old Eadgyth, completed the high table.

I had been chosen to be Earl Aldred's cup bearer, much to Durfel's annoyance, but I think that Aldred was afraid that the boy would be so nervous that he was likely to pour mead all over the king.

As Aldred was drinking sparingly I was getting bored and spent my time scouring the hall for faces I recognised. Of course, Cnut's housecarls were on duty alongside Siward's and I was alarmed to see one of then staring at Aldred with hatred in his eyes.

'There's one of the king's housecarls who is has been giving you malevolent looks all evening, lord earl,' I whispered the next time I topped up his goblet.

'Don't point but where in the hall?'

'By the door, lord.'

Without seeming to, Aldred looked in that direction as he took a drink.

'Regnwald,' Aldred hissed. 'We'll need to keep a close eye on him.'

I nodded and resumed my place again.

A little later I had the feeling in the back of my neck that I was the subject of someone's malicious stare myself. I again scanned the hall and with a start I saw that Iden was present. He lowered his eyes and turned to talk to his neighbour as soon as I looked in his direction but I knew that he'd been giving me the evil eye.

The last I'd heard of Iden he'd fled to Scotland, now here he was sitting with the thegns and minor nobility of Northumbria. How did that come about?

His neighbour looked vaguely familiar but I didn't think I'd met him before. Then I realised why his face rang a bell. He looked like a younger version of the man I'd fought and killed near Newsham – Thurbrand! It had to be the son who'd been absent – Carl.

My thoughts were interrupted when the king started to talk to Aldred.

'Have you heard from your brother recently?' Cnut asked.

'He sent me a letter three months ago, lord king. I gather that there are problems in Norway.'

'Yes, serious ones. The Norse are not a people who gladly accept rule by one king. They are too independently minded. That's why they always fight amongst themselves in Ireland. It's the same in Norway. Olaf Haroldsson declared himself king in competition with me after my father's death and had some success, especially in the north. Gunwald has managed to hold onto the south and, since his defeat at the Battle of Helgeå, Olaf's power has declined.'

I had heard about Cnut's naval victory near the estuary of a river called Helge against a combined Swedish and Norse fleet but I didn't know any details.

'You will know that Gunwald was wounded at the battle?'

'Yes, I'm sorry. Eadulf said the wound was quite serious.'

Cnut nodded and paused for a moment before continuing.

'He never really recovered and I heard a few days ago that he had died. I have already sent my eldest son, Svein, to act as my regent but I was sorry to lose Gunwald.'

Aldred didn't say anything. It was difficult to comment because he knew that Cnut had scarcely even acknowledged Gunwald as his son when he was a boy. He barely even recognised Svein because, although he was legitimate and the eldest, he was the son of his first marriage. He probably only regretted Gunwald's loss because he had been useful to him, rather than because he was his son.

'What happens to Eadulf now? He only went to Norway because Gunwald was his friend.'

Cnut shrugged and turned to talk to the queen.

I thought it was ill-mannered of him not to reply, but then I suppose kings have a great deal on their mind and he had probably forgotten Eadulf was with Gunwald.

✝✝✝

We left York at noon the next day. Aldred would have liked to have left earlier but everyone seemed to be suffering from overindulgence the night before, whether they'd been at the feast or not. Some of the militares didn't look as if they could put up much of a fight, which was a concern with so many of our enemies in York, and even a couple of the armigers looked distinctly unwell.

'We need to expect an ambush,' Aldred told us as soon as we were clear of the town. 'Carl and Iden left over an hour ago and although they headed south east towards Holderness, it would be easy for them to double back once they are out of sight and wait for us on the road north. Put your helmets on, ride with your shields ready and loosen your swords in their scabbards. Colby, you and Osric scout ahead.'

As the youngest of the militares I was riding at the rear, just ahead of Durfel and the armigers, who were leading the packhorses. Not long after we'd set out Acca rode forward to join me. We had been riding for about two hours and at long last Acca had run out of chatter when he suddenly pulled up his horse.

'What is it?' I asked as the other armigers also came to a halt.

'Hooves, can't you hear them?'

Now that he mentioned it I could just make out the sound of galloping hooves hitting the cobblestones of the old Roman road. There were a lot of riders by the sound of it and I realised that Carl had outwitted us. Aldred had been expecting to ride into an ambush. Instead Carl was planning to attack from the rear, slaughter the armigers and hit the rest of us whilst we were at our most vulnerable; we would be stationary and trying to turn our horses around.

'Durfel, ride and warn the earl. The rest of you grab a spear and a spare shield each from the packhorses, then form up back here; quickly now.'

It was probably less than two minutes from the time that Acca had heard the hooves until they appeared over a dip in the road behind us. They were riding six abreast across the full width of the road. I had formed the five armigers up beside me across the road with a dozen packhorses milling about in front of us.

I realised that it was hopeless when I saw that Carl had at least two dozen mounted warriors with him. Nevertheless, my duty was to protect the earl. We started to trot forward, driving the packhorses before us. Some of the packhorses tried to escape from the road but a drainage ditch ran alongside it and none were brave enough to leap it.

Then the attackers did something I hadn't anticipated: they dismounted. Of course, I should have expected it. We were the only housecarls in England who were trained to fight on horseback. Every other warrior might travel on horseback but they always dismounted to fight. Our adversaries hadn't finished forming their shield wall when the packhorses ran into them.

Unlike warhorses, they avoided people if possible but, in their panicked state, they barged their way through the line of men, causing a fair amount of chaos. Then we hit them. I picked my man and in the split second before he raised his shield into position I realised that it was Iden. I gripped my spear more firmly and aimed at the space between the top of his shield and the brow of his helmet. I felt the jar as the point struck his cheekbone and was deflected into his eye.

My horse reared onto its hind legs and lashed its hooves at the helmet of the man who had been standing next to Iden. The helmet crumpled and he fell dead on top of Iden's body. I spurred my horse forward as I let go of my spear and grabbed at the axe hanging by its strap from my saddle horn. I raised it to attack the man in the second row but he scuttled out of the way in terror. My stallion barged its way through the last two rows as I brought my axe down twice in passing. I felt it hit something both times but I'd no idea what damage it had done. Then I was in the clear.

The armigers had more sense than to charge a shield wall; they would have been slaughtered. Instead they threw their spears from a safe distance and then retreated, bringing down three men in the process. They galloped away as the shield wall broke and twenty furious men chased after them.

I scattered the enemy's horses and kicked my own mount into a gallop. I rode through the pursuing housecarls, using my axe with gusto as I passed through them. Then disaster struck. One of the housecarls had the courage to turn and face me. He thrust his spear into my stallion's chest. It was brave, but foolish. My horse reared up in agony and stamped on his attacker, turning him onto a bloody mess before it sank to its knees.

I jumped out of the saddle just in time and landed on my feet. Three housecarls who I'd overtaken now rushed at me and I thought my time had come. I was scarcely aware of anything behind me as I turned to face the three but suddenly a horse appeared at my side and the rider thrust his spear into the chest of the leading housecarl.

'Get up behind me,' a voice yelled.

With a start I realised it was Acca. He was threatening the other two men with his spear and they hesitated just long enough for me haul myself up behind him; not an easy thing to do wearing a hauberk but adrenaline gave me a strength I didn't know I had. The two men ran at us but Acca pulled his horse's head around savagely and headed back towards the rest of the enemy. I thought he was mad until I saw Aldred and his men charging down the road towards us.

The housecarls stopped chasing the fleeing armigers and formed up into a shield wall again to face the oncoming militares. We were now trapped behind the shield wall and there were a couple of enemy housecarls behind us. Tempted as it was to attack the rear of the shield wall, I decided that would be folly, especially with Aldred and the others about to smash into them in wedge formation. Instead we turned to face the two behind us.

I slid off the horse and grasped my axe, which thankfully was still hanging from my wrist by its strap. I had dropped my shield when I had mounted behind Acca so I drew my sword with my left hand. Acca went for one whilst I attacked the other. Out of the corner of my eye I saw my brother's opponent bat the spear away with his shield but then I had to concentrate on my own adversary.

I swung my axe at him and, as expected, he caught it on his shield, where it stuck fast. Meanwhile he slashed at me with his sword and I countered it before stabbing down towards his thigh. He knocked it away with his own sword and I swung it up whilst, at the same time, yanking his shield down with my axe. Before he could bring his own sword back into play I had thrust the point of mine into his neck and he collapsed onto the roadway.

I turned back to the other man, desperately hoping that Acca was all right. The man had managed to wound Acca's horse and it was on its knees. Evidently my brother had managed to jump clear and was frantically trying to defend himself with his spear. His arm was bleeding as was his thigh and I realised immediately that he was within seconds of being killed.

It went against my sense of fair play but that counted for little when Acca's life was at stake. I swung my sword from behind the housecarl's back and hacked into his neck. My sword had been blunted in the fight but it went deep enough to sever the man's spine. Acca dropped his spear and threw his arms around me, crying with relief. I hugged him back but then I become conscious that the shield wall had broken and the routed housecarls were heading our way.

✝✝✝

'Would you like a hand out of there?' Aldred asked with a smile.

We were trying vainly to claw our way out of the steep sided drainage ditch that ran beside the road. Rather than face Carl and his routed men I had dragged Acca to the side of the road and we'd jumped down into the ditch. I was hampered by my hauberk and Acca by his wounds so, try as we may, we were stuck there.

Someone threw a leading rein down to us and, with the horse backing up and me pushing, somehow we got Acca out of the ditch. I wasn't hampered by wounds and so I took my hauberk off and handed it up to someone and then, again with the horse's assistance, I managed to clamber out of there.

Durfel and the armigers were busy attending to other injured men and so I pulled out Acca's own wounds kit, washed his cuts, which thankfully were only flesh wounds, pulled out all the detritus from his clothing that had got imbedded in there, and sewed the cuts up.

During the whole time – from being pulled out of the ditch to having his wounds treated - he hadn't uttered even a whimper, which said a great deal about his strength of character. I was proud of him and I told him so, as well as thanking him for saving my life.

'I couldn't lose you,' he said faintly. 'Besides you saved mine too.'

With that he fell into unconsciousness.

Several of the militares rode off to find some carts on which to transport the wounded, others had chased Carl and his men and had killed two more as they fled on horseback. Only half a dozen managed to escape. The bad news was that one of them was Carl.

However, when we examined the dead – there were no wounded left alive – not only was Iden amongst them, but so was Regnwald.

'Does this mean that Cnut was involved?' I asked Aldred, who shook his head.

'He has no reason to want me dead; no, Regnwald was after revenge and acted independently. I shall have to let the king know, however. I need to tell him about Carl as well, before a different version of events reaches his ear.'

Once the carts arrived we returned to York where the wounded could be looked after by the monks. At least we had no shortage of horses, even if those who had belonged to the dead housecarls were inferior to ours.

When Aldred managed to see Cnut just before he himself departed the king's attitude was that his dispute with Carl was a blood feud in which he couldn't get involved. He was more concerned about the death of Regnwald, who had been the second in command of his housecarls. Emma confirmed Aldred's tale about the enmity between the two of them from the moment she had landed back in England. However, Aldred wisely said nothing about Regnwald's earlier attempt to kill him.

Chapter Eight – Scots Raiders

April 1028

Acca didn't take long to recover and, as he was now approaching his seventeenth birthday, Aldred decided to reward his courage by promoting him to join the ranks of the militares. We didn't want our group of friends to be split up so Acca joined Colby, Osric and me. That meant that our new armiger, a fourteen year old called Cynric, had four of us to cope with but he didn't seem to mind overmuch.

We had reached Melrose monastery the previous evening and stayed in the guesthouse and joined the brothers at mass the next morning. We broke our fast with them after the service before continuing our patrol.

Raids by the Scots, especially from Lothian, had got worse over the past year and so we spent a lot of our time out on patrol. On this day in April the world seemed very peaceful. Leafs were appearing on the trees, birds were singing somewhere and the crops in the strip fields around the villages were pushing up out of the earth. It was one of those days when the sun shone at times and it hid behind white clouds at others. As we were dressed in chainmail, albeit without helmets, we were thankful when we were able to ride in the shade.

We rode into St. Boswells, named after Saint Boisil, one of the original monks at Melrose in the seventh century and the tutor of the celebrated Saint Cuthbert. It was a small village with fewer than two hundred inhabitants and all of them seemed to be thronging the space outside the thane's hall when we arrived.

As soon as he saw us the thane pushed his way through the crowd and looked at us trying to determine which of us was the leader. Both Colby and Osric were in their mid-twenties, I was barely twenty and Acca was seventeen so none of us looked very old. He quickly decided to speak to Colby who perhaps had more of an air of authority about him. In truth we had no official leader and tended to decide things between us. However, I suppose that we looked to Colby for instructions in an emergency.

'You are Earl Aldred's men?' he asked, although who else he thought we might be I don't know.

Colby nodded.

'What's happened?'

'Those damned Scots have crossed the Tweed at Maxton and are raiding along the Ale Water,' he said spitting on the ground to show what he thought of them.

'Who is the thane at Maxton?'

'I am, and I own the vill of Riddell as well.'

I could understand his concern. Riddell was the only village of any size on the Ale Water, a tributary

114

of the Tweed, although there were various isolated farmsteads along the valley.

'How many, do you know?'

'These people are the only survivors of Maxton; they think that there were between two and three dozen men and a handful of boys but they are not used to estimating numbers, of course.'

He pointed to a group of a dozen people: a few men and women and rather more children.

'How many were killed at Maxton?' Colby asked.

'They say that most of the men were killed – perhaps fifteen. That means that they have taken over forty people as captives: women, older children as well as their slaves.'

'That'll slow them down, especially as I assume they have taken their livestock as well?'

The thane nodded.

'Perhaps ten head of cattle, a flock of sheep and quite a few pigs.'

'Very well, how many armed freemen do you have?'

'A little under forty, I suppose. But won't you send for help?'

'There's no time. It would take a messenger several hours to reach Bebbanburg. By the time that reinforcements could reach us it would be tomorrow morning. My guess is that the raiders will try and slip back across the Tweed during the night.'

'What do you suggest?'

'Is there another ford the Scots could use?'

'Not between Melrose and Kelso.'

'They'll want to cross back with their plunder quickly so they'll use Maxton ford again. Call your fyrd to arms and tell them to make their way to Maxton. Meanwhile we'll locate these raiders and try and whittle down their numbers somewhat.'

'We can't hold the ford against a sizeable force of Scots,' the thane said helplessly.

'Not with that attitude you won't, no, but you outnumber them and I presume you have bowmen?'

'Hunters, yes.'

'Then can I suggest that you use the time before dark to dig defensive works to deny them the ford; a rampart topped with either a palisade or, if there isn't time, sharpened stakes dug into the rampart at forty five degrees. Do you know what I mean?'

The thane nodded, but he didn't look at all certain.

'Acca, you understand what I mean?'

'Yes, Colby.'

'Then perhaps you could stay here and help erect the defences. Are you happy to do that?'

'I'd rather be with you but, yes, I can see that it's essential if we're to trap the raiders south of the Tweed.'

Both knew that Colby meant Acca should direct the work and, although the thane looked a little happier at Colby's suggestion, Acca would have to tread carefully. A thane was a noble whereas Acca was a junior housecarl in status and the thane had five older housecarls of his own.

'Cynric, you stay here as well,' I told him.

'But Oeric...' he started to say.

'Do as you're told,' I told him sharply. Then in a kinder voice I said 'you'll see plenty of action when the Scots get here. Can you use a bow?'

'Yes, Oeric.'

He had strong shoulders for his age and so I gave him my war bow and quiver of arrows. He nodded his thanks, then Colby, Osric and I set off to find the raiders.

†††

We saw the smoke before we saw the Scots. We dismounted and crept forward through the trees until we could see what was happening. It was, or had been, a large farmstead. There were eight raiders in all, five men and three boys, who were herding a few women and children and a large quantity of livestock away from the burning buildings. We hadn't reached Riddell yet but these Scots were headed for home, presumably satisfied with the plunder they'd already stolen.

Once away from the place, they divided into two groups: the boys herding the livestock and the men guarding the captives they'd taken as slaves. Gradually the men left the boys behind. We were shadowing the column in the woods along the narrow valley, looking for a suitable opportunity to kill the Scots without endangering the captives.

After an hour the column stopped and the men took the opportunity to slake their thirst in the river, leaving one man on guard. The livestock were half a mile behind them by this stage and presumably the men were waiting for the boys to catch them up.

Colby took careful aim from our position in the edge of the trees and his arrow flew true, catching the man guarding the captives in the stomach. He cried out in pain, doubled over and fell to the ground. He wasn't dead but it wouldn't be long before he was with a stomach wound like that.

Osric and I spurred our horses forward and made for the startled group of men by the river. They had put down their weapons when they crouched on the bank to scoop water into their mouths. Now they scrambled to their feet, hastily picking up their weapons and the small shields called targes that had a narrow blade protruding from the middle instead of a boss. Two had spears, one a sword and the fourth man an axe.

I made for the axeman. He futilely tried to chop at my spear but he was too slow and my spear struck him in the middle of his chest, throwing him back into the Ale Water. I let go of my spear and grasped the haft of my axe, which was dangling from my wrist. I batted away a spear with my shield and, ignoring the man holding it, I chopped down onto the bare head of the swordsman. He crumpled to the earth and I spun my horse around to look for another opponent; but Osric had already killed both of them.

Meanwhile Colby had remounted and galloped off towards the boys and the livestock. He killed one and the others ran. We couldn't let them warn the rest of the raiding party but I needn't have worried; Colby caught up with one and killed him before setting off once more.

The last boy made the mistake of looking behind him instead of looking where he was going. He tripped, sprawled onto the track and hit his head on a rock. When we reached him Colby was checking for a pulse.

'Still alive but he'll have a sore head when he wakes up,' he said grimly.

I knew he wouldn't have liked killing Scots this young but it was necessary. At least this one would survive and could be interrogated. We knew that the earl would want to know whose men these were so that he could complain formally to King Malcolm, although such complaints didn't seem to have done much good in the past. I'd never heard of anyone being punished.

We sent the women and children on their way to St. Boswells, where they could wait until the rest of the raiders had been dealt with. They took the livestock and the Scots boy with them, tied over the back of a plough horse. The women reluctantly agreed not to maltreat him, although it was obvious that they were itching to revenge themselves on him for the loss of their menfolk and their homes. He would be sent on to the ford at Maxton so that Acca could interrogate him. Little did I know how important he would turn out to be.

When we reached Riddell we tethered our horses in the trees and cautiously walked forward to the edge of the wood. From there we had a good view of the Scots encamped before the village. Unusually for such a small settlement, there was a palisade around the whole place, not just the lord's hall. It was evident from the bodies lying between the camp and the village that the villagers had beaten off the first assault. There were a couple of bodies who had obviously been killed trying to scale the palisade but the others were some distance from the palisade and riddled with arrows.

Between our viewpoint and the Scots campsite there was a crudely constructed enclosure in which a variety of captured livestock were penned. These were guarded by three boys who were kneeling in a group intent on a game of some kind. A little off to one side there was another group: captive women and children, tied up and guarded by two bored looking Scots. We settled down to wait for nightfall, hoping that the Scots wouldn't make for home until they had looted the village.

Having eaten some dry rations and taken off our armour because of the noise it made when we moved, we headed for the captives first. Our greatest fear wasn't the sentries; it was that the captives would make a commotion when they realised that they were about to be rescued. Inevitably that would alert the main body of Scots.

Whilst my two companions took care of the sentries I moved amongst the captives, whispering for them to be quiet when we freed them. Once I was sure that everyone was ready we cut through the ropes around their wrists and ankles one by one. We were aided by the light of the new moon, although it disappeared behind scudding clouds from time to time.

The last group of captives I freed consisted of a middle aged woman, two young boys and a girl who looked to be about fifteen. When I cut the ropes around the girl's wrists she grabbed my right hand and kissed it; not on the back of the hand but on the inside of my wrist. I was startled, but in a nice way. A shiver of excitement ran up my arm and then through my whole body. I looked at her face on which there was a radiant smile and then into her eyes. What I saw there made me even more excited. I had little experience with girls, although I had tumbled the odd one or two serving wenches but somehow it failed to satisfy me.

I had just turned nineteen and, unlike most of my comrades, I felt that making love should be something you did with someone you cared about. They seemed happy to satisfy their carnal desires. I didn't; I wanted it to be something more than pure lust.

I knew that Acca felt the same. He was coming up to fifteen but he was still a virgin. His approach to sex was the same as mine; something that bound us even closer together. Of course, he didn't brag about it. Most boys his age had acquired some experience of the opposite sex. Some seem to have done so almost as soon as they reached puberty.

Now I felt the stirrings of desire but I was dragged back to the present as Colby led the captives away to the safety of the trees. I stayed close to the mysterious girl and her family.

'What's your name?' I asked her as we entered the wood.

'Rowena,' she whispered back. 'What's yours, lord?'

It meant white haired. I could see that her hair was very blond but it was impossible to make out the exact colour by the pale light of the moon.

'I'm no lord, I'm one of Earl Aldred's militares, I replied. 'My name is Oeric.'

'Militares?' she queried.

'It's Latin. It means a warrior on horseback; a mounted housecarl.'

'I thought most housecarls could ride,' she said in surprise.

'Yes, but we are like the Duke of Normandy's knights. We're trained to fight on horseback, not just ride from here to there.'

'Do you like other types of riding as well, Oeric?' she asked with a twinkle in her eye.

I was not accustomed to flirting and I was confused. Thankfully she wouldn't be able to see my blushes in the darkness under the tree canopy. I was saved from looking a fool by Osric, who grabbed me by the arm to attract my attention.

'We need to leave the captives to make their own way to St. Boswells, Oeric. Colby thinks we should run off the livestock next.'

122

'Very well, but we should allow the women and children a head start before we kick over the hornets' nest,' I said.

'I agree. Who's their leader?'

I turned to the girl who had so captivated me.

'Rowena, who is the senior amongst you?'

'My mother I suppose; my father was the reeve of Pirnie before the Scots bastards killed him, together with the rest of our menfolk, including the priest would you believe.'

I was surprised at how far the raiders had roamed. Pirnie was on the other side of Ancrum Moor, a good four miles to the east of Riddell. Moreover the vill belonged to the Monastery of Melrose. It appeared that the Scots marauders had no respect for Church property or its clergy, despite the fact that they professed to be Christians.

I reluctantly said goodbye to Rowena, wondering if I'd ever see her again, and we crept towards the livestock enclosure. However, before we got there pandemonium broke out.

The Scots, impatient to get back north of the Tweed before dawn, had launched another attack against Riddell. It was a sensible move and presumably they thought that the bowmen defending the palisade couldn't see well enough in the darkness. However, someone in the village had some initiative because fire arrows streaked into the sky before the Scots were halfway to the palisade. By their light two volleys of arrows hit the Scots attackers before darkness returned.

We had stopped to watch and counted seven new casualties. By our calculations the Scots had lost nearly half their strength and they retreated once again. We heard a furious row break out as some were determined to have their revenge on the villagers whilst others just wanted to cut their losses and head for home. In the end the latter won.

The boys headed over to the enclosure to get the animals on the road whilst someone called over to the sentries guarding the captives to get them on their feet ready to leave. When there was no reply one or two went to investigate only to discover, of course, that the birds had flown.

A fresh outbreak of heated argument followed this discovery before the men set off in pursuit along the track towards Maxton, leaving the boys to deal with the livestock.

'The women and children have an hour's start,' I said quietly. 'I doubt that they will have gone more than two miles in that time with the children in tow. How far is it to Maxton?'

'A good seven miles,' Colby muttered. 'They'll probably overtake them half way there. We need to delay them.'

'I agree,' Osric said. 'Forget the boys and the livestock, we can come back for them.'

Two minutes later we were mounted and on our way back up the track. Shortly afterwards we caught up with the laggards amongst the Scots puffing their way on foot. We charged into them, spearing the rearmost three and chopping two more down with axe and sword before the rest realised what was happening. The shouts of alarm must have reached those in front because we were suddenly faced with more than a dozen warriors baying for our blood.

We turned and cantered back out of harm's way. The Scots chased after us for several minutes before giving up and turning around to resume their pursuit of the captives.

'That should have delayed them by a good quarter of an hour,' Osric said with satisfaction.

'Not nearly enough,' I said brusquely.

I was worried to death about the captives, and about one in particular.

This time when we rode back up the track we found ourselves facing a rear guard of eight. Evidently the warriors who were still alive had sent one group after the women and children and left the rest to keep us at bay. As they capered and hurled insults at us Osric and Colby dismounted and strung their bows.

The Scots were difficult targets in the poor light but my two companions sent three arrows each in quick succession in their general direction. The howls of pain told us that at least some had found a target. The Scots rushed at us and my companions quickly mounted. We cantered away from the infuriated enemy and then turned and charged back towards them.

The five survivors were bewildered by our tactics and, almost before they realised what was happening, we were amongst them hacking down with sword and axe. I felt something strike my shield and, almost by instinct, I brought my axe across my body and chopped down. I felt it strike something and then my horse took me clear.

It was only then that I realised that Colby was in trouble. His stallion had been killed and he was trapped under its dead body. I saw a man with a sword trying to kill him but Colby was holding him off with his shield. Osric was too preoccupied to help as he fought off two more Scots. I kicked my spurs into my mount's side and he leaped forward. As we came level with Colby's assailant I swung my axe with all my might and the raider's head leaped clear of his torso and went bouncing away into the trees.

I turned to help Osric but the last two men had run off.

It took both of us to lift the horse off Colby. He wasn't badly hurt: a twisted knee and a dislocated shoulder were his worst injuries. By the time that we had forced his shoulder back into place and bound up his knee we knew that we would be too late to help the fleeing women and children. The other party of Scots would have caught up with them by now.

✝✝✝

I helped lift Colby up behind Osric and mounted my own horse.

'What about the boys with the livestock?' Osric asked just as I was about to head after the rest of the Scots.

'They won't be able to cross the ford with them,' I replied impatiently. 'Our priority must be the women and children.'

'I agree,' Colby said over Osric's shoulder.

He must have been in a lot of pain but he didn't show it. We set off at a gentle canter to spare our tired horses and I tried to persuade myself that somehow Rowena would have survived. Together with the defenders of Riddell, we had accounted for most of the raiders but the survivors were more than enough to overcome their former prisoners. I only hoped that they would take them captive again and not slaughter them in revenge for their losses.

Suddenly Colby passed out and it was all that Osric could do to stop him falling off his horse.

'The jolting must have caused him to pass out from pain,' Osric said after we'd gently lowered him to the ground.

'I'll send some men back to take him to St. Boswells in a cart,' I said. 'Will you be alright waiting here?'

'You mean can I defend myself against a few boys?' he grinned.

'Let's get you into the trees so that they don't see you,' I said.

We carried the unconscious Colby fifty yards into the wood and then Osric went back for his horse.

'What are you doing?' he asked as I remounted.

'Find out what's happening ahead. Don't worry; I won't do anything stupid.'

As I rode off I thought that something idiotic but heroic was exactly what I had in mind. For Rowena's sake I was prepared to throw caution to the wind.

I wasn't wearing coif or helmet so that I could hear better, so when I clearly heard the lowing of cattle and the bleating of sheep ahead I was bewildered. How had the Scots lads and the livestock got ahead of me?

Then an uncomfortable thought crossed my mind. Supposing the sound came, not from the animals stolen from along the Ale Water, but from another collection of livestock. That would mean that the raiders we'd encountered were just one part of a much larger group of Scots. I pulled my horse to a halt, uncertain what to do.

Suddenly I was startled by a disembodied voice calling out 'Oeric, is that you?'

A moment later I looked down into Rowena's sweet face.

'Quick into the trees,' she said, pulling urgently at my leg.

I swung down from my horse and led him into the wood behind Rowena. We walked a hundred yards or so through the trees and shrubs before we came to a small clearing. I was relieved to see all the other women and children had made it to this place of safety.

'We heard the Scots coming up behind us and darted into the trees. When we reached here we thought we would be safe but I went back to the track to make sure that they went past. They did and I was just about to return here when I heard your horse neigh, so I waited.'

I hadn't even been conscious of the sound my horse had made so intent was I on listening for the Scots ahead. If he hadn't neighed Rowena wouldn't have stopped me and I would have blundered into the enemy when all the time my love was safe.

Perhaps I was premature in thinking of her as my love; we didn't know each other and had only exchanged a few words, but in my mind we were already betrothed. I chided myself for being a lovesick fool. I was behaving like a callow youth. Then she took my hand and whispered in my ear.

'I'm glad you're safe. I've been so worried about you.'

'And I you. I prayed to God all the way along the track that you'd be unharmed.'

She squeezed my hand but then the others were clustering around me asking what they should do now.

'Be as quiet as you can for a start,' I replied in a low voice. 'The Scots aren't that far away. You should be safe here. We have blocked the Scots' retreat back across the ford with defensive works but I need to find out how many more of them have joined those who held you captive. Wait here and I'll be back in a while; but keep quiet.'

I hated leaving Rowena again but I was worried about Acca as well.

Just after I left dawn broke over the hills to the east and weak sunlight percolated through the leaves above me. As I neared the ford at Maxton sometime later I heard the sound of fighting – the clash of metal on metal, the screams of the wounded and the competing battle cries which both sides used to bolster their courage.

I halted where the track emerged from the trees. I was still mounted but no one was paying me any attention. About thirty Scots were in the water or trying the scale the rampart on the far bank. Several dead bodies with arrows sprouting from them were being carried downstream and several more lay at the bottom of the earthworks that Acca and the men of St. Boswells had built.

As I watched I saw with alarm Acca and Cynric standing on the very top of the rampart; the boy was sending arrow after arrow into the massed ranks of the Scots and my brother was chopping down any of the raiders who managed to scramble up the slippery slope. Evidently Acca had had the sense to thoroughly wet the steep earthen bank to make it almost impossible to scale without help.

As I watched a Scot at the base of the rampart threw a spear at Acca but he knocked it away with his shield. The rampart had been built in a crescent shape so that the Scots were forced into a small space which had now become a killing ground. I was wondering what I could do to help when the Scots broke off their assault. They came running back and I

130

was in danger of being seen so I backed my horse further into the trees.

After a short discussion the Scots marched off to the west, no doubt making for the next ford at Melrose. I watched them go and then I noticed a dust cloud some two miles to the west. Presumably it was being kicked up by the livestock that the second group of Scots had stolen.

Of course, St. Boswells Village lay in their path but it was defended by a stout palisade, as was the monastery at Melrose. I prayed that they wouldn't try and storm either place. Hopefully all the Scots wanted to do now was to escape back over the Tweed to safety. The raid must have cost them well over half of the sixty men they had started out with.

'Acca, are you and Cynric well?' I called out as I rode forward to the southern bank of the river.

'Never better, although I suspect Cynric's arms might be a trifle tired after all the arrows he's put into these ruffians,' he said pointing to the dead Scots with his sword. 'Are you alone? What's happened to Colby and Osric?'

'They're fine; well, Colby is injured but nothing serious. Get on your horses and come with me; our work is not yet done.'

Ten minutes later we were cantering along the south bank of the Tweed after the remnants of the Scots. I had no intention of trying to avoid them; we were after the boys driving the livestock. Without those animals the people of the area would starve this winter and have no breeding stock for next year.

With Cynric in the middle the three of us caught up the rearmost Scots just after passing St. Boswells and increased our pace to a gallop. We didn't break our pace to hack them down and most scattered out of our way. One man tried to spear my horse but he was too slow and I was past him before he completed his thrust. Acca used his shield to fend off a blow from an axe and then we were through them.

We slowed our pace to a trot to allow the horses to recover and so it took another quarter of an hour to catch up with the livestock. Ignoring their young drovers, we spread out and herded sheep, cows, a few horses and quite a few protesting swine off the road. One boy was foolish enough to run at Acca with no more than a dagger. My brother used the flat of his sword to knock the lad onto his back in the dust. The others gave us a wide berth after that.

The Eildon Hills rose to our left and so we drove the animals up the hillside and inside the ramparts surrounding the remains of an old Roman camp called Trimontium. They would be safe there until the various owners could sort them out again. We rode to the crest of the hill and sat on skyline from where we could watch the retreating Scots. Thankfully they ignored Melrose Monastery and crossed back over the Tweed.

It was only then that we realised that half a dozen more Scots had crossed over the Melrose ford ahead of the rest. They were the ones guarding the captives taken by the second group of marauders and they had taken at least two dozen women and twice that number of children with them. I wept in frustration.

They were destined to become slaves to the bloody Scots. We had failed.

My only consolation was that at least Rowena and her family were safe; however, I had no idea whether I would ever see her again.

Chapter Nine – Cnut's Invasion of Lothian

Summer 1028

The news that the king was coming to Northumbria came as a surprise to everyone. The ostensible reason was to attend the marriage of Siward to Aldred's sister, Ælfflæd. To say that it was unexpected was to put it mildly; the bride was not yet twelve and the expectation was that she wouldn't be married until she was at least thirteen. However, the ceremony in York was really only a pretext.

Oh, the wedding was genuine enough, but Cnut's real reason for bringing the date forward was to hide his preparations for war. The Scots' raid a few months previously had been in greater strength than previous incursions but the boy we had captured and who Acca had interrogated had revealed a more sinister situation.

He turned out to be a boastful lad, full of arrogance and distain for the English, and Northumbrians in particular. Torture or threats weren't necessary to make him talk. He told us of his own volition, as if mocking us. In essence what he said was that the ten year peace agreed after the Battle of Carham was nearly at an end and King

Malcolm intended to seize the rest of Lothian in the coming few months.

By that he meant the rump of the old Goddodin territory that we Anglians had conquered centuries before and which lay north of the Cheviot Hills and south of the River Tweed. If he expected us to be frightened or cowed by his declaration he must have been disappointed. He was probably too stupid to realise that what he'd told us was the one thing that was likely to stir Cnut to action.

The king ruled a sizeable empire – England, Denmark and part of Norway; although he was having difficulty in hanging onto the latter. The loss of a small part of the far north of his realm paled into insignificance compared to the loss of Norway, but Cnut was a proud man and the thought that Malcolm of Scots could thumb his nose at him and expect to get away with it enraged Cnut.

Many of the leading nobles in England would be coming to York for the wedding and, naturally, each one would be bringing a sizeable escort with them. Secretly Siward and Aldred had also sent out word to their ealdormen and thanes to be ready to muster at Ancrum, a few miles south east of the crossing over the Tweed at Melrose.

There wasn't much at Ancrum, just a large farm steading, but it stood on the River Teviot and an adequate supply of water was a necessity for any muster point. From Melrose the way lay open along Lauderdale towards Malcolm's base at Edinburgh.

I hadn't seen Rowena again after the Scots raiders had fled. We had to return to Bebbanburg with all haste to acquaint Aldred with the situation and to allow him to question our Scots captive himself. I heard later that the women and children who we'd freed had reclaimed their livestock and returned to their respective villages and farmsteads to rebuild their lives. I longed to travel to Pirnie to see her again but the opportunity hadn't arisen before the other militares and I set off with Aldred for York.

✝✝✝

The wedding was a truly splendid affair; rather too splendid in my view. It was a chance for Siward to show off in front of the king and his fellow earls. I didn't like what I'd heard about the man and his display of ostentatious wealth was, I felt, vulgar. He appeared on his wedding day in a robe embroidered with gold wire and he wore a sword whose scabbard was encrusted in jewels. In contrast Aldred wore a sober dark blue robe and his normal sword. Even Cnut looked like a pauper compared to Siward and I don't suppose that the bridegroom's pretentious display endeared him to the king.

I had expected the bride to look demure and perhaps a trifle fearful, after all she was still a child and her new husband was twenty; nearly twice her age. However, she was anything but the shy maiden I had imagined. She appeared to be enjoying herself hugely at the wedding feast and, from what little I saw of her, she seemed to have inherited the character of her father – Uhtred the Bold. I suspected that Siward might well have his hands full with such a spirited girl.

I have to admit that the feast was magnificent. I had never eaten so well before, or ever will again I suspect. Like most there, I left the table after the king retired feeling bloated and I was seriously drunk. Strangely I felt much better after I had brought most of the rich food back up.

After a day for everyone to recover, Siward said goodbye to his bride and we left York to take the road north.

†††

We were the first to cross the ford over the Tweed at Melrose. Led by Godric, Aldred's captain, we had been deployed as a screen in advance of the main army, who were on foot. Only the king, his nobles and a few of his housecarls rode. Osric, Colby – who had now completely recovered – Acca and three more militares: Anson, Bryce and Heorot – had joined us together with their armiger, Leof. We ranged well ahead of the rest with Leof and Cynric leading our packhorses a hundred yards behind us. There were other sections on each flank as well. So far we had spotted nothing more interesting than a shepherd and a flock of sheep.

We were riding just below the ridge to the west of Lauderdale looking down on the Leader Water flowing along to join the Tweed between Melrose and St. Boswells. Inevitably my thoughts strayed to

Rowena when suddenly the others halted and I was brought back to the present with a jolt.

Below us in the valley lay a sizable village. It lay in the shadow of the old Votandani hill fort called Arcioldun and when it had been part of Lothian that had been its name. Now it was called Earlston, named before his death in honour of the treacherous Earl Hacca.

Most of the land around Earlston was pasture but there were also areas of cultivation where men laboured to weed the fields prior to harvest time. I thought it was odd as normally the women and older children would help the men with such tasks. However, I dismissed the thought without properly thinking through the possible reasons. It was an omission I'd later regret. No one seemed to have spotted us and so we withdrew to the far side of the ridge.

'Go and tell Earl Aldred that Earlston is unaware of our presence, Bryce,' Anson ordered.

He'd been designated as our leader but we didn't really know him or his two companions. We were used to working together by consent and Anson's somewhat officious tone jarred with our group of four friends. However Bryce must have been used to it and wheeled his horse to canter back to the army. Meanwhile we continued on our way, crossing back to the eastern side of the ridge once we were past Earlston.

Two smaller villages came into sight, one ahead of us on the lower slopes of the ridge on which we rode, and one up a small side valley to our right.

'They will take fright as soon as the main body sacks Earlston,' Anson said. 'Get ready to attack the first village down there. I don't see why others should have all the fun,' he added with an unpleasant smile.

'That's not our role,' Colby said firmly. 'We are scouts and that's all.'

'Are you afraid of a few villagers, is that it?' Anson sneered.

'Don't be a fool,' I told him. 'Colby's right. We need to press on and scout ahead, not get sidetracked.'

What I didn't say was that the last thing I was prepared to do, unless it was absolutely necessary, was to attack defenceless men, women and children.

'What about you two, are you as lily livered as your friends?' he asked Acca and Osric.

'None of us are cowards!' Acca said hotly. 'We have nothing to prove, least of all to an idiot like you.'

For a moment I thought that Anson was going to strike my brother and my hand went to the hilt of my sword.

'Come on Heorot. Let's leave these old women here and go and kill some Scots.'

Heorot didn't look at all certain and he gazed nervously at us and then back to Anson. In the end he rode over to Anson and the two militares cantered down the hill towards the village.

'Where are they going?' Cynric asked as the two armigers rode up to join us.

'To slaughter some innocent villagers,' I replied curtly.

139

'Come on,' Osric muttered, 'we need to press on.'

'Should I follow them?' Leof asked nervously.

'No, you stay with us,' Colby told him. 'You two drop back a bit.'

We continued on our way along the hillside just under the skyline, scanning the ground ahead of us but, occasionally looking down into the valley. There were no defences and Anson and Heorot rode straight into the village, which seemed strangely deserted. Suddenly men erupted from huts, barns and the hall and surrounded the two horsemen.

They never stood a chance. Before they could defend themselves they were pulled from their horses and killed. However, the men who attacked them didn't look like ordinary villagers; most wore chainmail vests or byrnies and helmets. They looked more like Earl Wigbehrt's warriors, or perhaps even King Malcolm's. Whoever they were it seemed that Cnut's surprise attack hadn't been that much of a surprise.

†††

Somehow word of Cnut's plans had reached Malcolm. When we rode back to rejoin the army that evening we found out that there had been a hard fight for Earlston. As our army advanced the men we'd seen earlier had fled and sought shelter in the village. That had encouraged our men to give chase but when they neared the palisade they found it was manned by hundreds of Scots, including quite a few archers. We had lost one hundred and fifty men before the defences were finally breeched and another fifty died before we secured the place. It had been a hard fight and our men were in no mood to be merciful. Without exception the surviving defenders were put to the sword.

There were no women, children or animals in the place; presumably they'd been sent up into the hills with the men who were too old to fight. Some of the dead were simple villagers armed with whatever they could get their hands on, but most were well trained warriors. Malcolm evidently meant us to fight for every inch of his territory.

Cnut burned the village to the ground before moving on up the Leader Water to camp for the night.

Aldred had listened to our tale of woe about Anson and Heorot impassively and dismissed us without commenting. We heard later that he had berated Godric for choosing to use the pair of them as scouts, and especially for putting Anson in charge. The next day Colby led the scouts. Much to our surprise Bryce joined us again, together with a new militar called Landry. Like Colby he was an experienced tracker and huntsman. Leof also stayed with us and he and Cynric looked after the six of us.

By the end of the next day we had coalesced into one tightly knit section, each one of us respecting the skills of the rest. It was a far cry from the first day.

Provisions were always a problem and, as Malcolm had systematically stripped the country bare of livestock, finding food became a priority. Some of the crops were nearly ripe in the fields and there were a lot of root vegetables to be had. We got used to a diet of pottage and gruel but occasionally our section got lucky and managed to kill the odd deer or sheep that had somehow evaded being rounded up. Leof also proved to be a dab hand at tickling trout and so we had venison, mutton and fish to enliven our meals. Of course, the deer hadn't had time to hang and so its meat was exceptionally tough, but at least it was meat.

Every village and farmstead we came across was deserted, even the town of Lauder after which the valley was named, was devoid of life. It was as if we were the only living folk left on God's earth. The deserted landscape began to unsettle the army. We were a superstitious lot at the best of times and now rumours about plague, pestilence and the wrath of God began to spread.

'The king has decided that we should stay here for a few days,' Godric told us when we camped near Oxton that night. 'Earl Aldred has been asked to send out patrols into the Lammermuir Hills to the east and the Moorfoot Hills to the west to see if we can find any hidden herds of cattle or flocks of sheep. Obviously you will need to keep an eye out for the enemy at the same time.'

Our section was divided into two to provide the scouts for the raiding parties. Colby, Osric and I went into the Lammermuirs whilst Bryce, Landry and Acca were sent with the other foragers. I had got used to doing everything with my brother and I missed him when we were split up. He told me later that he felt the same way. I had to smile to myself when I remembered how I had detested him when he was a snotty nosed young armiger.

At first we found nothing but, after two hours we rode over the shoulder of a tall hill that Colby identified as Hunt Law and there below us was an area filled with cattle, sheep, pigs and horses. The area lay at the headwaters of a small river called the Dye Water. We had found it by pure chance. The pasture where the animals grazed lay surrounded by hills to the north, south, east and west. The river rose in two different places and flowed around the hill to the south to meet up just beyond it.

This secluded spot was also home to several hundred women and children. Their tented encampment was spread over the lower slopes of the hills surrounding this natural basin. We rode back to brief Earl Aldred.

An hour later he led twenty militares down from Blythe Edge to the south-east of Hunt Law and into the valley some two miles from their target. Meanwhile our small group of scouts had ridden around to the back of Miekle Says Law, the hill to the north of the Scots' hideaway.

When we heard the horn, which signalled Aldred's attack on the camp, we rode around the hill to the saddle where the spring feeding the southern branch of the Dye Water bubbled out of the ground. Now we were directly above the Scots encampment and barring the easier of the two routes up into the hills. Our task wasn't to stop the Scots escaping; we were there to turn back any animal who came our way. Of course, these were being driven by women and children desperately trying to escape, but they lost hope of saving their livestock when they saw us waiting for them.

Thankfully only a few died during the assault on the camp and they were boys who were too brave for their own good. A few animals inevitably escaped our pincer attack, but we had netted some five hundred sheep, a hundred head of cattle, sixty swine and twenty plough horses. I wondered if Godric and the other group of militares had been as successful.

✝✝✝

By the time we reached Edinburgh Malcolm had fled westwards. At first we thought that we must have moved more swiftly than Wigbehrt had expected because he was still at Dunbar, according to some Scots we'd captured. Aldred asked Cnut for permission to go and deal with the Earl of Lothian and, barring some militares who stayed with the king as scouts, the earl took the Bernician contingent eastwards to confront Wigbehrt.

Our force consisted of forty mounted militares and a dozen armigers, seven ealdormen and forty three thanes, some two hundred of their housecarls and eighty hunters and other bowmen. Aldred was confident that a shade under four hundred well-trained fighting men would be enough to deal with Wigbehrt and however many men he had with him at Dunbar. It therefore came as something of a shock to be confronted by a sizeable army in the foothills of the Lammermuirs.

Colby, Acca and I had been scouting forward on one side of the track along which our main force advanced whilst Osric, Bryce and Landry were checking the woods on the other. We had taken Cynric with us whilst Leof was following the other three. In the early afternoon we spotted a dust cloud coming towards us. It hadn't rained for some time and so the ground was very dry. By the size of the cloud there had to be a considerable number of warriors in front of us.

Acca went back with Cynric to inform the earl whilst I drew my sword and carefully angled the blade to catch the sun so as to signal the others in the trees without giving our position away to anyone else.

A few minutes later the other four crossed the track and rode up to join us. They too had seen the approaching dust cloud. There was an old hill fort on the spur above us called Dunbar Common and so we made for that. It would give us a good view down into the valley of the Papana Water, a small river, along which the track ran.

Once inside the fort we dismounted and climbed up to look over the earthen ramparts. From here we could see beyond the small village of Garvald and we watched in amazement at the column wending its way westwards. All but the first part of the column was hidden in the dust being kicked up by those at the front. Extrapolating numbers from the part of the column we could see and the length of the dust cloud, we realised with dismay that the enemy's strength was somewhere around four times ours. We slipped away and made for the rest of our men as quickly as we could.

Earl Aldred suspected that it was a trap as soon as we told him what we had seen; not for us, but for Cnut. Malcolm wasn't retreating; he planned to ensnare our army in a pincer movement.

✝✝✝

When we re-joined Cnut's army just as dusk was falling that evening we discovered that Malcolm was waiting for us at a place called Allenmuir Hill. Evidently he planned to hold us there until Wigbehrt could attack us in the rear. Our scouts estimated that his numbers were slightly more than ours, but of course the majority of our army were trained and well-armed warriors superior to most of those in the Scots force. In normal circumstances the advantage would lie with us, despite the fact that we would be attacking uphill. However, Cnut had no intention of engaging Malcolm; not yet at any rate.

By the time that dawn broke over the land we were already on the move back to the east. So far the weather had been benign with sunshine much of the time. Now the blue skies had been replaced by dark scudding clouds and the wind blew strongly from the west. You could almost feel the rain in the air, although it was still dry for now.

We had left a dozen militares and their armigers behind to make themselves obvious on the east bank of the River Esk. Malcolm needed to think that they were waiting for our army to arrive to give us enough time to deal with Wigbehrt. Once he had been eliminated as a threat we would return and deal with Malcolm.

Once more our section were ranging ahead of the vanguard. Wigbehrt's men were crossing the Binns Water by the time we found them. He had now deployed his own scouts and we spotted a dozen men on hill ponies a mile ahead of his main body. However, they were down on the low ground whereas we were on the upper slopes of the Lammermuirs high above them.

I rode back to let Aldred know where Wigbehrt was and he went to confer with the king. Of course, I wasn't privy to their discussions but shortly afterwards Cnut split his army in two. He led half to confront Wigbehrt directly whilst Earl Siward took the rest away to the south. They would swing round and attack Wigbehrt in the flank. Cnut was using Malcolm's own tactics against his underling.

Meanwhile we rode along the base of the Lammermuirs to take up position behind Wigbehrt's army. Our job was to stop his men from retreating; Cnut needed to eliminate the threat he posed before attacking Malcolm.

As we rode the heavens opened. With the wind behind us it didn't affect us that much, but we knew that our enemy wouldn't be able to see as clearly with the driving rain in their faces.

As it turned out, we weren't needed. Wigbehrt was outnumbered but his men fought bravely. It was difficult to make out what was happening but we later found out that they attacked our shield wall bravely but could make little impression on it. As soon as they withdrew to regroup Siward hit them in the flank. Cnut then charged into them whilst they were disorganised. The battle didn't last much longer; the Scots were routed and fled. Small groups broke away at first and then the trickle became a flood.

We had drawn up our forty militares in extended line and charged towards the oncoming horde. Seeing us, men started to run to the left and right of our line. Some made it, but we crashed into the remainder before they could run clear. Many had thrown away their weapons in flight and so were defenceless as we chopped and hacked them down. Soon the sheer press of numbers slowed us down and Aldred gave the order to withdraw.

We lost one man in the fight, although that was too grand a term for what was basically the slaughter of defenceless men. Osric had seen what had happened. Our dead comrade had been pulled from his horse and hacked to pieces by Scots who still had their daggers.

More and more of the desperate Scots were making their way around us, many heading up into the Lammermuir Hills to the south. In truth we had little appetite for slaying a beaten foe but Aldred had his orders from Cnut. He wanted to kill as many of them as possible to eliminate the threat of another invasion of Northumbria for a generation. It made strategic sense but carrying it out was unpleasant work.

Once more we charged into the men fleeing the battle but this time there didn't seem to be so many of them. We probably killed another hundred or so before, thankfully without further loss to ourselves, before we arrived at the area where the main battle had taken place.

It looked more like a killing ground. Piles of Scots bodies littered the ground whereas there were far, far fewer of our own dead. We had just come to a halt when Cnut rode up looking furious.

'What are you doing here?' he yelled at us. 'Wigbehrt is escaping.'

He pointed to the south where a small group of horsemen could be seen galloping away. Without replying, Aldred turned his horse and set off in pursuit with us streaming behind him.

Our mounts were tired whereas those of Wigbehrt and the men with him, presumably some of his thanes as few Scots owned horses, would be relatively fresh. One thing in our favour was the fact that they were galloping away and they wouldn't be able to keep that pace up for long before the horses would be blown. We, on the other hand, followed them at a gentle canter. As long as we kept them in sight we would catch them eventually.

By now we wore soaked to the skin. You can't fight encumbered by a cloak so we had no protection against the driving rain. Mercifully it started to ease up as we neared the foothills of the Lammermuirs and by the time that we were climbing up a narrow valley in pursuit of our quarry the rain had stopped altogether.

We slowed to a walk as the incline became greater. Two of the Scots horses had collapsed with exhaustion. Their riders tried to surrender but Aldred had no time to take prisoners so he and Godric killed them as they passed by. I didn't like it but I appreciated the necessity.

By now we were no more than a hundred yards behind the rearmost of the group ahead of us. Three more horses gave up, one sinking to its knees and the other two standing with heaving flanks refusing to take another step. At least their riders put up a fight and so it was easier on my conscience to kill them. Unfortunately they were determined to sell their lives dearly and one of them succeeded in stabbing me in the thigh before Acca cut him down.

At first I felt nothing but then the pain was so intense I nearly fainted. I swayed in the saddle and nearly fell off. Luckily Acca was there and he came alongside me and grabbed me around the waist until I nodded to tell him I was back in control. He stayed with me as the rest rode away in pursuit of the last half a dozen Scots.

Once he was confident that I wasn't going to topple to the ground he let go and dismounted. He helped me off my horse and pulled out a spare tunic from my saddle bag to staunch the bleeding until Cynric, who was following on with the rest of the armigers, reached us.

Needless to say, my wound continued to hurt like hell and it hurt even more as the boy probed it to extract bits of cloth from inside it before washing it clean, and then sewing it up. I'm told that I cursed the boy to Hell and back but he stoically ignored my ranting. The good news was that, deep as the cut was, nothing vital had been severed.

I suffered even more agony when they helped me back onto my horse; so much so that I nearly passed out. Every step back down the valley sent a jolt of pain through my leg but after an interminable time we reached the battlefield.

Of course Cnut was no longer there. He and the army had already departed to confront Malcolm, but there were priests and monks attending to our wounded along with a few of our men who were busy cutting the throats of the enemy wounded and looting the bodies. Crows, buzzards and other carrion birds had already descended to feed on the corpses and I watched in disgust as they plucked out the eyes first.

People talk about the stench of death. That day I found that I could break it down into its components: the smell of blood, faeces, urine and sweat assailed my nostrils. I was glad when we rode clear and shortly afterwards arrived at the place where the wounded were being treated.

A monk took off Cynic's temporary dressing and examined the wound. He grunted in satisfaction and re-bandaged it with a clean dressing before moving onto the next man. Acca and Cynric helped me into a cart and I must have fallen asleep until I woke to the jolting motion as I, along with a dozen or more other wounded, were taken to where the army was now camped.

I looked up to see Acca and Cynric riding either side of the cart before falling asleep again.

✝✝✝

There was no battle against Malcolm and the rest of the Scots. When Cnut confronted Malcolm across the River Esk he asked to negotiate. He started proceedings by giving the Scots king a present: a casket containing the severed head of Earl Wigbehrt.

The Scots were in no position to resist Cnut's army with the men they had left and Malcolm capitulated. I heard all this from Acca as I lay recovering in our tent. What surprised me was the news that Cnut hadn't demanded the return of Lothian. Perhaps he thought that, if he had, it would remain a bone of contention for the future.

The King of Scots swore fealty to Cnut as his overlord and agreed a further treaty which was intended to ensure peace for another ten years. I gather that Earl Aldred had managed to get Malcolm to agree that he would hand over for trial anyone found to have led a cross-border raid, though no one had much faith that the arrangement would be honoured in practice.

To seal the agreement a marriage was arranged between Malcolm's grandson, Maldred, Earl of Cumbria, and Eadgyth, who was Queen Emma's granddaughter and Aldred's half-sister. At least this time the bride was fourteen, not still an immature child.

Mention of marriage drew my thoughts back to Rowena. I had planned to visit her once the campaign against Scotland was over, but now it looked as if I would have to wait months until I was fully mended before that was possible.

Chapter Ten – The Struggle for Moray

Late 1028 – Autumn 1029

Despite Cynric's best efforts to clean my wound I developed an infection. Shortly after I arrived back at Bebbanburg in a cart with other wounded men it started to ooze yellow and green pus. The earl's chaplain, a priest called Father Beadurof, had something of a reputation as a healer. Whilst some were of the opinion that my wound needed to be cauterised, Beadurof maintained that it would be better to treat it by washing it thoroughly with vinegar and binding a pad coated with honey over it.

He continued to do this every morning for two weeks and gradually the amount of pus decreased until one day the wound was clean. He continued to treat it with honey until he was satisfied that the infection wouldn't return and then I just had to wait until it was fully healed. By then the muscles of my legs had wasted away through lack of use and I found that I was as weak as a baby when I tried to walk.

Recovery was a slow process. In addition to losing the strength in my legs, I was out of practice with the skills I needed as a militar. Even Cynric could beat me with sword and shield at first. I was equally hopeless on a horse as it hurt a great deal to grip its flanks with my knees. Once I could best the armiger I started practicing against Acca. By the time I was fully fit again winter was upon us and the first snows had started to fall.

'No.'

My request to visit Pirnie to see how Rowena was faring was flatly refused by Godric.

'We've been without your services for long enough as it is, Oeric. It's time you started to earn your keep amongst the militares.'

'You know that's not fair, Godric,' Acca said hotly. 'Few have earned their place amongst the earl's men like my brother.'

'Watch your tongue, boy,' the captain of militares shot back.

'Can I make a suggestion before someone says something they'll later regret?' Colby said calmly.

Godric flashed him an angry look before nodding.

'We all know that the Scots have been chastened by Malcolm's submission and the loss of Wigbehrt. The new earl seems to be keeping his ruffians from launching even small scale raids across the Tweed, so far at any rate. However, Earl Aldred has other responsibilities as well as defending his borders. Unlike some nobles, he cares for his people.'

'I didn't ask you to make a speech, Colby,' Godric cut in. 'Get on with it.'

'The people of the Ale Valley have suffered grievously from the burning of their homes and the lack of menfolk to help them survive. With the onset of winter don't you think it would be a good idea if we sent a patrol to check on their wellbeing?'

Godric looked thoughtful for a moment before making up his mind.

'You have a point, Colby, and I could probably spare a few men for a short time from border duty. However, it doesn't have to be you and your friends, does it?'

I felt despondent and could have cheerfully punched our captain on the jaw at that moment. Then a grin suddenly lit up his face.

'Go on then, but you only have four days and you are to visit all the villages and farmsteads that suffered, not just Pirnie. And I want a full report when you return. I'll ask Earl Aldred to draft a letter for you to take with you. I don't need to tell you that you need to report to the Thane of St. Boswells first as the main landowner.'

†††

As we approached Pirnie on the third day after leaving Bebbanburg my heart was in my mouth. Suppose that Rowena had forgotten all about me? Perhaps she was betrothed to another? Although the absence of any eligible males between the ages of fourteen and fifty made that unlikely.

St. Boswells hadn't been affected as it had escaped attention during the raid eighteen months ago. It was a different story elsewhere in the area. I was disgusted to find out that the thane had evidently taken bribes from some of his wealthier freemen to allow them to marry the widows who had inherited land from their dead husbands. Inevitably if the new husbands gave their wives children this would disinherit those boys who had survived the raid and they would grow up resentful and rebellious.

New reeves had been installed to look after the other vills he owned and, although it had been hard on the women and children, they had managed to harvest enough to see them through the winter.

Pirnie was different, of course, as it belonged to Melrose Monastery. I was certain that the abbot would have appointed a new reeve by now. No doubt the new man would have turfed Rowena out of the hall and installed his own family so, although I was confident that the vill as a whole would be alright, it didn't mean that the previous reeve's family were.

As soon as the village hove into view I scanned the area in the hope of seeing my love. It was a vain hope, of course. It was early December and a thin layer of snow covered the empty fields. As we rode the final couple of hundred yards towards the outermost huts a new flurry of snow hit us, obscuring our view.

Suddenly I saw someone walking along the track ahead of us with a wicker basket on their back full of twigs and fallen branches. It was difficult to tell if the figure was that of a man or a woman but somehow I knew it was Rowena. I dug my spurs into my horse's side and he leapt forward past the wood collector. I jumped out of the saddle and turned to confront the solitary figure. I wasn't mistaken; it was Rowena but not the girl I remembered. This Rowena was careworn and the life seemed to have gone from her eyes.

She looked at me without comprehension for a moment until I threw back the hood of my cloak.

'Oeric?' she asked dubiously, looking at me as if I was an apparition.

I nodded dumbly, longing to take her in my arms but I hesitated, not wanting to seem too forward.

'What are you doing here?'

'I came to see how you are.'

She threw the heavy basket off her back and crumpled to her knees.

'How I am? Can't you see? Poor wretch that I am.'

'What's wrong?'

Before she could reply a man appeared out of the swirling snow.

'What are you doing girl? The reeve is asking why there's no more wood to put on the fire. Get up now or do you want another beating.'

'Who are you?' I demanded, annoyed at the way the wretch had ignored me and even more irate at the way he'd spoken to Rowena.

'I'm the reeve's steward; what's it got to do with you? Who are you anyway?' he peered at me and then at my seven companions watching from their horses behind Rowena.

'You're the earl's men? You have no business here. This is Church land.'

'That may be, but Melrose is in Bernicia and the earl has a care for all its inhabitants. He sent us to see how his people are faring after the Scots' raid last year,' Colby replied before I could say anything.

'Well, you can go and tell Earl Aldred that he needn't bother himself about us,' the man who called himself a steward replied brusquely.

'Whoever heard of a reeve having a steward?' Bryce said with derision. 'Only ealdormen, earls and kings have stewards. Has your master got delusions of grandeur?'

'I look after the reeve's affairs for him,' the so-called steward replied stiffly.

'Why? Is he incapable of carrying out his duties?' I asked.

'He's an important man,' he blustered. 'He has better things to do with his time.'

'Such as?'

'He spends his time hunting,' Rowena explained when the man said nothing.

'Hunting? Does this vill have lands on which to hunt then?' I asked.

The man looked uncomfortable but didn't reply.

'Answer the question,' Colby demanded with an edge to his voice. 'Where does this reeve hunt?'

'On Ancrum Moor,' he mumbled reluctantly.

Colby and I looked at one another. The moor was part of the vill of Ancrum, which belonged to the earl.

'And does this reeve of yours have the earl's permission to hunt on his land?' Colby asked softly.

The answer was obvious and the man just hung his head.

'Come,' Landry said, 'let's get out of this blasted snow and go and have a word with this poacher.'

I mounted and held out my hand for Rowena to grasp so that I could pull her up in front of me.

'What are you doing,' the reeve's man exclaimed. 'She's a slave.'

'A slave?' I asked incredulously. 'That's where you are mistaken, my friend. She is my betrothed and no one's slave and I'll kill anyone who says otherwise.'

We left him standing there in the middle of the track with his mouth open and the snow swirling around him.

'What happened?' I asked Rowena as we rode our horses into the village.

'The reeve forced my mother to marry his brother, a brute of man who raped her repeatedly,' she replied. 'In the end she killed him with his own dagger. She couldn't pay the weregild so my two brothers and I are now slaves.'

'What about your mother?'

Rowena sobbed quietly for a few moments before she recovered sufficiently to reply.

'Dreogan, the reeve, worked her and whipped her so severely that she fell ill. He did nothing to help her and she died last winter,' she said bitterly.

I felt as if my bowels had turned to water. Slavery was the prescribed penalty for a family who couldn't pay the weregild due. I had acquired quite a lot of silver and coins over the past few years and I had spent little on myself. Had I known, I would have gladly paid what was owing to this damned reeve.

The eight of us dismounted outside the hall, though in reality it was little more than a large hut. Cynric and Leof took the horses off to the stable to

dry and feed them whilst we entered the hall. I
looked around as my eyes adjusted to the gloom.
Apart from the reeve and his family sitting at the high
table there was a trestle table with two old men
sitting at it quaffing ale. They wore swords but no
armour; nevertheless they were probably the reeve's
housecarls. They regarded us warily but continued to
sit.

The hall was nothing special – a floor of beaten
earth, bare timber walls and a central hearth. Snow
fell in lazy flurries from the hole in the roof through
which most of the smoke escaped, landing spitting in
the fire below. There were four slaves and I
recognised the two boys, one about ten and the other
twelve; both were Rowena's brothers. The younger
was turning the spit over the hearth on which a
haunch of venison was cooking. He wore a pair of
ragged trousers and his bare torso was so red from
the heat that I suspected he was close to being burnt.
His brother stood some distance away, in a similar
state waiting for his turn to take over. Evidently they
were both employed as spit boys.

'Who are you?' the reeve barked at us as we
entered his hall.

We had put on our helmets and picked up our
shields before entering. The shields were painted red
with the earl's black wolf's head emblem in the centre
so the question was superfluous.

He sat behind the only table in the place beside a
thin woman with a mean face and a chubby boy of
about eleven. The man had a large frame with a
round face that made him look fatter than he was. He

was dressed in an expensive robe that looked as if it should have been worn by a noble, particularly as it was trimmed in rabbit fur which was forbidden for a man of his status. The man evidently had ideas above his station.

The woman, presumably his wife, was dressed poorly in comparison but the son wore a tunic of fine wool embroidered at the neck and hem. The two old housecarls nervously fingered their sword hilts but wisely decided not to intervene.

'I'm Colby, one of Earl Aldred's militares, and who might you be?'

'Dreogan, I'm the abbot's reeve. You have no business here.'

'On the contrary, this vill might be the property of the Church but it lies within Bernicia, whose earl is Aldred. Are you a priest or a monk?'

'No, of course not!'

The question had taken the man by surprise.

'Then you are subject to the earl's jurisdiction are you not?'

Dreogan shifted uncomfortably in his chair but didn't reply. Suddenly his wife spotted Rowena standing by my side.

'What are you doing there, slave?' she barked at her. 'Where is the wood you were sent to fetch? You'll be beaten within an inch of your life for your disobedience.'

The woman had got up from her chair and had gone red in the face with rage, whilst Rowena trembled with fear by my side.

'Lay one finger on her and it is you who will be punished,' I retorted. 'Rowena is my betrothed and I'm here to pay the weregild so that you can release her and her brothers.'

'Suppose I don't accept payment for my brother's murder?' Dreogan asked with a grin of triumph. 'She remains a slave, together with these two idle urchins.'

'You don't know the law very well, do you Dreogan?' Osric asked with an unpleasant smile. 'Slavery is only permissible if Rowena's family can't pay the weregild. If you refuse to accept payment, then honour dictates that the only alternative is a blood feud. Either way, weregild having been offered, slavery is not an option.'

'A blood feud?' Dreogan said faintly.

'We'll accept payment then,' his wife said quickly. 'The price is six hundred shillings for killing a freeman,' she added triumphantly.

'Very well, Cynric go and felt my saddle bags.'

The boy ran outside and, as he left, I noticed the man calling himself the steward slink into the hall and stand, nervously wringing his hands, by the door. Whilst we waited Colby went over to inspect the meat cooking on the spit.

'This smells like venison,' he remarked. 'Is it?'

'Er, yes,' Dreogan replied nervously.

'I see. Does this vill have land on which to hunt?'

'It strayed onto our fields,' his wife said quickly.

'Really? Osric, would you mind going with the man who calls himself a steward and see what's hanging in the meat store?'

Osric dragged the unwilling retainer outside and asked him where the meat was kept. Landry went with him in case of trouble. Whilst they were away Cynric came back and I counted out six hundred shillings. It was almost all the coinage I had saved up but it still left me with a decent amount of hack silver.

'Rowena, gather your possessions and those of your brothers. You'll all need something warm to wear in this weather.'

'We only have what we're wearing. That bitch took the rest of our clothes saying we wouldn't be needing them.'

'Then go into their sleeping chamber and choose what you need to replace what was stolen from you. The fat boy's clothes might be a little large for your brothers but they'll have to do. Don't forget cloaks.'

The look that Dreogan and his family gave me could have curdled milk. Osric and Landry came back accompanied by the steward and two men carrying the remains of one deer and two more complete carcasses.

'We found these in the food store, Colby. Looks as if a lot of deer have strayed into this vill, eh Dreogan?'

'Or perhaps you like to go hunting on Ancrum Moor?' I suggested.

'Poaching on the earl's land is punishable by blinding,' Osric pointed out.

'You cannot prove it,' Dreogan blustered.

'No, but the evidence points to poaching and I think I can guess what finding the earl would reach when you appear before him,' Osric responded with a smile.

'I shall appeal to the abbot,' the reeve declared.

'Don't bother. We are heading to Melrose to spend the night. I think Earl Aldred would be satisfied if you were deprived of your position here and you and your family were sent packing with just the clothes on your backs.'

Colby and Leof went and fetched our horses and we mounted with Rowena riding pillion behind me and her brothers seated in front of Osric and Acca.

'You do realise that Dreogan will take whatever he can and flee with the shrew and their brat before we reach Melrose?' Landry asked Colby.

'That's what I'm counting on. Intruding in Church affairs is always fraught with difficulties,' he answered with a grin.

††††

Rowena and I were married a week after returning to Bebbanburg. Perhaps I was presumptuous to have told Dreogan that we were betrothed but Rowena never mentioned it and seemed just as eager as I was for our union. The snow still lay on the ground but on the day itself the sun shone and I don't think I'd ever felt happier.

Of course, I couldn't continue to live in the warriors' hall and so I had bought a hut in the village below the stronghold, together with two slaves - a girl of sixteen and a boy of twelve to look after it. It wasn't much but it would be our first home together. Cynric continued to look after my horses, my armour and my weapons, even though it meant traipsing backwards and forwards from the fortress to do so.

Of course, my new wife and I had never had the opportunity to get to know one another properly and our sudden union could have proved to be a disaster. I was also worried that Rowena would feel an obligation to me for having rescued her and her brothers. That was no basis for a life together and it came as a great relief to find that she was truly in love with me as, of course, I was with her.

It didn't mean that we didn't have arguments. She was strong willed and had very fixed ideas about certain things. Whereas I would have made love whenever and wherever the mood was right, she would only do so in bed. I found that frustrating.

One other thing that bothered me was that her brothers were completely under her sway. Perhaps it was their spell as slaves that had knocked all the mischief and sturdy individuality that characterised most boys out of them. After all the eldest, Æsc, was twelve and the other boy, Beorhtric, was nearly eleven. They needed to be allowed to grow up and they wouldn't do that under my wife's thumb. In the spring I arranged for her brothers to go to Durham to be educated by the monks until they were old enough to start training as armigers. Rowena was against the idea initially but then inexplicably she changed her mind. It puzzled me and I pressed her to explain why she had relented, but she wouldn't say. It vexed me and we argued. She could be stubborn if she wanted to be and I realised that I wasn't going to get her to explain, so I dropped it and told her I was sorry, though I'm not quite sure what I was apologising for. Once I had done so she was equally contrite and that night celebrating our reconciliation exhausted both of us.

And so we settled down to a life as a happily married couple. It didn't last long.

'I have had a request from Macbeth to help him to recover Moray from Máel Coluim – one of his two cousins who murdered Macbeth's father,' Aldred told us one rather chilly day in May.

We had gathered outside the earl's hall to say farewell to Godric who had been our captain since before I had become a militar. No one seemed to know quite how old he was, but he'd been a contemporary of Earl Uhtred, Aldred's father, so he was probably approaching fifty. The earl had given him a vill in the Cheviot Hills as a reward for his long service and so he would end his days as a thane.

The new captain of militares was a man in his early thirties called Eadwyn. Our section had had little to do with him before so he was a bit of an unknown quantity, but those who did know him well spoke of him as fair but demanding.

The number of militares had grown over the last eighteen months as several of the older armigers were promoted. More and more boys wanted to join us as armigers as well and now there were enough for us to share one between two. Cynric stayed with Acca and me and Leof was allocated to Osric and Colby.

Maintaining sixty mounted warriors, thirty armigers, another twenty men as the permanent garrison of the fortress of Bebbanburg and another hundred housecarls spread out between the twenty or more vills that Aldred owned was expensive. Consequently the earl was always looking for more ways to earn income. I suspected that he'd just discovered another one. I couldn't see why else he would want to go to Macbeth's aid.

Eadwyn looked as intrigued as the rest of us at the earl's announcement so it didn't look as if Aldred had confided in him beforehand. I wondered why.

'The less you know at the moment the better. I'm sorry not be able to say more but I will brief your leaders once we are on our way north. For the moment all I can say is that you are to prepare for a month's campaign. We will be travelling by sea and our horses will be transported in several knarrs that I've hired. We leave at dawn the day after tomorrow.'

I bade Rowena goodbye and she did her best not to cry, not altogether successfully. It goes without saying that I was sad to be leaving her, but part of me was eager for this new adventure. Whilst I loved being married to Rowena, life had been devoid of much excitement recently. Even our patrols were uneventful and the usual round of training was becoming tedious. I was only twenty three and deep inside I missed the exhilaration of combat.

We embarked on two birlinns and, after the horses were loaded onto two merchant ships – a knarr and a karve - we left Budle Bay and rowed against a stiff wind out into the North Sea. What made it even more strenuous was the need to tow the knarr and the karve out of the bay.

Once we had rounded the Holy Island of Lindisfarne all four ships hoisted their mainsails and we headed north-north-west for the mouth of the Firth of Tay and Dundee, the port which lay closest to Macbeth's lands.

✝✝✝

'Why does this Macbeth need our help against the Mormaer of Moray,' Acca asked me as the prow of the birlinn plunged into another wave, throwing salt water over everyone in the ship.

'Because he and his brother, Gillecomgan, murdered Macbeth's father, Findlay, and took the mormaership from him. He has two reasons for wanting both his cousins dead. Firstly because a blood feud exists between them after the slaying of his father, and secondly because Macbeth feels that he is the rightful Mormaer.'

'Mormaer?' Acca queried.

'I suppose the nearest we have is earl, but in the past they were more like kings, albeit vassals of the high king. I gather that Moray still regards itself as independent of the rest of Malcolm's Scotland.'

'I see, though why we are involved is less clear.'

'Macbeth is a friend of Earl Aldred's.'

It sounded a rather lame reason even to my ears but I wasn't about to voice my suspicion, even to my brother, that in reality we were little more than mercenaries hired by Macbeth.

I need hardly have bothered to keep my thoughts to myself. When we landed at Dundee we were met by one of Macbeth's chieftains who handed over a chest full of gold and silver. Of course, word soon got around that the earl was being paid by Macbeth for our support, but he avoided any awkward questions by promising a share of it to every man once the campaign was over. The fact that we were fighting solely for money, rather than in defence of our land, didn't seem to bother most of my fellow militares. Even Acca didn't seem to think that there was anything wrong with it. The only person who thought like me was Osric. Even Colby seemed happy enough.

The rest of the day was spent unloading the horses; then we had to spend the next morning exercising them to get them fit after the sea voyage. Finally we set off for Macbeth's hall at Glamis with his men leading the way

I soon discovered that a thane in Scotland had a rather different status to an English thane. Our thanes were men who owned one or more vills. They owed fealty to an ealdorman, an earl or in some cases directly to the king. In Scotland a thane was a man, often the chief of a clan, who held land from their king and ranked socially with an earl's son. He was more akin of our ealdormen. In Macbeth's case he was lord of almost a third of Angus, including a stretch of the border with Moray.

Cuncar, Mormaer of Angus, was now a very old man and all three of his sons and his wife has pre-deceased him. His steward was essentially in charge of Angus but he didn't interfere with Macbeth. The latter therefore had a free hand in raising an army to attack Moray.

It took us less than two hours to reach Glamis, which was no more than a collection of hovels with the thane's hall standing slightly separately to the north of the village. The hovels were built with walls of what seemed to be cut turves with thatched roofs. There was a doorway but no windows which must have made them very dark inside. Macbeth's hall was rather different. The walls were made of alternate layers of undressed stone and thin turves. The stone was bedded into the turf above and below it, thus making a windproof wall without the need for mortar. Like the hovels, the roof was thatched.

Like our halls there was a hole in the centre of the ridge to allow the smoke to escape but there were boys pouring water into the straw around the hole, presumably to stop the straw catching fire. It must have been a boring and laborious life, but they were slaves and I supposed it was better than being spit boys. At least they got a respite when it rained.

The hall also had a number of windows. These were simple holes in the wall with a timber lintel to support the weight of the structure above it. They were quite small, presumably to keep the worst of the rain, wind and snow out as there were no shutters.

Macbeth came out to greet Aldred, who would presumably be staying in the hall, whilst Eadwyn led the rest of us off to set up camp. There were already several hundred Scots encamped between the village and the hall along a stream which I later learned was called the Glen Ogivie Burn. We headed past the hall to a small river into which the burn flowed called Dean Water and camped upstream from the confluence with the burn to avoid the waste from the Scots' camp.

We divided the river bank up into sections; drinking water being furthest upstream, then a section where we could wash and the section for our waste furthest downstream. The Scots didn't bother to partition their burn and I wondered that they didn't all go down with the bloody flux.

That night I lay in the tent that I shared with Acca and Cynric and listened to the rain beating down on the oiled leather above my head. I slept badly and when I did fall asleep I dreamed of Rowena. Somehow our little hut at Bebbanburg seemed very attractive at that moment and I wondered if I was growing old.

The next day dawned fine and clear and Cynric set about his usual tasks whilst Acca and I decided we wanted to go and explore the countryside. Eadwyn wasn't happy about letting us go until the other members of our section said that they would like to accompany us. After a lecture about avoiding confrontation with any Scots we came across, the ten of us set off, along with our five armigers.

Aldred had reorganised us into six sections of ten men recently. Four other young men, all newly promoted to militar from armiger, had joined us and we had unanimously elected Colby as our leader.

Inevitably he wanted to scout the ground we would be travelling over once the muster of Macbeth's men was complete and we set out towards Moray. He had already asked the guides who had accompanied us to Glamis about the way north and was told that there were two possibilities: up Glen Clova and over the hills down into Glen Muick, or north-west to find the River Isla, follow it for ten miles and then cross over the mountains into Glen Shee.

The former sounded like the easier route without a guide and so we rode due north to another of Macbeth's villages, called Kirrimuir, and then continued until we came across the South Esk, the river which ran through Glen Clova.

We took to the high ground to the right of the river when we reached what we believed must be Glen Corsa and followed it for a little way. By then it was just after midday, judging by the sun's position in a cloudless sky, and Colby called a halt.

'I think this is probably far enough for today,' he said. 'Perhaps tomorrow we might try and see if we can find this River Isla.'

'There are riders over there,' Acca suddenly called out, just as we were about to turn back.

'Yes, he's right. They're some distance away down in the valley,' one of the new militares – a young man called Uuffa – said excitedly. 'They're riding small horses.'

'Hill ponies; it's difficult to tell at this distance but I think that there's about half a dozen of them,' Acca added.

'They're scouts,' another of our new companions called out.

His name was Ricberht and he probably had the best eyesight of all of us.

'Why do you say that?' Osric asked, squinting in an effort to see more clearly.

'Because there is a long shadow in the distance, perhaps two miles behind the scouts. I think it's probably a column of people on the march,' Ricberht replied.

'There's no dust cloud,' Uuffa said dubiously.

'That could well be because the ground underfoot is soft or covered in grass, unlike our well-worn roads,' Colby said thoughtfully.

'Of course, it could be more men coming to join Macbeth,' suggested Æðelbert, another of our new militares.

'How many do you think there are?' Colby asked Ricberht.

The latter studied the moving black snake for some time before replying.

'The path along the river bank appears to be quite narrow and so I doubt they are walking more than three abreast, perhaps only two in places. I estimate that the column is probably half a mile long, so if there is a couple of feet between one man and the man behind, and allowing for camp followers, pack animals with supplies and so on, there must be at least two thousand warriors there, possibly more.'

'Then it's hardly likely to be reinforcements for Macbeth; I gather that he's only waiting for about another five hundred men.'

'Then it must be the men of Moray,' I exclaimed.

'It certainly looks like it,' Colby said grimly. 'Come on, we need to get out of sight before one of those scouts has the bright idea of looking up at the surrounding hills.'

✝✝✝

'Tell Macbeth what you have just told me,' Aldred said.

Colby, Ricberht and I stood in front of the Thane of Glamis and the earl in the former's hall. My eyes had just about adjusted to the dingy light, as had my nose to the peculiarly earthy smell of a building with turves in the wall, damp straw for its roof and a floor of beaten earth.

Colby told him briefly what we had seen and Ricberht added a little more detail. I wasn't quite sure why I was there, but Aldred had wanted me along for some reason.

'Where do you think they'll camp tonight,' Aldred asked our host when he'd finished questioning Ricberht.

'They'll need water, so on the South Esk north of Kerrimuir where it turns and heads east,' Macbeth replied.

'That's about a day's march from here for men on foot?'

'Ten miles; so rather less than a day for highlanders. They're used to covering long distances at speed, even over rough terrain. They'll want to catch us by surprise, so I expect that they'll aim to leave at dawn and hit us in the middle of the afternoon.'

'If Ricbehrt's estimate of numbers is anywhere near accurate they'll outnumber us.'

'Yes. Somehow my cousins must have got warning of my intentions and they've stolen a march on us. They must have mustered every man and every boy over twelve in the whole of Moray, which means that they've left it defenceless.'

'How does that help us?'

'Perhaps if they got word that somewhere like Elgin or Inverness was under attack they'd turn around and run home?' suggested someone I hadn't paid much attention to before, presumably one of Macbeth's advisers.

'If we could manage that we could attack them on the way,' I suggested, then realised that I had spoken out of turn.

'It's a good idea,' Aldred said thoughtfully, giving me an appraising look. 'But would he believe that you'd managed to get there without him knowing?'

'Not me, no; but an attack by the Norse of Caithness and Sunderland is much more likely.'

'How will you get a message to him?'

Macbeth smiled.

'I have a few men from Moray who are loyal to me; they have the right accent and they can go through their camp tonight spreading the word that Inverness if being besieged by Jarl Thorfinn Sigurdsson. At the very least it will unsettle them.'

'Colby, take your section out again and keep an eye on the enemy. Let Macbeth and I know if they either break camp and head back up north or, more importantly, continue towards Glamis.'

'If we are to surprise my cousin I think I need to take a calculated risk,' Macbeth said, frowning. Let's hope our ploy works so that we can ambush his men on their way back north.'

I was surprised that he was willing to risk losing his home if Máel Coluim didn't take the bait. However, it wasn't my problem and I turned to follow Colby out, but Aldred stopped me.

'Oeric, I just wanted to thank you. I gather the idea to ride out and scout to the north was yours.'

'Well, I wanted to go for a ride but it was Colby's idea to scout our possible route towards Moray.'

'Thank you; your honesty in not claiming the credit when you could have done says a great deal about your character.'

I left feeling very virtuous.

†††

I didn't think that the ploy would work but just after dawn we watched as the Moray scouts set off back towards Glen Clova. The rest of the Moray army followed them, not in any formation, but in dribs and drabs just as soon as a group was ready.

'Oeric, you and Acca ride as fast as you can and let Macbeth and Aldred know,' Colby ordered.

We scrambled back down the reverse side of the hill from our viewpoint to where Cynric held our horses. Minutes later we were riding up Glen Prosen, the valley that ran parallel to Glen Clova. Glen Prosen branched after five miles and we turned left into Glen Logie heading for the side of the mountain called Cairn of Barns.

The ground was strewn with boulders so we had to travel slowly and I began to worry that we wouldn't reach Macbeth in time. He and Aldred had led their forces around the enemy camp and north-west up Glen Prosen during the night. By now they should be in position on the reverse slopes of the oddly named Cairn of Barns.

I had thought of the Cheviot Hills as a wilderness but they were tame compared to the Braes of Angus. The wild landscape consisted of barren heather covered mountains, rocky cliffs and screes. The mountains were intersected by river valleys but areas of bog could trap the unwary at relatively high altitude. There were few roads or even paths, except animal tracks, and the whole place had an aura of desolation. To add to the gloom engendered by the land, it soon started to drizzle; but thankfully the clouds stayed on the hill tops. Had they descended we would have quickly become lost in the mist.

As we rode up Glen Logie we came around a bend and we could see our army huddled on the rock strewn saddle between Cairn of Barns and the neighbouring mountain, Cairn Inks.

'Máel Coluim took the bait, lord earl,' I told Aldred when we reached him.

He was standing next to Macbeth who thanked me.

'We had hoped to see down into the glen but this damned rain limits visibility to a few hundred yards,' he added.

'Well, now we know that our gamble paid off, perhaps we can move down the slope until we can see the river?' Aldred suggested.

Macbeth nodded and sent for his chieftains.

'You and Acca might as well stay and join us, Oeric,' Aldred said. 'Our task is to block the road along the valley whilst Macbeth's lads charge into the column from above.

'Should we attach ourselves to any particular section, lord earl,' Acca asked.

'No, stay with me. You can be my bodyguards this day,' he grinned.

Acca sent Cynric to join the other armigers and we followed the earl down the steep hillside to the valley floor. Once there we headed north-west along the South Esk, two sections of militares on the far bank and three on the near one. Then we waited.

'Advance in line when you hear the horn, pass it on,' Aldred called softly. 'You can have the honour of blowing it, Acca,' he said giving my brother a hunting horn made of bronze. 'Three short blasts followed by a short pause and then three more; keep blowing until I tell you to stop.'

We sat waiting nervously in the light rain, which seemed to find its way into every crevice in our clothing. I shivered as cold water trickled down my back. Then suddenly the drizzle stopped and, although the cloud still sat on the hill tops, a light breeze was dispersing the last wisps of moisture in the valley so that we could see much further ahead of us.

The clearing of the drizzle came just in time. The enemy scouts were barely a hundred yards from us and the first of the men on foot scarcely two hundred yards beyond that. I could just make out a party of men on horseback behind the vanguard. They had to be the mormaer and his chieftains. At that moment Acca blew his horn for all he was worth and we were galvanised into action.

We were lined up in three rows, stretching all the way across the flat area either side of the narrow river. At first we walked slowly forwards whilst the dozen Moray scouts milled about, unsure what to do. If they retreated their way was blocked by the first of their own warriors on foot. If they charged us they faced certain death. Two of them made a break for it, riding at an angle up the hillside to our right. However, unlike us who had picked our way through the boulders carefully, they urged their horses forward at speed and the one in the lead broke its foreleg, tumbling to the ground and, not only crushing its rider to death, but also bringing down the horse and rider behind it.

The others were still dithering when we hit them. I aimed my spear at a red bearded man with a look of panic on his face. He did nothing to try and counter my attack and I lifted him clear of his pony with my spear protruding from the centre of his chest. I let go of the spear and grasped the haft of my axe.

I felt a blow on my shield and turned my head to look into the frightened eyes of a beardless boy. I felt compassion for him but I had learned long ago that you never hesitated to kill an enemy if you wanted to live. I brought my axe around horizontally over my horse's head and felt the jar as it crushed his ribs and embedded itself into his side. I yanked my axe free and then I was through the scouts.

I looked for the earl and saw him cut down another Moray scout, but he was the last. Now we were faced by about a hundred yelling warriors thirsting for our blood as they sprinted towards us.

We withdrew at a canter until we were a good two to three hundred yards clear of the enemy, then we reformed. I took my place on one side of Aldred with Acca on the other. I looked across and grinned at my brother and he grinned back. Then I noticed to my horror that he was covered in blood.

'It's not mine,' he called with a laugh when he saw my worried face.

Then Aldred gave an order I hadn't anticipated.

'Archers dismount,' he called.

I swung down from my horse and grabbed my bow and quiver, quickly stringing the former. Another fifteen of the militares had also trained as archers and we stepped forward without being told and aimed our first arrows up at an angle of forty five degrees.

'Loose,' called Aldred and our shafts arced gracefully up into the sky before plummeting down amongst the advancing enemy.

Not all scored a hit but at least a dozen of the Scots fell dead or wounded. By then our second volley was in the air and ten more fell. Now they were less than a hundred yards away and our next volley hit the leading warriors head on. More dropped to the ground and those behind stumbled over the bodies of their fellows. We sent one more volley into the enemy and then unstrung our bows and remounted.

The enemy numbers had been halved and now that numbers were more or less even, their courage failed them. A few fled up the steep hillside and others ran back towards the main part of their army.

I was well aware that Máel Coluim had many more men than his cousin but, strung out as the enemy were, they hadn't been ready for Macbeth's onslaught. He'd swept whole sections of the enemy off the track and into the river, where most of them drowned. Those who made it to the far bank tried to escape to the north, only to run into the militares on that side of the river.

When they saw the horsemen charging at them their only thought was to get away. They scrambled up the steep slopes of Ben Tiran on the opposite side of the valley from Cairn of Barns and Cairn Inks. It was hardly terrain for men on foot and no place for horses so they escaped. However, they were few in number.

As we advanced on horseback towards the various skirmishes now taking place over a mile-long stretch of the valley, we saw another group of horsemen fighting their way through the confused mass of men fighting each other, chopping men out of their way indiscriminately – friend as well as foe. This had to be Máel Coluim trying to make his escape. He was on the same bank as Aldred and I and looked to be protected by about forty mounted nobles and bodyguards. They outnumbered us by about four to three but they weren't skilled in fighting on horseback, nor were they in any sort of formation.

'Wedge,' Aldred yelled and Acca blew three quick notes on the horn just in case someone hadn't heard the order.

Those on the wings slowed down so that within twenty paces we had smoothly changed formation and the point struck the leading enemy riders. We carved into them like the prow of a longship plunging through the waves, stabbing and chopping down men and horses as we went. Suddenly I saw a man directly ahead of me dressed in a polished byrnie and a helmet on which a band of gold had been riveted. He carried a round shield on which a stylised blue eel had been painted. It had to be Máel Coluim, the Mormaer of Moray.

I raised my axe and brought it down with all my might but Máel Coluim managed to raise his shield and my axe was deflected. He swung his heavy broadsword at me, which was half as long again as mine and, had it landed, it would probably have cut me in two. I positioned my own shield to block it, knowing that the weight and force of the blow was likely to break my arm, but thankfully it never landed.

I'd lost contact with the earl but Acca had stayed with me. Now he thrust hard with his spear, which he had somehow managed to retain, into the mormaer's side. The point parted the links of the expensive chain mail byrnie and lodged deep in his bowels.

He screamed in agony and toppled from his horse. He wasn't dead but death was coming and it would be agonisingly slow. I waved my thanks at Acca and we both turned as one to seek out the man we had been tasked to protect. Aldred was fighting off two men mounted on ponies, presumably part of Máel Coluim's bodyguard. Acca and I attacked them from behind and cut them down. It wasn't very fair but war isn't a fair business.

Aldred thanked us with a nod and the three of us turned to seek new opponents. However, the fight with their mounted contingent was over. Five riders had managed to get away up the valley but the rest were dead, or soon would be.

Over half the men of Moray also managed to escape but four hundred surrendered and were taken prisoner and, when we did the body count, we found over a thousand of the enemy had been killed or, if they were seriously wounded, soon would be.

Unfortunately one of the riders who escaped was Máel Coluim's brother, Gillecomgan. As soon as he reached Moray he declared himself to be the new mormaer and he set about raising another army from those who had escaped and those few who'd remained at home. However, there wouldn't be enough to make another attempt to invade Macbeth's lands until today's young boys grew up. In any case he'd be more worried about the Norsemen in his weakened state.

Macbeth had partially avenged the murder of his father but the actual killer had escaped and he was no nearer recovering Moray. His immediate impulse was to continue with his original plan but Aldred and his chieftains persuaded him otherwise. The element of surprise had been lost and Macbeth had also suffered many hundreds of casualties in the Battle of Glen Clova.

Chapter Eleven – The Hall Burning

1031 - 1032

I returned to Bebbanburg and to Rowena to find out that she was pregnant. Naturally I was overjoyed and I fear I fussed over her rather a lot.

'For Heaven's sake, Oeric, stop fretting!' she told me one day. 'Childbirth happens all the time and to most women several times during their lives. It's nothing special. Sometimes I wish you were back in Scotland!'

'Well, it may not be special to you, but it is to me,' I told her heatedly. 'I've lost one family and you can hardly blame me for worrying about my second.'

'You're not alone in losing your parents, are you? Or have you forgotten that I'm an orphan too?'

'That's not fair! We've both lost our parents but you still have your siblings,' I retorted.

'And what's Acca then? I sometimes think you care for him more than you do for me!'

It was our first real row and I stormed out to spend the night in the warriors' hall. I got drunk with Acca and felt very sorry for myself, especially the next morning when I awoke with a thumping head.

'You'll have to go back and apologise you know,' Acca said as I dunked my head into a bucket of water in a futile effort to clear it.

I knew that he was right but my pride wouldn't let me. Rowena was even more headstrong than I was and I'm not sure how we would have been reconciled if something hadn't happened to bring us back together.

We had rowed at the start of November 1031. The weather had been unseasonably mild in October but suddenly the wind veered around to the north and the temperature dropped significantly. It wasn't cold enough yet to snow but a combination of rain and a chilly wind made riding unpleasant.

Colby, Acca, Osric, Uuffa, Cynric and I were on our way back from collecting the annual taxes from the Ealdorman of Catterick when we came across two boys taking shelter during a thunderstorm under a large oak tree.

'Haven't you more sense than to sit under a tree when there is lightening about. Do you want to die?' I asked scornfully.

'Oeric? Is that you?' the elder of the pair asked.

Only then did I realise who the boys were: Rowena's brothers, Æsc and Beorhtric. I hastily dismounted and pulled the two boys to me. They were chilled to the bone and I realised that they were only wearing woollen under-tunics and thin trousers. I yelled at Cynric to hand me my spare cloak and that of Acca so I could wrap them in the thick dry material. They were still ice cold but, once they were riding pillion behind Acca and me, the combination of the cloaks and our body heat began to warm them.

They were still cold when we arrived outside my hut, but at least they had lost that blueish tinge which had so worried me. Acca and I took them inside and I told them to sit near the fire but not too close. They needed to warm up slowly.

'Ah, you've come back to ...' Rowena began to say when she saw her brothers. She forgot about me and rushed to deal with the boys, taking off their cold clothes and wrapping them in thick blankets whilst yelling for the servants to bring hot pottage.

'Where did do you find them,' she asked me eventually.

Both Acca and I were standing near the fire sipping mead that Cynric had fetched by that time.

'About five miles north of Alnwick, sitting under an oak tree in a thunderstorm. They were near to death; no heat in their bodies at all. I dread to think what might have happened had we not chanced by.'

'Thank the Lord God that you did,' she said with a smile, then she came and kissed me and hugged Acca as well.

We never mentioned out quarrel but as soon as the two boys had recovered sufficiently she started to question and scold them at the same time. The younger boy burst into tears.

'Perhaps if I have a quiet word with them, my dear,' I suggested mildly.

'Yes, of course. I'm sorry Beorhtric; I was just so concerned when I saw you. I couldn't bear it if you had both died.'

I got their story out of them, albeit slowly. When Æsc reached the age of fourteen he had asked the abbot for permission to write to me and ask to return to Bebbanburg so that he could become an armiger.

To my shame I had forgotten my promise and even failed to realise that had now passed his fourteen birthday. Rowena hadn't reminded me and, although she never admitted it, I suspected that she preferred her brothers to remain safely in the cloister rather than risk their lives as warriors. That would explain the sudden change in her attitude just before the boys left.

Of course, the gift of enrolment wasn't in my hands, but I was confident that Eadwyn would look favourably on my recommendation and had told him that. The captain was always on the lookout for suitable boys to be trained to eventually join the ranks of militares.

If Æsc was unhappy as a novice monk, Beorhtric positively hated the life. He was a boy who craved excitement and the humdrum round of prayers throughout the day and night, the learning of Latin, listening to tales from the Scriptures over and over and the rigid discipline and hard work that was his lot drove him mad, or so he said. He refused to stay if his elder brother abandoned him, as he put it.

Æsc didn't know what to do, but in the end he didn't need to make a decision. The Master of Novices refused to let him write to me and told him that both he and Beorhtric were destined for a monastic life. It wasn't true of course, but no doubt he was being spiteful to two boys who were a constant trouble to him.

In the end, after a painful beating given to Beorhtric because he fell asleep during the service of compline, the two brothers decided to run away together. One night they sneaked out of the dormitory where all the monks slept, stole some bread and cheese from the pantry and hid in the town until the gates opened in the morning. Then they ran, evading the sentries, and headed north.

They foolishly discarded their hated, but thick, homespun habits, leaving them dressed only in a thin woollen under tunic and trousers. At first the weather during the day was mild and they usually found a barn to shelter in at night. They had taken some bread and cheese with them and stole a few apples from an orchard so they had food, at least initially.

When they reached the River Tyne they were forced to abandon the old Roman road as they had no money to pay the ferryman to cross and had to walk inland for miles until they found a ford they could wade through.

By now the food had run out and they were hungry, tired and the weather had turned colder. They had a stroke of luck when a wool merchant's servant travelling to Alnwick with cloth ordered by the ealdorman's wife passed them on the road. He offered them a lift in his cart and gave them stale bread and apples to eat. By now the weather had really changed for the worse. They tried to see the ealdorman and ask for his help but the housecarl on duty outside the hall looked at the two scruffy urchins dressed in what were by then little more than filthy rags and threatened to beat them if they didn't clear off.

As they left Alnwick it started to rain and then, after they had trudged a few miles soaked to the skin and shivering with cold, the thunder storm had started. They had given up at that point and took shelter under the tree, cuddling together for warmth. No doubt they would have died there, and quite quickly, had we not found them.

If I thought that they would quickly recover I was mistaken. The next day their health deteriorated. They complained that their limbs ached and of a headache and a sore throat. As the day wore on they both developed a fever and started to shiver violently. They became listless, had a dry, hacking cough and thick green mucus ran from their noses.

Rowena sent for the village priest but he was at a loss to know how to treat them. In something of a panic I rode up to the fortress and sought out the chaplain. Before he'd had become Aldred's chaplain he had been the assistant infirmarian at Melrose Monastery.

'I've seen this before many times,' he told us calmly. 'Keep them in bed and away from the hearth, smoke in their lungs isn't going to help. Make sure they drink plenty of water and give them hot soup to keep their strength up. Keep them off solid food; they'll only vomit it back up. Pray to God and the fever should go away after a few days of its own accord.'

Both of us were worried but the priest's words were reassuring. Rowena was more concerned than I was, after all they were her brothers, but the next day she had something else to worry about. The baby was on its way.

We called him Cerdic, meaning one who is loved. It was an easy birth but the baby was small. However he was a fighter and had a pair of lungs on him that could wake the Devil. The goodwife who had delivered him said that he would soon put on weight and, as the boys were getting better every day, I went up to the church in the fortress and told the priest that I would like to make a donation to his old monastery at Melrose in thanksgiving.

He suggested that I should make a pilgrimage there on foot in order to make my offering and I reluctantly agreed. As a horseman I didn't travel anywhere on foot if I could avoid it but I could see that it would add more meaning to my gift if I suffered in the process. However, it was winter and the roads were like a river of mud thanks to incessant rain. I decided to wait and I eventually left in late March the following year.

Acca decided that he would accompany me. I told him it was unnecessary but he insisted and I grudgingly agreed. In truth I was glad of the company. We dressed appropriately in black robes that came down to mid-calf and black cloaks with black felt hats so that we looked just like any other male pilgrims. However, we were warriors and didn't intend to travel completely unarmed. We both wore seaxes hidden under our cloaks and carried stout staffs that would serve as cudgels as well as walking aids.

When we set off we found that we had a shadow. Cynric appeared with a haversack stuffed with bread and cheese.

'And where do you think you are going?' I asked him, not unkindly.

'With you and Acca, of course, Oeric. After all, I am your armiger.'

'What's in the haversack?'

'Food for our journey.'

'Part of being a pilgrim is that we have to depend on the charity of others in order to eat and find somewhere to sleep. You may come with us if you are that keen to do so, but go and get rid of the food first.'

We hadn't gone more than two miles and were climbing the ridge that lay between Bebbanburg and the road from Berwick to Alnwick when we were stopped by two horsemen. Neither looked particularly pleasant. They wore trousers that had seen better days and leather gambesons that had been badly sewn up in several places. One wore a leather arming cap and the other a dented helmet. The horses looked badly cared for and hadn't been groomed recently. In all they looked what they were: mercenary Danes.

'Have you come from Bebbanburg?' the one in the helmet asked.

'Yes, we are poor pilgrims on our way to Melrose Monastery. What do you want with us?'

'Don't be afraid, pilgrim,' the other said with a reassuring grin that exposed a mouth with several missing teeth. 'We're merely after information.'

Acca and I had resisted the temptation to put our hands on our seaxes when they had first appeared and I still felt that they could be trouble. Nevertheless I did my best to look relaxed and I returned his smile.

'If we can help...'

'We have a petition to give to Earl Aldred but the sentries on the gate won't let us past,' he began.

'And who would blame them,' I thought to myself, but I continued to smile.

'We thought that it might be best if we could approach him whilst he was out hunting. Did you hear anything to indicate that he was thinking of doing so soon?'

'No, I'm afraid not, but then we stayed with a kind family in the village and I don't suppose that they concern themselves with such things.'

'I see,' he said, not troubling to conceal his disappointment. 'On your way then.'

'Could you spare us a crust or a coin to aid our journey,' Acca asked as they turned to go.

'You'll get a kick up your arse to help you on your way, would that help?' the man in the arming cap said scornfully.

We watched them go.

'Hired by Carl?' Acca suggested as they rode beyond earshot.

'Possibly, or someone else who means our lord ill.'

'There's smoke coming from the wood in the valley there,' Cynric said pointing the way that the riders had gone.

'There's a lot more of the bastards then. We need to warn Aldred.'

'Once we've sworn to go on pilgrimage and started out, we can't turn back or we risk imperilling our immortal souls,' I said gnawing my lip in frustration.

'I haven't sworn an oath,' Cynric pointed out.

'Good lad. You know what to say?'

He rehearsed the gist of what he'd heard and then set off dropping down the slope to the north, away from the mercenaries, towards the shore of Budle Bay. From there he could make his way to the Sea Gate of the fortress without being seen.

We pressed on towards our goal for the night – the village of Wooler at the edge of the Cheviot Hills - but I continued to worry about the ruffians who I strongly suspected had been paid to kill our lord.

As the day wore on the clouds got darker but the rain held off. I found that walking used muscles not exercised much whilst riding, particularly my calves. By the time we'd walked a dozen miles they felt as if they were on fire. The Thane of Wooler allowed us to sleep in his hall that night and fed us well, but then he did know who we were. I awoke feeling stiff and my calves ached. However, once we started walking again I loosened up. Now my problem was my feet. I took my shoes off after a few miles and Acca laughed at the blisters I had acquired. He quickly used a needle to burst them and, although they still felt sore, walking was easier after that.

At last we arrived at Melrose on the afternoon of the fourth day. The abbot greeted us himself as soon as he was told that we had come to make a gift to his monastery in thanksgiving for the survival of my family.

That evening we ate in the refectory with the monks. The meal itself was fish soup and bread, the day being a Friday, and we ate in silence whilst one of the brothers read to us from the Bible. However, once the meal was over a hubbub of conversation broke out. I had long since discovered that monks were inveterate gossips but the subject of their animated discussion that evening was all about someone Acca and I knew well – Macbeth. Of course, Melrose lay just south of the Tweed and they had a great deal of contact with the Scots over the other side of the river, so it wasn't surprising that the news had reached them first.

✝✝✝

It took a little time for me to sort out exactly what seemed to have happened in Moray three weeks previously. After the Battle of Glen Clova Gillecomgan had taken over as mormaer from his brother with little opposition. However, he proved to be far less popular than Máel Coluim. He rewarded his favourites by giving them land taken from those who disagreed with him, he increased taxes and, most importantly, he cheated King Malcolm out of his share of those taxes.

It was pure supposition on my part, but in the light of what followed it was reasonable to presume that Macbeth's subsequent actions were supported by Malcolm, at least tacitly.

This time he didn't raise an army but gathered a force of a hundred men, all mounted on horses or hill ponies for swiftness of travel. Gillecomgan was staying at Doldencha whilst hunting in the Lochnagar area in the south of Moray. The monks didn't say so but the implication was that the local thane was either in the pay of Macbeth or he was one of his supporters.

What was known was that Macbeth arrived at the hall where Gillecomgan was staying, along with some fifty of his warriors, chieftains and servants, in the dead of night. If the local thane was present, as no doubt he was as his mormaer's host, he must have left the hall with his family and his men before the attack as apparently they all survived. No doubt he was complicit in the plot.

Macbeth's men laid piles of dry brushwood all around the timber hall and set it alight. Some reports said that they also threw flaming torches up onto the straw roof. Gillecomgan and his men tried to escape but Macbeth had nailed the doors and the shutters over the windows shut. None had escaped.

Evidently Macbeth had prepared the ground well because the thanes and chieftains of Moray who had suffered at Gillecomgan's hands rallied to his side. If anyone opposed Macbeth's claim to Moray they were apparently wise enough to keep quiet.

The last the monks had heard Macbeth was on his way north to Inverness, the principal town of Moray.

✝✝✝

We stayed at Melrose for two days whilst we arranged to purchase two horses for our return journey. Our pilgrimage was over and I had no intention of walking all the way back to Bebbanburg if I could avoid it. The two mounts we eventually paid over the odds for were no better than nags, but I supposed that I could sell them as pack horses when we got back.

I regretted having delayed our departure shortly after we set out. It had turned much colder and I wondered if it was about to snow. It didn't; instead we were bombarded by hailstones, some as large as a small pebble. We took shelter in a shepherd's hut until the hail ceased and then set out again in a world turned white by the lumps of ice.

Shortly after that it started to rain and then it sleeted. By the time we reached Carham village, near the site of the famous battle a dozen years previously, we were tired, cold and wet. Our sorry nags were in a poor state too. Acca and I were very glad of a fire to dry out by and warm up. I expect our horses were equally appreciative of a dry stable.

Our host had more tidings about Macbeth as well. It seemed that he had married Gruoch, Gillecomgan's widow as soon as he reached Inverness. The fact that she was Malcolm's niece, and therefore his first cousin once removed, didn't seem to bother him. Officially Macbeth needed a Papal dispensation to wed her but that didn't prevent the Bishop of Elgin from conducting the ceremony.

Gruoch had a son by Gillecomgan, Lulach, and by marrying his mother and adopting the boy, he had cleverly brought the blood feud between him and his cousins to an end. It also prevented those opposed to his rule from using the boy as a figurehead for a future rebellion.

✝✝✝

We reached Bebbanburg just as the sun was setting. Rowena rushed to greet me and then gave Acca a hug as well. Her brothers stayed shyly in the background and waited to be greeted, which I did next. Then I went and looked at my sleeping son. He looked very peaceful and I was pleased to see that his cheeks had a healthy glow. We had feared that we would lose him and the two boys but you wouldn't think that to look at them now. Once more I thanked the Lord for their recovery and I was pleased that we had made the pilgrimage.

'The earl wants to see you,' she said once we had divested ourselves of our cloaks and moved nearer the fire to get warm.

'What? Now?'

The servant boy brought each of us a goblet of warmed mead with a dollop of extra honey which both of us sipped appreciatively.

'Well, I don't suppose that he would be best pleased if he heard that you had returned and had ignored his summons,' Rowena pointed out a trifle sharply.

I sighed. 'I suppose not. But we'll eat first and I'll change my clothes. I don't suppose he wants me to appear as a pilgrim.'

'I'll go on up to the fortress and change as well. Collect me from the warriors' hall when you're ready.'

'Stay and eat with us first,' Rowena insisted.

Acca nodded gratefully and he told my wife about our journey to Melrose whilst I went and changed. My brother left to change his clothes as soon as he'd finished but I stayed for a while longer enjoying being back in the bosom of my family.

Aldred was eating when we appeared in his hall. His wife, Synne, sat on one side of him with their daughter Edith, now a pretty girl of twelve, on the other. Another girl who I hadn't seen before sat beside Edith. Her eyes flickered over me but lingered on Acca before she demurely looked down at her food again. A slight blush spread over her cheeks and I sensed that her evident interest in him was reciprocated by my brother. She glanced up again and smiled at him before looking down again.

The exchange between the two hadn't been missed by Synne. She whispered something in her husband's ear and he looked at Acca speculatively. I wondered what on earth was going on.

'I asked to see you to thank you both. Cynric's message undoubtedly saved my life. We took their camp by surprise at dawn the next day and wiped them out. There is no doubt in my mind that Carl sent them to try and avenge his father's death. He looked at me as he said that because, of course, I'd been the one to kill Thurbrand.

'Take a seat and drink some ale whilst we finish our meal,' Aldred said waving us to join a second table at which Eadwyn and several of the senior militares sat.

We discussed our pilgrimage and listened to all the current gossip. One thing I learned which I hadn't heard before was that Aldred's half-sister, Eadgyth, had given birth to a boy who she and Maldred had named Gospatric. It wasn't Aldred's first nephew as his other half-sister, Ælfflæd, and Siward already had a baby boy – Osbjorn.

As Aldred had only been blessed with daughters – at least so far – there was much speculation whether one or other of his nephews might succeed him in the fullness of time.

'What about Eadulf,' I asked, surprised that no one had mentioned him.

'No one has heard from him for some time,' Eadwyn replied. 'Cnut seems to have lost Norway now that Olaf Haroldsson has returned to claim his father's throne. Perhaps he is dead?'

'Perhaps,' another man said. 'But I have it on good authority that Olaf was killed in a great sea battle and Svein now rules unopposed as his father's regent.'

At that moment our interesting discussion came to a halt as Aldred rose from the table and gestured for Acca and me to follow him into his private chamber.

'I wanted to reward you both for your timely warning,' he said giving each of us a pouch of silver coins.

'Thank you, lord earl,' I replied, 'but it was only our duty. We would have returned ourselves but we had already embarked on our pilgrimage.'

'So Cynric told me.'

He paused and I wondered what else he had to tell us.

'As you may have heard my own armiger is now eighteen and I have allowed him to join the militares. I wish to reward Cynric by making him my next armiger.'

It was a great honour for Cynric, of course, but I would miss him, and I knew Acca would too.

'I am told that you wish your wife's two brothers to train as armigers?'

'Yes, lord earl. Æsc is old enough now but Beorhtric is only twelve,' I replied.

'He's young but I've made an exception before, as you know full well. If you are agreeable Æsc can become your armiger, Oeric, and Beorhtric can serve Acca.'

I looked at Acca, who looked pleased. He and Beorhtric had a close bond ever since the boy had ridden pillion behind him after we rescued them. I glanced at him and he smiled and nodded.

'Thank you, lord. They will be pleased.'

He hesitated and I wondered whether we should take our leave but instead he invited us to sit down.

'I know that you are happily married, Oeric, but you are still single Acca. Is that through choice?'

'No, lord. I just haven't met the right girl up to now.'

'And is that still true?'

'Pardon, lord?'

'My wife tells me that she noticed an exchange of looks between you and Mildred in the hall.'

'I, yes, well,' Acca blushed. 'If she was the girl at the high table, yes. Perhaps I did show an interest in her. Please forgive me if I am being impertinent.'

'No, that's not why I raised the matter,' Aldred paused and cleared his throat, plainly feeling ill at ease. 'Would you like to meet her, chaperoned of course, to see if she improves on closer acquaintance?'

Acca's face lit up.

'Yes, thank you, lord. That is, yes, I would like the opportunity to meet her properly, but...'

'You wonder who she is and why I have singled you out?' he asked with a smile, relieved that Synne's intuition had proved correct.

'Something like that, lord.'

'Well, her name is Mildred and she is the heiress of a vill called Lesbury near Alnwick. She has had a difficult time; her mother died young and she nursed her sick father for the past six months. She has managed the vill on her own for some time, but now her father is dead, she's being pressured to marry the youngest son of one of Earl Siward's ealdormen. From what I can gather he is only interested in acquiring the land and has threatened to force her into marriage if she doesn't accept him willingly. It's not exactly an uncommon situation but the girl fled to me for protection.

My wife took her under her wing and keeps pestering me to help her, even though I should really have sent her to see her own ealdorman. We were at a bit of a loss as to what to do without upsetting everyone involved when Synne spotted that there may be an attraction between the two of you.'

'You mean that, if we feel the same way about each other once we get to know one another, you would allow me to marry her and become a thane?'

Acca sounded incredulous, as well he might be. Even if he wasn't attracted to the girl it would be a wonderful opportunity for him to better himself. Then I had a thought. If he went to live in Lesbury we would no longer be serving together. I told myself I was being selfish and pushed the thought to the back of my mind. Besides Mildred might refuse him.

She didn't. After a week they were betrothed and a month later they were married. Even at the time I wondered about their relationship. They might feel attracted to one another but I didn't get the feeling that it was love exactly. Rowena put her finger on it.

'Mildred sees Acca in the light of a handsome young hero riding to her rescue whilst Acca is infatuated with a pretty girl who has the added attraction of owning land. It may turn into lasting love between them, but I have my doubts.'

Time would prove her right but for now they seemed happy enough. The morning after the wedding feast my section, our armigers and I accompanied Acca and his new bride to Lesbury.

Such a strong escort for a short journey might have seemed excessive, but I didn't want to take any risks just in case the bullying suitor had seized the vill anyway. However, there was no sign of him when we got there. We saw Acca and Mildred settled in and returned to Bebbanburg. I knew I'd miss Acca, but I hadn't appreciated quite how much.

Chapter Twelve – The Death of Kings

1034/35

Another wedding was about to take place in the church in the stronghold of Bebbanburg. This time Aldred's fourteen year old daughter Edith was marrying a wealthy thane called Ligulf. I had expected the earl to aim higher and perhaps use his only child to forge an alliance with a powerful family outside Bernicia. He and his wife doted on Edith and he had allowed his daughter to marry for love. The fact that Ligulf owned no less than six vills probably helped.

Macbeth had been invited to the wedding but at the last moment a messenger arrived to say that he wouldn't be there. He was coming by sea and so I was surprised that he couldn't spare the three or four days that his visit would take. Then I learned the reason: King Malcolm was dead.

There were three possible claimants for the vacant throne, all grandsons of the late king. The eldest was Duncan, who had been made Earl of Lothian after Wigbehrt's death in addition to holding the meaningless title of King of Strathclyde. The others were his brother Maldred, Earl of Cumbria, and Macbeth of Moray. Macbeth had lodged his claim but Maldred sided with Duncan and the other Mormaers chose the latter.

The throne of Scotland wasn't the only one to change hands that year. Cnut's son, Svein hadn't proved to be a popular ruler of Norway and several of his jarls had invited Magnus - the son of a previous king who Cnut's father had deposed - to return. A majority of the jarls rallied to his side and Svein had fled to Denmark without offering battle. None of this affected us in Bernicia, of course, but we did wonder what had happened to the earl's half-brother, Eadulf. On the second of September we found out.

A lone longship had been sighted from Bebbanburg's watchtower on the afternoon of the wedding when everyone was in the earl's hall getting drunk to celebrate the occasion. When the alarm bell rang at first no one moved. Then there was a mad dash to the ramparts to see what all the fuss was about. Rowena and I joined the throng, along with Acca and Mildred who had come to attend the wedding.

The weather was fair but the easterly wind was blowing a gale and the ship was corkscrewing its way towards Budle Bay. It was running under bare poles as the sail would have been ripped to shreds no matter how many reefs there were in it. The oarsmen struggled to keep the ship from broaching as every wave lifted the stern, pushing it one way, then surging down the length of the ship before pushing the bows in the opposite direction.

Aldred called for horses and rode down to the beach with Eadwyn and several armigers leading spare horses to meet the longship when it docked. Thankfully the tide was in and half an hour later the ship came alongside the sheltered jetty. One man disembarked and Aldred threw his arms around him, slapping his back. Aldred would only greet one person like that – Eadulf had returned.

†††

Acca and Mildred returned to Lesbury two days after the wedding but they left Beorhtric behind. Acca had little need for an armiger anymore and the boy would be trained better at Bebbanburg.

The newly married couple departed before I met Eadulf again. Of course, he had changed a great deal in the dozen years since I'd last seen him. Then he'd been one of a group of militares and I'd been their armiger. Twelve years changes everyone. I'd liked the old Eadulf but I scarcely recognised him now, not visually, although of course he'd aged, but his character was so different. He had become embittered and taciturn and sat brooding much of the time. I had little sympathy with him until I found out that he had set out with two ships. The other had been a rather more comfortable karve on which his Norse wife and eight year old son, Oswulf, had travelled. The assumption was that they had been lost in the storm. I imagined how I'd feel if I lost Rowena and Cerdic.

It was Acca who brought the news to Bebbanburg. The wreck of a longship had been washed ashore on the sands to the north of the mouth of the River Aln about a mile and a half from Lesbury. There were only three survivors, two men and a young boy. One of the men had died shortly after he was rescued and the other only spoke Norse. The boy was exhausted and barely alive. Acca had been asked to translate as he spoke Danish and, although not identical to Norse, he and the surviving sailor could converse well enough. As soon as he heard that the boy was Oswulf he had him taken to his hall so that Mildred could care for him whilst he rode to Bebbanburg to inform Eadulf.

The transformation in Eadulf was miraculous. Even though his wife was presumably dead, his son's survival changed the irascible malcontent into the man I remembered from a dozen years before. He rode down to Lesbury with Acca and found that his son was recovering well under Mildred's care. Two weeks later Eadulf returned to Bebbanburg accompanied by Oswulf.

By that time Duncan had been crowned as King of Scots and had consolidated his position by making his brother Earl of Lothian in his place. He'd also taken the unusual step of making Maldred's son, Gospatric, Earl of Cumbria. It was a surprising appointment as the boy was only two years old. Perhaps Duncan thought that allowing his brother to hold both earldoms might be unpopular, or perhaps make him too powerful? The new king appointed a council of regency for Cumbria until the boy grew up.

Maldred's wife was Aldred's half-sister and, although she hardly knew her brother, having been raised at Cnut's court, she had grown up with Eadulf and evidently used her influence to keep the border relatively quiet. The other sister, Ælfflæd, didn't appear to exercise the same sort of sway over her husband. Siward made no secret of the fact that he detested Aldred and wanted to be Earl of Northumbria, not just Deira.

However, for the moment Aldred had Cnut's support and our life continued on its untroubled course unmindful of the storm clouds that were gathering overhead.

†††

That winter was a relatively gentle one with only two weeks of snow to keep us confined indoors. The weather at Christmastide was mild and Acca and Mildred invited us to spend it with them. I was meant to be on duty for two days over that period but Osric kindly volunteered to change with me so that I could take ten days off.

'I hear that Synne had another baby girl,' Mildred said as we walked back to the hall from the church after mass on Christmas Day.'

'Yes, that makes four. It makes you wonder if they'll ever have a son,' Rowena replied.

Talk of babies normally didn't interest me very much but the fact that Aldred had no son to follow him as earl was something of a concern. Even if he and Synne had a boy in the next year or so Aldred would be lucky to see his son grow to maturity. He would be forty soon and few men lived to reach sixty.

Of course, his brother Eadulf was ten years younger and he already had a son who was eight, so Uhtred's line seemed secure. I wouldn't have been so sanguine if I'd known then what the future had in store.

'I'm with child again, husband,' Rowena told me one evening after I returned from patrolling the western border.

I was immediately all concern. Cerdic had been lucky to survive his own birth and I worried about the next one. Many women died in childbirth and, now that I had a son, I was content. Of course we were a passionate couple and so I suppose that a second child was inevitable.

'How long?'

'I think I must be nearly four months gone; it's just beginning to show, which is why I had to tell you.'

'Why wait? Why didn't you tell me immediately you knew?' I asked, angry that my wife had kept the news from me until now.

'Because I knew you'd fuss and fret and I couldn't face that for any longer than I had to.'

I was hurt and resentful, although I knew deep down that she was right. I'd worry now until the baby was born and I would insist that she took things easy. Rowena wasn't the type of woman to sit by the fire and embroider. She had to be active and she would even insist on riding until it became too uncomfortable. That was something she knew I'd forbid.

I glared at her and went outside for a long walk to cool my temper before I said something I'd regret. Instead of being a reason for celebration, her pregnancy had turned out to be a cause of dissention between us. What made it worse was I knew that it was my fault. However, I could no more change my nature than Rowena could change hers.

Eventually I concluded that the best thing I could do was to absent myself for the next five months. I was sure that Rowena, instead of being angry, would be relieved.

'Are you sure about this?' Eadwyn asked me when I told him of my decision. 'Very well, I'll talk to the earl.'

A week later I joined the crew of one of the two birlinns that Aldred used to escort his merchant ships across the sea to ports on the Continent and to Inverness. Shortly after Macbeth had become Mormaer of Moray Aldred had concluded a trade agreement with him whereby we shipped our fleeces to him. The women of Moray produced various grades of woollen bales for making clothes and even sails. We bought the cloth and marketed it far and wide.

There was one other commodity which we bought at Inverness and that was furs. We had wolves in Bernicia, of course, but not in the same quantity as existed in the Scottish Highlands. Bears had disappeared from England a century or so ago, but they could still be found in the remote glens of Moray. Furs were highly prized by those who could afford them for bedding. Even with a woman to cuddle up to winter nights could be cold, but that wasn't what I wanted a quantity of bearskins for. The Vikings were well known for wearing bear and wolf skin cloaks and I had a feeling that they would be much warmer and better at coping with rain than oiled wool. I bought three bearskins and, although they cost me most of the coins I had on me, I counted it money well spent.

Moray also had four small gold mines: at Elgin, Knock, Rynie and in Glen Clova. Picts had produced gold ornaments for centuries but our Anglo-Saxon goldsmiths produced much finer jewellery and gold objects that any craftsman in Moray. We therefore bought gold and carried it south so that the jewellers of Bebbanburg and Durham could produce items for sale.

Of course, you couldn't keep such trade a secret for long and both birlinns were used to escort the knarr carrying the gold ore. It was July before we ran into any trouble. Three ships were waiting for us as we passed the entrance to the Firth of Forth: a longship whose sail displayed the yellow and blue alternating horizontal bars of Carl of Holderness and two birlinns with faded marron sails onto which a yellow sun had been embroidered. The latter was the device of Maldred of Lothian.

Our little fleet was commanded by a former housecarl called Freomund. He had no hesitation in deciding what to do and he ordered us to row towards the three enemy ships. The other birlinn swung into line behind us whilst the karve pressed on heading south under sail.

In total our two warships carried no more than seventy warriors whereas Carl's longship, a type termed a snekkja, probably carried upwards of forty men and each of the birlinns, although smaller than ours, would be manned by at least twenty men.

As we pulled for all we were worth towards the enemy one of their birlinns changed course to cut off the fleeing karve. There was nothing we could do about it and so we concentrated on the two ships ahead of us. We were close enough now to see the warriors packed onto the bows of the two ships. Evidently they intended to close on us under sail, dropping it at the last moment so that they could drift alongside us. Only an inexperienced sailor would try such a tactic and our confidence grew.

Four of our rowers shipped their oars and pulled their bows and quivers from their oiled leather bags. We had more archers but there wasn't room for more to operate in the bows. At a range of eighty yards they started to pepper the warriors crowded into the bows of the nearest ship – the snekkja. Arrow after arrow streaked into the sky so quickly that three were in the air at once. Their targets were so tightly packed in their eagerness to get at us that they didn't have the room to raise their shields and many of them were killed or wounded. Some fell overboard and sank below the waves, others fell back into those behind them, causing chaos.

Someone on the snekkja panicked, perhaps one of the ships' boys, and let go of the mainsail halyard too early. Without the sail to power it the longship lost momentum and slowed to a halt. It was now a sitting duck and we rowed slowly around it as several more of our archers exchanged their oars for bows and subjected the longship to a continuous hail of arrows. Satisfied that there wasn't enough of a crew left alive to pose a threat, we left the stricken vessel and raised our sail again to head for the karve and the third enemy ship.

By then our second birlinn had engaged the other Lothian ship and had boarded it. They seemed to be winning but, even if they weren't, our duty was to protect the gold. What the karve's attackers didn't know was that there were ten archers on board their quarry. Once more arrows rained down on the crew of the enemy ship but this time someone had decided to risk lighting a fire in a barrel on deck and now fire arrows struck the Lothian ship's mainsail and the wooden hull. It did little damage to the hull but two stuck in the gunwale and flames licked up the tarred rigging.

The crew frantically drew up leather buckets of sea water to douse the flames; all in vain. The hull suffered no damage other than a little charring, but the rigging and the mainsail continued to burn spectacularly. With a rending crash the mast, freed of its supporting rigging and still under pressure from what was left of the sail, came crashing down. We watched as the crew leapt into the sea to escape the burning wreckage. Few could swim and, in any case, they were so far from shore that only the strongest swimmers would make the distant beach.

The karve was safe and Freomund breathed a sigh of relief. I looked behind us where the fight between the other two ships continued. Freomund gave the order and we returned to our oars. Someone on the Lothian birlinn must have spotted us because shortly afterwards they broke off the fight and tried to make their escape. However, the captain of our other ship wasn't going to allow them to get away and grapnels snaked across from the Bernician birlinn and they pulled the Lothian ship back alongside.

By the time we got there it was all over. The remaining crew of the enemy ship had surrendered and we turned once more to shadow the gold ship until it reached the safety of Budle Bay.

Everyone was surprised that Maldred would join Carl in attacking Aldred's ships but we learned from those taken prisoner that Carl's captain had stolen the two Scots birlinns from Leith and manned them with hired mercenaries. Not that turning informer did the captives any good. Aldred hung them from the walls of Bebbanburg that faced the North Sea as a warning to any passing pirates.

✝✝✝

I spent that night back in my own hut and I was surprised at how big Rowena had become. She was

216

now seven months into the pregnancy but instead she looked as if the birth was imminent. When I asked her about it she gave me a worried look.

'The good wife thinks it may be twins, Oeric,' she said, anxiously scouring my face for my reaction.

'Twins?'

It was something I hadn't considered. It made things much more perilous, for the babies as well as the mother. I didn't know much about twins but I knew that they tended to be born smaller and earlier than single children. And it stood to reason that giving birth to two was more exhausting and more painful than one.

'Are you sure?'

'I'm not, but she seemed to be.'

'Did she say when?'

'Any time really.'

I nodded.

'I'm going to the church.'

'The church? Now? Why?'

To pray for a safe delivery and for God's blessing on us.'

I had never been particularly religious. Oh, I attended mass and did all that was expected and I believed in Christ but somehow it wasn't an important part of who I was; until that night. I prayed with the village priest and then after an hour or so our slave boy came running to fetch me.

'It's started,' was all he said, but it was enough.

I hurried back to our hut but the good wife and the other women told me to get out. I paced up and down outside and I didn't even notice that it had started to rain. Then I heard a baby's cry. It sounded lusty and loud. Ten minutes later, just after the crying had stopped it started again but this cry sounded slightly different.

'Master, you have twins, a boy and a girl,' Rowena's maid told me from the doorway. I rushed inside and straight to my wife's side, ignoring the babies.

'Are you well?' I asked Rowena, stroking her hair back from her sweaty forehead.

'Yes, just tired,' she replied, smiling up at me.

I kissed her on the lips, ignoring the giggles from the women, and went to inspect the new arrivals.

✝✝✝

We gave them the names Oswin and Cille when they were baptised and I quickly came to two conclusions. We needed a wet nurse if Rowena wasn't to get exhausted and it was time to get a larger hut.

By late autumn that year I had built a small hall house and bought two more slaves, a girl and a boy to add to the two we already had. I never did find a wet nurse but Rowena quickly learned to cope with two hungry mouths.

Life had been quiet since the birth of the twins but all that was about to change. We'd just moved into our new home when Aldred sent for me. When I entered his hall I found several ealdormen and senior militares already there.

I waited patiently at the back as more men arrived. Eadwyn whispered something in the earl's ear and shortly afterwards Bishop Edmund of Durham entered accompanied by Eadulf.

'Thank you all for coming. Word has reached us that King Cnut is gravely ill and is not likely to see out the year. That is grave enough but the question of succession is far from clear cut. He has nominated his son by Queen Emma, Harthacnut, as his successor but, as you all know he is only seventeen and is living in Denmark. Cnut's other son, born of his first wife, Harold Harefoot, is two years older, already living here in England and his mother is a Saxon and not a Norman.'

Aldred paused and looked around the room.

'Æthelnoth has called a meeting of the Witan and I am summoned, as are the other earls and every ealdorman.'

'Why Æthelnoth?' someone called out, 'and why now if Cnut still lives?'

'Because Æthelnoth will preside as Archbishop of Canterbury if the king is unable to do so,' Aldred explained. 'The reason I've called you here is to discuss who our ealdormen and I should support as Cnut's heir at the Witan. It goes without saying that I expect everyone from Bernicia to support whichever candidate we choose here today.'

'What about the Æthelings?' someone shouted. 'King Æthelred's sons, Ælfred and Edward; they have a better right to the throne than any usurping Dane.'

'I think we have to accept the realities of life. Both boys have been brought up in Normandy and have little or no powerbase here. They live there as dependents of Queen Emma's nephew, Duke Robert.'

The bishop coughed politely.

'I'm afraid that is no longer the case, Earl Aldred. Duke Robert died recently.'

Aldred frowned. The bishop should have made him aware of that fact before the meeting.

'I see. Who is duke now?'

'Robert's heir is his bastard son, William, but he is only seven years old and the Normans are fighting amongst themselves over the succession. The two Æthelings will get no support from that quarter.'

'Then our choice is clear. King Cnut should be followed by one of his surviving sons: Harthacnut or Harold Harefoot. One is the son of an English noblewoman and the other of a Norman, albeit one who is our queen and grandmother to my two sisters. Furthermore, Harthacnut has been brought up as a Dane and is heir to that kingdom. Will he remain there and neglect England?'

Aldred looked around the meeting, waiting for someone to break the silence. Eventually Eadulf got to his feet.

'It's a difficult choice, brother,' he said. 'As you have pointed out, our family is connected to Queen Emma and therefore to her son Harthacnut. However, Harold has been raised to manhood in England and is nineteen, whereas his brother is younger and less experienced. In any case, it's doubtful if Harthacnut is in any position to come to England in the near future. Magnus has consolidated his position as King of Norway and now he threatens Denmark as well.'

'You believe that we should support Harold?' Aldred asked.

'It seems the logical choice, although we ignore the esteem in which Queen Emma is held, especially in the south of England.'

'You think Godwin of Wessex will support Harthacnut?'

Godwin was known to be an ambitious man, and one with few scruples. His father had been a wealthy thane in Sussex and Godwin had been amongst the first of the English nobility to support Cnut when he had invaded in 1016. His reward was to be made Ealdorman of Sussex and two years later, when Cnut re-organised England into five earldoms, he had been given the largest – Wessex.

'Godwin will do whatever he sees as being in his best interests.'

'Then surely we need to be united in our opposition to the power of Wessex?' one of the ealdormen asked. 'What does Earl Siward say? Or Leofric of Mercia?'

Leofric was another man who had risen in status thanks to his early support of Cnut. A younger son of the Ealdorman of Gloucestershire, he had been chosen by Cnut to succeed the treacherous Eadric Streona. He had married twice, his second wife, Godiva, had gained some notoriety by championing the cause of the people against the onerous taxation imposed by her husband. He was greedy as well as ambitious but he was the strongest curb on the power of Wessex that there was.

'For once Earl Siward and I are in agreement. We both think that Harold is the better choice. I don't yet know who Leofric supports. I suspect it will be whoever Godwin doesn't favour.'

He paused to look around the room.

'Does anyone want to add anything or are we all in agreement that the ealdormen and I should vote for Harold Harefoot?'

There were a few nods which Aldred took to be acquiescence. Only the bishop looked dubious. Time would prove his doubts to be well founded.

✝✝✝

In late November word reached us that Cnut had died on the twelfth of the month, not in London as we had supposed, but at Shaftesbury in Dorset. Apparently he'd expressed a wish to die in Winchester and was being carried there in a cart, or so the story went, but it didn't make sense; Shaftesbury was some distance to the west of Winchester and, as London was his capital, it didn't lie on the route between there and Winchester.

It was much more likely that Godwin had made sure that the king died within the boundaries of Wessex. Traditionally the Witan selects a new king immediately after the funeral of the old one. It was a sensible arrangement as the senior nobles of the kingdom would be present for the funeral. However, had Cnut died in London the convenor of the Witan would have been Archbishop Æthelnoth as London was in no particular earldom. As it was, Godwin would now play the host.

Aldred was displeased by the venue for another reason. Although late in the season, he had planned to sail down to London. Now we would have to travel on horseback. We could follow Roman roads for some of the way, especially as we got further south, but inevitably part of our route would be across country. Winchester was almost four hundred miles from Bebbanburg; a journey that would normally take the best part of two weeks - and that was supposing that the weather was kind, something you couldn't rely on in late autumn. Even Siward would have to travel some two hundred and fifty miles from York. Obviously Godwin's intention was to hold the Witan without the two northern earls.

'If each of my escort takes an armiger and each armiger leads two spare horses as well as a pack horse we could probably cover sixty to eighty miles a day, depending on the roads and the weather,' Aldred told the thirty men he intended to take with him.

'What about the ealdormen?' Eadulf asked.

'They all live south of here and messengers have already left telling them to travel with all haste and the minimum escort to meet us at Oxford. Those that are there when we arrive can join us. The rest will have to follow on and hope that they arrive in time.'

'When is the funeral, lord earl?' I asked.

'On the first Sunday of Advent.'

We all looked at each other in consternation. The sixth of December was only eight days away. Even if we left tomorrow we would have to average near on sixty miles a day. It would be tight, and that was assuming that the weather would hold.

'Well, what are you waiting for?' the earl asked. 'We leave in three hours, get moving.'

So much for leaving tomorrow I thought as I cantered down the hill to our new hut. Æsc sorted out the five horses we would be taking with us whilst Rowena and I sorted out what we would need to take with us. She had made a new bearskin cloak for me out of the three I'd bought in Inverness. In return I gave her brother my old one of oiled wool which was of a much better quality than his present one. It was much too big for him, of course, and Rowena was going to cut it down until I stopped her.

'It won't matter on horseback,' I pointed out, 'and he'll grow into it in a couple of years.'

As we finished loading the packhorse Beorhtric came running up to say that the cavalcade was just leaving the fortress. I kissed Rowena and my children, said farewell to Beorhtric and mounted. We reached the column just as it reached the road south and I slotted into place beside Osric whilst Æsc waited for the armigers in the rear of the column to reach him.

'My God, Oeric, you look like a bloody Viking,' Bryce called from behind me, to the amusement of everyone.

I ignored him. I would be warm and dry when their cloaks were sodden and their teeth were chattering with the cold. We were on our way to Winchester. Even at my age I was excited as I'd only been south of Northumbria a few times before.

✝✝✝

The journey started well. The weather continued to smile on us and we made good time. All of us were used to riding long distances but by the fourth day we were all sore between the thighs, our muscles ached and we groaned at the prospect of another long day in the saddle. The horses were also suffering but, thanks to the remounts we'd brought along, we'd only lost a couple to exhaustion.

On the fifth day we left Leicester with the aim of spending that night at Oxford, the muster point for the rest of the nobles of Bernicia and their entourages. We took it as a good sign that we hadn't passed any of them on the road but not all would have taken the same route as we had. From there we could follow Roman roads all the way to Winchester.

We alternated trotting and gentle cantering to travel as quickly as possible without killing our mounts. Every two hours or so we changed horses. Using this method we could travel at between ten and twelve miles every hour. It was eighty miles from Leicester to Oxford and, even though we set out just before dawn each day, there were only nine or ten hours of daylight at this time of year. Allowing for stops to change horses and to have a short rest now and then, we should arrive with an hour in hand. We needed that to find a campsite and settle in for the night.

Just after noon we encountered our first problem. We came up behind a long column of marching men and carts. I could just make out a group of mounted men at the front, but not the details on the two banners flying over their heads. Taking Eadulf and Eadwyn, Aldred cantered forward yelling for me to get out of his way. We plodded along at barely three miles an hour until Aldred and the others came back.

'It's Siward,' Eadulf explained succinctly.

'He won't move his column out of the way to let us past,' Eadulf added.

'There's a track off to the left which looks as if it runs due south,' I said, indicating with my arm. 'We are heading south west at the moment. If I remember correctly, the Roman road to Towcester and then Oxford turns off this one. If so, then that track should intersect with it. If we follow it we should be able to get ahead of Earl Siward.'

'Well done, Oeric. It's worth a try anyway.'

Our high spirits as we headed away from the other contingent were dampened somewhat as it began to rain for the first time since we had left Bebbanburg. At first it was quite light but soon it became a downpour. I pulled my bearskin hood up over my head and wrapped it more tightly about me. Apart from the rain from my face trickling down inside my cloak and my exposed knees, I was warm and dry.

The track quickly became muddy and slippery so we were reduced to a trot. Nevertheless we emerged just ahead of Earl Siward and he was forced to wait until the last armiger had emerged back onto the Roman road. I don't suppose he appreciated the cheeky grin that I was told my armiger gave the earl as he passed in front of him.

The rain lessened and after a while it stopped completely and the sun came out. There wasn't sufficient power in it to dry woollen cloaks out but I smiled inwardly. I didn't have that problem.

We reached Oxford in daylight to find that all but the ealdormen of Alnwick and Otterburn had made it ahead of us.

†††

Earl Godwin tried to get the Archbishop of Canterbury to convene the Witan immediately after the funeral but Æthelnoth refused, saying that it would be unseemly and he also felt that they should wait until at least all the earls and bishops were present. Siward, his ealdormen and Archbishop Ælfric of York had yet to arrive. However, Bishop Edmund of Durham had managed to join us at Oxford and he had further to travel than the contingent from Deira.

That evening a group of us were allowed into Winchester to explore. It was larger than York, and smelt even worse. Used to the clean air of Bebbanburg, I had never got used to the stench of urine, faeces and rotten animal corpses that seemed such a feature of towns and cities.

Osric, Colby, Bryce, Landry and I found a tavern that wasn't full of shady looking characters and whose ale was at least palatable; mind you we had visited three others first and so were a trifle merry. A group of Godwin's housecarls were drinking near the fire and, being cold, we went and sat at the next table so that we could warm up.

'Who are you?' one of the housecarls called across. 'This is our tavern and we don't allow ruffians in here.'

'We are militares, the mounted housecarls of Earl Aldred.'

'Militares? Never heard the term, nor of any earl called Aldred either.'

'Militares is Latin, but you would need to be educated to know that,' Bryce said, his voice a little slurred.

The six Wessex housecarls got to their feet and their hands went to the hilt of their swords. We didn't move.

'You will have to excuse my friend, he is enjoying your Wessex ale a little too much. Let me buy you another flagon,' Colby said smoothly.

'Cowards are you?' one of the housecarls sneered.

'You wouldn't say that if you knew how many men we have killed,' Landry said coldly. 'How many have you put into the ground?'

'Where have you done all this killing?' the sneering housecarl asked.

'Wessex has been at peace for so long now I don't suppose any of you have faced a man intent on depriving you of life, have you?' Colby said. 'We've

228

killed hundreds of Scots, Norsemen and Danes in our time. The far north isn't a peaceable land like this. You have to be quick to kill a man, you can't hesitate as you're doing it or you'll wind up dead. Now do you want to die or join us for a drink?'

They looked at one another, unsure of what to do. I think that perhaps our calm demeanour in the face of their aggression must have unnerved them. I imagine that they assumed, correctly, that our confidence stemmed from years of defeating our enemies. The other reason for our lack of reaction was Aldred's strict instructions that we weren't to get into a brawl with the locals.

One by one the housecarls let go of their swords and they came and joined us at our table. Perhaps we boasted a little about our exploits but they seemed fascinated by our tales of battles, especially our campaign against the Strathclyde Britons before the fateful Battle of Carham, and we parted the best of friends.

Siward and Ælfric arrived at noon the next day and the Witan met that afternoon. Of course I wasn't present and I had to piece together what had happened from the gossip and rumour that circulated afterwards.

Godwin of Wessex and his twenty ealdormen, together with the bishops of the nine dioceses in Kent, Sussex and Wessex, supported the absent Harthacnut, although Æthelnoth abstained. The other earls, ealdormen and six bishops voted for Harold Harefoot. Those abbots present voted with their bishops.

Given the number of Wessex men present the outcome was hardly a surprise. Harthacnut won, but only by a narrow majority. However, he would need a regent to rule England until he could leave Denmark. Perhaps Godwin saw himself in that role but even some of his own nobles and bishops baulked at that.

In the end a compromise was agreed. Harthacnut would be recognised as king but remain uncrowned until he landed in England. In the meantime Harold would act as regent for his half-brother. Aldred said that Harold was furious about it, but there was little he could do.

Chapter Thirteen – The Disputed Succession

1036

When we returned to Bebbanburg Aldred found out that he had become a grandfather. His daughter Edith had given birth to a son who she and Ligulf had named Morcar.

Life carried on as normal in the early part of 1036. The twins learned to walk and I spent my time out on patrol, training the armigers and enduring the occasional boring stint guarding the fortress.

Following the success of my bearskin cloak, Rowena had the clever idea of using seal skins. We couldn't afford more bearskins and even wolf skins were expensive but seals abounded on the rocks of the Farne Islands offshore. A few even came ashore to sun themselves on the beaches to the north of the fortress. She soon had a profitable business killing seals, skinning and curing them and then sewing them into cloaks. It wasn't a simple process and at first it was a question of trial and error.

After skinning the animals the pelt had to be salted, soaked in a weak solution of acid, shaved to the right thickness, tanned and then oiled. This made it supple enough to make into waterproof cloaks soft enough to wear.

We bought two more slaves to help my wife do the work so the initial expense was high and I had little silver left in my chest before we sold the first cloak. The sealskin cloaks were so much better at keeping you dry that soon demand began to outstrip supply. Of course, others tried to copy us but getting the process right had taken us time and money. Our competitors produced inferior, stiff products which often shed their hair. Warriors would rather wait for one of Rowena's cloaks than buy someone else's.

Our chest began to fill with silver again and I thought about buying a farmstead for us to live on when I got too old to be a militar. What stopped me was the thought that I would then be a poor farmer whilst my brother was a rich thane. I wasn't consciously jealous of Acca but I didn't want my children to live hand-to-mouth when I was dead whilst their cousins were minor nobility.

Later that year Earl Aldred's extended family grew again. His half-sister – Eadgyth – gave birth to a second son, Walteau. Eadgyth's husband, Earl Maldred of Lothian, kept his word and there were no large scale border raids. There were, however, numerous small scale incursions across the Tweed to steal livestock and occasionally take slaves. It was whilst chasing a group of these raiders that I was nearly killed but something significant had happened just before that.

Our captain, Eadwyn, was only in his late thirties but one day he clutched at his chest and started to vomit for no apparent reason. He fell to the ground, struggling for breath. I was one of the first to reach him but I had no idea what was wrong or what to do. His face had taken on a white, almost waxy, look and he was sweating profusely even though it was a chilly day.

He continued to moan and clutch at his chest. I could tell that he was in great pain but I had no idea what the reason was. The chaplain arrived at that moment but he didn't know what was wrong either. Eadwyn thrashed about and then lay still, his eyes staring sightless up at the sky. The priest listened to his chest and asked me for my dagger. He held the polished blade under Eadwyn's nose but it didn't fog over with moisture. He wasn't breathing. The only thing the priest could think of was that his heart had suddenly stopped, although he didn't know the reason.

Aldred chose Colby as the new captain, which left a vacancy for the leader of our section of ten militares. To my surprise my comrades asked Aldred to appoint me to succeed Colby. Needless to say I was delighted.

In addition to Osric, Bryce and Landry there were six other members of my section: Faran, Durwyn, Bartulf, Roweson, Wynchell and Tedmund. I had served with five of them for some time and we knew each other well. However, I didn't know Tedmund, who replaced Colby, at all. He'd been the armiger in another section who had just been promoted. It soon became apparent that he had a problem with the rest of us.

He was seventeen and the second son of a wealthy thane. On the other hand most of us had been born

lower down the social scale. The section he had
served as an armiger had evidently been from the
same social class as he was and included two sons of
ealdormen. He looked down on us and resented
being allocated to our section. I thought he'd be
trouble and I was soon proved right.

†††

The first time that we were out on patrol together
we saw smoke coming from somewhere several miles
south of the river that divided us from Lothian and
Scotland. The nearest settlement was Jedburgh, near
the junction of the River Teviot and the Jed Water,
which was some six miles away.

We set off at a canter towards the smoke and
splashed through the ford where the Roman Dere
Street crossed the Teviot. Half a mile away we could
see that raiders had set a large farmstead alight and,
as luck would have it, were still there. Several men
were searching the barns and outlying huts whilst the
hall burned brightly. However, something told me
that not all was as it seemed.

There was much more smoke coming from the
hall than I would have expected, and it was black. It
was almost as if the raiders wanted us to see it.
Furthermore, the three mounted men I could see
were riding horses, not the hill ponies favoured by
the Scots. Only wealthy chieftains and nobles could
afford horses north of the border.

234

'Halt,' I commanded holding up my hand. 'Something isn't right.'

'Got cold feet have you, Oeric,' Tedmund sneered. 'They'll see us and get away, come on, ignore him!'

So saying he galloped towards the nearest group; three men coming out of a hut pulling a young girl with them.

'Bloody idiot,' I muttered. 'Faran, Wynchell and Roweson dismount and get your bows ready; look out for men coming up behind us. The armigers are to stay behind them. Durwyn and Bartulf follow me. Our task is to save Tedmund from his own folly, then we get out of here. Clear? Right, let's go.'

As Tedmund approached the two men holding the girl let her go and drew their swords and the third man levelled his spear. All three were wearing byrnies and helmets of a style typically worn by Danes. My suspicions were correct. These were no Scots raiders.

The man with the spear thrust it into the chest of Tedmund's horse and jumped to the side as the stallion fell to its knees mortally wounded. Tedmund kept his head and cut down the swordsman to his right as he jumped clear of the stricken animal. He was fast, I'll give him that. He fended off the other swordsman with his shield and at the same time cut the head off the spear.

I was conscious of a score of men on foot closing in on us as we reached Tedmund. I thrust my spear into the second swordsman whilst Durwyn took care of the spearman. Thankfully I managed to keep hold of my spear and, as I rode clear, it came out of the swordsman's corpse.

'Up behind me, Tedmund and quickly,' I yelled as we wheeled to face back the way we'd come. Half a dozen men blocked the road north but my immediate worry was the three riders.

'Kill the horsemen,' I shouted throwing my spear at the nearest one. Few warriors other than Aldred's militares were skilled at fighting on horseback and these three had made the mistake of leaving their shields on their backs. It was the best place for them whilst travelling, but they should have brought them around to protect their bodies before charging us.

Our spears struck all three riders and two of the horses were hit as well. A groan went up from the raiders and I knew that we had killed their leaders. However, there was no time to congratulate ourselves and we dug our spurs into our mounts' flanks and headed for the shield wall blocking our exit.

Tedmund jumped down from behind me and managed to catch the last of the horses that been ridden by the raiders. He pulled himself into the saddle and raced after the rest of us. My attention switched back to my front.

I saw that another ten or so of the ambushers had appeared beyond my three archers and the armigers. A volley of arrows streaked into the sky quickly followed by two more and just before I dragged my eyes back to the shield wall I saw two of the enemy fall. Doubtless subsequent volleys would reduce their numbers further before they could get near to my archers, but the warriors immediately in front of me now demanded all my attention.

I had chosen my axe in preference to my sword and as two spears were thrust at me I knocked one away with my shield and chopped at the other with my axe. The stallion I was riding was of a type called a destrier by the Normans. They were both large and trained for war. It now reared up whilst I held on grimly and its front hooves kicked out at the two spearmen immediately in front of me.

It struck the shield of one and the helmet of the second man as he cowered in fear. The latter dropped dead and the other man was thrown back into the second rank of the shield wall. My stallion went to bite the man to my right but he jumped out of the way, leaving a gap. Now I was faced by the second row.

I hauled the head of my destrier around so that I could chop down with my axe and it connected with the helmet of one man, crushing the metal like an eggshell. Meanwhile my destrier bit another man who was trying to stab him. He screamed in pain as the powerful jaws crushed his shoulder.

My fellow militares had similar successes and the shield wall collapsed. We were through. We regrouped on the far side and I glanced about me. The archers and the armigers had also won against their group of adversaries. Two of the raiders were running away but Faran, Roweson and Wynchell had remounted and were chasing after them.

'Bring one back alive,' I shouted after them but I had no way of knowing if they had heard me.

I turned back to the remainder of the enemy but they too had fled.

'Shall we chase them down?' Tedmund asked eagerly.

'No, we need to attend to our wounded and see if there are any inhabitants of this place left alive. I will want to speak to you later,' I said angrily.

At least Tedmund had the grace to look abashed.

Both Durwyn and Roweson had been wounded; not seriously but they needed stitches. Several of our horses had also been injured and Bartulf's destrier had been killed. Tedmund had replaced his, although his new mount wasn't a destrier. However, Bartulf was now without a mount and even the big destriers would soon tire if they had to carry two armoured men any distance.

†††

The girl was the only survivor and she had only been spared to use as bait; something only the naïve Tedmund had fallen for. She was in a state of shock but she did manage to tell us that she had relatives in Jedburgh. I sent Bryce and Landry off to the nearby village with the girl riding pillion. They would find her relatives and also buy a horse of some sort for Bartulf.

Most of the ambushers had been killed or had fled but three had been too badly wounded to run. One had a gut wound which would shortly kill him so Faran cut his throat to put him out of his misery. The other two were less seriously injured. The younger one had been knocked out but otherwise seemed unharmed. The third had a deep cut in his thigh. It was a miracle that an artery hadn't been severed.

I got them both patched up by two of the armigers whilst the rest of us dug a mass grave for the dead residents of the settlement. We had no priest and so Osric, a former novice monk, said what he could remember of the burial service over them. The enemy dead were stripped of anything useful or valuable and their corpses were left for the carrion crows and the animals to eat.

Once they had been treated I noticed that the two surviving ambushers seemed very close. They were talking quietly in Danish, a language that several of us spoke in addition to English. I soon picked up that they were uncle and nephew. The man's brother, and father of the youth, had been killed and the uncle was trying to comfort his companion who I guessed to be about fifteen or sixteen.

I went over to them and demanded to know who they were and why they had ambushed us. At first neither said anything so I put my dagger to the uncle's throat and threatened to kill him if the boy didn't start talking. The uncle started to order the boy to say nothing but I sawed my blade against his neck until I drew blood. He quickly shut up.

It took a little time to get the full story but I eventually learned that they were Danes from Holderness, Carl's men. They had been sent to ambush one of the regular patrols from Bebbanburg. It seemed the plan was to kill us for our distinctive armour and destriers. They would then ride back into the fortress pretending to be us and secure the main gate so that Carl and his men, who were hiding nearby, could attack and capture Bebbanburg.

They didn't need to tell me that the ultimate object was to slaughter Aldred, Eadulf and both their families.

The plan was doomed to failure from the outset, even if their plan to kill us had worked. What Carl evidently didn't know was that there was a second gate at the end of a passage between the outer palisade and an inner stone wall. The passage between the two gates was called Death Walk and it was designed specifically as a killing area.

The other thing we learned was that Carl's younger brother, Arne, had been the leader of the ambushers. He and his two sons had been the three riders who we'd killed. The blood feud had just intensified.

†††

Aldred had sent out his militares to find Carl and his men as soon as we had reported to him, but evidently the ambushers who had fled from us had told him of their failure and he was long gone by the time we found his campsite.

I had lectured Tedmund about his insubordination and disobedience but I might have just as well have saved my breath. As far as he was concerned he'd done me a favour by springing the trap and so I asked

Colby to move him from my section. He did so, but with reluctance. He sent newly promoted Cynric to us in place of the disruptive Tedmund and I was happy to have him back within our section again. I had liked him when he'd been our armiger and he had only improved with age.

Several other armigers had been made militares and our mounted force now numbered eighty. It was a severe strain on Aldred's finances, of course, but his small fleet now brought in a good profit from trading to supplement the taxes he levied on freemen, thanes and ealdormen and the income from vills he owned personally.

Part of the reason for increasing our strength was to defend our lands, not so much from the Scots or the Norsemen in the west, but from Aldred's brother-in-law, Earl Siward. Rumour had it that he had petitioned the regent, Harold Harefoot, to demote Aldred and to make Siward Earl of Northumbria in fact as well as in name.

However, Harold had more important issues on his mind. He had never accepted that the absent Harthacnut should be king whilst he had to be satisfied with the post of regent. Tensions between Emma of Normandy, Harthacnut's mother, and Earl Godwin of Wessex on the one hand and the other earls grew until there was a real danger of civil war.

I was enjoying a rare moment playing with my children when Colby sent for me one sunny day in July 1036.

'Oeric, prepare your section for a long journey. Earl Aldred is summoned to a meeting of the Witan in

241

London,' he told me without preamble. 'We'll take the two birlinns and sixty of the militares as crew.'

Colby had changed since he was appointed to be our captain. Before, when he in charge of our section, he'd been relaxed and friendly towards us and we followed him because we liked and respected him. He'd tried to retain his informal style of leadership but those who didn't know him well took that as a sign of weakness and either ignored what he said or challenged him. As a result he'd swung too far the other way and was in danger of becoming a martinet. Naturally that made him unpopular.

It made me reflect on my own qualities as a leader. I knew the members of my section and they knew me. I was able to continue to run the section in much the same way as Colby had and it worked, except of course when it had come to Tedmund. I could see now that getting rid of him had been the easy way out. What I should have done was rise to the challenge and encourage him to become a member of our team. I knew now that Earl Aldred had been disappointed with me and no doubt Colby was too.

I took my place on my sea chest and ran my oar out ready to row as we left the jetty feeling low and depressed. Because I was disappointed with myself I took out my anger by rowing hard and I was soon exhausted. Everyone else had the sense to row in a more relaxed manner knowing that we were likely to be rowing for a long time into the south-easterly headwind. I had no option; I had to persevere. By the time that the wind backed to the east and we could raise the sail I was on the verge of exhaustion.

My armiger, Æsc, was now sixteen and serving as one of the ship's boys. He was well aware of my distress and brought me water as soon as the mainsail was hoisted and set. However, I waved him away.

'See to my section first, Æsc,' I told him, though I could hardly speak.

'The others are seeing to them. I shouldn't say this to you but sometimes you're an idiot, Oeric. Why were you forcing yourself to put twice as much effort into rowing as the rest?'

'You're right. You shouldn't talk to me like that. Now do as I say and serve me last or I'll have you flogged for disobedience.'

It took all the willpower I had to say that to him. I was desperate for a drink but warriors think less of leaders who think of themselves before their men. Of course, my threat of a flogging was an empty one. Rowena would never forgive me if I had her brother whipped for a start! I shouldn't have spoken to him like that but I had nearly succumbed to the temptation he had put my way and that made me angry.

After taking my turn to drink a ladle of water I began to recover from my exertions and went to sit by myself in the bows. I knew that I was making poor judgements and I wondered whether I was fit to lead my section. I blamed Tedmund and then realised that I was being unfair. He seemed to have fitted in perfectly well in his new section; no doubt joining us when we all knew each other was difficult for him. I should have done more to make him feel welcome.

'What's wrong?'

Someone had come to sit next to me without me being aware of it. I saw to my surprise that it was the earl's brother, Eadulf.

'Nothing, lord.'

'I recognise when someone is in trouble. It's been many years since we knew each other well, Oeric, and we've all changed, but it wasn't like you then to bottle things up inside you and I suspect it has to be serious for you to punish yourself like that.'

I sighed. I trusted Eadulf and I needed to talk to someone about what was bothering me.

'I'm new at command of men and I'm making mistakes. I'm beginning to wonder if someone else should lead my section,' I confessed.

'You think we don't all make mistakes? You think my brother's judgement is impeccable? He doubts himself all the time, as do I. What he does, and what I try to do, is to learn from those mistakes and put it behind us. Now stop moping and come and join me in a game of nine men's morris.'

I smiled and thanked him for his good advice and we set up the board on his sea chest. It was a game I'd often played and I considered that I was quite good at it, but that day he beat me by five games to one. It took my mind off things and when we put the board away I realised that I had regained my equilibrium.

✝✝✝

The meeting of the Witan was a disaster. Archbishop Æthelnoth and Earl Godwin maintained their support of Harthacnut whilst Archbishop Ælfric Puttoc and the rest of the earls wanted Harold as king. In the end they partitioned the country between the two sons of Cnut. Harthacnut was recognised as king south of the Thames whilst Harold would rule north of the river. It weakened England and it wasn't a situation that could endure for long.

When Aldred left London to return to Bebbanburg Eadulf asked for permission to visit their step-mother, Ælgifu, and Queen Emma at Winchester. Of course, the younger brother had been brought up by them at Cnut's court and had a natural affection for them. Aldred didn't have the same close relationship; his last association with Emma had been when he'd escorted her from Normandy to marry Cnut.

So it was that we sailed around to Southampton in one ship whilst Aldred returned home in the other. The majority of the birlinn's crew stayed in the port, enjoying its various attractions, whilst Eadulf and a small escort hired horses to ride north to Winchester. For some reason he chose me and my section of militares and armigers to be his escort. We were still there three weeks later when the two surviving sons of King Æthelred launched separate invasions in an effort to regain the English throne for the House of Wessex.

Chapter Fourteen – The Æthelings' Invasion

1036

I never understood why the two æthelings, Ælfred and Edward, didn't launch a joint invasion. Perhaps they couldn't agree on who should be king if they succeeded in conquering England, but invading separately doomed their bid for power from the outset.

Edward, nicknamed the Confessor for his piety, had landed at Southampton with a force composed of exiled companions, mainly Saxons from Wessex. Earl Godwin had ordered the Ealdorman of Hampshire to muster his fyrd to oppose Edward and he had done as he was bid. Perhaps he and his men were unwilling to fight against one of the last surviving æthelings but, whatever the reason, they had been routed by Edward.

We arrived two days after the battle when the port was still buzzing with the news. There were ten warships anchored in the estuary of the River Test just off the port itself and at first they were somewhat alarmed by our approach.

A grizzled greybeard challenged us as we came within hailing distance of the first one and Lord

Eadulf called back that he was the Lady Ælfgifu's stepson and had been the ward of Queen Emma as a boy. That seemed to reassure everyone and they ceased shortening the cables ready to up anchor.

Each ship seemed to be manned by a few boys and several elderly warriors and they would have found it difficult to fight us had we been an enemy. We rowed past them and pulled into the jetty amongst several merchant knarrs and karves.

Southampton wasn't quite what I had expected. I'd been told that it was the major seaport of Wessex but, if so, it was insignificant by comparison to the port that served London. There was but one jetty and that could hold no more than a dozen ships at once. That was no doubt the reason that Edward the Ætheling's fleet lay at anchor out in Southampton Water.

There were a number of warehouses which lay along the jetty, but each was quite small. Behind that lay several buildings: no doubt brothels and taverns for the most part. Then a little way behind them lay the fortified town itself. As far as I could see it was no bigger than the village of Bebbanburg.

I later learned that there were other ports all along the south coast and so Southampton served only as Winchester's port.

Eadulf and I shared a room with our squires at one of the better taverns and the rest of the crew found accommodation where they could. I wondered at being selected as Eadulf's companion over the other two section commanders manning the birlinn - both of whom were older and more senior to me -

until he explained that he wanted my section to serve as his escort when we left to visit Winchester. The rest would stay and guard the ship.

It took us a little time to hire the necessary twenty three horses the next morning and some of the armigers were less than impressed by the hacks they were given but they were better than Fiske's mount. Eadulf's body servant had to make do with a donkey borrowed from the town's priest. By the time we left it was early in the afternoon but thankfully Winchester was only a dozen miles away and we arrived well before dark.

If Southampton had been something of a disappointment Winchester was the opposite. I suspected that it was even bigger than London. As we rode in through the King's Gate – the main entrance through the defensive palisade from the south – the stone built cathedral loomed ahead of us. There were very few stone buildings in England and most were churches but this one was more imposing than any others I had seen.

To the west and north of the cathedral and the monastery lay the town itself. I later found out that it followed a grid pattern using the layout of the old Roman town of Venta Belgarum, which meant market place of the Belgae. Of course that town had been abandoned six centuries before but the Saxon town that eventually replaced it followed the same layout. Instead of the narrow streets and alleys of other towns this one had broad roads between the blocks of huts, shops and the larger halls belonging to nobles and wealthy merchants.

We turned right and rode into the monastery. Eadulf asked the porter for directions to Queen Emma's lodgings and the monk directed us towards the buildings that lay near the river. We headed for the imposing hall constructed of stone as the man had said that the queen's hall was beside it. The one in stone had replaced the previous timber hall in King Alfred's time and he had expanded the complex into a palace. Now the main hall was the residence of Earl Godwin, but he wasn't there, which was something of a relief.

Outside the queen's hall four men stood on guard. Two were evidently Emma's housecarls but the other two were dressed as I was; as Norman knights. Not all of our militares wore Norman armour and helmets; after all there were now over twice as many as the original warband which had accompanied Aldred from Normandy as Emma's bodyguard decades before. However, the smiths and armourers of Bebbanburg had copied the original sets as closely as they could. Only Eadulf was dressed differently. As he had lived in Norway for most of his adult life he wore the armour and helmet made for him there. Consequently he looked more like a Viking than the Angle he was.

We dismounted and a groom and his stable boys came running to help our armigers with the horses.

One of the knights asked Eadulf a question in Norman French, a language none of us spoke.

'This is the queen's hall, not the ætheling's.' The elder of the two housecarls told him angrily.

'What did he say?' Eadulf asked, amused at the evident antipathy between the two pairs of guards.

'He asked who you are,' the man replied uncertainly. 'You look like Franks but you speak English, albeit with a strange accent.'

'I am Eadulf of Bernicia,' he replied. 'Northern Northumbria,' he added when the man still looked mystified.

'You're a long way from home.'

'I was in London with my brother, Earl Aldred, and I've come to see my stepmother and my former guardian, the queen, on my way home. Now let me pass.'

'Who is your step mother?'

'The queen's daughter, the Lady Ælgifu.'

'Wait here. I'll let them know that you're here. However, you may only enter with one companion and you must surrender your weapons first.'

'Of course,' Eadulf said impatiently and the housecarl scurried away.

He turned to me.

'You may accompany me but your men must wait here until the chamberlain assigns us some accommodation.'

Both Queen Emma and Lady Ælgifu came to greet Eadulf, who they hadn't seen for sixteen years. Then he had been a gangling youth, now he was a man who had just turned thirty with a son of his own. My eyes strayed from the reunion to two figures who had hung back. One was a man in his early thirties dressed in a richly embroidered robe. The other was a woman who I vaguely recognised but who I couldn't put a name to.

'This is my son Edward. I suspect you must have met in Normandy when you were both boys?'

'Yes, lady. Many years ago now, of course. I think I was about nine at the time and Prince Edward was a few years older.' Eadulf replied, bowing briefly to the young ætheling.

Edward smiled back.

'I'm pleased to renew our acquaintance, Eadulf. When I last heard of you, you were in Norway with my half-brother, Gunwald.'

'Yes, it was a sorry business. I hear that the usurper Magnus, who defeated us, now threatens King Harthacnut in Denmark.'

Edward scowled at the mention of Emma's son by Cnut.

'Another of my half-brothers who lays claim to my throne,' he said bitterly, looking at his mother with distaste.

'Edward,' she said sharply, 'we've been over this. You have no support amongst the nobles of England. It is bad enough for the kingdom to have Harold and Harthacnut squabbling over it without you and Ælfred adding to the turmoil.'

'I'm trying to persuade Edward to return to Normandy where he'll be safe,' she explained to Eadulf. 'He thinks that just because he defeated a peasant rabble he can beat Earl Godwin as well.'

'The people of Wessex will desert the traitor Godwin and rally to my banner, mother. After all,

251

who is he? The jumped up son of a thane who kissed Cnut's backside to get where he is today,' Edward sneered.

'Edward! Watch your language. You forget that Cnut was my husband and Godwin is co-regent with me on behalf of Harthacnut, who the Witan have recognised as king.'

Edward retreated into sulky resentfulness whilst Emma make an effort to regain her composure.

'Do you know this lady, Eadulf?' Ælgifu asked to break the awkward silence.

'No, I'm not sure that I have had the pleas...'

He broke off and stared at the woman who had come forward.

'Sigfrida,' he muttered in astonishment.

Sigfrida was Aldred's half-sister but, as she didn't share a parent with Eadulf, she was no blood relation of his. She had been his detested Uncle Eadwulf's widow but he couldn't blame her for his misdeeds. She had hated him and had been having an affair with Aodghan, Eadwulf's body servant behind her husband's back. The last time I'd seen her had been when she and her lover had left Bebbanburg shortly after Eadulf had killed Eadwulf. I seemed to remember that Synne had persuaded Aldred to grant the couple a vill in Teesdale, but I couldn't remember the name of it.

'Hallo Eadulf. It's good to see you again,'

She gave him a smile which lit up her face. I tried to remember how old she was. She must have been in her early thirties, probably a few years more, but she looked ten years younger. I thought she looked extremely pretty and evidently Eadulf thought the same, judging by the stupid look on his face.

'Sigfrida came seeking my help. Her husband, Aodghan, was thane of Thornaby in Teeside but unfortunately he died a few months ago. Ever since a thane named Wermund, who owns the neighbouring vill, has been pressuring Sigfrida to marry him.'

'He only wants me for my land; he's one of Carl's adherents and, because I'm related to Earl Aldred, he's promised to make my life hell because my half-brother slew his father, Thurbrand.'

'I'm sorry, both for the death of Aodghan and for the predicament you find yourself in. You didn't have any children?'

'Yes, two: a boy and a girl. They died with my husband,' she said sadly, and then added, 'of the plague.'

'You survived. What about Ceatta?'

He'd been the captain of Uhtred's warriors and then of Aldred's militares but he had gone to serve Aodghan and Sigfrida as their head housecarl when he retired.

'He died seven years ago. He left a widow and three children. None survived I fear. A third of the vill perished before the plague ended.'

'I'm sorry. Let me think about this, would you? I'll see if I can find a way to help.

We stayed for a month at Winchester during which time Eadulf spent a great deal of time in Sigfrida's company. I was getting worried about sailing home as the weather gradually worsened with the approach of winter. The news reached us of Emma's other son, Ælfred.

It appeared that, as he and his men, mostly Normans but also a number of minor thanes and their housecarls who had declared for him, approached the town of Guildford in Surrey, they encountered Earl Godwin and a sizeable force. However, instead of attacking Ælfred, he swore fealty to the young prince and stayed with him in the town.

According to the merchant who brought the news, Godwin had promised to conduct the young ætheling to London, where he said that the Witan were awaiting him so that they could elect him as their king.

However, Godwin had played him false and led him and his men to Guildown on the road to Winchester, not London. Godwin's army were waiting in ambush and Godwin's housecarls seized the ætheling and bound him. His men were surrounded and Godwin threatened to kill the prince unless they surrendered.

A few elected to fight and were killed but the majority surrendered on condition that they were allowed to go free. Godwin released the Normans and his men escorted them back to their ships so that they could return to Normandy. The rebel thanes were killed, along with their housecarls.

Both Emma and Edward were upset by the capture of Ælfred and she cursed the treacherous Godwin, her supposed ally and co-regent, but what the merchant told us next appalled us. He said that Ælfred was tied to a horse and taken to the south coast where he was put aboard a ship belonging to King Harold. This surprised everyone as Godwin was a supporter of Harthacnut, not Harold. It seemed possible that he had turned his coat and that was what finally convinced Edward that the time had come for him to leave England again.

Unfortunately the merchant knew no more and it was another week before we heard what had befallen the unfortunate prince. By this time Edward and his men were long gone. His brother had been taken to the monastery of Ely in East Anglia, whose earl supported Harold. Ælfred was supposedly offered the choice of becoming a monk or death. He chose the former but, to make sure that he didn't change his mind and cause further trouble, Harold gave orders that he was to be blinded.

Whoever did the job was incompetent and Ælfred never recovered after the mutilation. A few days later he died.

✝✝✝

Eadulf went to see Emma as soon as he heard that Earl Godwin was on his way back to Winchester. It was time our pleasant sojourn in Winchester came to an end, but first he had to persuade the queen to leave.

'Lady, don't you consider it strange that Godwin surrendered Ælfred to Harold Harefoot, considering that he is regent with you on behalf of Harthacnut?'

'You think that he's changed sides?'

'If not, why else he would hand your son over to Harold?'

Emma started to pace nervously up and down the hall.

'Lady, Eadulf, would it help if some of my men and I frequented the taverns in the town tonight to see what the gossip is?' I suggested.

It wasn't necessary as, when I visited the warriors' hall, my men clustered around me and told me sotto voce that there was a rumour amongst Godwin's men, with whom they shared the hall, that Lyfing, Bishop of Worcester, had convinced Godwin to hand Ælfred over to Harold's men. Apparently he had now persuaded the earl to recognise Harold as king. Now only Queen Emma and the Archbishop of Canterbury supported Harthacnut.

I reported back to Eadulf and the queen and they quickly came to the conclusion that Godwin was on his way to imprison Emma and seize the royal treasury, which she was holding in trust for Harthacnut.

Eadulf was in a quandary. His brother supported Harold but he felt honour bound to protect Emma, Ælgifu and especially Sigfrida, to whom he had just announced his betrothal. No doubt the queen and her ladies would be confined to a convent if Godwin got his hands on them. Flight into exile was the obvious alternative but the palace and the town were manned by Godwin's men.

'We can't sneak out,' Eadulf said when he, Queen Emma and I met to discuss our escape. 'We need to ready our horses and a carriage for the ladies and that's not something we can do surreptitiously with so many guards about.'

Edward had an army with him and no one had dared stop him from leaving; we only had a handful of warriors.

'I'm not going without Harthacnut's treasury,' Emma said with determination, adding to our difficulties.

The royal treasury was traditionally kept at Winchester, the ancient capital of Wessex, and, as Harthacnut was still the recognised king, technically it belonged to him. However, with Godwin's change of allegiance I didn't think it would be long before his half-brother Harold was crowned, with or without Archbishop Æthelnoth's approval.

'We'll need a cart or two as well then,' Eadulf said, chewing his lip in thought.

'We're going to have to eliminate the housecarls within the palace and capture the King's Gate, then hold it for long enough to allow us to leave,' I concluded.

'How many horses does the garrison have?' Eadulf asked.

Neither Emma nor I could answer that and so I sent Æsc to see if any of my men knew. He came back within a few minutes to say that those he had managed to have a quiet word with thought that several of the garrison could ride. There were over a dozen horses in the palace stables, in addition to ours, which we would need to take with us. That would avoid pursuit as well as providing us with the extra horses we needed. We would leave Fiske's donkey though, now that he could choose a proper mount.

The queen had fifteen housecarls as her personal bodyguard and, although only a handful could ride, the rest could travel in the cart or drive the carriage.

The latter was scarcely more comfortable than a cart. It was basically a wagon with a leather roof to give protection from the elements. Its body was suspended on chains to save it from the worst of jolting on the uneven roads; even so it jolted you quite badly and threw you about, so I wasn't surprised when Sigfrida asked to ride the short distance to Southampton.

We made our plans just in time. Durwyn and Roweson, who I'd sent out to watch the road from the east, came riding in late in the afternoon to say that Godwin had camped for the night about ten miles away. That meant he would reach Winchester the following afternoon. We had to act tonight.

✝✝✝

Dusk had just fallen when Faran and Durwyn cut the throats of the two sentries outside the warriors' hall efficiently and quietly. They were helped by the incessant rain which hid any slight sound that they might have made. As soon as they had lowered the corpses to the ground the rest of my men ran forward and hammered nails into stout planks of wood to keep the door – the only entrance to the hall – shut.

Meanwhile the queen's housecarls slammed the shutters closed and did the same. I prayed that it would keep them imprisoned for long enough to enable us to make our escape. It was a risk, but both Eadulf and I thought it was a better solution than trying to kill the thirty off-duty warriors now confined in the hall.

As soon as I was certain that hall had been sealed I raced off with Bryce, Roweson, Landry, Osric and Wynchell to capture the King's Gate. Thankfully the heavy rain kept all those without good reason to be abroad inside their homes. The armigers and the queen's servants were busy saddling our horses, hitching up the carriage and the cart and loading the latter with coffers containing the treasury, the ladies clothes and the queen's jewellery. I estimated that would take half an hour with the help of those who I'd left behind at the warrior's hall. I prayed that it wouldn't take any longer than that because timing was critical.

The two guards on the gates to the palace compound were sheltering from the rain in the base of the gate tower. Osric and Landry ran inside and emerged seconds later with bloody daggers. We left the gates open and ran on.

The porter was asleep when we got to the monastery gates and so we quickly tied him up with the rope around his habit and gagged him. Once more we left the gates open and moved on.

My hope had been to use my archers to slay the sentries on top of the King's Gate and on the palisade near the gate but the heavy downpour made that impossible. Instead we waited in the shadows near the gate until I judged that the time was right. There were five of us and so killing the six men sheltering in the small gatehouse was easy.

They scarcely knew what was happening and only one managed to draw his sword before all were slain. However, the noise had alerted the sentries on top of the gate and they gave the alarm. Thankfully the rain deadened the sound somewhat and only the two sentries on the palisade either side of the gate heard them.

I led my men up the steps onto the walkway but three men had gathered at the top to oppose me by the time I got there. I was out of breath and anticipated a difficult fight, but they were no warriors. They were members of the town watch who did duty once a month to guard the perimeter and patrol the streets after dark. One made an ineffectual attempt to stab me with his spear which I batted away with my shield without conscious thought. I lunged forward with my sword and gutted the spearman.

It wasn't immediately fatal – gut wounds their take time to rob one of life – but he fell off the walkway and landed on the ground below with an audible crunch as several bones broke. The other two were shocked by the quick death of their companion and drew back from the top of the steps, allowing me to step onto the walkway.

One, braver than the other, thrust his spear toward my face. I lifted my shield and he changed his attack to aim for my legs. Had I been a callow youth he might have succeeded but I swung my sword down and its sharp edge deprived the spear of its metal point. He was left holding a useless wooden haft.

He didn't know what to do and before he could drop it and draw his sword I thrust the point of mine into his exposed neck. A moment later Osric appeared beside me and the third man fled.

We had a moment's respite but then I heard men coming towards us along the walkway from both directions. I heard a bell being rung further along the palisade, presumably in the watchtower. Despite our greater skill as warriors, we risked being overwhelmed by vastly superior numbers.

† † †

I left two men to hold the top of the steps and the rest of us ran down to open the main gates. We had just succeeded in doing so when I heard the clash of weapons on the parapet above me and I saw armed men massing across the main street between the palace and monastery complex and the King's Gate. Then I heard the wonderful sound of galloping horses.

My militares, led by Eadulf, struck the rear of the men blocking the street and burst through them chopping several down who were too slow to get out of the way. Other armed men now appeared at the entrance to the side streets, but they halted when they saw my men wheel around to face them.

The carriage and two carts careered through the gates. They were followed by our armigers, each leading several horses. Æsc pulled back on his reins and brought his horse to a sudden halt as he reached me and I gratefully took the reins of my horse from him. Meanwhile my militares rode forward a few paces and threw their spears into the men who were trying to summon up the courage to attack us. They drew back in alarm as several of their fellows were killed or wounded, giving us time to mount and follow the carriage and the two carts through the gates.

The last out were those of the queen's housecarls who could ride. By that time several of the braver citizens had run forward to try and unseat them. The housecarls weren't trained to fight on horseback, but they managed to kick out at those trying to stop them or else to bring down their swords or axes onto the heads and shoulders of those nearest to them. Only one man was dragged from his horse and butchered before the last housecarl fought his way clear.

We regrouped a few hundred yards outside the town and then we headed for Southampton. It was only then that I realised that the rain, which had been such an ally, had stopped.

Chapter Fifteen – Thornaby

1036 - 1037

Queen Emma had intended to flee to the place of her birth – Normandy – but when we arrived there after an unpleasant winter crossing we found that Duke Robert had just died and his successor, Robert's nine year old bastard, William, had fled into hiding. Half the nobles had risen in rebellion and William's own life was in peril.

Eadulf found out that Edward had gone to the court of Count Eustace of Boulogne, who was married to his sister Godifu and so Emma decided to join him.

We were stormbound in Boulogne for a week and so we spent Christmas there. It was pleasant enough and Eustace made us welcome, though having so many more mouths to feed at an expensive time a year, and when food was in short supply, must have been a burden.

I missed my family at this time of the year and I was relieved when the winds abated and we could set sail once more. It was bitterly cold and it snowed several times during our voyage home to Bebbanburg but the voyage passed without incident.

Sigfrida had remained on board and shortly after we arrived at Bebbanburg she and Eadulf were married. Although Eadulf had decided to build a hall next to his brother's for them to live in when they were at the fortress, he planned to spend most of his time at Sigfrida's vill. Following their marriage he had now become Thane of Thornaby and it was only natural that he would want to be his own master rather than living in his brother's shadow.

It came as something of a surprise when I was sent for early in February 1037 and found both brothers and Colby waiting for me.

'Oeric, Lord Eadulf has asked for you to be his captain now that he has land of his own. I have granted his request and I hope that you will accept the post. You may take six of your section with you, together with their armigers of course, but they should be given the choice whether to stay here or go to Thornaby.

'Of course, you will remain as members of my militares and my brother will recruit a few housecarls to protect his vill as and when you are needed here. Are you agreeable to this?'

I would have liked to discuss this with Rowena but that wasn't something a man like the earl would have understood. Synne was known to be a strong personality but she invariably followed where Aldred led. Perhaps she had never quite put her humble start in life behind her? Whatever the reason, she had never to my knowledge disputed his decisions.

'Yes, lord. Of course, I am honoured,' I said and prayed that Rowena would see this as an opportunity, rather than a disruption to her comfortable life.

I can't say that she was happy to be moving, but she was at least pleased for me. Instead of being a minor figure in the big world that was Bebbanburg, I would be rank second after the thane at Thornaby, along with the reeve.

Faran, Bryce, Landry and Durwyn would accompany me, along with Æsc, who was now eighteen and had just been promoted to the rank of militares. That meant that both he and I needed new armigers. His brother Beorhtric was happy where he was, and in any case he would be eligible for promotion himself in a couple of years. I accepted the younger son of a Danish jarl, a fourteen year old boy called Rathulf, as one and decided that he would serve Æsc. I still needed an armiger myself but Eadulf solved that for me.

His son, Oswulf, was now thirteen and his father decided that it was time he learned to be a warrior. Of course, being a noble's son, Eadulf could have had someone train him to fight, but he didn't want special treatment for him. He therefore offered him to me as my armiger.

I was dubious as I didn't want an obnoxious, arrogant boy who I'd have to treat with kid gloves just because he was a noble's brat. Fortunately my fears were misplaced. Oswulf turned out to be a pleasant boy eager to learn and we got on well from the start.

The ride down to Stockport was cold, wet and miserable and we were all thankful when we arrived at the small port on the River Tees. This was the southernmost point of Bernicia. When we crossed by ferry the next morning we would be entering Deira, Earl Siward's territory.

'What's the ealdorman like?' I asked Sigfrida as we sat eating in a tavern that evening.

All I knew was that Thornaby, which had originally been one of Uhtred's vills when he was earl of all Northumbria, lay just inside in the shire of Cleveland.

'Ketil is a Dane. The previous ealdorman was an Angle but, when he died, he left a ten year old boy as his heir. Siward disinherited him and put Ketil in his place. It wasn't a popular move but Ketil dealt ruthlessly with any opposition. It is said that he had the previous ealdorman's son killed and the body disposed of at sea but there is no proof. At any event, he was never seen again and his mother was sent to a monastery to become a nun.'

'It sounds as if he might be an enemy when we take over Thornaby,' Eadulf mused.

'He certainly failed to support me when Wermund tried to force me to marry him,' she replied with some heat. 'He tried to convince me that marrying the man was my only option.'

I don't think either of us had anticipated any opposition in view of the fact that Sigfrida was the lawful owner of the vill, but it now seemed as if Ketil supported Wermund, the Thane of Stainton, which was the vill to the south-east of Thornaby.

'I think it might be an idea if you visited Thornaby first, Oeric, just to see how the land lies,' Eadulf said. 'Take Oswulf with you but don't wear armour. Pretend that you are just passing through on your way to York.'

✝✝✝

The two of us crossed the Tees on the ferry early the next morning. Oswulf was excited and I had to reprimand him and tell him to calm down. It was only a two mile ride from the crossing point to the village; in fact we had entered the vill of Thornaby as soon as we had landed from the ferry. At first we rode through trees before emerging onto a meadow on which both sheep and cattle grazed. A muddy track crossed it and took us into an extensive area of cultivated strips of various crops: wheat, barley, rye and cabbages. There were also strips devoted to roots crops, presumably onions and parsnips as they were the common ones.

The vill exuded an aura of prosperity, echoed by the village itself. All the huts were well built, being of timber or timber beams with wattle and daub infill on stone foundations and with thatched roofs in good repair. The church was built similarly but it was quite large and had a stone tower at one end. This evidently served as a watchtower because I could see a bored looking housecarl leaning on the parapet and gazing to the east.

The hall was surrounded by a stout timber palisade with a single gateway on the southern side. Only one of the two gates was open and two more housecarls stood in front of it barring our way. Through it I could see a hall made of infilled timber beams and a roof made of red tiles. This was quite unusual and I surmised that they had been taken from the ruins of a Roman villa at some time. There was the usual opening in the centre of the ridge to allow smoke out but it had a small roof of its own above it to keep the worst of the rain and snow out.

It was quite large for a thane's hall and had been extended to one side. Sigfrida had said that this was to provide a separate chamber for her and her late husband. It was another indication that this was a rich vill; indeed, many an ealdorman's hall wasn't as grand as this.

'Who are you and what do you want?'

The elder of the two sentries had spoken in Danish and so I replied in the same language.

'We're passing through on our way to York and would appreciate some refreshment and water for our horses.'

The man turned to his companion, who looked scarcely older than Oswulf.

'Go and tell the thane that he's got visitors. Wait, what's your name?'

'Oeric of Bebbanburg,' I replied.

I saw no reason to lie. A traveller from one seat of an earl to another wasn't that unusual, though Siward and Aldred could hardly be said to be on friendly terms. The fact that the man had described the occupant of the hall as the thane made me suspect that he was the Dane Wermund who had wanted to wed the Lady Sigfrida. When she had fled he'd presumably seized the property anyway.

'I have a message from Earl Aldred to his sister,' I explained, feeling that that sounded plausible enough.

The boy scuttled away and five minutes later he returned, followed by a portly man in a fine red woollen over tunic embroidered in silver thread around the neck and hem. Like most garments of its type it was short sleeved and so I could tell from the sleeves that under it he wore a yellow tunic. The man was a peacock.

'Greetings lord, I'm a messenger from the Earl of Bernicia to his sister, the Lady Ælfflæd, in York. I crave refreshments for my servant and me and water for our horses.'

The thane looked at me suspiciously.

'I don't know you and I don't play host to every messenger who passes by here. Be off with you.'

'Very well, lord. It is your right to deny me hospitality, of course, but I was under the impression that the Lady Sigfrida owned this vill. I'm sure that, as Earl Aldred gave it to her and her late husband she would not mind sparing us a little water, bread and cheese.'

'You are misinformed. Ealdorman Ketil has given me this vill. Now leave before I get my men to force you to do so.'

We turned our horses and rode out of there slowly whilst I tried to see how many more housecarls I could spot. The answer was none but I pulled my horse to a halt beside a boy aged about eleven weeding a strip of land beside the road. I looked back at the vill so as not to be seen talking to him.

'Don't look up boy, but tell me how many housecarls the thane has?'

The boy was startled by my question and went to look up at me, but checked himself just in time.

'Seven, lord. Why do you want to know?' he replied as he dislodged a particularly large weed with his hoe.

'Just curious. Thank you. What is your name?'

'Dunstan, lord.'

'Thank you Dunstan. I'll remember you.'

✝✝✝

'I agree, we could just arrive at Thornaby and demand that Wermund and his people leave,' Eadulf said after I'd made my report. 'However, he could refuse and make a fight of it. I want to avoid that if possible.'

'What other option do we have?' I asked. 'He is the one in the wrong.'

'Yes, but apparently with Ketil's blessing. We must remember that Thornaby lies in his shire and Siward's earldom. I don't want to give them cause to act against me. No, the first step is to seek redress from the ealdorman, Ketil. This needs resolving lawfully.'

The next morning we arrived at the gates of Middlesbrough, Ketil's base. It lay on the south bank of the Tees a mile or two nearer the river mouth than Stockton. It might seem odd that there were two ports so close together but goods bound for or exported from southern Bernicia used one and goods to and from northern Deira the other.

We didn't seek conflict but it was important that Ketil took us seriously. The sentries on the town gates tried to stop us but they were intimidated by armed horsemen and their efforts were half-hearted. We used our horses to push them out of the way before riding on towards the ealdorman's hall. The children and the wagons had been left in Rowena's care at Stockton, but Sigfrida had insisted on coming with us. This time she rode a horse instead of riding in a carriage. She didn't even glance at the protesting guards as she rode past them.

The land here was flat and there was no hill on which to site the hall. Perhaps because of the palisade around the town and the port, there were no defences around the hall. A housecarl sat on a stool half asleep outside the door of the hall but he soon woke up when sixteen riders arrived.

'Thane Eadulf and the Lady Sigfrida to see Ealdorman Ketil,' Eadulf told the startled man brusquely.

Stable boys came running but Eadulf waved them away. Three of the armigers dismounted and took the reins of my horse and those of Eadulf and his wife. The three of us then marched past the bewildered sentry and into the hall.

'Who the devil are you? How dare you come bursting into my hall like this?' a man who had to be Ketil demanded.

He was sitting at a table with a man in clerical garb studying a scroll when we burst in. Several housecarls were sitting at another table drinking and a boy was turning a lamb on a spit over the open fire. Otherwise the hall was empty.

'Forgive my unannounced arrival, lord,' Eadulf said with a slight bow, 'but my wife and I have a matter of the utmost urgency to bring to your attention.'

'Who are you? Do I know you?'

'We met once when I was a boy at the court of King Cnut. I was Queen Emma's ward in those days.'

'That still doesn't tell me you name, or am I meant to guess?' Ketil replied with a sneer.

'You asked if we knew each, other not my name,' Eadulf pointed out. 'My name is Eadulf, brother of Earl Aldred, husband of the Lady Sigfrida and thereby Thane of Thornaby. I'm here because my vill has been appropriated by another, a man called Wermund, who claims that he was given it by you. As I have the deeds to the vill here there has clearly been some sort of misunderstanding.'

'I see. You had better come in and sit down.'

He dismissed the cleric and Sigfrida sat down on the vacated chair. I pulled over a bench for Eadulf to sit on and stood behind him.

'Let me see the deeds.'

Eadulf handed the leather cylinder in which the deeds were lodged to Ketil and he pulled out three sheets of vellum. The first was the original deed from King Æthelred grating the vill to Earl Uhtred some thirty years before. The second was the transfer of ownership by Aldred, as Uhtred's heir, to Aodghan and Sigfrida jointly and the third was the deed of transfer to Sigfrida as sole owner after Aodghan's death.

'As the Lady Sigfrida is now my wife I have come to register my title to Thornaby as its thane. However, it is my wish that it should be owned by us jointly. No doubt your steward can draw up the appropriate deed?'

'Um, er, yes. I suppose so,' Ketil said uncertainly.

'Why? Is there a problem with the documents, ealdorman?'

'No, no. Of course not Eadulf. They seem to be in order. Er, when were you married?'

'At Bebbanburg on February the twelfth this year. We were married in Earl Aldred's presence by his chaplain,' Sigfrida said, giving Ketil a sweet, but entirely false, smile.

'I see. Well then, I'll ask my steward to draw up the deed. You can collect it at your convenience.'

'We'll wait if you don't mind. I'm sure Wermund will ask to see it before he leaves.'

'Ah yes, quite so.'

It was simple as that. An hour later we rode out of Middlesbrough with a fourth deed to accompany the other three. The only sour note was that Ketil didn't offer us refreshments and stomped out as soon as he had instructed his steward to write the deed. No doubt he'd gone to send a messenger to let Wermund know what had transpired. By the time we arrived at Thornaby the next day there was no sign of him or his housecarls.

✝✝✝

I think we all expected there to be some come back from the ejection of Wermund but as the months passed this seemed less and less likely. He had withdrawn to his smaller, and less prosperous, vill of Stainton and occasionally he and Eadulf would encounter one another, either at Middlesbrough or at York, but they studiously ignored each other.

My life was taken up with training the armigers, improving the defence of Thornaby, building a new hut for myself and my family, collecting the annual taxes from the three villages, four hamlets and eight outlying farmsteads that made up the vill and trying to turn our small fyrd into something approaching warriors.

I hadn't forgotten Dunstan and, although the information he'd given me wasn't useful in the end, I still gave him a silver penny. It was probably worth a quarter's rent or more to him and his family. After that I seemed to see him wherever I went.

'That boy has got a bad case of hero-worship,' Oswulf said to me one day as I was training him to use sword and shield on foot.

I turned around there was Dunstan watching us from the alleyway between two huts. When he saw me looking at him he disappeared from sight like a scalded cat. The next time I saw him I beckoned him over.

'Isn't there something you should be doing?'

'Yes, lord. I should be helping in the fields.'

'Then why aren't you?'

'Because I'd rather watch you training the boys, lord.'

By boys I presumed he meant the armigers.

'Doesn't your father punish you for evading work?'

'He's not pleased with me but he's been more lenient since I handed him that coin you gave me, lord.'

'Dunstan, for the last time I'm not a lord. My brother is a thane and entitled to be called lord but I'm not.'

It was something I'd not minded at first - in fact I was pleased for Acca's good fortune – but as time had gone on and I'd got older I started to have the odd twinge of jealousy. I never made it obvious when our families visited each other from time to time but it was there just under the surface none the less; especially when I was entertained in his hall and I saw how well he'd done for himself.

'Yes, lord. Oh, what should I call you then?'

'My name is Oeric, use it.'

'Oh, I couldn't do that.'

'Then don't call me anything. In fact, there shouldn't be any occasion when a freeman's son need to speak to the thane's captain; at least not until you are old enough to start training with the fyrd.'

'Then I won't have long to wait!' he said excitedly.

'What do you mean? Boys don't start to train until they're fourteen.'

'I'm fourteen next month,' he said proudly.

I looked at him. Oswulf was slightly younger than this lad and yet he was nearly a foot taller and much broader across the shoulders. I supposed that it was a question of diet.

'Well then, I'll see you next month; but I don't want to catch even the merest glimpse of you before then.'

'Yes, lord,' he called back as he scurried away.

†††

Christmas came and went. We spent it with Acca, Mildred and their two young children at Lesbury. I tried not to draw comparisons with the hut that Rowena, the children and I lived in. It suited us but it was no hall. We had just the one girl servant and her main task was looking after the children and helping my wife prepare the food. Mildred had several servants, mostly slaves, including two spit boys to cook the haunches of venison, whole sheep and pigs. We seldom dined so lavishly and what meat we did have was boiled, not roasted. It didn't taste the same, of course.

There was a downside and that was having to share the hall as living quarters with the servants and his housecarls. They had overcome the question of privacy by building a platform at one end of the hall with a curtain. It was accessed by a ladder, which was a problem for Mildred in the latter stages of pregnancy, as she was now, but it seemed to me to be a neat solution to the problem. I wondered that more nobles didn't adopt it.

When Acca and I found ourselves alone on the walkway of his palisade looking out over the bare winter landscape I was surprised when he said that he envied me.

'Why? You have everything I don't have,' I replied, trying to hide the bitterness I felt. 'You are a noble, you have a fine vill and a hall of your own, and you are much richer than I am. Why would you envy me?'

'Because you are in love with your wife. I'm not. I married for all the things you just mentioned but I would give it all up for a loving relationship. It's something I have never experienced and I doubt I ever will now. To tell you the truth Mildred and I are barely on speaking terms when we don't have to put on a front for guests.'

After that I found I didn't envy Acca quite so much.

My son Cerdic was now a robust little fellow of four and a half, so unlike the frail little scrap of humanity he'd been at birth. The twins, Osric and Cille, were nearly three and just at the age when they were beginning to get up to mischief. I loved them all desperately, just as I did Rowena, and wished that our tranquil life at Thornaby would continue for ever. Of course that was a foolish hope and in the summer I was off to war again.

Chapter Sixteen – The Campaign in Cumbria

Summer 1037

In recent years the border between Bernicia and Lothian had been quiet; well, as quiet as it ever was. There were still occasional raids both ways across the border but both Maldred, Earl of Lothian, and Aldred severely punished those who were caught and that helped keep such incursions to a minimum. Of course, the fact that Maldred was married to Ealdgyth, Aldred's half-sister, undoubtedly helped.

However, now King Duncan was flexing his muscles. After years of internal turmoil Scotland was, in the main, quiescent under his rule. He had even managed to subdue the Norse in Cumbria and therein lay the problem. To the east of Carlisle the border between Cumbria, which was part of Strathclyde, and Bernicia ran along the River South Tyne as far as Alston Moor, where both the South Tyne and the River Tees had their source.

The border elsewhere was ill defined but there were settlements to the east of Whitfield Moor and Middlehope Moor that were definitely inside Bernicia, one in Hexhamshire and the other in the shire of Durham. The ealdormen of both had complained to Earl Aldred that Norsemen had attacked the whole area, killed the families that lived there and taken over their land. Not only isolated farmsteads and hamlets had suffered, whole villages had been seized and four dispossessed thanes had added their voices to the protests. Aldred had to act, and act decisively.

The Earl of Cumbria was the five year old Gospatric, Maldred's son and Aldred's nephew. Of course, he was still far too young to manage his earldom and that task was entrusted to a council of regents, the leader of which was now Jarl Øybjǫrn, the most influential of the Norse chieftains. As Aldred was fairly certain that he was behind the migration eastwards of his people there seemed little point in seeking to negotiate with him.

Aldred tried to enlist the support of Maldred but he seemed reluctant to help. Aldred suspected that his brother-in-law was coming under pressure from Duncan to be less friendly towards the Bernicians. There were even rumours that Duncan wanted to invade the portion of Lothian that lay south of the Tweed and which was still part of England.

In view of the situation Aldred called a meeting of his ealdormen in May 1037. Eadulf wasn't an ealdorman but he was also summoned and I accompanied him together with Faran, Æsc, Bryce and Landry as his escort.

I took Dunstan along as well. The boy had turned fourteen and, as was the case with all freemen, he now trained as a member of the fyrd. However, he was small and lacked the weight to be of any use in the shield wall, nor did he have the strength in his shoulders and arms to become an archer. However, he was clever and had a natural skill to move through the landscape unobtrusively. He reminded me of Colby in the days when he was a scout and so I decided to train him in the skills required.

We arrived at Bebbanburg and I felt surprisingly nostalgic when the gaunt stronghold hove into view. The first person to greet Æsc and me when we arrived was Beorhtric who, he told us with pride, had just joined the ranks of Aldred's militares. Old friends came and made us welcome and that night I got exceedingly drunk, something I hadn't done for ages.

Eadulf took me with him to the council of war the next morning, though I would have much preferred to have remained curled up on the floor of the warriors' hall feeling sorry for myself. Many ideas for dealing with the problem were proposed but the common theme was an invasion of Cumbria in strength to drive the Norsemen and their families back where they came from, though others were in favour of harrying the whole of Cumbria, destroying their homes, their crops and their livestock and killing as many of them as possible, even small children, to prevent a repetition of the problem at some future date.

I was appalled at the idea, knowing that such barbaric treatment would unite the Norse of Ireland, the Isle of Man, Caithness, Sutherland and the Orkneys against us. It would also give Duncan the excuse to invade. Thankfully Aldred didn't consider such a plan for an instant.

In the end it was decided that we should launch an attempt to conquer Cumbria and bring it back within the borders of Bernicia, just as it was in the days of King Oswiu four centuries before. Gospatric could remain as the titular earl so as not to alienate his father, Maldred, but Aldred would appoint new ealdormen for the shires of Cumberland and Westmorland to govern in the boy's name.

It seemed a sensible plan, especially as Aldred said that he would warn Maldred so that he didn't rush to his son's assistance, thinking he was in danger. Nevertheless, Aldred decided to remain at Bebbanburg with a sizeable force just in case of trouble from Lothian, or from King Duncan. Colby would remain with him and Eadulf was chosen to lead the invasion of Cumbria and I suddenly found myself as the captain, not of a handful of militares, but of a force some fifteen hundred strong.

✝✝✝

It was mid-June before the army was mustered at Hexham. Five ealdormen and thirty nine thanes had joined the host together with their housecarls and fyrds. Acca was amongst the thanes and I was overjoyed to be serving with my brother again. Aldred had given his brother four section of militares and so, with mine and Acca's, we had fifty mounted warriors. It was the same number that Aldred had led at the Battle of Carham and I was sure that Eadulf would make the same effective use of them.

I would have dearly loved to have led them but, as his captain, that wasn't possible and Acca was given command as the only thane who was a trained militar. I was pleased for him but also slightly envious.

Eadulf's plan was bold. I thought that he might have advanced hoping that the Cumbrians would meet us in open battle. Their defeat would have made conquest easy, but it also had its risks. If we caught them by surprise we should have the advantage of numbers but, if they employed delaying tactics whilst mustering their army, they could probably field more than two thousand, many hundreds of which would be Norse warriors hardened by raiding and fighting in Ireland.

Instead he drove straight towards Carlisle, where we believed the seat of government of the earldom lay. Acca and his men formed a screen to our front and flanks and, although they encountered some slight opposition, the speed of our advance had taken the enemy by surprise and they fled before us in the main.

We foraged but we didn't loot, pillage and burn as we went. Some of these vills and farmsteads would be given to Eadulf's followers as a reward, and of course to settle the area with loyal Bernicians.

Carlisle was a mere fifteen miles from where we had crossed the border. The weather was fine, if chilly, and the ground was dry so even those on foot made good time. On the afternoon of the second day we arrived before the walls of Carlisle.

In the days of the Romans six centuries before the walls had been of stone, but they had crumbled away over time and the gaps that formed had been repaired with timber. The town had expanded in size as well and now there were huts, taverns and workshops outside the walls. Some had been built up against the wall and this gave easy access to the parapet for an agile man.

I had expected us to camp but to my surprise Eadulf told me to get the housecarls organised into groups with the fyrd behind them. He intended to make an immediate attack on the walls. By the time that the parapet had filled with shocked townsfolk and those living outside the walls had fled inside we were ready.

Acca hadn't even blooded his sword so far and I intended to beat him to it. I joined the group led by Beda, Ealdorman of Durham. I was surprised to see Bishop Edmund was also there armed only with his crozier. I hoped that he was just there to lend us spiritual support. I didn't think a wooden pole topped with an ornate hook would fare well against spear, sword and axe.

The abbot of Durham Monastery, Æthelric, stood beside him. I had heard than he had been brought to Durham by Edmund and appointed as abbot to correct the laxity of the monks in observing the Benedictine rule. He certainly looked fierce enough, and he had the good sense to wear a helmet and carry a sword and shield, which was painted with the arms of the Durham diocese – a gold cross on blue.

A horn blew away to my right somewhere and we advanced at a slow walk towards the huts in front of us. As we entered the narrow alleyways between the buildings we came within range of the archers on the walls and arrows rained down on us. They did little damage, however, as we raised our shields above our heads and kept going.

When we reached the huts built against the old town walls the leading rank stood against the front of the building, out of sight of the archers, in groups of three. Two men hoisted the third onto the sloping thatched roof and he then ran up it and jumped up into the crenels cut into the top of the stone wall, which gave it its characteristic toothed appearance.

I saw to my alarm that the man beside me fell through the thatch into the room below. Evidently the roof had been poorly made. I hesitantly stepped forward with my shield held before me to protect me from arrows and thankfully felt something firm, presumably a beam, under the thatch. The next man was clambering up onto the roof behind me so I threw caution to the wind and ran forward, trusting that I was running along the beam.

My luck held until my final step when my right foot punched through the straw. I nearly lost my balance but I managed to push off with my left foot and, holding my shoulder against the shield I propelled myself into the two defenders standing behind the crenel. One was armed with an axe and the other a spear. The point of the spear struck my shield head on and my momentum drove the haft backwards and out of the spearman's grasp. The axe was still somewhere above my head when I barrelled into the man wielding it.

He cannoned into the other man and they both fell backwards off the wooden walkway behind the parapet to land on the earth below. They landed with a sickening crunch that meant that, if they weren't dead, then they had several broken bones and would be playing no further part in the fight. As there were no screams they'd either been killed or were unconscious.

I staggered as I landed on the walkway and very nearly followed my two opponents off it. That probably save my life as a youth with a sword stabbed at where I'd been a moment before. I whirled to my left and brought my sword across in a horizontal arc, chopping into the lad's side. He collapsed onto the walkway with a cry of agony and I ignored him.

I had two fresh assailants, one to my left and one to my right. I used my shield to fend off a sword thrust and caught the downward motion of an axe with my sword. I twisted my sword down and round and the axeman let go of his weapon as it spun away. I jabbed him in the stomach with the point of my sword and forgot about him. The Cumbrian on my other side tried to cut at me above and below my shield but he couldn't get past it. With a scream of fury he jabbed at my feet instead. It was a mistake.

He had no shield and so I was able to bring my sword around and chop into his neck. I looked around for my next foe but realised that the walkway was filling up with the men of Durham. It was only then that I realised how out of breath I was and how much my muscles ached. My throat felt as if I hadn't drunk a drop of liquid for months and I became aware of several minor cuts to my arms. More and more of our men were pouring over the wall and the defenders fled into the town. Carlisle was ours.

✝✝✝

Despite Eadulf's edict that there should be no pillaging there were many instances of looting and rape before night fell, by which time we had finished consolidating our hold on the town. He hung three of the fyrd caught burning a house to hide the fact that they had raped and murdered the occupants before taking everything that they had. It served as warning that Eadulf meant what he said, but in truth the three were unlucky to have been caught. Carlisle wasn't exactly sacked but there were plenty of other instances of plundering houses and treating their occupants abhorrently.

Carlisle was ours but it soon became evident that the boy earl wasn't there. We eventually discovered that the administrative base had been moved by Jarl Øybjǫrn to a town called Penrith about twenty miles to the south-east of Carlisle. Naturally Gospatric would also be there.

'We need to seize the earl and, if possible, kill Øybjǫrn, before Penrith are warned that we have captured Carlisle,' Eadulf said that evening.

'Some of the townsfolk will have fled. Some will doubtless have headed for Penrith,' I pointed out.

'But they will be on foot. Oeric gather together as many horses as you can find. Many housecarls can ride, even if they've no experience of fighting on horseback. Head for Penrith with as many men as you can. Take only warriors. The armigers can give their horses up to housecarls for now. Your task is to seize Gospatric and capture or kill Øybjǫrn and any other advisors the boy has.'

With packhorses we had a hundred and forty horses with us and we found another fifty or so in the town. As dusk fell I left Carlisle with nearly two hundred mounted men and followed the River Petteril south east.

When I asked for scouts to lead the way I was surprised to see Dunstan amongst them. I had assumed that he would remain behind with the armigers but Osric assured me that he would be useful, so I agreed. His pony wouldn't be of much use as a mount for an armoured housecarl anyway.

Once we reached the point where the river turned to the west we stopped. I knew from interrogating the people of Carlisle that Penrith now lay some three miles ahead of us. We were helped by a nearly full moon in a relatively cloudless sky that night and I could dimly see the mountains with a dusting of snow on the tops beyond the town.

Whilst the men camped and allowed the horses to rest Landry, Dunstan and I rode on to reconnoitre. I had discovered little about the town, except that it lay on the Thacka Beck, a small river that ran into the River Eamont a few miles south of Penrith. I also knew that there was an old Roman fort at Brovacum to the south east. There was a jetty on the Eamont which served the town and from there it was only a few miles before the river ran into an inlet of the Irish Sea. Penrith's defences were nothing compared to those of Carlisle, or so we had been told. Our informants claimed that there was a palisade but it was only about ten feet high.

The three of us dismounted a mile short of the town and Dunstan ran forward to verify what we'd been told. I sent him on his own because Landry and I might be spotted in the bright light of the Moon. The boy moved like a wraith, flitting from one patch or cover to the next and we soon lost sight of him.

I could just make out a few details, though the place was hidden in front of the dark hills beyond. It was unfortunate that the snowline wasn't lower down; that would have silhouetted the town nicely. We waited impatiently and it seemed like forever before Dunstan returned, but it was probably less than an hour.

'It's as we were told, Oeric, the palisade is only nine or ten feet tall but there is a tower at each corner. There are also towers each side of the two gateways: one on the north side and the other on the south with a track leading down to the jetty and warehouses on the river.'

'How many sentries did you see?'

'Only one in each tower. There didn't seem to be any patrolling along the top of the walls.'

Scaling the palisade sounded as if it would be easy; the problem was the towers. A few archers in each could catch us in enfilade as we tried to scale the walls. It wouldn't stop us but I only had two hundred men and I didn't know how big the garrison was. I couldn't afford to lose too many men gaining access.

I rode back and told Acca what I intended to do.

'It's risky, Oeric, especially at night. We'll have to leave the horses at least two miles away or risk their neighing alerting the sentries and men could get lost in the darkness.'

As luck would have it clouds had started to scud across the sky as we returned to re-join the rest and now the Moon appeared only briefly. I suspected that the cloud would only get worse and we might even have some rain before dawn. Not that I minded if there was a downpour; it would make the archers far less effective. Wet bowstrings lacked power.

'We'll walk in single file. Each man is to hold his spear horizontally so that the man behind can grasp the end. That way we shouldn't lose any.'

†††

Surprisingly it worked. As we walked the sky clouded over completely and soon it began to rain. Moderately at first and then more heavily. Men cursed as they got soaked and more than a few stumbled over the rough ground as we approached the town away from the road. But we arrived without a single man getting lost.

The rain was a godsend. The sentries in the towers cowered below the ramparts under their cloaks trying to keep dry and so we reached the palisade undetected. A dog started to bark somewhere but it ended abruptly with a yelp as someone threw something at it. Otherwise the only sound was the drops of water hitting hard surfaces.

We reached the palisade undetected and spread out along it. Two men hoisted a third up so that they could grasp the top of the palisade. They pulled themselves up and swung their legs over the top of the wooden wall and jumped down the other side, expecting to land on the walkway behind the parapet. It was then that we discovered why Dunstan hadn't seen any sentries patrolling along the walkway. There wasn't one.

Half a dozen men had fallen onto the hard ground beyond the wall before their screams of agony alerted us to this fact. Four had broken their ankles, one had shattered his leg and one was lucky enough to get away with no more than a sprained ankle.

I pushed my way through to the base of the palisade and called up as quietly as I could to the men sitting atop the timber wall.

'What's happened?'

'There's no walkway, Oeric,' one man yelled back.

'Quietly, you idiot. How far is it to the ground?'

'About ten feet,' he replied in a more hushed voice, though I suspected the damage had been done.

'Lift me up,' I told two men standing beside me.

Once astride the top I could hear the alarm being sounded from one of the towers and the sound of men shouting to each other, asking what was happening. I put my hands on the top of the wall and lowered myself down the other side. At full stretch there was only a drop of four feet or so and I landed safely by bending my knees on impact.

'Do what I've just done,' I called up the men still astride the palisade.

By now the first light of dawn had just appeared over the mountain tops in the east and others further along had seen what I'd done. They quickly told the others and men began to drop beside me. Those with broken bones called to us pitifully but they would have to wait. I could see a mass of men heading our way through the narrow alley ways of Penrith.

The town resembled a Scandinavian settlement rather than an Anglo-Saxon one. Whereas most of our streets, though narrow, were wide enough for a horse and cart, here the gaps between rows of huts were no more than alleyways. The one advantage I could see as the light strengthened was that, instead of being inches deep in mire, the people here had laid duckboards down over the earth, so keeping most of the mud at bay.

The duckboards clattered as armed men ran towards us. More and more men were dropping beside me but I had to get the gates open to allow the other half of my little army to join us quickly.

'Follow me,' I yelled to those closest. 'We need to open the gates. The rest of you keep that rabble at bay.'

They were only twenty yards away from us but my men formed a shield wall in time to protect my

little group as we pounded towards two startled gate
sentries. They had been huddled over a brazier for
warmth when we appeared. It was still roaring away,
although it was now spluttering and hissing in the
rain, and the light silhouetted the two sentries.

They didn't try and defend the gates when we
appeared; they ran. Just as the clash of arms
indicated that our shield wall was now being attacked
I reached the gate and three other men and I heaved
the stout beams out of their brackets and threw them
aside. We dragged the gates open and I yelled for the
men still outside to join us.

Acca led the rest of the men through the gates and
we had to flatten ourselves against the open gates to
avoid being knocked over and trampled on. There
must have been a hundred men in that charge and
they tore into the disorganised enemy in a loose
wedge formation. Most of the opposition were men
who had picked up the first thing to hand: axes,
butcher's cleavers, knives and a few hunting spears in
the main. It was less than five minutes before they
broke and ran leaving perhaps sixty or seventy of
their number dead and dying on the ground.

We reformed and I sent a few men to tend those of
our warriors with broken bones by the palisade.
Meanwhile I led the rest at a fast jog towards where I
calculated the centre of town must be. According to
my information, the earl's hall and the warriors' hall
lay on one side of the square in the middle of Penrith
with the church opposite it.

We burst into the square to find at least sixty
housecarls and Norse warriors standing in front of

the two halls. In front of them stood two figures: a boy of about five, who had to be Gospatric, and a Norse chieftain with several gold and silver arm rings encircling his two brawny biceps. He would have looked like a giant in any company. Next to the small boy he looked enormous. He had to be Øybjǫrn.

'Earl Gospatric, we mean you no harm. It is the Norsemen you surround yourself with that our quarrel is with. They invade our lands, kill our people and take our vills for their own,' I shouted across the intervening space. 'Jarl Øybjǫrn, let the boy go; or do you need shelter behind a five-year old?' I sneered.

As I'd hoped that remark needled him.

'I need no one to protect me, you Saxon cur. You are very brave with so many men at your back. I dare you to settle this in single combat.'

I swallowed hard. He was bigger and stronger than I was, but he was also older and, I hoped, slower.

'Get your men to swear that they will surrender when I kill you.'

'More to the point, I want your oath that your men will depart quietly when I part your head from your body.'

'They will. You have my word. Will your men surrender if you lose?'

'What will happen to them if they do?'

'They will be given a choice: depart to Man, Ireland or the Orkneys or stay and swear fealty to Earl Gospatric and the new ealdormen who Eadulf of Bebbanburg will appoint.'

There was a murmur amongst the men behind the giant Norse jarl at this and I had a feeling that his men would indeed surrender if only I could manage to kill Øybjǫrn.

'Very well,' he called across. 'I'll allow you the choice of weapons.'

'Sword and shield.'

'So be it.'

We advanced towards each other and suddenly my opponent darted to one side with a speed that belied his age and bulk. I nearly perished in those first few seconds as he whirled around and charged in from the right side – the side unprotected by my shield. I managed to parry the blow from his sword more by luck than skill, but it jarred my arm to the point of numbness. I needed time to recover and so I went down on one knee and raised my shield above my head.

He should have either waited for me to stand again or moved behind me. Instead, thinking he had me, he battered my shield with his sword trying to split it so that it became useless.

I swept my sword around horizontally just above the ground and felt the blade connect with his boots. Like mine they were protected by vertical metal strips but, unlike mine, the strips were only sewn into the front of the boots. My blade cut into the base of his calf and continued until it met bone. It was clumsy blow, and not one I was proud of. Had I been able to put all my weight behind it, the blow would have broken the bone. As it was, it must have cut through his Achilles tendon.

He hopped clear on his good leg, gritting his teeth against the pain. Blood began to seep out of the cut in his boot. I sprang to my feet. Now the advantage of mobility lay with me. However, the jarl wasn't finished yet. He whirled around on his one good leg and swept a sideways cut towards my face. I ducked just in time and the blade clanged on my helmet, deafening me, before glancing away. I had avoided serious injury but I felt dizzy. I shook my head in an effort to clear it.

Øybjǫrn hopped to my right, dragging his useless leg with him. I spun around just in time to catch his sword on my shield. Suddenly I sprang forward, thrusting my own shield into the Norseman's body. Normally it would have been an ineffective move but he was caught off balance and he stepped back onto his injured leg. It gave way as he grunted in agony and fell flat on his back.

I trapped his blade under my foot and went to push the point of my sword into his neck, but he wasn't finished yet. He brought his shield into play, deflecting my blade and cracking me on my left shin with the metal reinforced edge. It did no serious damage but my shin was badly bruised, despite the protection afforded by the metal reinforcing strips in my boots. I found that I couldn't put much weight on it but I was still on my feet and Øybjǫrn was struggling to get to his.

I stood back and allowed him time to get upright again, which met with murmurs of approval from the men standing behind Gospatric and groans of disappointment from my own warriors. The jarl stood on his one good leg with his shield hanging by one side of his body and his sword at the other. He bowed to me. I wasn't sure if it was in thanks or respect, but a moment later he adopted a fighting stance once more.

He didn't try to move but just stood there daring me to attack him. I walked around him forcing his to turn on the spot, something that evidently caused him pain. Suddenly I jumped towards him, ignoring the pain in my shin, and made as if to cut at his neck. He raised his shield and brought his sword up at the same time. I stooped, holding my shield to take any counter stroke, and chopped sideways again – this time into the thigh of his good leg just below the bottom of his byrnie.

The blade had been dulled a little during the fight but it was still sharp enough to slice into the vastus lateralis muscle and it must have also severed one of the femoral arteries. Blood spurted out under pressure soaking my blade and arm and he collapsed onto the ground with a shriek. I could have left him to bleed to death but I took pity on him and sunk my blade into his throat to finish him off quickly.

My men gave cheer after cheer as I raised my gory sword in victory whilst the Norsemen and Gospatric's housecarls regarded me with sullen bewilderment.

They had never expected Øybjǫrn to lose.

'Will you keep your word, Saxon?' a high treble voice asked, barely audible above the tumult.

'I'm an Angle like you, Earl Gospatric, not a Saxon, so you don't need to ask. You are to wait with me for the arrival of your uncle Eadulf. Your men must make up their own minds whether they want to continue to serve you or be escorted to the coast. Naturally I expect them all to give their oaths to abide by the conditions of their surrender.'

'We will abide by the terms,' one of the Norsemen said as he came to join us. 'I'm Jarl Vøgg, the senior Norsemen now that Øybjǫrn is dead. I can't speak for all but my family and I are happy here and it doesn't much matter to me whether we are ruled by a Scot or a Northumbrian, just so long as we are allowed to live our lives in the traditional way and to retain the lands we now have.'

'That is not within my remit; it will be for Lord Eadulf to decide. However, the terms you have been offered are his.'

'Very well. We will wait until he arrives.'

I didn't know what to do until Acca came and whispered in my ear.

'Get the housecarls to come and give their oath, that'll leave the Norsemen isolated. Then get them to go and wait in the old Roman fort for Eadulf's arrival. If they don't submit we can surround them and wipe them out.'

I nodded to my brother gratefully and invited Gospatric and his housecarls to come and join us.

'What about those amongst us who are nobles, not housecarls?' a voice called out.

'Who are you?'

'Ealdorman Deorwine of Cumberland.'

'I have no instruction on that score, I'm afraid, but I ask you to release your men from their oath so that they may choose to serve Gospatric and Eadulf.'

There was a hurried discussion amongst a few of those opposite us. It was only then that I realised that the rain had stopped.

'Get the archers to prepare their bows,' I told Acca, 'just in case.'

He nodded and disappeared.

'I'm sorry,' Deorwine answered eventually. 'It's evident that you intent to dispossess us of our shires and vills and we would rather die that let that happen.'

'I think you are being very foolish but so be it. Jarl Vøgg, what is your decision?'

'We will wait in the old fort for Eadulf.'

'Very well, leave your weapons here and some of my men will escort you there.'

Acca and twenty men led them away leaving just over a score of men in the square.

'I ask you one more time, do you wish to surrender or die?'

I raised my hand and forty archers stepped forward and levelled their bows at the group. The men facing us reacted in a variety of ways; some shouting defiance and others groaning in despair.

'You intend to slaughter with arrows and deny us a fair fight?' Deorwine asked incredulously.

'Why should I risk any of my men's lives for your stupidity?' I replied.

'Wait! At least spare Gospatric.'

'My men are expert bowmen. No arrows will touch the earl,' I snorted scathingly.

'Wait. We will submit.'

I signalled the archers to relax and the few nobles and their housecarls started to divest themselves of their weapons. I breathed a sigh of relief just as one of the men I'd left to guard the gates came running to say that Eadulf was approaching with a small group of riders.

††††

We had taken two of the major towns of Cumbria and had custody of its earl, but it was far from over. We still had to capture the shire town of Westmorland – Kendal – which lay thirty miles due south of Penrith through the mountains. Furthermore the vast majority of Norsemen who had settled in the area were still at large.

Finding a way through the wilderness of moors and hills wasn't easy. The only inhabitants seemed to be sheep farmers and there were numerous valleys that led nowhere. We tried to find a guide in Penrith but it seemed that no one was familiar with the area to the south.

We set out but our scouts failed to find an obvious route through the mountains, so we returned to Penrith feeling more than a little dispirited. It seemed that normal contact with the southern shire was by sea from Carlisle, but we had no ships.

I suggested that we sent out a few of our best scouts to discover a feasible route to Kendal and I was amazed when Dunstan came back first. He had found an overgrown Roman road that led to an old fort called Low Borrowbridge. It was occupied by a large family of shepherds who had seemed friendly enough. They told him that there was track from there to Kendal, where they went occasionally to sell some of the sheep and buy essentials like flour and salt.

Dunstan had followed their directions and eventually came across a town little bigger than a large village nestling in the hills beside a river, which we later discovered was called the Kent. There was another Roman fort about two miles south of the settlement which had been re-occupied at some point. The fort was called Watercrook and was apparently now the stronghold of the Ealdorman of Westmorland. Kendal itself had no defensive wall or palisade.

As we'd found out, most commerce between Westmorland and Cumberland was by sea but Kendal wasn't on the coast. However, Dunstan was told that there was a port on the coast called Barrow. From there a road ran through the hills to the shire town.

When he left Kendal he hadn't retraced his steps but had followed a track north west until he reached a long lake. There was a drover's road due north from there which took him to another long body of water which was called Ullswater. It curved to the right half way along and turned into the River Eamont, which led to Penrith.

I congratulated Dunstan on his success and took him to see Eadulf.

He decided that the route Dunstan had taken on his return sounded the easiest, even though the drover's road climbed up to a high pass halfway between the two lakes.

News of our coming must have reached Kendal before we did because we found the town half deserted. When we went to Watercrook Fort it was empty; the ealdorman had fled along with his housecarls. We left a small garrison, as we had at Carlisle and Penrith, and marched on to Barrow. There we were told that many of the Norse who had lived in the area had left a few days before on their longships, including the jarl who had controlled Barrow. The second son of the Ealdorman of Catterick volunteered to remain at Barrow as its thane and Eadulf left a few housecarls with him to impose his rule on the area and we returned to Kendal.

He installed one of the thanes as the new Ealdorman of Westmorland and the rest of us returned to Penrith. It had all seemed too easy so far and so I suppose we should have expected things to turn nasty at some point.

When we arrived back at Penrith we were told that Carlisle had been recaptured by King Duncan and the Scots.

Chapter Seventeen – The Witan at York

Late Summer 1037

Contrary to what we'd been told, Carlisle wasn't held by King Duncan. It had been captured by his brother, Earl Maldred of Lothian. By this time our army had shrunk somewhat. In addition to those we had left in Westmorland and Penrith, there were the usual injuries, illnesses and desertions. Surprisingly there had only been one fatality – the housecarl who had broken his legs getting over the palisade at Carlisle had developed an infection which led to fever and eventual death. We had just over twelve hundred men and Eadulf and I believed that Maldred must have more than that.

We prepared to attack Carlisle once more but Maldred didn't stay inside the town. The morning after we had set up camp outside the gates they opened and he rode out accompanied by about thirty horsemen and perhaps fifteen hundred warriors on foot.

Eadulf and I rode forward accompanied by the five ealdormen in our army and Gospatric. We rode under both the banner of Bebbanburg and the boy earl's banner.

'I'm pleased to see you unharmed, Gospatric,' Maldred began.

'And I am pleased to see you father. It's been a long time.'

The boy's reply was delivered in a treble voice but was a mature comment for one so young. The way he said it implied a criticism for his father's abandonment him.

'How is my lady mother?'

'Well, she sends her love.'

'I would dearly like to see her again.'

My heart went out to the little boy. He had been forced to play a political role ever since he was two years old and I doubted if he could even remember the Lady Ælfflæd.

'What are you doing here, Eadulf?' Maldred said, changing tack.

'My brother's patience at the incursions of the Norsemen from Cumbria into our lands has worn a trifle thin. As you seem incapable of controlling them I'm here to expel them and to make sure that they don't return to trouble us. Why are you here, brother-in-law?'

'This is my son's earldom. I am here to protect it,' he replied brusquely.

'Your son's earldom is still his, Maldred. True, he now has new ealdormen to assist him but at least he's not a puppet of the Norse jarls anymore.'

'You haven't deposed him and taken Cumbria for yourself?'

Maldred sounded puzzled.

'No, it is still your son's and it remains part of Duncan's kingdom – for now. It is the Norse we had a quarrel with, not the Scots.'

304

'If this is true then I am content. Who is the new ealdorman of Cumberland?'

'I am, Maldred. Unless you have any objection?'

I started. I knew nothing of this, but one thing I did know. I had no intention of living in Cumbria. I felt that it was too perilous to settle there with my family. However, events were to prove that we would have been safer there than in Bernicia in the years to come.

More negotiations followed but eventually Maldred was satisfied and Eadulf swore allegiance to Gospatric. The garrison we had left behind were released and the Scots withdrew, as did most of the Bernician army. Unfortunately my old comrades, all except Æsc, elected to stay with Eadulf. I explained my reasons for not joining them and Eadulf seemed to accept them. Nevertheless I sensed a new coldness between us.

I returned to Bebbanburg with Æsc, our armigers and Dunstan wondering what the future now held for me and my family.

✝✝✝

I washed my face and tried to make myself as presentable as I could after a long journey on horseback before reporting to Colby. He welcomed me back and took me to see Aldred. The earl sat in his hall in earnest conversation with Synne and his steward. I waited patiently whilst Colby went and had a quiet word in the earl's ear. He looked up and studied me for a moment. My heart was in my mouth. What sort of a reception would I receive after leaving his service to serve his brother? I breathed a sigh of relief when Aldred smiled and beckoned me forward.

'Oeric, so the wanderer returns? I have heard good reports of your conduct as Eadulf's captain during the Cumbrian campaign. What brings you back to Bebbanburg?'

'Cumbria is controlled by your brother for now, lord earl, but the situation is volatile. Maldred has accepted him as ealdorman of Cumberland but the attitude of King Duncan is unclear. I would have stayed but I miss my family and Cumbria is not a place I would take them at the moment.'

'Well, you are honest, I'll say that for you. How did my brother take your desertion?'

I didn't like the word desertion and it worried me. There is nothing worse in the sight of an Anglo-Saxon than the breaking of an oath, especially one of fealty.

'Ealdorman Eadulf released me from my oath and allowed me to leave with my brother-in-law, Æsc, our armigers and the scout Dunstan,' I replied stiffly.

'Ah, yes Dunstan. I gather it was he who found the way through the wilderness from Penrith to Kendal.'

'You are well informed, lord.'

'I make it my business to be,' he said brusquely. 'I am willing to accept you back into my service, if that is what you seek, but I need to think about your exact role. Report back to Colby tomorrow.'

'Yes, lord earl.'

I left the hall wondering what exactly Aldred was thinking about. Surely if he was going to accept me back as a militar he would have said so there and then. I allowed myself to hope that he might be deliberating whether to make me a section leader again, but that was more than I had dared hope for and I firmly closed my mind to that possibility. There was no point in building up my hopes only to have them dashed.

I wanted to send for my family but I decided that would be foolish until I knew exactly where I stood with the earl. Instead I rode down to the hut I owned to see the tenants. It would take two weeks before Rowena and the children could join me and I warned them that I would need our hut back then. I can't say that they were particularly happy; in fact the man swore at me and threatened to stay put.

'This is my hut and either you leave peaceably within the next two weeks or I will force you out, and none too gently either,' I told him angrily.

He swore at me again and my hand went to the hilt of my sword. At that his wife pulled him into a corner and whispered urgently to him. When he came back he apologised and said that they would leave but he refused to pay me any more rent. The reeve of the vill had already told me that he was three months in arrears but I decided to waive it just to get rid of them.

I returned to the warriors' hall still angry at the way the man had treated me and concerned about my future. I'm afraid I snapped at Æsc when he asked what was happening and he stormed off. I was sitting with my head in my hands feeling sorry for myself when Dunstan appeared and came and sat beside me.

'Are you alright, lord?'

I had got him to stop calling me lord some time ago but his evident concern for me caused him to lapse back into his old ways.

'Yes, thank you, Dunstan. It's not been a particularly good day so far.'

'Aren't you pleased with your new appointment,' he asked with surprise.

'What new appointment? What are you talking about?'

'Why as head of scouts, of course.'

'Where did you hear that?'

'It's common gossip in the stables. As soon as Earl Aldred heard you were back he discussed the best way to employ you with Colby. A servant overheard them and, of course, it was all over the place within minutes.'

'I see. Thank you Dunstan. You have lifted a weight off my mind.'

The next day Aldred and Colby explained their thinking in more detail. Up until now we had used militares as scouts, aided by the odd boy like Dunstan. In fact Colby himself had been a scout when he was a boy. Aldred wanted me to select and train both boys and men as a scouting force. They would relieve the heavily armoured militares from the role and also act as messengers. Because they would be only lightly armed they would be able to move more quickly than the militares and I was to train them as light cavalry, armed with both a bow and two javelins.

I thought that the concept was inspired but later learned that it was the chaplain's idea. He was an avid reader of any Roman texts he could lay his hands on and he had discovered that was how the horsemen attached to the legions operated.

I had assumed that the strength of my new command would be ten, the same as the sections of militares, but Colby said that eventually he wanted me to train a force of at least twenty. Furthermore he wanted me to train them as trackers.

'But I know nothing of the skills required,' I protested.

'That is why I've engaged Pæþ to help you.'

The name literally meant tracker and my heart sank. It was the name of the tenant I had just ejected from my hut.

✝✝✝

Before I had to deal with Pæþ, Aldred sent for me again.

'You'll need to train your scouts in suitable country,' he began. 'I own a farmstead at a place called Akeld at the edge of the Cheviot Hills. I've decided to make a gift of it to you on two conditions.'

'Yes, lord. Thank you. That's most generous. Er, what are the conditions?'

I didn't really care. I was euphoric. At last I would be a landowner, perhaps not a thane like Acca, but now I had property I could pass on to my sons.

'Firstly, you are become my oathsworn man and are never to leave my service again. Secondly you are to build a fortified hall there to defend the valley of the River Glen.'

That didn't seem to me to be a problem. Presumably I would have to stand the cost but I already knew that Aldred proposed to pay me more than he had done when I was a section leader.

I next went to see Pæþ. He greeted me warily, wondering how I would treat him now that I was his commander. I smiled and told him that his family could now stay in the hut, provided he paid me the rent overdue, but that he would be required to live with me and the scouts at Akeld. He thought for a moment whilst his wife whispered in his ear.

'Would it be permitted for me to build a hut there for my family? I don't really want to be parted from them for long periods,' he asked.

'I can do better than that. I'll ask the reeve to find me a new tenant and you can move into the hut that I'm told is already there, but,' I paused, 'only after everyone had built me a hall so that I, my family and the scouts have somewhere to live.'

He smiled and held out his hand. I shook it and that was that. Past rancour was behind us and in time we became good friends.

†††

Akeld was a pleasant spot. It nestled on the northern foothills of the Cheviots near the River Glen.

The main occupation of the other occupants of the farmstead was sheep farming though each hut had a vegetable plot and there were other livestock as well – cattle, pigs and chickens and a dovecote. It was a hamlet rather than a simple farmstead and the main hut had been used as a hunting lodge in the past so it was more than ample for Pæþ's needs.

There was an empty barn which was used for lambing in the spring which we used as temporary housing. The shepherds and their families were welcoming when they realised that I was going to build a fortified hall there. Occasional raids by the Scots were always a hazard and now they and their livestock would be able to take refuge inside the palisade when necessary. Furthermore, with armed warriors present most small raiding parties would give us a wide berth.

It was August before the hall was completed and Rowena and the children joined us. By then I had four hunters and nine boys under training in addition to Dunstan. Pæþ wasn't just a skilled tracker he was also a hunter and part of his task, and that of the other three, was to train the boys to hunt. The shepherds kept their sheep for the wool and to trade any surplus flocks for the necessities of life at the market in nearby Wooler. They rarely ate meat themselves and so when we had a deer that had hung long enough I gave a feast for everyone in the place. Needless to say it enhanced my popularity.

With Æsc and our armigers, I now had nineteen scouts in my section. A boy of fifteen who was the son of one of the shepherds was a good hunter and when he asked to join us I agreed. I now had my twenty.

By September I felt that my scouts were ready, although some were better trained than the rest. I rode to Bebbanburg and told Colby and he immediately tasked me with mounting two patrols: one along the western stretches of the Tweed and the other into the heart of the Cheviots in search of a pack of wolves which had been taking sheep from a farmstead at a place called Alwinton.

The patrol along the Tweed led by Æsc was uneventful but the wolf hunt was rather more exciting. My boys managed to track the pack to their lair without Pæþ's help, which pleased both of us. As we approached seven wolves appeared at the entrance to the cave and stood in a semi-circle with fangs bared, snarling at us. Behind them I could see several cubs moving about. They advanced and retreated repeatedly, indicating that they were both curious and fearful.

Had we been there for sport we would have tackled them with spears, but we weren't. Our task was to eliminate a menace, so we stood off at a safe distance whilst they continued to confront us. We launched our attack using bows and javelins and by the time the wolves realised that they were in serious trouble five of them were dead or badly wounded. It was then that we were taken by surprise.

The two largest wolves had evidently slunk off into the trees before we saw them. Now one charged and pounced on Pæþ whilst the other attacked me. I was scarcely aware of what was happening as it knocked me to the ground and went for my throat. I was saved by my chainmail coif as its fangs closed around my neck, trying to tear out my windpipe. Nevertheless, it was making a good job of ripping the coif to bits and I didn't think it would be long before it reached bare flesh.

Its fetid breath filled my nostrils as I struggled to strangle it but my feeble efforts weren't having much effect. Then, with a roar of rage Dunstan threw himself on top of the wolf and stabbed it repeatedly in the neck with his dagger.

'I think it's dead,' I said as Dunstan's stabbing frenzy continued.

The boy tried to drag the corpse off me but it was too heavy for him.

'I thought you were dead for sure,' he sobbed.

'No, I'm alive thanks to you.'

Two of the men came and helped him lift the dead creature off me. It was the largest wolf I'd ever seen – almost certainly the alpha male - and I thought inconsequentially that its skin would make a good cloak for Dunstan.

'Are you hurt, lord?' the boy asked, his face a mask of concern. 'Your face is covered in blood.'

'No, it's the wolf's; and stop calling me lord.'

'Yes, lord,' he said grinning in relief.

I put my hands on his shoulders.

'I owe you my life, Dunstan. I won't forget it.'

I looked around me and groaned.

Whilst my own drama was playing out the other two animals at the cave mouth had charged but fell dead with several arrows and a javelin in them before they were halfway towards us. However, Pæþ hadn't been so lucky. I suspect that the one who had attacked him had been the alpha female. She had eaten half his neck away before two boys and one of the men managed to kill her.

I regretted his death as much as that of anyone in the past. After that first initial confrontation he and I had got to know each other well. I liked him as a man and I respected his skills as a tracker and as a hunter. I also felt that I had failed his wife and children by allowing him to die. We should have been more cautious in our approach.

Thankfully he had passed on enough of his tracking knowledge to enable others to fill his shoes and most of the section were now proficient hunters; nevertheless he would be sorely missed.

We brought the horses forward and wrapped his body in a leather tent to disguise the worst of the smell; horses don't tend to react well to the stench of blood. We'd take him back to his family so that he could have a proper funeral. I would have to think about the future of his wife and small children now that Pæþ was unable to provide for them, but that would have to wait until another day.

There were four young cubs in the lair. We were reluctant to kill defenceless animals but wolves were impossible to tame and, had we allowed them to live, they would either have died slowly through starvation or else grown up to be a problem in the future.

That was the major excitement of the year and life continued in much the same vein until early May

1038 when Aldred was summoned to a meeting of the Witan at York. Siward was no friend to Aldred and we didn't trust him, so Aldred decided to take a strong escort, including my scouts. However, it wasn't Siward who tried to ambush us; it was Carl.

†††

We had stopped for the night at the old Roman fort at Morbium when they came for us. Morbium was a large fort on Dere Street about halfway between Hexham and York. It lay just south of the old Roman bridge over the River Tees, which formed the present border between Bernicia and Deira. The old bridge had long since collapsed and had been repaired in timber, but using the original stone piers.

Once across we would be in Siward's earldom and I sent my scouts over first. They ranged five miles in all directions south of the river but found nothing. By the time they had returned we had set up camp in the ruins of the fort.

At one stage it had been a major stronghold, no doubt built to control the crossing over the Tees. It might even have been the base of a legion, or at least several cohorts, to protect the south before the wall was built by the Emperor Hadrian along the Tyne Valley. Aldred's chaplain had read somewhere that it was one of the last forts to be evacuated when the legions withdrew from what they called Britannia several centuries before.

Now little remained except the foundations of the perimeter wall, its corner towers, the four gatehouses and the commander's villa. These had all been constructed in stone; perhaps the accommodation blocks, granaries and stables had been built of timber and had now rotted away? There was no village on the site and when we arrived as dusk was falling it had a certain eerie quality.

I don't think anyone was happy staying there. Although we were Christians, most were of us superstitious and we worried about the ghosts of those who had died here long ago. However, it was nearly dark, it had started to rain and the gatehouses, parts of the commander's house and a building just outside the walls that no-one knew purpose of offered us shelter. More importantly it was defensible.

The armigers and the horses shared the strange building outside the walls. The latter were fed on oats that night as Aldred didn't think it sensible to let them graze in a makeshift paddock. I went to visit them and inspected the building by torchlight to satisfy my curiosity. It seemed to have consisted of several large rooms including one that might have had a large sunken pool, another with a much smaller pool and a room where part of the floor had collapsed revealing odd little pillars underneath which presumably supported the stone slabbed floor. I couldn't imagine why they didn't just lay the slabs on the earth, as we would have done.

The wooden gates had long since disappeared but the remains of the stone fortifications were at least ten feet high at the lowest point so we stationed the two sentries on one of the towers at each entrance and gathered thorn bushes to block three of the gateways. We used the two carts we had along with us to carry equipment, tents and the like to block the northern one.

I divided my twenty scouts into four watches and five men or boys went out on foot for two hour stints to watch for anyone approaching the fort. Aldred had an intuition that we might be attacked there as it was an obvious place to spend the night. His suspicion was well founded.

Sometime in the early hours of the morning Dunstan and another scout, a man called Chad, clambered over the cart barricade and ran to the commander's house where most of us were sleeping.

'Oeric,' Chad said breathlessly, 'men are sneaking towards the fort.'

'How far away?'

'Perhaps three hundred yards away by now,' he replied uncertainly.

Dunstan gave him an impatient look.

'Nearer than that by now, but they are moving cautiously so as not to make any noise. I would say we have seven or eight minutes before they reach the walls.' The boy panted.

'How many and from which direction?'

'Difficult to say. Two score at least. They're coming from the east.'

'Right, go and warn the armigers in the building where the horses are. They are the ones who are in immediate danger. Æsc, take ten men to help them defend it.'

'What's going on?' Colby demanded, looking less than pleased that I seemed to have taken command.

'I was just coming to find you. We have about five minutes before we are attacked by at least forty men,' I replied tersely. 'I've sent ten men to help defend the building where the horses are stabled.'

'Good. You four go and warn the sentries in the towers. The rest of you come with me. Armigers stay here. I'll go and wake the earl.'

He needn't have bothered. No one could have slept through all the commotion as we donned our helmets and picked up shields and weapons.

'Are we under attack,' he demanded.

'Imminently, lord,' Colby replied.

'What have you done?'

'Oeric has sent men to reinforce the stables; I've warned the towers and was just about to set off for the gate where the carts are.'

'Good. Well done both of you. Oeric, you take ten men to defend the low patch of the wall. Colby, you and the rest head for the main gate. Armigers, divide yourselves into three and go and watch for men scaling any of the other walls. Now move!'

We barely made it in time. Dunstan's estimate was spot on. Just as we approached the low section of wall we could hear noises coming for the other side. I signalled my men to keep quiet and we flattened ourselves against our side of the wall. As the first two men landed on our side we quietly slit their throats. We did the same for the next two pairs and then one of the enemy managed to shout a warning before he died.

Two more men were already on top of the broken wall about to jump down. Hearing the warning they made to go back the way they had come, but two of my men were too quick for them. They thrust their spears upwards and caught one in the thigh and the other in the calf. They were still alive but they wouldn't be taking any further part in the fight.

We could hear an excited babble of voices speaking Danish the far side of the wall but my men started to ask questions so I couldn't make out what they were saying.

'Shut up!' I hissed and then listened intently.

'There is another section of wall that's twelve foot high. They are going to try again there. Anyone know where that might be?'

'The west wall. I spotted it when we arrived,' a boy's voice replied.

'Dunstan? What the hell are you doing here? Never mind; show me.'

We sprinted across the fort using the thoroughfare connecting the east and west gates to avoid tripping over the ruins. We arrived in plenty of time and just at that moment the moon appeared from behind the clouds. It was just after the new moon but still the shallow crescent provided enough light for us to see moving shapes. I glanced over towards the North Gate where Aldred was managing to hold the enemy at bay.

The part of the west wall that had fallen down was quite short and the stone walkway behind the crenulations on either side looked to be intact. We rushed up the two stone staircases at either end of that section of wall and looked down. There was no sign of our foes as yet.

'How many have bows?'

Only two men had the wit to bring them but they were both good archers.

'Shoot down at them as soon as you are certain of scoring a hit. They'll quickly raise their shields so get as many arrows off as you can before they do that.'

Three of the attackers were hit before they hurriedly withdrew with their shields above their heads. We waited but they didn't attack again and I began to think about the place where they'd make their next assault. I soon found out. The attack on the North Gate had also ceased but we could now hear the sound of combat coming from the strange building outside the walls.

We raced back to the centre of the fort and then along the road to the gate. By this time Aldred's men had pulled the carts out of the way and he was already leading them towards the sound of fighting. My men and I raced after him.

The building only had one entrance and it was only wide enough to admit one man at a time. However part of the side wall had fallen down and I could see men clambering up the rubble. Aldred was about to attack the men trying to fight their way through the door so I headed for the other group.

We were all winded and it took the two archers a little while before they could calm their breathing in order to use their bows with any accuracy. Then they calmly sent arrow after arrow into the back of the men scrambling up the rubble. They tried to turn and descend but those who rushed broke an ankle or a leg. None made it down again. However a few had got to the top before the archers were ready and I could hear the sound of combat coming from inside.

'Come on,' I said, starting to scale the pile of bricks and stones.

It took time but eventually I reached the top and breathed a sigh of relief. Only half a dozen men had managed to get inside and they had all been killed by the boys and the warriors I'd sent to assist them.

As I descended the rubble again I realised that the sounds of combat from the doorway had ceased. I led my men back to join the earl just in time to see about a dozen or so of the enemy fleeing into the darkness. We had won and with few loses on our side. There were some with flesh wounds and two of the armigers had been killed. However, so had the militar who had held the doorway against the attackers until Aldred arrived. It was only when I looked at his face that I realised with horror that it was Æsc.

Chapter Eighteen – Murder at Rise

Autumn 1037 to Summer 1038

My first thought was that I was mistaken; it couldn't be him. But, of course, it was. I didn't know how I was going to tell Rowena that her brother was dead. I fell to my knees beside him and cradled his bloodstained and battered head in my lap. I loved my brother Acca, even if I was jealous of him some of the time, but I had grown to love my brother-in law almost as much.

I was dimly aware of someone else kneeling beside me and holding Æsc's gory head in his hands. I glanced up and saw that it was Beorhtric. I might have been the dead man's brother-in-law and close companion but Æsc had been his brother. I put my arm around his shoulder and he sobbed before turning away so that I shouldn't see his tears. He shook his head as if to clear it; we both knew that this wasn't the moment to be maudlin. Those who had fled might be reforming for another attack.

We got to our feet and Aldred said how much he regretted the loss of Æsc. I nodded my thanks, unable to speak at that moment. Aldred turned away and told Colby to find out how many of our assailants had been killed and whether there were any wounded men available for questioning.

'I'd like to join you, Oeric, if I may,' Beorhtric said to me quietly. 'I know I'm not my brother and I know little of scouting, but I had been thinking of asking to join you two for a while. I just wish I'd done so whilst my brother was still alive.'

'I hope you aren't thinking that, had you been with him, you might have been able to save him? He died heroically and, had you been with him, I might have lost both of you.'

'No, I suppose you're right. But, will you take me?'

'Of course, nothing would please me more.'

It was midday before we left Morbium. Now there were more ghosts to join the Romans. We had killed nineteen of the attackers and another seven had been wounded. Aldred had no compunction about torturing them and we found out that there had been around sixty attackers. Carl was the instigator, not Siward as Aldred had supposed. A few were his housecarls but most were mercenary Danes and cutthroats he'd recruited in return for silver.

The latter weren't brave men, unlike the housecarls who died without saying a word. Aldred took two of the mercenaries along to testify in front of the king and Earl Siward. The rest we killed.

York was, of course, filled to capacity and beyond. Not only was the king and his entourage there, but also every earl, most ealdormen and various bishops and abbots. Each had brought servants, housecarls and, in the case of the churchmen, numerous priests and monks.

The earl and a few servants and his guards would be found somewhere, either in Siward's hall or in the monastery in view of his rank, but the rest of us would be camping outside the town. The campsites of those already there spread along the River Ouse and Colby took one look at those collecting drinking water downstream of where others were washing and defecating and decided to camp elsewhere. There were two rivers at York: the Ouse and the Foss. They became one just south of York. The ground at the confluence was marshy and so the other campsites were on both the banks of the Ouse to the north west of the walled town. The River Foss was smaller and so far its banks upstream of the marsh were deserted.

I was about to choose a suitable site for my tent when Colby summoned me and said that Aldred had chosen himself, Beorhtric, Osric and myself to guard him. When I saw the small monk's cell that was supposed to house four housecarls, the earl and his body servant, Durfel, my tent seemed a much more attractive prospect.

Aldred took the small, narrow bed whilst the rest of us made do with the floor; not that there was a lot of difference. The bed was almost as hard. There was just room for us all to squeeze in as one of us always stood guard outside the door as a precaution. The attack on us at the fort had made us extremely wary.

The Witan didn't meet on the appointed day as Godwin of Wessex was still to arrive, nor were his ealdormen or the bishops of Sherborne, Winchester and Selsey present. However, most of the abbots from south of the Thames were already at York, as were the Archbishop of Canterbury and the Bishop of Rochester; all of which made Godwin's non-appearance even more intolerable.

In the meantime Aldred requested a private audience with the king. It was to prove an unwise decision. I pieced together what had happened from what I learned afterwards. The earl outlined the attack on us at Morbium Fort and produced the two prisoners to corroborate his complaint against Carl of Holderness. Once he had heard their evidence Harold ordered the captives' summary execution. This inevitably angered Aldred, who had promised to pardon the two men if they told the truth. He remonstrated with Harold and probably said things that were unwise.

That didn't improve Aldred's standing with the king and, instead of taking Aldred's side against Carl and fining him, as Aldred had expected, Harold decreed that the blood feud must end and summoned Carl so that he and Aldred could come to terms. In doing so Harold went against established Anglo-Saxon tradition. A blood feud was a matter of honour between the two families involved. It wasn't something that the king should resolve. Nevertheless Harold seemed determined to bring harmony to the northern part of his realm, come what may.

Godwin and his entourage arrived the next day and the Witan convened in the nave of the cathedral. The Earl of Wessex didn't explain his tardiness or apologise for it and Harold let it pass. As far as I could gather the business conducted over the next two days was merely routine except for one matter. Godwin raised the question of the succession as the king had no legitimate offspring. His only child was Ælfwine, a bastard son who was just three years old.

According to Aldred, Harold lost his temper with Godwin and declared that, as he was only twenty two years old, he had decades of life in front of him in which to marry, produce sons and for them to grow to maturity. How wrong that prediction proved to be.

When the Witan dispersed Aldred was told to stay behind. The next day Carl arrived and both men were summoned to see the king. Each could take two supporters with them as witnesses. The audience was held in the refectory of the monastery which had been turned into a throne room for the day. Each man was invited to state his grievance against the other and both did so; Aldred calmly and with reasoned argument, Carl heatedly and with much exaggeration.

He denied that his father was at fault for Uhtred's death, claiming that he was carrying out the execution of a traitor. When Aldred pointed out that his father was carrying Cnut's safe conduct Carl claimed that was a lie. Harold seemed content to allow the argument to continue until it petered out before he pronounced his decision.

'It is obvious that Thurbrand was involved in the murder of Uhtred of Northumbria,' he began, holding up his hand for silence when Carl started to protest. 'I tend to believe that Uhtred did have my father's safe conduct and was merely answering a summons to attend him. Thurbrand's act was therefore unlawful. As to motive, I can only conclude that Uhtred's brother, Ealdred, paid him to do it.

'Aldred was perfectly justified in killing Thurbrand; indeed the code of honour which binds all demanded it. However, that should have brought the feud to an end. Carl, your attempt to kill Aldred on his way here was ill advised and unnecessary.

'My decree is that you should both put past enmity behind you and give each other the kiss of brotherly love.'

Both men went to protest but the king held up his hand for silence once more.

'I'm sure that you need to get to know one another in order to become more tolerant towards each other. I therefore direct that you to swear a sacred oath to go on pilgrimage to Rome together. Ask our Holy Father, the Pope, for forgiveness for your sins and return as friends. I appreciate that you will need time to make the necessary arrangements for the management of your lands whilst you are away, but you will incur my severe displeasure if you do not set out within the next twelve months. Now do as I say and exchange the kiss of friendship before Archbishop Ælfric takes your oaths.'

We were all stunned. The idea of Aldred and Carl making peace just because the king said so was ludicrous. Nevertheless the two men had no alternative. It was either obedience or revolt and neither man wanted the latter. They took the oath, perfunctorily kissed each other's cheek and made arrangements to meet in July the following year in order to set out for Rome.

✝✝✝

Of course the forced reconciliation between Aldred and Carl meant little in reality. They decided that they would have to travel to Rome together, but they would do so each on his own birlinn; and they would travel by sea along the Atlantic coast of France and Iberia and through the Mediterranean Sea. That way they would fulfil the king's orders, and perhaps more importantly to them, fulfil the sacred oath that they had sworn, but avoid having to put up with each other's company.

It might have worked too, had it not been for the weather.

Aldred's birlinn needed a crew of thirty seven: thirty two rowers, a steersman, a captain and three ships boys to handle the sail and carry out the menial tasks. However, the voyage to Rome was a long one; two weeks given fair winds, or so we were led to believe. Therefore Aldred took two extra men as spare rowers and a fourth ship's boy. He also took his body servant, Durfel.

I was chosen as one of the rowers, as were Colby and Beorhtric. The spare ship's boy was Dunstan and, much to my delight, the steersman was my brother Acca. Although a thane, he had spent some time at sea in recent years and was now one of Aldred's best sailors. There were others more experienced, of course, but I suspected the earl wanted men around him that he trusted completely. After all we were heading into the snake pit.

The two nobles had agreed that Aldred would call in at Carl's port of Brough-on-Humber and then we would sail in company, fulfilling the king's command, if not in quite the way he had anticipated. I had half expected that the port we used would be the pirate's lair near Newsham, where Acca had killed Thurbrand fourteen years before, but Newsham was no longer Carl's base and he claimed to have foresworn piracy. Whether that was true or not I didn't know, but he no longer operated out of the hidden harbour in the marshland south of Newsham.

The voyage from Budle Bay started well enough. There was a brisk easterly wind and an azure sky dotted with occasional white fluffy clouds. We let the sail do the work and sat on our sea chests chatting and joking amongst ourselves. We stopped for the night at Whitby and were made welcome by the monks and nuns at the monastery. Whitby wasn't the only monastic establishment where both men and women lived together, but it was perhaps the most well know. It had been at Whitby nearly four centuries ago, when Saint Hilda was the abbess, that the famous synod had been held. The momentous decision reached then meant that we Northumbrians adopted the tenets of Roman Catholicism in place of the practices and beliefs of the Celtic Church.

As the second day wore on the wind picked up a little and the clouds overhead became more numerous and eventually the sky turned an ominous dark grey. We could see the first squall scudding over the sea towards us and the ship's boys ran to get the sail down. Meanwhile we unshipped our oars and began to row.

Storms were not unknown in the summer, but they were rare. Because the waves were hitting us sideways on we began to ship water and the ship's boys and the two spare rowers began bailing. However, water was filling the bilges faster than they could get rid of it and we had to change tack and head further out to sea into the teeth of the gale.

My back felt as if it would break and my arms ached with the effort of driving the ship into the ever higher waves. The wind whistled around the mast and through the rigging and saline spume soaked us every half a minute or so. Just when I thought I couldn't go on Acca pushed the steering oar over and rowing became easier as we ran with the wind on our rear quarter. We corkscrewed through the sea but the wind was pushing the ship along so my task, and that of the other rowers, was to just keep her on course, as far as we were able to that is.

Dunstan, who was the lookout in the bows at the time, suddenly yelled and pointed, but his voice was carried away on the wind. Aldred made his way carefully to the bows and looked to see what the boy was pointing at.

'Land dead ahead, less than a mile,' he shout to the earl, trying to make himself heard over the howling wind. Aldred nodded and carefully made his way back to where Acca was wrestling with the steering oar. 'It looks as if there is sea between two headlands,' I heard him shout to my brother. 'With any luck it's the mouth of the Humber.'

'If it is,' Acca replied with a grin, 'it's more by luck than judgement.'

Aldred nodded.

'If it isn't the Humber at least it will give us shelter whilst this storm lasts.'

Thankfully it was indeed the Humber estuary and we pulled gently up the wide river until we saw a small port to our right. It had to be Brough. There were two knarrs and a birlinn already moored to the small jetty but there was just room for us to come alongside. The three boys leapt ashore to secure us to two posts and we rowers collapsed where we sat.

Carl's birlinn was there but, it was unmanned, apart from the ship's boys who had been left to guard it. The village lay behind the jetty and two warehouses. When we got there we discovered that it was quite small; just two dozen huts and a tavern. There wasn't even a thane's hall. However, we couldn't care less. We were exhausted and just thankful to be alive. We made a meal out of the provisions on board and then repaired to the tavern to slake our thirst.

It was a mean hovel of a place: a dirt floor stained with vomit and other liquids I didn't even want to think about. It stank and the tables and benches were sticky with spilt ale. The few customers in there gave us suspicious looks and then returned to talking amongst themselves. We guessed that their sniggers were aimed at us but no one had the energy, or inclination, to take them to task over it. We each

331

bought a tankard of ale or mead and stood swilling the truly awful local brew. No one fancied a second tankard of the stuff so we returned to sleep on the birlinn's deck.

It wasn't a comfortable night. The wind grew in strength and, although we were sheltered from the worst of it, it shrieked in the rigging. We huddled under our cloaks as the rain lashed the ship. I went to relieve myself over the gunwale at one point and was nearly blown over the side by a sudden gust. Clearly the pilgrimage wasn't likely to commence for a few days yet.

The next morning the rain had ceased and we found a spot ashore to light campfires on which to cook and to dry our clothes. Around mid-morning, just as we were beginning to feel a little more comfortable, Carl arrived with an escort of mounted housecarls. These weren't militares like us, but warriors who rode to get from one place to another and then fought on foot.

'I'm sorry I wasn't here to greet you lord earl,' he said to Aldred without dismounting – itself a sign of disrespect – 'but it wasn't the weather to venture outside my hall yesterday.'

'Nor to be out at sea I can assure you,' Aldred replied sourly.

'I don't think we'll be setting out for a day or two yet,' the Dane replied. 'The wind has abated somewhat but it's still blowing a gale and the waves out there are higher than your masthead. Come, you'll be more comfortable in my hall at Rise whilst we wait for calmer conditions.'

Carl rode off, saying that he needed to prepare a feast for tonight, leaving us to follow him on foot. Aldred could have hired a horse but he said that, if we had to walk, then he'd walk with us. We left five warriors and all but one of the ship's boys to look after our birlinn and the rest of us, including Dunstan, who we sent ahead as a scout in case we were ambushed, set off.

I thought that Rise was a strange name for a village but when I saw it I understood. The ground all around was completely flat but the place itself was built on a small hill. It was a good twenty miles from Brough to Rise and it took us most of the day to get there.

I'll say this for Carl, he didn't stint on entertaining us. The ale and the mead was excellent and there was roast boar, venison and mutton to eat with fresh bread and a broth made of barley and various root vegetables. We slept in the hall that night and most of us woke feeling a little sorry for ourselves. I dunked my head in a bucket of water and felt a little better but both Carl and Aldred seemed fresh and in good humour.

Carl invited the earl to walk around the vill with him and they set off with two of the local housecarls, Colby and Acca following at a discreet distance. As they disappeared I saw Dunstan shadowing them and I wondered what the boy was up to.

I ate some bread and cheese washed down with a flagon of ale and had just gone outside the hall to relieve myself when I saw Dunstan running back as fast as his legs would carry him.

'Oeric,' he called to me breathlessly as soon as he was in earshot. 'Aldred and Carl fought and the earl is dead, as are Colby and Acca.'

I stood there dumbfounded for a few seconds. I had trouble in taking in what the boy had said.

'I was behind them,' he blurted out, struggling to get his breath back. 'Carl asked Lord Aldred if he really wanted to go on pilgrimage or whether he was prepared to settle the feud there and then, like men. The earl accepted and they fought with sword and dagger. At first they were evenly matched but then Carl rolled on the ground and chopped at Earl Aldred's lower legs with his sword. I think he must have managed to cut the earl's Achilles tendon.

'After that there was no doubt as to the outcome. As soon as Carl delivered the killing blow both Acca and Colby rushed at Carl with shouts of rage. Undoubtedly they would have killed Carl had they reached him but the two housecarls attacked them from behind. In the ensuing melee one of the housecarls was killed and the other wounded but Carl escaped without a scratch. He went to attend to the wounded man but I didn't wait any longer and came back to warn you.'

'Warn us?' I asked stupidly.

I just couldn't believe that my brother was dead, nor that Aldred and Colby were too.

'Yes, Carl is hardly likely to let us leave and spread the tale, is he?'

Then it hit me with all three dead that left me as the senior man. I ran back into the hall.

'Gather up your kit,' I shouted to our men.

Carl's warriors and servants looked at us in bewilderment. By their reaction I guessed that Carls' offer to fight Aldred had been a spur of the moment thing. Even if it was planned, he evidently hadn't ordered his men to detain or kill us.

'The earl has already left to return to Brough,' I explained. 'We are to follow on as quickly as possible.'

We walked out of Rise and I waited until we were out of sight before stopping and explaining what had happened. Like me the men were incredulous at first but Dunstan's eye witness testimony convinced them. Most were in favour of returning and killing Carl in revenge but I pointed out that there were twenty five of us, excluding Dunstan, and there were nearly fifty men back in Rise – counting the fyrd as well as housecarls. We'd be throwing our lives away pointlessly. Grudgingly they accepted the logic of fleeing so that we could take our revenge another day.

'We need to get back to the ship and away from here before they come looking for us,' I urged them. 'I must get word to Eadulf too; he should be the earl now.'

As we neared Brough we heard sounds of pursuit behind us. The bastards were using dogs to hunt us! We piled aboard our birlinn, thankful that those left with the ship were on board, whilst two men went and cut through the mooring lines of Carl's birlinn with axes.

As our pursuers arrived on the jetty their ship drifted out into the river, leaving them cursing and swearing at us. A few ran to the two knarrs before they realised that the wind was still blowing from the east. They wouldn't stand a chance of catching us in a merchantman with three oars a side and the wind against them.

We had got away safely, but that was small consolation for the loss of Aldred, Colby and Acca. I was lost in a pit of despair. I had lost my brother, my lord and one of my oldest comrades. Life would never be the same again.

Chapter Nineteen – The End of an Era

1039 to 1040

In the absence of an earl – at least until Eadulf arrived – I was elected captain to replace my old friend Colby. It was an honour, of course, but one I could have done without in the present crisis. I was well aware that Siward had always wanted to become Earl of Northumbria and to reduce the lord of Bernicia to his deputy; or even do away with a separate Bernicia altogether and rule us through our ealdormen.

Aldred's death gave him a golden opportunity to do this and so I had to move quickly if we were to maintain our independence. However, I was worried about making a wrong move so, before I did anything, I needed to consult the section leaders of the militares and, more importantly, my wife.

'You must notify the ealdormen immediately and get them to support Eadulf as the new earl,' she advised. 'Of course, the king will have to confirm the appointment but, without the support of the ealdormen, he may well be inclined to unite Northumbria under Siward.'

'You think some of them might be in Siward's pocket?'

'Perhaps not now, but I'm sure a few might be susceptible to bribery. Hence the need to act before Siward does,' Rowena said firmly.

'You're right. I'll send messengers with a letter from me first thing tomorrow.'

'No, today. There's no time to lose.'

'Very well. The other thing I must do as soon as possible is inform Eadulf.'

'Who will you send?'

'I think I should go myself. He trusts me and he's more likely to listen to what I have to say. He could well be tempted to delay until he's put other arrangements in place in Cumbria. He needs to understand how urgent it is that he returns and takes over the earldom.'

'Who will you leave in change here?'

'I've called a meeting of the militares; the section leaders will need to elect a deputy to command the fortress whilst I'm away.'

There were eight section leaders now, including Beorhtric who had taken over command of the scouts. The two most senior were Kjetil, who was Norse by birth and his friend and fellow Norseman, Hakon. It might seem odd to leave the most important stronghold in Northumbria in the hands of a former Viking, but the two had been twelve and thirteen respectively when they'd been captured and enrolled as ship's boys. Both had served Aldred for the past two decades and the only Norse thing about them now was their names.

Before I went into the hall to speak to the men I called on Synne to explain what I was doing. Her eyes were red from weeping and I felt sorry for her, not just because she'd lost the man she'd loved, but also because I suspected that her own future might be uncertain. It all depended on what provision Aldred had made for her in his will.

'Will you be alright, lady?' I asked her when I'd finished explaining what I proposed to do.

'Yes,' she sighed. 'I propose to leave before Eadulf and Sigfrida arrive. Aldred left me the vill of Aycliffe in Teesdale and so I'll go there. I'd be grateful if you would arrange for a small escort and then I can leave the day after tomorrow.'

'Of course, lady. May I say how sorry I am?'

'Thank you Oeric. You were always one of my late husband's best warriors.'

Her grief had depressed me anew and I went for a walk along the ramparts to shake off my melancholy. I gazed out over the leaden grey sea and that made my mood even darker. I took a deep breath and headed for the warrior's hall.

Before I spoke to the others I took Hakon and Kjetil aside and asked them individually whether each of them would be prepared to accept the other as my deputy. Both said yes without hesitation.

When I explained to everyone why I thought it necessary to go and see Eadulf myself a few argued against it, but most could understand my logic.

'Who will command us whilst you're away, captain?' someone called out.

'It's for the section leaders to decide; the two most senior are Hakon and Kjetil but if anyone wants to nominate another candidate they may do so.'

No one did.

'Very well, I suggest we decide this by a simple show of hands.'

Inevitably four voted for each of the two men; Hakon voting for Kjetil and vice versa.

'Very well. Hakon is the elder by a year so he will be my deputy whilst I'm away.'

†††

I took two sections with me together with the scouts, now commanded by Beorhtric. The sections I chose were those led by Osric and Kjetil; one because it had been my old section and I knew the men well, and the other so that there was no awkwardness between Hakon and Kjetil. I know the two had said that they would accept the other as the senior but I thought it was better for a number of reasons that it shouldn't be put to the test.

The scouts came en masse because Bernicia would be unsettled after Aldred's death and I didn't trust Siward not to try something. With the scouts acting as a screen around us, we could travel swiftly without having to be too cautious.

With the armigers there were sixty of us and as we neared Penrith Beorhtric came riding in to report that we were being shadowed by a half a dozen men on ponies. I hoped that they were Eadulf's scouts but we donned helmets and brought our shields around from their travelling position on our backs just in case. I also ordered Hereward to unveil the wolf banner of Bebbanburg just in case there was a misunderstanding about our identity and purpose.

We were shadowed all the way to Penrith but no one tried to get too close and we arrived at the earl's hall without incident.

'Oeric?' Eadulf said from the steps of the hall. 'This is a pleasant surprise. Have you come to ask to serve me once more?'

He asked in a jocular manner but you could tell that he knew that wasn't the case. The size of my escort told him that something serious was afoot. I dismounted and went to kneel before him and the boy earl standing beside him. Of course Gospatric had grown since I'd last seen him and he now came up to Eadulf's shoulder. He was tall for seven and the way he stood beside his cousin told me that the two had developed a close relationship. Alas that wouldn't last once Gospatric grew to manhood.

'I fear I am the bearer of grave tidings, lord.'

'Then you'd better come into the hall. I'm sure you'd appreciate some refreshment after your journey.'

He gave instructions to one of his housecarls to look after my men and I followed him and Gospatric into the hall. We sat down around the high table and a servant brought us ale and bread. I was surprised to see that the young earl drank his ale undiluted but at least his goblet was smaller than ours.

'Now, what brings you to Penrith in such haste? Eadulf asked as soon as the servant had departed.

'As you know your brother was to have set out on pilgrimage to Rome with that turd Carl to cement their reconciliation.'

'Yes, of course. What has happened?' he asked a trifle impatiently.

'Their departure was delayed by a storm and they went to Carl's hall at Rise to wait for better weather. I'm not sure of the details, but they decided to fight a duel the following morning and Carl killed the earl.'

Eadulf was stunned for a moment, then I saw his features harden as he fought against his grief.

'What happened then? Were you there?'

'Not when they fought, lord, no. My brother and Colby were and they were both killed by Carl and his housecarls. We were heavily outnumbered by Carl's men and I took the decision to flee in our birlinn. No others were lost.'

'You were right to leave immediately. There would have been nothing to be gained by throwing the lives of valuable militares away needlessly. I'm sorry that you too have lost your brother.'

'Thank you, lord.'

'Wait a minute. How do you know that Aldred was killed in a duel if Acca and Colby are also dead?'

'It was witnessed by one of my scouts, a boy called Dunstan. He'd followed Earl Aldred and saw the whole thing from behind cover.'

'I see. Is he with you?'

'Yes, shall I send for him?'

Dunstan came in looking nervous and blinking in the gloomy interior of the hall.

'Don't look so apprehensive,' I told him with a smile. 'Tell Lord Eadulf what you saw at Rise that day.'

'So it was a fair fight between my brother and Carl Thurbrandsson, even if he did use low cunning,' Eadulf mused when the boy had finished. 'How did Colby and Acca die?'

'Colby and Acca were obviously enraged by Aldred's death and they tried to kill Carl in revenge. Unfortunately the two housecarls were expecting that sort of reaction and they attacked them from behind whilst Carl parried their attack from the front.'

'So they too died in a fair fight?' he said.

'Yes, although it was three against two. Acca did kill one of the housecarls and Colby badly wounded the other before Carl killed them.'

I hadn't thought about it before. I had assumed that I had a case against Carl for the death of my brother. It was unlikely that Carl would pay weregild to me, especially as it was twelve hundred shillings in the case of a thane, and so I would be honour bound to declare a blood feud. However, I wasn't sure whether Acca's killing had been lawful but it seemed that Eadulf thought it was. In any case, that wasn't a priority at the moment.

'Lord Eadulf. The reason I came in haste was to prevent Earl Siward laying claim to all Northumbria. I have summoned the ealdorman to a meeting at Bebbanburg so that they can swear fealty to you and so we need to return there as quickly as possible.'

'You have summoned the ealdormen? In what capacity?'

'The militares elected me as their captain and Synne endorsed their choice,' I replied. 'But if you would rather appoint another...'

'No, no. You have been my captain before and I have utmost faith in you.'

Just at that moment his wife, Sigfrida, entered the main hall from one of the bed chambers to the rear of the building.

'I thought I heard voices...' she started to say. 'Oeric? So you have come crawling back.'

'My love, Oeric has come to inform me that Carl has killed Aldred,' Eadulf said before she could say any more.

It was evident that she resented the fact that I had left her husband's service and returned to Aldred's.

'Aldred dead?'

Her face paled but then the look of shock was replaced by one of determination.

'Then you are the next earl. We must return to Bebbanburg immediately.'

'That is precisely what Oeric and I were discussing. As captain of the militares he has already summoned the ealdormen to meet me there to confirm their loyalty to me.'

'Captain? Oeric?' she exclaimed with a frown. 'What's happened to Colby?'

'He died with my brother when the earl was killed,' I told her.

I was disgusted with her attitude; after all Aldred was her half-brother. She showed no signs of

344

remorse; instead she made it obvious that she disapproved of my election as captain of militares. Nor did she offer any words of sympathy for Acca's death.

We needed to travel speedily so we set out the next day; Sigfrida would follow on later. Eadulf made his son Oswulf ealdorman and advisor to Gospatric in his place and so he stayed in Penrith along with a few of Eadulf's warriors. The boy was only thirteen so I wondered at the wisdom of leaving Cumbria in the care of two boys, but I suspected that the earldom in the west was the last thing on Eadulf's mind at the moment.

'What happens about your brother's vill? Where is it again?'

'Lesbury, lord. He has a three year old son who will inherit it in due course. For now Acca's widow, Mildred, will look after it.'

He nodded.

'You have a farmstead in the Cheviots?'

'Yes lord, although I haven't visited it in a while. It's where we train the scouting section. My brother in law, Beorhtric, will be there more than me now as he is the head scout.'

He said no more and we rode on in silence until we reached Hawick, where we were staying the night. I sensed a slight coolness between us and I suspected that, whatever Eadulf might say, he hadn't really forgiven me for leaving his service and now I was foisted on him as his captain without his agreement.

These thoughts depressed me. Life since we'd fled from Rise had been hectic, but now I had more time the loss of Acca really hit home. I mourned my brother deeply and, despite the fact that I had Rowena and our three children, I felt alone in the world. Up to that moment I hadn't appreciated how much Acca had meant to me.

I couldn't sleep and went over things in my mind until finally dawn broke and everyone started to get ready to leave. At least tonight I'd be back in the arms of Rowena. I desperately needed her comfort at the moment.

✝✝✝

The meeting of ealdormen went well. One suggested that we'd be stronger united with Deira, as were in the days of Uhtred, but his was a lone voice. No doubt he was in the pay of Siward but, apart from him, no one thought having an earl as far away as York would be a good idea. He was unlikely to pay much attention to the defence of the Northumbrian part of Lothian, which was still part of Bernicia, or to the situation in Cumbria.

Eadwulf wrote to King Harold to ask for him to approve his succession to the earldom and life returned to normal for a while. Sigfrida arrived and to everyone's surprise she brought my successor as Eadulf's captain in Cumbria with her. I had assumed that he would stay in Penrith and serve Oswulf but I suspect that she brought him to force a confrontation with me.

The captain, whose name was Kaden indicating his Norse heritage, was a housecarl pure and simple. He could ride, but badly. He was certainly no horse warrior and he looked down on those who were. Initially he was made garrison commander but he made it obvious that he was less than happy with that and started to agitate for reinstatement as Eadulf's captain.

He kept pointing out how much money the earl could save if he got rid of most of the large number of horses necessary to keep eighty militares and the same number of armigers mounted. Kaden accepted that the scouts should be retained, or some of them, and that a few horses for border patrols were necessary, but he wanted the bulk of Eadulf's warriors to fight on foot as every other Anglo-Saxon and Scandinavian warband did.

Of course, Kaden had little or no support amongst the militares or the armigers, but he had the ear of Sigfrida. In fact they were so close I wondered if the two of them might be cuckolding the earl.

By Christmas nothing had changed, thankfully, and then other events drove the squabble about the militares out of our minds. King Harold had suddenly succumbed to a fever. No one seemed to know how serious it was and we prayed for his recovery. He had confirmed Eadulf as earl, despite strong protestations from Siward, but if Harold died that acknowledgement would be worth very little.

The next thing we heard was that King Duncan had invaded Moray. If he defeated Macbeth he would eliminate the threat in the north of his kingdom, leaving him free to bring Cumbria back under his direct control and to invade Bernicia; something he had often threatened to do.

We spent the first two months of 1040 anxiously waiting for news. When it came it was both good and bad. We heard in early April that Harold had died at Oxford on the seventeenth of March. Everyone assumed that Harthacnut would come to England to claim the crown almost immediately but, despite being offered the throne by the Witan, he remained in Denmark.

The war between Duncan and Macbeth dragged on. Macbeth retreated before Duncan, expending his lines of communication and launching pinprick attacks to weaken Duncan's forces with minimal losses himself. It was a tactic used so successfully by Aldred before the Battle of Carham and perhaps Macbeth had learnt it from him when we supported him in his bid to regain Moray a dozen years previously.

†††

In June Kaden made his move. He and Sigfrida had finally worn Eadulf down and he sent for me to give me the bad news.

'Oeric, you have served my brother and me well over many years and I feel that it is time I gave you a better reward for your loyalty than a single farmstead tucked away in the Cheviots,' he began.

I knew what was coming; I was about to be bought off.

'I have therefore decided to give you one of my vills so you can become a thane and live out your retirement in comfort.'

'I am grateful, lord earl, but I'm not yet ready to retire. I'm only thirty one and I feel I can serve you as a warrior for several years yet.'

'Then serve me as one of my thanes,' he said coldly. 'Kaden will take over from you as my captain.'

'But he is no horseman, lord earl. How can he lead militares?'

'He has convinced us that keeping so many horses is a needless expense,' Sigfrida cut in. 'We will keep some for patrols, of course, but most of the so-called militares will become proper housecarls. Using mounted warriors may suit those on the Continent but we fight on foot, like our ancestors.'

I wondered what she knew about fighting but I held my tongue. She and Kaden had obviously convinced Eadulf to go down this road and there was nothing I could say to alter things.

'Very good. I understand,' I said, trying to keep the bitterness out of my voice.

Everything that Aldred had built up was being thrown away. Other warriors, even housecarls, feared the militares. The earl was making himself more vulnerable but, if he couldn't see that, then there was little point in me saying so.

'Where is this vill?' I asked.

'At Wooler, which stands at the entrance to Glendale and so it's strategically important,' he said with an attempt at a smile. 'And it's not too far from the farmstead you already own.'

'Thank you, lord earl.' I paused before asking my next question.

'May I ask if I might recruit a few of your militares to help patrol the area?'

'Housecarls,' Sigfrida snapped. 'There are no more militares.'

I bowed to acknowledge her statement, not trusting myself to speak. I would doubtless say something I'd regret, not that I minded for myself but I had Rowena and the children to think of.

'Who do you want?'

Cynric was no longer an armiger, having been made one of the militares some time ago. Now, of course, he was termed a housecarl, like the rest. I decided that I had nothing to lose by asking for those I felt closest to. No-one would need armigers any more. Most boys would be sent back to their fathers, but a few would stay to train as housecarls; another of Sigfrida's cost-cutting measures. My armiger at the time, Hereward, was one of those who had asked to stay.

'Osric, Durwyn, Beorhtric, Cynric, Hereward and Dunstan.'

'Dunstan's not a housecarl, nor is Hereward.' he said, surprised.

'No, but Dunstan is an excellent scout and Hereward will be old enough to become a housecarl in a few years.'

Eadulf shrugged and then nodded.

I was dismissed and left the hall feeling depressed. Although I was pleased that I would become a thane, the changes at Bebbanburg, especially the malign influence of Sigfrida, troubled me. Eadulf was too much under her thumb. Certainly he was no Aldred.

✝✝✝

Wooler turned out to consist of a sizeable village tucked into the eastern end of the Cheviot Hills. The River Glen turned from its east west course to run south at that point and the vill extended along both valleys from the farmstead at Akeld in the west to another at Roseden in the south.

The previous thane had died heirless a few months ago and so the vill had reverted to Eadulf's ownership. It already had a reeve and five housecarls who had stayed on in the hall after the thane had died. The hall was basic but at least it had a palisade around it. The first thing I intended to do was to spend some of my silver on making it a lot more comfortable. I also began to build a separate warrior's hall for the three militares and the existing housecarls. Hereward, now my armiger once more, would live in the hall and Rowena insisted that Dunstan did the same as he was still a boy. However, for now we would all have to sleep together in the only hall.

Wooler lay within the shire of Alnwick whose ealdorman was called Alwyn. I had met him a few times and I'd liked him. He was in his early twenties and, as yet, unmarried. When I rode over to present a copy of the deeds to my vill to him he seemed delighted to see me. I had a feeling that he was a little in awe of me, which made me uncomfortable. I had never liked people admiring me; it made me feel as if I had to live up to their expectations. That was probably why I had disliked Acca at first.

When I left I decided to visit my brother's widow as her vill was only a few miles to the east of Alnwick. Mildred was pleased to see me and we spent a pleasant hour or so reliving old times. She seemed content and her children were thriving. I made a fuss of her son, Nerian, who wanted me to fight him. He had a wooden sword and I pretended to spar with him for a while. For such a young boy he already had a good grasp of the basics. I left feeling happier than I had done since the death of Acca and Aldred.

Nothing much happened for a few months and then news reached us that Macbeth had killed King Duncan in a battle near Inverness on the Moray Firth. I had thought that Maldred might make a bid for the throne but apparently he had accepted his cousin as the next king. Macbeth had always been a friend to Aldred and I hoped that he would prove to be Bernicia's ally now. We would need one if the rumours were true. Harthacnut was on his way to England to be crowned as our next king and Siward had gone to London to meet him.

Chapter Twenty – Betrayal

1040 - 1041

I learned what had happened next when Alwyn invited me to go hunting with him. He had been summoned to Bebbanburg with the other ealdormen of Bernicia when Siward was thought to be mustering an army to take Eadulf's earldom by force. It was rumoured that he had applied to Harthacnut to become Earl of Northumbria and the king had agreed provided that he could overrun Bernicia without any help from him.

'I understand that Siward's plan is to install his elder son, Osbjorn, in Bebbanburg to rule as his deputy,' Alwyn told me.

There was some sense to that as Osbjorn might be acceptable to many Bernicians as he was Uhtred's grandson. However, he was Siward's son and Siward was far from popular. Then something struck me. Alwyn had said elder son. As far as I knew, Siward and Ælfflæd only had one son.

'Has Siward had another boy then?'

'Yes, hadn't you heard? They've called him Waltheof in honour of Uhtred's father.'

I thought that was somewhat ironic as Uhtred had hated his father by all accounts and Waltheof the elder had disinherited Uhtred in favour of the despised Eadwulf Cudel. In the end that hadn't mattered as the king at the time, Æthelred, had removed Waltheof and made Uhtred earl of all of Northumbria.

Things looked a bit bleak for a while but in the autumn of 1040 a visitor had arrived at Bebbanburg. Macbeth had sailed down from Edinburgh with his cousin, Maldred of Dunbar, to visit Eadulf. He had evidently assured Eadulf that he would support him if Siward tried to overrun Bernicia. Of course, he wasn't being altruistic, he probably saw it as a means of gaining the part of Lothian south of the Tweed that various kings of Scots had coveted for several decades. At any rate the threat was enough to change Siward's mind and he disbanded his army.

In the autumn of 1040 I received complaints from my tenant at Akeld that a pack of wolves were taking the sheep which were grazing in the hills above the farmstead. That in itself was nothing new but they were getting bolder and a few days ago they had attacked a shepherd boy, badly mauling him and killing his dogs.

I set out with Osric, Durwyn, Beorhtric, Cynric, Hereward and Dunstan together with two huntsmen and four wolfhounds. The day was pleasantly warm and, although the hill tops were shrouded in cloud, the indications were that the weather would stay fine. As the day wore on it got hotter. It was October but our route was sheltered from any cooling breeze and we began to swelter in our hauberks. We stopped to allow the horses to drink in a stream and we took the opportunity to divest ourselves of our armour.

When we arrived at Akeld we discovered that the
boy had died of his wounds. That hardened my
resolve to exterminate the whole pack. Our
warhorses weren't suited to mountain terrain and so
we were riding the smaller local type. They were
sturdy and surefooted but they tired more quickly
when carrying a man in chainmail.

We followed the muddy path between two tall
hills, winding ever upwards until it petered out in an
upland pasture. It was the route taken to bring the
animals down to lower ground in the winter but most
sheep still dotted the hillsides above us. The place
where the boy had been attacked was on the side of
the hill to our right. We stopped to let the horses rest
whilst I deliberated which way to go.

If we went to the right we would eventually arrive
at the old royal summer palace at Yeavering. There
hadn't been any kings of Northumbria for over a
hundred and fifty years and the buildings had fallen
into disrepair; all except for a few which housed some
twenty people. Essentially Yeavering was now a
farmstead which belonged to the Thane of
Kirknewton, my neighbour to the west.

The wolves would steer clear of the place, as they
would the hills above Wooler which lay to the east.
The most likely place to find them would be in the
hills to the south of where we were and that was
where we headed.

Today was cooler, for which we were thankful as
we were now wearing both hauberk and chainmail
coifs to protect our heads and throats. I was ever
mindful of the last time I had hunted wolves when

only two things saved my life: my coif and Dunstan's bravery.

As we ascended ever higher into the hills the land changed from pasture to a wilderness dominated by the brooding bulk of the mountain known as the Cheviot, which gave its name to the long range of hills running some forty miles across the country from Wooler into Strathclyde. The whole area was virtually uninhabited. The next settlements lay in the Coquet Valley well to the south of where we were. The wolves' den could be anywhere within an area of two hundred and fifty square miles.

However, my gut feeling was that it was within a few miles of where the boy had been attacked. Furthermore, the den was likely to be within fairly easy reach of water. We started by exploring the stream that flowed down from a boggy area on the east side of Newton Tors. The dogs found no tracks there so next we went along a stream that had its source on the saddle between Preston Hill and Newton Tors. The dogs got excited and we followed them up the valley until they lost the scent near the top.

By now it was late afternoon and so we set up camp beside the stream a little further down, where there was a small area of flat ground. There were very few trees in the vicinity - not enough to provide sufficient firewood at any rate – and so we dined on dried venison, stale bread and hard cheese. It required a great deal of chewing and the huntsmen, both of whom had rotten or missing teeth, moaned until I sent them to eat out of earshot.

The night was uneventful and when dawn broke we broke our fast with the same fare. We started by checking two more streams in the vicinity of Preston Hill and its neighbour, Cold Law, but without finding anything. We had a similar lack of success along Harthope Burn to the south of the Cheviot.

By now we were getting rather dispirited. I decided to try the headwaters of the River Breamish between Comb Fell and Bloodybush Edge before calling it a day. We had just reached the area below Cushat Law when the dogs picked up a strong scent. Their handlers had difficulty in restraining them as they yelped with excitement and strained at their leashes, wanting to charge up the steep slopes of the hill. We dismounted and followed the impatient dogs in extended line.

I insisted that Hereward and Dunstan stay with the horses. They weren't happy but, as I explained to them, wolves were cunning creatures and I was worried that some might evade us and pick up the horses' scent. The last thing I wanted was to be stranded in the middle of the Cheviots on foot. That seemed to satisfy them. In truth I thought the scenario I had painted was unlikely, but it was a possibility. However, my real concern was to keep the youths safe. I wanted no more heroics from Dunstan.

My companions and I wore our hauberks and were armed with bows, spears, swords and daggers. We moved into extended line behind the dogs and their handlers and strung our bows. After nocking an arrow in place we set off. The handlers were now having real difficulty in restraining the dogs and I knew we must be close.

Initially clouds had covered the sun, parting from time to time to allow it to bathe us in sunlight. It wasn't nearly as hot as it had been on the first day, but it was pleasant enough. Slowly the sky changed as the day wore on and now it was a uniformly grey. The summit was hidden in low cloud and now, as I watched, wisps of mist rolled towards us. Five minutes later we were enshrouded in a whiteout.

Not only did the temperature drop considerably, it was dangerous. We could no longer see the wolves at other than very close range and our bows would therefore be useless. I called everyone back and began to descend to below the cloud ceiling. Then I heard excited barking followed by the yowl of an injured dog. More barking and cries of distress followed. Then suddenly the two huntsmen reappeared running downhill fast, but without the dogs. One had a gashed arm and the other was splattered in blood.

'Come on,' I shouted. 'Forget your bows, loosen your swords in their scabbards and ready your spears.'

I made my way cautiously back into the mist with the others in line beside me. Suddenly as quickly as it had appeared the cloud parted and we saw the wolf pack straight in front of us.

They didn't see us at first. They had cornered the last two wolfhounds and were busy circling them. The other two dogs lay dead nearby, but so did one of the wolves. I quickly did a count; there were six of the beasts left. I cursed. Leaving our bows lower down the slope had been a mistake.

Suddenly the wolves closed in on the dogs and I ran forward with my spear levelled. Thankfully the wind was blowing downhill and they didn't smell us. The first the wolves knew about us was when I thrust my spear into the flank of the nearest beast. The point grated on its ribs before piercing its lungs. The heart of a wolf is quite hard to hit from the side as it's partially surrounded by the lungs. This one would die, but not immediately. I pulled my spear free and plunged it down again, this time into its back, breaking its spinal cord. It was now immobilised and I looked around me to see how the others were fairing.

As I swivelled my head to the left my vision was filled with the head and gaping jaws of another wolf as it leaped towards me. I twisted to the side and it landed beside me. It was too close for me to use my spear and I just managed to draw my sword as it's its teeth fastened about my thigh.

Thankfully it had bitten me high enough for the skirt of my hauberk to have protected my flesh. Nevertheless the power of those jaws made me scream in agony. It was as if my thigh had been caught in a man-trap. I was struggling to stab it with my sword but all I could do was hack at its rear haunches and that didn't have any effect at all.

I drew my dagger and stabbed the brute repeatedly in the neck until finally its jaws parted and it slumped dead at my feet. I gingerly tested my leg.

It was painful and I expected to have a badly bruised thigh but I could at least move, albeit with a limp.

I looked around for the others but the mist had descended again. I tried shouting but there was no response. I moved a little further uphill and yelled again, asking if everyone was alright. A few muffled shouts came back but it was difficult to tell where they came from. Being surrounded by mist is always disorientating and I decided the most sensible think was to stay where I was and wait for better visibility.

Suddenly an injured wolf appeared out of the mist. I don't know who was more startled: me or the beast. I drew my sword and crouched down holding both sword and dagger in front of me. The wolf was injured and it was dragging its half severed right hind leg behind it, nevertheless it was still extremely dangerous.

It couldn't jump at me but it limped towards me snarling and growling. I moved to the left and the beast turned its head to watch me. I was scarcely more mobile than it was but I managed to continue to circle it until I was behind it. It was still trying to turn to face me when I gritted my teeth and jumped forward, slashing down with my sword at the other rear leg.

The wolf collapsed, unable to use either of its rear legs and I leapt onto its back. I let go of my sword and grabbed it around the neck, pulling its snarling head back. I sawed at the thick hair around its throat and eventually blood spurted out all over my right arm and left hand.

I got off its back, shaking in reaction as the adrenaline wore off. I'm not sure how long I sat there beside the dead wolf but it was probably no more than a minute or two. It seemed longer. When I looked about me all I could see was mist and I cursed. I got to my feet with difficulty, thanks to my injured thigh. As I did so I felt a breath of air on my cheek.

The mist swirled and eddied as the wind picked up and suddenly it cleared. The others were standing together some distance away and I could now hear them calling my name. I counted four more dead wolves, making seven in all. None of the other men had more than the odd scratch, much to my relief. We found the den after a bit of searching but, thankfully, there were no cubs this time. We'd destroyed the whole pack.

✝✝✝

That winter was harsh. The snows came in the middle of January and, although it got milder in February, the bitterly cold weather returned and lasted until the middle of March. We had laid in enough provisions, but they were running low by the time the weather improved enough to travel. My horsemen and I rode out to check on the surrounding farmsteads and, although several of the elderly had died, together with two infants, everyone else had survived.

Two of my old companions from the days of the militares arrived a week later. Eadulf had sent all those who could ride out to check on how well his ealdorman and thanes had survived the worst winter any of us could remember. Unfortunately not everyone had done as well as we had. Some vills had been decimated and we learned later that Ealdorman Beda of Durham had been one of those who had succumbed.

Spring arrived and the annual agricultural cycle started with ploughing and sowing the seeds. The livestock were taken up to the summer pasture and I went hunting to replenish our meat larder.

We heard that Earl Eadulf had been summoned to the king's court, which was at Nottingham at the time. Eadulf hadn't attended Harthacnut's coronation and so I assumed that he was required to attend to pledge his allegiance. I heard nothing further for a time and, in any case, Eadulf was far from my mind that summer. Rowena had suddenly collapsed whilst out picking mushrooms with our daughter in the woods outside Wooler.

Cille wasn't yet seven but she had the common sense to realise that there was nothing she could do for her mother and so she ran to the nearby fields and got help. I was discussing our finances with the reeve when there was a commotion outside the hall and four men carried my wife in on a makeshift stretcher. Her face had a lopsided look and when she tried to speak her words were slurred and I had difficulty in understanding what she was trying to say. I took her in my arms and she tried to hug me but there was something wrong with her arms.

I didn't know what the matter was but I felt sick to my stomach with worry. Dunstan appeared at that moment, though I was barely aware of him. He took one look at my wife and disappeared again. He returned ten minutes later with Merwenna, the village wise woman, in tow. Some priests were versed in basic healing but the one at Wooler wasn't of that ilk. Everyone in Wooler relied on Merwenna and her daughter for herbal remedies, the treatment of injuries and childbirth.

She asked the men to take Rowena through to our bedchamber so she could examine her in private. I went to follow but she pointedly shut the door in my face. I paced up and down until Dunstan came and handed me a goblet of mead. In my agitation I drank it quickly but when the boy went to top it up again I shook my head. The last thing I wanted to do at that moment was to get drunk.

When Merwenna eventually re-appeared her face was glum.

'Something has happened which has partly paralysed her,' she explained quietly.

'What can you do to cure her?' I asked, not that I had much hope that even Merwenna could restore my wife to the women I loved.

'Nothing I'm afraid. I can give her something for pain but that's all. We will have to wait and see what happens. It's in God's hands now.'

I went to the church and prayed but it didn't do any good. Rowena stayed the same.

'Your children need you as well, lord,' Dunstan told me the next morning, 'they don't understand what's happening.'

'No more do I,' I said bitterly.

I nearly struck him for his impudence, but he was right. Cerdic was a sturdy little chap of eight and the twins were six. They were frightened and had been ignored whilst we all fussed over their mother. They didn't know what was happening and huddled in a corner of the hall, keeping out of the way. I went over to them and hugged each one in turn. I needed some fresh air and so I took them outside.

'What's wrong with mother?' Cerdic asked timidly.

'We don't know. Something seems to have robbed her of movement all down her left side so she can't speak properly and her face looks funny,' I replied.

'Will she get better?' Oswin asked anxiously.

'Don't be silly,' his sister chided him 'how can father know that.'

I thought my younger son was going to burst into tears at Cille's chiding.

'No one knows, Oswin. All we can do is pray that mother recovers.'

Our prayers did no good. That night as I sat beside our bed she had another seizure and died in my arms.

✝✝✝

It rained on the day of the funeral. I was surprised how many made the effort to attend. Many of my old comrades from Bebbanburg came, as did Ealdorman Alwyn, several of my neighbouring thanes and my brother's widow, Mildred. At the wake afterwards Alwyn sat next to me with Mildred on his other side. After the usual words of condolence he spent the rest of the meal talking to Mildred. I didn't mind. I was in no mood to be sociable.

I had hoped that Eadulf might attend but I was told that he was still away at Nottingham. I thought it strange at the time. The Witan met all over England but it never lasted more than a day or two at the most. Even allowing for travelling time, it shouldn't have required the earl to be away for nearly three weeks.

I didn't learn what had happened until a week after the funeral. Then I received a message requiring me to attend a council at Bebbanburg.

As Dunstan and I approached the all too familiar main gates into the fortress we had to pull into the side of the road to allow a carriage escorted by six mounted housecarls I didn't recognise pass to us going the other way. I looked into the carriage out of curiosity and saw that it contained Sigfrida and her maid. Eadulf's wife had a thunderous expression on her face and she didn't even look my way as she passed.

My foreboding increased as I dismounted and Dunstan took my horse to the stables. The atmosphere can best be described as one of sullen animosity. I saw Alwyn standing outside the earl's hall talking to two of his other thanes so I went over to join them. When I heard what they were talking about I was astounded. It was not surprising that Eadulf hadn't yet returned to Bernicia. He'd been murdered.

✝✝✝

I learned the full story in bits and pieces over the next hour or so. Eadulf had taken Kaden and the one section of Militares he had retained with him as escort. As he had had Harthacnut's safe conduct in his pouch he thought he had enough protection for the journey, but he wasn't under threat on the road.

He was shown into the king's presence accompanied by Kaden the morning after his arrival. He was surprised to see that the king was alone apart from two men and the housecarls standing on guard behind the throne and at the door. He must have suspected trouble when he saw that the two men were Earl Siward of Deira and Carl of Holderness.

No one else was present and so it was difficult to know exactly what happened but the outcome was clear. Both Eadulf and Kaden were killed and Siward was created Earl of Northumbria, the separate earldom of Bernicia being abolished.

Eadulf's heir, Oswulf, was safe in Cumbria for the time being but his cousin, Gospatric, was growing older each year and one day he would want to rule without Oswulf standing at his shoulder. One thing was clear, Oswulf couldn't return to Bernicia if he wanted to live.

Carl's revenge was now complete. There were still members of Uhtred's family who could pursue the feud, of course: not only Oswulf but also his other grandsons – Gospatric, Osbjorn and Waltheof. Not that the latter two, being Siward's sons, were likely to act in view of their own father's complicity in the slaying of Eadulf.

'What I don't understand is why Harthacnut would want Earl Eadulf dead,' I said to Alwyn.

'I don't know for certain but the earl always supported Harold.'

'But so did Siward and the other earls.'

'Yes but they all wrote to Harthacnut when Harold fell ill pledging their support to him. Eadulf wasn't astute enough to do so, and then there is Macbeth.'

'Macbeth?'

'I heard a rumour that Carl went to the king to say that Eadulf and his son Oswulf had pledged loyalty to the King of Scots and that there was a plot to make Bernicia part of Scotland.'

'But nothing could be further from the truth!'

'You and I know that but it sounds plausible enough, especially since technically Cumbria is part of Scotland and Oswulf is an ealdorman there.'

I pondered what Alwyn had said and I could imagine both Siward and Carl whispering such a falsehood in Harthacnut's ear.

'Riders approaching,' the sentry shouted from the watchtower, 'lots of them.'

'What banner?' Alwyn called up.

'Blue with what looks like three gold crowns on it.'

367

That was the old banner of Northumbria; the three crowns symbolising the ancient kingdoms of Deira, Bernicia and Rheged – now called Cumbria.

'Siward,' I hissed.

The cavalcade swept into the stronghold, up the road known as the Death Walk and through the upper gate. Stable boys ran to take the horses but there were so many that they had to make several trips. The riders were mainly housecarls, but not militares. Most had trouble staying on a horse at more than a gentle trot.   It was then that I noticed the absence of any faces I recognised amongst the garrison. I learned later that the section with Eadwulf had been killed and the rest had left to serve Oswulf in Cumbria as soon as the news of the earl's demise reached them. No doubt the garrison were now all Siward's men.

Siward swept into the hall followed by his eldest son, Osbjorn, and a handful of ealdormen and thanes who had accompanied him from Deira. He took his place in the earl's chair with his son and his captain of housecarls standing on either side of him. The nobles who had accompanied him from Deira arranged themselves in a semi-circle behind them. As we all filed in he stared impassively at us.

'Thank you for coming,' he said curtly. 'As you will have no doubt heard by now, the king had made me earl of all Northumbria. There is to be no more Bernicia, just one earldom. The ealdormen north of the Tees are to swear fealty to me and anyone who feels unable to do so is free to resign their post and leave Northumbria. I will appoint replacements, with the king's blessing, and the thanes of that shire will be expected to swear an oath to the new ealdorman.'

He paused to look around the hall before continuing. I felt his eyes pause when they reached me, but that may have been my imagination.

'Because the earldom is so vast I have decided to make my son Osbjorn the High Reeve of Bebbanburg. He will command this fortress and be responsible for the security of the border with the damned Scots. Now each ealdorman in turn is to come forward, kneel and take the oath of loyalty to me.'

That was it. Bernicia was no more and the long line of the House of Bebbanburg had come to an end. Oh, Osbjorn might be Uhtred's grandson but he wasn't one of us. He was a Deiran and we loathed them more than we did the Scots. There was, however, one man left alive who could truly claim to be of Uhtred's line and that was Eadulf's son, Oswulf. Had I been free I would have joined him in Cumbria and prayed for the day when he claimed his birth right as Earl of Bernicia, but I wasn't. I had sworn an oath to Alwyn as my ealdorman and I had my children to think of.

The next day Dunstan and I returned to Wooler wondering what would happen to Bernicia now.

Epilogue – The Massacre at Settrington

November 1073

Morcar rode through the late afternoon, the first snow of winter stinging his face, but it made little impression on him. He was the son of Ligulf and Edith and thus Aldred's grandson. He had been brought up by his mother to hate Carl of Holderness and his family but had had to wait a long time for revenge. Now, at long last, he was about to avenge the deaths of Aldred and Eadulf.

Waltheof, son of Siward and now Earl of Northumbria, was Uhtred's grandson and the nephew of the two dead brothers. He was the instigator of the raid led by Morcar, but not through any reasons of honour or desire for vengeance. It would have been hypocritical of him to pretend that he had any motivation except for pure greed as his own father had been involved in Eadulf's murder. The blood feud was no more than a convenient justification for the raid. Of course, that didn't mean that Morcar himself was undertaking this raid for purely altruistic motives. He too planned to profit from this night's work.

The men who followed him, in addition to his own housecarls, were the scum of the streets of York – assassins for hire, petty criminals and cutpurses. Many hadn't been on a horse before and hung on grimly. More than once they had to stop because someone had fallen off, despite the fact that Morcar had set a gentle pace. One had broken his shoulder and had been left behind with his throat cut. It made the rest try a lot harder to stay in the saddle.

They skirted Malton just before the sun set, keeping out of sight in the woods. Now their destination lay a mere four miles ahead of them.

†††

I learned what ensued that dreadful night at Settrington in Ryedale, some twenty five miles north east of York, second hand, but I have no reason to doubt the tale's veracity. Of course, much had happened since Eadulf's murder and the events at Settrington some thirty years later.

It took me some time to get over Rowena's death but eventually I was forced to the conclusion that my children needed a mother and, if I'm honest, I missed someone to share my bed. I married for the second time in 1042, the year of Harthacnut's death. I was still only thirty four and I found a merchant who was eager for his fifteen year old daughter to marry a thane, even one over twice her age.

I suppose he thought that his grandchildren would be nobles and that was a step up the social ladder, even though he was far richer than I was. The girl was called Hilda and was willing enough to marry me, mainly I suspect because it allowed her to escape her domineering mother.

We were happy enough, although it was scarcely a love match. Perhaps I was incapable of loving again after Rowena. I watched what was happening in the outside world with a detached interest, glad that I was no longer involved; although there were times when I was required to muster my fyrd and lead them and my housecarls off to fight in wars that held no interest for me, but these are tales for another time.

Edward the Confessor of the ancient House of Wessex followed Harthacnut onto the throne in 1042. Then Norman William killed the last Anglo-Saxon king, Harold the Second, at Caldbec Hill near Hastings. Most of the old nobility were slain during the battle and those who survived were slowly dispossessed so that Normans, Flemings and Frenchmen could take their land. My vill escaped the savage retribution King William meted out to the North after the slaying of the man he had appointed as the new Earl of Northumbria – Robert de Comines – and his men at Durham.

For now we seem to be secure here on the edge of the Cheviots but I often wonder whether Galan, the child I had late in life with Hilda, will be allowed to inherit my estate when I'm gone. He is the only one left now. The sons that Rowena had given me died fighting, one at Durham fighting Malcolm Canmore and the other with King Harold at Caldbec Hill. I was sixty when William the Bastard invaded and far too old to fight anyone. Galan was, thankfully, too young in 1066.

Hilda died a year ago, although she was much younger than me. I'm sixty six now and I doubt that I'll survive another winter, but I digress. I was going to tell you about the massacre at Settrington in the autumn of last year - 1073.

✝✝✝

Carl had died at Stamford Bridge, killed by Oswulf or so rumour had it, but his sons survived the battle and were still on their way south with the bulk of the army when tidings of Harold's defeat at the hands of the Normans reached them. They returned to Holderness and, after much argument, three of them divided Carl's properties between them. The fourth brother, Somerled, had retreated from the world after the slaughter at Fulford Gate to become a monk at Whitby. Whether his decision was taken through cowardice or horror at the realities of warfare I couldn't say. The other three brothers were Thurbrand, Gamel, and Cnut - named in honour of the old king.

They in turn had sons; seven in all aged from eight to twenty. They gathered as a family at Settrington on the thirtieth of November to celebrate the wedding of Gamel's son, Wigmund. This place was the largest vill owned by Thurbrand, the eldest brother.

Morcar and his band of ruffians left their horses with two of their number in a wood a mile from Thurbrand's hall. By now darkness had fallen and the night was pitch black under the leaden skies. The only illumination, such as it was, was provided by the snow which covered the ground and painted the trees and shrubs a ghostly white.

At first Morcar wasn't sure that they were heading in the right direction, then he heard the sounds of merriment coming from ahead. The wind had drifted the snow so that in places it barely covered the ground and in others it was two feet deep. The snow was coming down harder now and the flakes were getting bigger. Morcar was sweating with exertion under the thick woollen cloak he wore over his chainmail hauberk but his face and hands felt as if they were lumps of ice. His feet weren't in much better state.

Snow wasn't something he was used to. Winters had been severe when he was a young boy but over the past two decades they had gradually become warmer and he couldn't remember when there had been more than a dusting of snow for a few days, and that had been in January or February, not November.

The men who followed him were less well protected against the elements and, although they were more used to hardship, the snow had come as an unpleasant surprise. They did nothing but complain until he whispered hoarsely for them to shut up.

He could now see the lights of the villagers' huts up ahead. The palisade around the hall stood out starkly, black against the surrounding white of the snow. Morcar couldn't believe his luck. The gates stood wide open and, as far as he could see, they were unguarded. His men closed the gates behind them and Morcar left two men to ensure that they stayed shut. The rest crept towards the hall.

Just when he thought they were going to reach the hall without being detected, the door opened and a man staggered out, his hands already fumbling at the fastenings of his trousers. He stood, swaying, barely two feet from the hall entrance and turned the snow in front of him yellow without noticing the figures some fifty feet away. Morcar had held his hand up when the door had opened and his men stood stock still; all except one of his housecarls who slowly drew an arrow out of the quiver on his back and nocked it to his bow. Just as the man was tucking himself away his eyes widened in shock and he crumpled to the earth with an arrow in his chest.

He had left the door to the hall open and, just as Morcar reached it, someone came to close it. Without thinking Morcar reacted by instinct and thrust his sword into the chest of the person in the doorway. It was only when the body fell to the floor that he realised that the person he'd killed was a woman. He swore. Earl Waltheof's instructions had been quite clear: only Thurbrand's male descendants were to be killed. Quite apart from being able to gain their property, he wanted an end to the blood feud. The last thing Waltheof needed was the enmity of the other leading families in the south east of his earldom. Luckily for him the girl that Morcar had killed was a servant.

He rushed into the dimly lit hall, followed by his men whose blood was now up. Morcar had passed on the earl's instructions that only those who attacked them were to be killed but he was less than confident that they would obey him. Hopefully his housecarls would be able to deal with any of the hired thugs who got out of control.

At first no one paid much attention to the commotion at the door. Then a cry of alarm went up as Morcar's men ran into place around the walls.

'Stay where you are and you won't get hurt. We are here for Carl's family; that's all. The rest of you are safe.'

Morcar's voice stilled the uproar in the hall for a moment, but then men scrabbled for weapons and women screamed. He knew how nervous his men were and feared that they would start a massacre at any moment.

'Silence!' he roared. 'The first man to pick up a weapon will get an arrow in his chest.'

He pointed to the two archers standing just inside the door with arrows nocked to their bowstrings and aimed at the centre of the hall. That seemed to do the trick and a deathly silence descended, although everyone was still on edge.

'Now sit down.'

No one moved for a moment, and then one person obeyed; slowly the rest sank back onto their benches. However, five men at the high table at far end of the hall remained standing.

'Who are you? How dare you interrupt this wedding feast?' the one in the centre demanded.

'Never mind who I am. What's your name?'

'Thurbrand, Lord of Holderness. I will have your head for this outrage.'

'I doubt that very much. Who are the others who have disobeyed my order to sit down?'

'I'm Gamel, father of the bridegroom. We will hunt every one of you down and kill you.'

'You talk bravely, Gamel of Rise, but you have to be alive to do that.'

The other three identified themselves as Cnut, the third of the brothers; Horsa, the bride's father; and Evoric, the newly married husband of the young girl sitting beside him and weeping piteously.

'Everyone at the high table except Horsa and the women are to go outside with my men.'

Several of Morcar's housecarls walked up to the high table and pushed the three brothers and Evoric towards the door. As soon as they were outside Cnut produced an eating knife from his sleeve and stabbed the housecarl who was holding him in the neck. Before the others could react he raced away into the trees.

For a second the stunned housecarls stood there as their comrade's lifeblood stained the snow crimson. Then they swiftly cut the throats of the other two brothers and Evoric before chasing after Cnut.

Inside the hall Morcar was unaware of the drama which had just taken place outside. The rest of his housecarls were moving through the hall collecting weapons whilst the hired thugs continued to glower at the angry, but impotent, men and the fearful women and children.

Suddenly a boy of about fifteen grabbed a dagger from the sheath hanging from the belt of one of the housecarls and tried to stab him with it. It was an act of stupid bravado. The dagger slid off the chain mail protecting its wearer's chest and a second later another housecarl cut the boy's head from his shoulders with one blow of his axe. His body slumped to the floor, his head bouncing once on the table before coming to rest with the eyes staring up at the roof.

Pandemonium broke out as men tried to get hold of weapons and women, clutching the hands of their children, stampeded for the door. The archers let fly with their arrows but, apart from wounding a child in the arm, it achieved nothing. The archers dropped their bows and drew their swords, desperately hacking at the crowd surrounding them.

The cutthroats around the walls launched themselves into the fray with cries of glee. They cut down men, women and children indiscriminately. Morcar cried out for his men to desist but they ignored him. He groaned; this was what he'd wanted to avoid at all costs. He saw that one of his thugs had pinned a young girl down on a table and was about to rape her so he thrust his sword into the man's back and pulled his body off the terrified girl. Instead of thanking him, she launched herself at Morcar and tried to claw his eyes out. He was forced to defend himself and, more in reaction than with intent, he chopped at her arms. He severed one cleanly at the elbow and cut down to the bone in the other forearm. The girl stared at him in horror before collapsing to the floor.

By now the hall was a place of carnage with many of the wedding guests either dead or badly wounded. A few of the hired ruffians had been killed as well, but Morcar couldn't have cared less about them. He sunk to his haunches in despair, dropping his gory sword in the process.

An hour later the corpses had been laid out on the tables in the hall and the wounded were being attended to by the village priest and those women who'd survived. His housecarls had failed to find Cnut and so, to that extent, the raid had been a failure. Morcar had a list of the sons of the three brothers and checked it against the bodies. In addition to Evoric, the bridegroom, three more of the seven had been killed during the slaughter and two had been wounded. Morcar cut the throats of the injured pair himself. That left the last of them, a petrified boy of eight who sat in the corner by the body of his dead mother.

Morcar desperately wanted to spare him but he was only too well aware that young boys tend to grow up into strong men. It was bad enough that Cnut had escaped. If he wanted to end the blood feud and wipe out Thurbrand the Hold's brood the boy had to die.

He pulled the boy to him and gave him an encouraging smile. Unbelievably the boy smiled back; no doubt thinking he was to be spared. Morcar let go of him and the boy turned to run away, but Morcar grabbed his long fair hair in one hand and cut his throat from behind with the other. At least that way he didn't have to look into the boy's shocked eyes as he died.

No one ever found out what had happened to Cnut. Perhaps he died somewhere in the snow that night, his body providing a feast for animals and birds. He might have survived, but if so he must have decided to disappear.

Morcar gathered all the coins, hack silver and jewellery he could find in order to pay those he had hired and he gave his housecarls some of the silver. That didn't leave enough to meet the weregild he was forced to pay to the families of the innocents who had died. It would take ten years' income from his vills, both newly acquired and those he'd inherited, to meet the rest of the cost, but at least that would avoid further blood feuds.

Morcar was never the same after that night and after a few months he made his vills over to the Archbishop of York on the understanding that the Church would pay off the remainder of the weregild he owed. He became a monk at Jarrow but he remained a troubled man. They found his body hanging from a meat hook in the monastery storeroom exactly a year after the massacre at Settrington.

THE END

The story of the Earls of
Northumbria will continue in

Year of the Three Battles

Due out later in 2019

Historical Note

Weregild and Blood Feuds

There was no such thing as imprisonment for committing a crime in Anglo-Saxon England. Crimes were punished by execution, fines or the payment of weregild to the wronged party or, if dead, his family.

Weregild, also known as man price or blood money, was the value placed on every human being and piece of property. If property was stolen, or someone was injured or killed, the guilty person would have to pay weregild as restitution to the victim's family or to the owner of the property.

If someone was unable to pay the weregild owing he would become a slave, the property of the person or family to whom the weregild was due.

A blood feud is a dispute, usually between families, with a cycle of retaliatory violence. It is formally defined as avenging the wrongful death of a person's kinsman by killing the murderer. This duty of exacting revenge was passed down from generation to generation. Although weregild was the preferred manner of resolving matters, in cases where the guilty party refused to pay, or if the wronged party refused to accept weregild, then a blood feud would follow.

During the medieval period all European nations had similar customs concerning murder. The closest next of kin to a person who had wrongfully died at the hands of another had the primary duty to obtain recompense or else retaliate against the killer. It was a matter of honour. This obligation was subject to certain laws and customs concerning the type of vengeance, the amount of compensation that could be exacted and the circumstances in which compensation was not required.

For example, a blood feud was not appropriate if the person killed was a convicted thief or if the person who did the killing did so to defend his lord or a close female family member; nor was it necessary if a husband found his wife in bed with another man and killed the adulterer.

There is some debate as to what extent a blood feud was legal in Anglo-Saxon England. King Alfred enacted a law whereby a feud would only be lawful after an attempt was made to exact weregild, but that probably only applied in Wessex.

The Church ruled that a death should be avenged through the payment of weregild, not further violence, but blood feuds continued throughout England until after the Norman Conquest.

The Deaths of Aldred and Eadulf

After Aldred killed Thurbrand the Anglo-Saxon Chronicle says that the latter's son, Carl, laid ambushes for Aldred and he did the same to Carl, presumably without success. Someone, it might have been the king, the Archbishop of York or some other influential person eventually arbitrated between the two and they signed a pact by which the blood feud would end and they would go on pilgrimage together to Rome. They planned to sail to the Continent from one of Carl's ports in Holderness but were delayed by storms.

They went to Carl's vill at Rise to wait for better weather and he seems to have been a generous host. However, something went wrong, or perhaps Carl was playing a duplicitous game. When he was showing Aldred around his estate he murdered him in Rise Wood.

It was unusual for important men to be unaccompanied; there were always retainers and usually guards on hand but the written records of the killing say nothing about this, or indeed what happened to the rest of Aldred's party. All we know is that a cross was erected to mark the spot where he fell. We don't know who erected this cross or why Carl permitted this memorial to be placed on his land. After all, it commemorated his betrayal of the pact he'd made with Aldred.

We knew even less about the murder of Eadulf. He had been summoned to court by King Harthacnut a year after he'd become king. Evidently Eadulf and the new king were in dispute, though over what is not recorded, and Harthacnut had sent Eadulf a safe conduct. One source states that the murderer was Earl Siward of Northumbria.

The motive for Eadulf's murder isn't clear. Siward was married to Eadulf's half-sister (or possibly niece) but that didn't mean the two men were close. It's possible that he was killed over a land dispute or because Siward wanted to be Earl of Northumbria.

There was no separate Earl of Bernicia again until 1065 when Earl Morcar of Northumbria appointed Eadulf son, Oswulf, as his deputy in the north.

The Northumbria Novels by H A Culley

985 to 1016 AD

The Battle of Carham
1017-1018 AD

Blood feud
1018 – 1041 AD

Printed in Great Britain
by Amazon